THE THIRD FLOOR

C. DENNIS MOORE

C. DENNIS MOORE

For Jennifer,
who was there when it happened.

C. DENNIS MOORE

Acknowledgments:
Cover photo taken by C. Dennis Moore
Manipulated by David G. Barnett

C. DENNIS MOORE

Chapter One

The Kitches entered Angel Hill the same way everyone did: US 169. They came from the south, having arrived after an almost two day drive from Houston. They spent the night just over the Missouri border in a small town they couldn't remember the name of and drove the rest of the way to the northern part of the state in one stretch. Jack was ready for bed. Liz was ready for something besides sitting in the car. Joey was asleep in the back seat.

Once they entered town, Liz was ready to find the first motel and search for the house in the morning.

"Come on," Jack said. "We're in town now; we'll just find the house. We'll be there in twenty minutes."

"We don't even know the streets here," Liz said. "Let's just get some sleep and we'll find the house in the morning."

"I've got directions," Jack countered, pulling directions from his breast pocket. He handed it to Liz, then turned on the dome light. "Read it to me."

Liz took the paper and tried to focus her eyes in the glare of the light.

"Turn right when you get to Vogul," she said.

"Then what?" he asked.

"Then turn left when you get to Seventh Street."

Jack followed her directions, turning when he found the street she mentioned, then looking for the next one. And, like Jack had said, before they knew it, the Kitches were on Fourth Street, pulling up in front of their new house. Liz looked past her husband to the three-story block standing thirty feet back from the street. Even with a street lamp in front of their house, it was dark. Not just the house, but everything around it, as if the house sucked up any light that dared come near it.

"That's it?" Liz asked, sounding less than thrilled.

"That's it," Jack said. He didn't sound entirely convinced, himself.

"Is there going to be electricity?"

"Of course," he said. "I had it turned on two days ago. And the Realtor said they'd have it aired out for us. The only things we'll be missing tonight are beds."

They got out and Liz lifted Joey from the back seat while Jack got the sleeping bags from the rear compartment. He closed the door and went up to the porch. After some jiggling and fighting, they got the door opened and were inside. Jack locked the door behind them.

"So they aired it out," Liz asked, "or they were supposed to air it out."

"She said they did," Jack said, wincing at the smell of dust. He found a light switch and flipped it. Nothing happened. "Nice to know quality work is alive and well in Angel Hill," he said.

"Where are we going?"

"Downstairs," he said, leading the way.

The porch entered onto a landing between the first two floors and the way down looked, to Liz, like a physical invitation to Hell. "You didn't bring a flashlight, did you, Mr. Genius?" she teased.

"We weren't supposed to need one." He missed the last step and stumbled, spilling the sleeping bags and his keys all over the dark hall. There was a jangling and Jack said, "Shit!"

"What," Liz asked, shifting Joey to her other shoulder.

"I think I just kicked the keys down the cold air vent."

"Nice."

"Hush up."

They found one of the bedrooms--at least, they thought it was a bedroom--in the dark by running a hand along the wall until coming to a doorway. That was where they spent the night. They spread the sleeping bags on the floor, slept on one, covered with the other. In the middle of the night Jack woke up when he heard a door close, then footsteps padding down the hall. He reached over and felt Liz next to him. Joey had to pee, he thought, then was asleep again before his son came back. He woke up again, what seemed like only seconds later, to Joey's screams.

Shit, Jack thought, he's realized he doesn't know where he is. He's lost in the hall in the dark.

He began to get up, then realized Joey was right next to him. Liz was already comforting the boy who was crying over a nightmare. Jack put his head back down and fell asleep again instantly.

By the time he woke up, Joey and Liz were gone. Jack raised his head and looked around, trying to force focus on the room. Liz had opened the windows, and Jack's first Angel Hill summer breeze blew by. He leaned up and realized they'd spent the night in the living room. He could see Liz in the kitchen just ten feet from him. She had her back to him, staring out the back door. From outside, he heard Joey laughing.

"What time is it?" he asked.

She didn't answer, so he asked it again, louder. Liz jumped and caught herself before she yelled. "Shit, you scared me." She looked at her watch. "It's almost nine."

"Good, the movers should be here by noon. We can get something to eat and be back with plenty of time"

"Plenty of time for what?" she asked.

"Good point," he said.

Then Joey rushed in, slamming the tin storm door behind him. "Dad," he said. "Is this whole house ours?"

"It sure is," he said, sitting up and smoothing the wrinkled length of his pant legs. "Will this be enough room for all your toys, do you think?"

"It might be," Joey said. Then he turned to Liz. "Who lives up there?" He pointed toward the ceiling.

"Nobody lives up there," she answered. "The whole building is our house. And nobody else's."

"Wow," Joey said, his eyes wide with childish joy.

"Yep," Jack said, pulling his shirt down over his stomach, "all ours, babe. And we can do anything we want to it. What color would you like your bedroom to be?"

"Pancakes," Joey said.

"Pancakes."

"Yep," he said, smiling wide. "Then if I wake up some day before you and Liz, I won't be hungry waiting for you to get up and fix my breakfast."

"I see," Jack said, smiling as he stuffed his feet into his shoes. "Tell you what, how about we have pancakes for breakfast now, and while we do that, we can pick a color for your bedroom."

"Okay."

Jack went to brush his teeth, and when he came back he said, "Shit, I forgot I dropped my keys last night."

"I've got a set in my purse," Liz said. "We can look for yours when we get back."

"And we don't know where the restaurants are."

"Just drive. We'll find something, or someone who can tell us. Stop at a gas station, if you see one."

While Jack drove the unfamiliar streets of Angel Hill and Joey played in the back seat, Liz whispered to Jack, "It's been a year now, Jack, and he still calls me Liz."

"I'm sorry," he said back, quietly. "Give him time. He's six. For the first five years of his life, the boy didn't call anyone Mom. He met you as Liz. When he's ready, all right? Just relax. At the very least, you're more mother to him than his real mother ever was."

"That doesn't help. That's all the more reason, in fact."

"He will. I'm telling you. Just let him do it when he's ready. Here's a gas station. Let me fill up and we'll find out where the closest restaurant is."

Jack came back from paying for the gas, holding a map under his arm. "The guy inside said there's a diner on . . . " he unfolded the map and scanned it, starting in the top left corner and moving across, then down an inch, and back again until he found, "tenth and Marshall. Well, that's easy to find." He started the car and pulled away, heading for breakfast.

They were soon walking into the Grand Prize Diner and heading for a booth. Jack and Liz grabbed menus and Joey pulled the dessert card from the wire mount against the wall, staring with big eyes at the ice creams and pies.

"Pancakes, first," Jack said. "If you've got room left, we'll think about ice cream."

"Okay. I'm gonna eat twelve, or maybe a dozen pancakes," Joey said. "I'm starving to death."

"We'll see," Jack said.

A waitress came and wrote down their orders, smiling at Joey as she walked away.

"Did you have a hard time finding the bathroom last night, Joe?" Jack asked.

"What?" Joey replied.

"When you got up last night to pee," Jack said. "Did you get lost, not knowing where you were?"

"I didn't get up," Joey said. "Except when I had a bad

dream."

"No, I heard you close the bathroom door and come back down the hall."

"Huh-uh," Joey said. He was still eyeing the desserts.

"Was it you?" Jack asked his wife.

"I didn't get up," she said. She stared out the window at the strange new city. "It's not a very . . . what's the word I want? . . . classy place, is it?"

"Angel Hill? I don't suppose it's any different than any other city. It's smaller than Houston, but it's big enough."

"But it's nine-thirty in the morning. It's the beginning of summer. Where's the sunshine, the birds, and the sounds of lawnmowers?"

The food came and Joey dove into his pancakes, stuffing half of one into his mouth before Jack had the chance to ask if he wanted syrup. Liz and Jack ate hungrily, but civilly, unlike Joey who acted as if he hadn't eaten his own dinner the night before, plus the half of Liz's cheeseburger she didn't finish.

"What's the rush?" Jack asked.

"I'm hurrying up so I can have ice cream."

Back in the car, Jack asked Liz, "So you didn't get up last night?"

"No," she said. "And I'm pretty sure he didn't, either."

"Man, I was sure I woke up for a second and heard him coming back down the hall."

"I don't think he would have found the bathroom that easily by himself, in the dark, in a house he's never been in before."

"I didn't think so, either. But I was sure I heard him. What was his nightmare about last night, did he tell you?"

"No," she said. "He just said he was scared, as if we couldn't guess that. Did you hear that scream he let out?"

"No, it only scared the shit out of me. I woke up thinking he must have cut an arm off or something."

"Me too--turn left here--I about had a heart attack myself."

Jack glanced into the mirror and saw Joey watching out the window, his head moving from side to side, and his mouth moving in silent song.

They pulled in front of the house and looked at it again, this time in the full light of day.

"Well, I guess it doesn't look so bad," Liz said. "It sure is big."

"Sure is," Jack said. "But you were the one who wanted a house you could work on. They said the top two floors needed a lot of work, so have at it."

"I meant I'd like to paint a couple walls, maybe get new carpet in the living room. I didn't mean I wanted to do an entire house."

"I'll help you, of course," he said.

"Sure you will."

They got inside and had just decided which of the two bedrooms would belong to whom when the banging started. Jack slid Joey off his back and went up to the front door to let the movers in. Their house in Houston hadn't been a third the size of this one, so everything they had fit on the first floor. Liz directed traffic, while Jack helped unload the truck and bring boxes and lamps, the microwave cart, and an end table up to the house.

Meanwhile, Joey explored.

The bottom floor consisted of two bedrooms, a living room, kitchen, a bathroom, and a hall that divided the floor, with the bedrooms on one side, the rest of the rooms on the other. At one end of the hall stood a wall, at the other end the stairs went up to the landing at the front door. A 180-degree turn led to the second floor. There were four more rooms up here and another bathroom. A third flight of stairs ran to another landing and another 180-degree turn that led to the third floor. This floor had one large central room that branched off to four smaller rooms and a final bathroom.

Joey stood on the top landing, staring up at the third floor, not wanting to go all the way up. He looked up at the ceiling that seemed to rise forever above him. It was easy to feel so small in this house. It would be easy to get lost. He couldn't believe they had this whole place to themselves. Maybe there were people who lived here nobody knew about. It would also be easy to hide, especially up here, without anyone finding you. Joey took a step up, then froze when he heard movement up above, from somewhere on the third floor.

He was too short to see over the top of the stairs without going further. He stopped and listened, but the sound didn't come again. He waited, then decided he really had heard something, but didn't want to see what it was. He didn't have to see to know it scared him.

Only silence came. He didn't even hear his dad and the other men coming in and out of the front door with their things. Joey turned and bounded back down the steps, hurrying as if being chased, and he knew if he turned around, he just might see something coming down after him. He raced to the bottom floor and into the living room, leaping onto the couch.

"What's the matter, Joey?" Liz asked. She scooted a box of dishes into the kitchen.

"Do you promise my bedroom is down here?"

"Of course, silly-head. All our bedrooms are down here. It'll be a while before we move anything upstairs."

"Do you promise, even if Dad says I have to move my bedroom upstairs, do you promise I can stay down here?"

Liz looked at him crookedly, wondering what was the matter.

"Of course. He wouldn't make you sleep upstairs unless you were older and you decided you wanted to."

"Promise?"

"What's wrong? Did he say you were going to sleep up there? He was just trying to scare you. He's being silly."

"He didn't say anything. I just don't want to go up there."

"Okay. Now come here and help me put up these dishes."

Joey ran into the kitchen where he was safer with Liz than on the couch.

Liz put away the last plate and closed the last cabinet as Jack came into the room, rubbing his eyes.

"All done."

"You got everything?"

"I hope so. If I didn't, it's still in Houston. The truck's empty. Wow, you got all this stuff put away already?"

"Already? You've been unloading that truck for over two hours. I didn't even think we had two hours' worth of stuff."

"Well, we put some of it away as we went. The beds are put together and . . . listen."

Liz was quiet, head cocked.

Jack held his breath and waited. After a minute, he said, "Maybe not. I thought I heard a mouse in the wall. I didn't even think to check for mice."

"Well go get some traps," Liz said. "We're not sleeping here with mice. I'm not coming in here in the morning to find mouse poop on the counter. Go, go. There's a store in town somewhere. Don't come back without at least half a dozen."

Jack groaned and rubbed his head.

"But I'm so tired from carrying every single piece of furniture we have out of the truck, up to the house, and down all those stairs," he whined. "Can't I do it later? Or tomorrow? Tomorrow sounds like a good time."

"No," she said. "I'm telling you, if I see a mouse run past me I'm gonna freak out. Please."

"Well," he assented, "we do need food, too. I'll grab a few things for the next couple days. Then you can go get all the good stuff once we get settled. How's that?"

"Whatever," Liz waved him away, "just don't come back without traps."

"I won't," he said, kissing her head. "I'll see if Joey wants to go. Where is he?"

Liz scanned the kitchen. "He was in here, helping me. I don't know."

Jack found him asleep on the couch. Joey's two middle fingers hung limply from his mouth and his knees were tucked up underneath him.

"I guess he doesn't want to go."

"That's okay. I'm kind of beat, myself. I'm gonna lay down for a little bit, too." Liz stretched and yawned, mocking Jack who wrinkled his face and growled at her. He kissed her again and was gone.

Liz found their bed, unmade, of course, in the bedroom directly across the hall from the living room. If she kept the doors open, she'd be sure to hear Joey if we woke up. She stretched out on the bare mattress, covering her head with her arms, and drifted off immediately.

Her mind went far away and her thoughts made

16

everything a jumble, mixing Joey calling her Liz with the thought of Alex. Things could change completely in one year. It took Alex only that long to decide their marriage wasn't working. So why, after a year, did Joey still call her Liz? Jack was probably right, Joey would call her Mom when he was ready. And what if he never did? Was it really a big deal? Liz had already been more mother to him than the real one. Everyone knew that. What he called her shouldn't matter that much. She knew he already thought of her as a mother, and that would be enough.

She came half out of her doze when the bed squeaked and she felt someone lying behind her. She didn't want to wake up, not yet.

"Jack?" she murmured. When he didn't answer, she decided it was Joey. She smiled in her sleep and felt fine.

She woke up later when she heard Jack coming down the hall and the crinkle of grocery sacks in his arms. She rolled off her side of the bed, stretched, and looked down at the empty spot where she'd expected to see Joey. Where was he?

He must have heard Jack coming and got up, too.

Liz wandered into the kitchen to put the groceries away while Jack finished carrying them in. She stopped in the doorway and her fingers came away from her eyes, suddenly clear, her vision fine.

Joey lay sleeping on the couch, his two fingers still hanging from his mouth.

He must have come back in here after I fell asleep, she thought. That had to be it. Because she knew she felt someone on the bed; the mattress squeaked, and she felt the weight behind her. Then again, there was every possibility she'd dreamed it.

Liz pushed it away and went into the kitchen to make sure Jack hadn't forgotten the traps.

"So what do you really think?" he asked, pulling a package of traps from the bag.

Liz took the traps and opened them, knowing this would be the only time she touched them. Once set, they were Jack's domain. And once used, she didn't want to see them.

"Think about what?" she asked.

"The house? Honestly?"

He pulled a jar of peanut butter from the bag, handed it over.

"I told you. I think it's big." She set the peanut butter on the counter next to an unwrapped trap. "God, I just realized I haven't even been upstairs yet. All I've seen are the few rooms down here. Why don't you finish with the traps and I'll go see the rest."

Liz rounded the first landing and saw the huge open room in the middle of the second floor.

"Wow," she said. "That's a big room."

She continued up and wandered the second floor, marveling at the spaciousness of the rooms. Each room boasted high ceilings, clean white walls. There was a door leading off from the main room. Liz opened it to find the perfect study. Even though the room was empty, one wall held a five-shelf built-in bookcase and Jack could move his desk in here and have an official home office.

There were two windows in the room, one looking out on the front yard, the other on the front porch. Liz was leaned over, watching the houses across the street when she heard thumping. She stood up straight and listened. It came again, from above. Joey was upstairs? She hadn't heard him coming up, but she heard him now, and he sounded like he was having fun up there.

She poked her head out of the room. The stairs were there in front of her and the space was open all the way to the third floor ceiling. She heard him making play noises, the rrrrrrrrr of an imaginary car engine. He chuckled. She smiled. He made another sound, something she couldn't distinguish, and then he screamed, loud and high. Liz leaped up the stairs three at a time, yanking herself around the post when she reached the landing, then up to the top.

When she reached the third floor, she found herself confronted with four choices. Each door was closed and Joey was nowhere. She entered the first door on the left and found an empty room. Another door in here led to a corner room. It too was empty. Liz went into the next room and found nothing except ugly yellow walls. Then another empty room, and finally a dirty, but no less empty, bathroom.

So where was he? She made the rounds of the rooms again, calling, "Joey. Come on out. What's the matter?"

He wasn't up here. But she'd heard him.

Just like you felt him get into bed with you?
But I did feel him, she told herself.
So where is he?
I don't know, she thought.

Then, before Liz could move, the scream came again, directly behind her. She whirled, expecting to see Joey lying half-dead, by the sound of that scream. But she was alone.

Liz turned and went down the stairs quicker than she'd come up them.

When she got to the bottom floor, she found Jack in the hall, shining a flashlight down into the cold air vent.

"I gotta get my keys out of there," he said.

"Where's Joey?" she asked, ignoring his search.

"On the couch, last I saw. He was waking up a bit, but he was still in there. Why, you find something upstairs he'd like?" Again she didn't respond, but if Jack had bothered to look up, he would have wondered why his wife was staring at him like he'd just crushed her cat's head with a hammer.

Liz went into the living room. Joey was awake, a toy car in his hand, driving it along the edge of the cushion.

"What'cha doing?" she asked. She sat next to him, just behind his outstretched feet.

"Playing."

"Did you have a good nap?"

"Uh-huh." She nudged his feet and he kicked back, a game they had.

"Did you just wake up?"

"No, I been awake fifteen hours already. I'm hungry."

"We'll eat in a bit. Did you go upstairs to play when you got up?"

"Huh-uh." He rolled his car along the couch and didn't bother to look back when he said, "I don't like it upstairs."

"You don't?"

"No."

"Are you sure?"

"I know I don't like it up there."

"I meant, are you sure you didn't go up there?"

Of course he's sure, she told herself. What's he going to do, forget? Stupid question. No, he said he hadn't, so he hadn't. Didn't explain what she'd just heard, but something would, she was sure. She hadn't had a decent night's sleep since they left Houston three days ago; her mind was messing with her. It was a bird outside, or in the ceiling, that's all it was.

Didn't sound like any bird I ever heard of.

Then again, who knows what kinds of birds were common to Angel Hill. A Screaming Banshee bird might be a common sound in this town. She hoped not.

Was it just a couple hours ago he'd come to her begging not to have to sleep up there? She wondered now if he'd heard something up there, too.

You know, not all big houses are haunted, she told herself.

"I don't think they knew I was listening," Joey said.

"What?" She hadn't been listening, either.

"The ones upstairs, I don't think they knew I was listening."

"There's no one upstairs," she told him.

He didn't respond, just turned back to his car and drove it over the bumps in the cushion.

She wanted to continue with this and see what he meant, but instead she took a lesson from Jack and tried to think it through. He heard people upstairs. Of course he did, she thought, the movers were in and out. Maybe they were talking about something and didn't know Joey was listening. It's not impossible, is it? That's what he meant.

She didn't ask what he'd heard, a conversation, a thump, a scream--bird, she reminded herself--and she wouldn't ask because it was their first day in their new house, the first day of their new lives and right now the uneasy feeling in her gut had her so clenched--from a stupid bird?--she knew she'd be sore tomorrow.

She put it aside and went into the hall

Jack pointed the flashlight into the cold air vent in the floor, still searching for his keys.

"Are you hungry?" Liz asked. He left the beam pointed where he had it and looked up.

"What?"

"You want a sandwich?"

"No. Thanks. I'll get something later."

Liz turned away, leaving Jack to his keys. In the kitchen, she made Joey a peanut butter and jelly, set it on a plate next to a couple of cookies and called him into the kitchen.

"But there's no table," he said.

Liz realized he was right and looked around. Surely with all these boxes, he could sit on something other than the couch.

"Can I eat outside?"

Liz smiled at his ingenuity. "Yes, that's a good idea. It's an awful nice day."

The backyard had two levels and they sat together on the step from the higher to the lower. Liz wondered at the huge back yard that included the empty lot next to their house. Jack will have a ball mowing this thing, she thought.

Joey chewed loudly, mostly playing with his sandwich and munching the cookies.

"Put the cookies down," she said. "You can eat those after your sandwich."

"Just one more?"

"No. Now eat."

Joey nibbled the bread. A drop of jelly oozed from the bottom and dropped to his leg. He didn't notice it.

She turned around to stare at the house and noticed for the first time another door, about ten feet to the left of the back door. She got up, asking, "Where's this go?"

Joey sat staring at his food. He stayed put as she reached the door, turned the handle. It was locked, but she pushed against the door anyway. It didn't budge.

Just then Joey laughed and pointed.

"Look, Liz," he said, smiling, "a naked woman!"

Liz looked and sure enough there was a naked woman, an old naked woman from the looks, staring at them from the window of her apartment in the building just across the alley from the Kitch house.

"Joey, don't look at that!" She tried not to laugh. Liz covered Joey's face and the old woman ducked behind her curtain. Her face peeked out again, just enough for her to see Liz was still trying not to watch.

"Come on," Liz said. "I think we can go inside now."

"Did you see her?" Joey laughed. "She was naked." He laughed with childish hilarity and almost dropped his plate. A cookie slid toward the side, but stuck in a smear of peanut butter. Joey kept laughing as Liz carried him in and set him on the couch. She plugged in the television, then went looking through the maze of junk for the DVD player and Joey's cartoons.

Jack came into the room, tossing the flashlight onto the couch, asking, "What's so funny?" She told him and Jack said, "Great. Nice to know we picked the good neighborhood."

"Did you find your keys?"

"No. I'm going to have to take the vent cover off and get down there myself. Those keys are down there, I just can't see them from up here."

"Why don't you just make copies of mine?"

"Because my keys would still be down there and it would bug me."

"I see," she said. She spotted the DVD player and pulled it from the box it had been stuffed into. She was unraveling the cord when she remembered, "Do you know where that other door outside leads?"

"What other door?"

She told him and Jack said, "That goes to the laundry room. It's downstairs."

"There's another floor?" she asked.

"Two, actually," he explained. "The basement has two levels. The laundry room on one, and then another level down to the furnace and the water heater."

"This house is just too big. And you have to go outside to get to it?"

"No," he laughed. "You can get outside from the laundry room. There's a door by the stairs in the hall that leads down."

Liz shook her head at the floor and asked, "How did I miss all this stuff? I was up before you, I looked around. I was even outside earlier this morning. I'm just not paying attention to anything." She searched for an outlet to plug the television into.

"There's one by the window," Jack said, then. "You just gotta realize, babe, I got the brains of the marriage, you got the body."

"Oh, so I'm stupid, but hot, right?" She plugged in the television, then set the DVD player on top of it, hooked it up, and plugged it in.

"Hey, I didn't say stupid."

"You didn't have to." As she talked, she tried to find the

box with Joey's cartoons. She should have packed them with the DVD player.

"What I meant was, um, see, uh, what I--"

"That's okay," Liz smiled. "I know what you were trying to say. We'll just leave it like it is for now." Jack groaned and frowned at Liz. She raised her eyebrows at him, then turned toward the bedroom. "You can look for Joey's movies. I'm gonna do some unpacking."

"Do you want to go out for a little bit instead?" Jack asked.

Liz stopped in the doorway. "What did you have in mind?"

Jack shrugged. "Just a drive around. I've got a week until I start work, we might as well get as used to Angel Hill as we can."

Liz shook her head. "Naw, I'd just as soon get this mess out of the way. But why don't you take Joey for a ride around town? When you get back, I should have the bedrooms livable and then I'll start dinner."

Jack asked Joey if he wanted to go and Joey leapt at the chance.

Liz started by shoving her dresser into place against the wall and filling it with her clothes. Jack's dresser would go against the opposite wall, on his side of the bed. She put the clothes away and made the bed. She was about to start on the bedside table, setting the clock, locating outlets for the lamps, when the front door slid open then clicked shut. She yelled, "You guys are back soon. I'll be done here in a minute. Why don't you start on Joey's room while I'm cooking?"

She'd found an outlet on her side of the bed for the clock and now her lamp stood next to it on the table. Jack's side didn't have an outlet. She'd either have to get an extension cord to another outlet, or he'd have to forego his bedside lamp.

She realized then that no one had come downstairs yet. She stepped into the hall and called out, "Are you guys coming down or what?"

But no one answered and, in fact, when Liz listened, she didn't hear anything at all. No feet moved around upstairs, no boards creaked overhead. She walked closer to the stairs and listened again, then called, louder, "Are you guys coming down?

I'm gonna be making dinner in a minute. What do you want?"

Again there was no answer. She stepped up to the landing, annoyed that they were ignoring her. "Joey," she said, "who wants candy?" When Joey didn't come running and screaming, she decided Jack had told him to keep quiet and they'd scare her. But she was smarter than that.

"It's not going to work, Jack," she said. "I'm going downstairs." With that, she clomped back down to the first floor and into the bedroom. She moved into Joey's room to start his unpacking.

Before she even got started on his clothes, she heard the front door again.

"Nice going," she yelled into the hall. "I can hear the door from down here, you know."

"Liz?" a voice called down. It sounded like Joey, kind of. But he sounded odd. Had he hurt himself, she wondered. I'd better go see if he's okay, she thought.

Liz dropped his clothes on the floor and went upstairs to the landing. They weren't here. Maybe Jack had taken him up to the second floor bathroom for whatever reason. The voice came again, "Liz," from upstairs. She went to the second floor bathroom, but it was dark, empty. The door stood open and as she leaned in to close it, the voice came again, "Liz," from behind her. She turned, expecting to see Joey in the open main room, but Joey wasn't there. No one was. But the voice had been right behind her. She let go of the bathroom door and stepped toward the main room when it came, "Liz," right behind her again. This time it had come from the bathroom and Liz could see clearly that the bathroom was dark and empty.

Panic welled in her; her heart skipped a half dozen beats and her stomach wanted to hide in her knees. Her breath caught and she turned to dart down the stairs. She almost rounded the landing and leapt to the bottom floor, but she bolted through the front door instead. Liz sailed down the porch steps to the walkway, down the path across the long front yard and finally down another small set of steps leading to the street. She stopped and turned back to look at the house, expecting any of a dozen horror movie scenes to be playing out in front of her eyes. Instead, she saw their new house. Nothing else.

The upper windows didn't glow with eerie light, nor did

macabre figures stare out at her. She caught her breath, calmed herself down, and looked up at the house again. She stared at it then, waiting, daring something to show itself. When nothing did, she decided she had come all the way from Houston to live in Angel Hill with her husband and son and this was their house now. No matter what may lie in the shadows of this house, it was theirs now and if she heard a noise every now and then, well, what house didn't make noises?

How many houses call you by name?

Shut up, she told this inner voice. Lots of things sound like *Liz*. There's biz, quiz, wiz, fizz. And when she thought about it, she wasn't entirely sure what she'd heard had been a voice. In all the recorded history of ghost hunting, no one had yet to supply any kind of proof solid enough to convince all the world's skeptics. Why was that? Because everything was always explainable some other way.

Another Angel Hill bird. The Talking Liz bird maybe.

But you heard the door open.

No, she told the voice. I heard something. I've been in this house, what, fifteen hours, suddenly I know all its noises? No. I heard something, but that's all. It could have been a breeze blowing against the door.

Just then, their Jeep rolled up behind her. The horn honked and Liz turned, glad to see Jack and Joey home again.

"Wanna get some supper?" he asked. "We found a good restaurant."

Liz ordered a pot roast dinner while Jack and Joey both had hamburgers. Liz thought about telling Jack about the noises, but decided it wouldn't be a good idea in front of Joey, so she kept quiet. They laughed and talked about the new town and Jack's new job. He would take part of tomorrow and go visit the plant, an electronics company that built control panels for utility trucks. After paying the check, Jack let Joey leave the tip and the six-year-old bounded back to them at the door. They drove around for a while, sightseeing and familiarizing themselves with their neighborhood. While it darkened outside, Joey dozed in the back seat. Jack said, "I wonder if there's a music store in town."

"Didn't you just change those strings a few weeks ago?"

"Yeah," he said. "It was my last set, though. I like to have them on hand, just in case."

"Oh." Liz turned her attention back to the window. Angel Hill was now a blur of light and dark patches whizzing by.

By the time Jack pulled up outside the house, Joey was asleep and Liz also felt exhaustion coming. Her head rested against the glass, enjoying the coolness of it after the summer heat of the city. All thoughts about the sound earlier that might have been her name being called--or might have been the Talking Liz, native to Angel Hill--were forgotten.

Jack got the door open and Liz carried Joey. They let him sleep with them since theirs was the only room close to done.

In the middle of the night, Jack roused just long enough to hear Joey coming back down the hall. While he was almost asleep again instantly, he was conscious enough to know he didn't remember feeling Joey actually climb onto the bed.

Chapter Two

Over the next few weeks, the house became theirs. The first floor was unpacked and decorated, pictures on the walls, plants in the windows, the couch pushed against the wall and the cable hooked up.

The bedrooms were arranged and the sheets covered the mattresses. Joey only occasionally asked to sleep with Jack and Liz. Usually they let him. Sometimes they told him to sleep in his own room like a big boy.

The front door was usually locked, Jack and Liz opting to use the back door instead of dealing with the stairs, especially with an armload of groceries. Jack's keys were still lost, and it drove him crazy like he knew it would, but they simply couldn't be found. He'd copied Liz's and had been able to get another house key from the realtor's office.

Liz had begun making plans for the second floor restoration, spending as much time as she could at McCauley's Hardware, choosing paint colors, light fixtures, a good varnish for the hardwood floor that drew your attention in the open main room. It was easy to concentrate on the house; being new in town, they hadn't found time to meet anyone who might steal their free time. Jack had found a music store and found, not only new strings for his guitar, but a big white acoustic with a pearl pick guard and gold edging. He was thinking of buying it as soon as the big checks started coming in.

A week after moving in, he'd taken his guitar and amp to the third floor, thinking up here he could turn up the volume a little without blasting out his wife and son's eardrums. He plugged into the corner room wall socket, flipped the power switch and waited. When the amp never warmed up, he checked the plug. It was in, but nothing was coming out. He flipped the breaker in the basement, but still the outlet didn't work. Nor did any of the other outlets on the third floor.

He went to the second floor, but the best he got there was a crackle with the intermittent whine of guitar strings. On the first floor, closed off in their bedroom, he played. The headphones were on, so all Joey and Liz heard was the strumming.

A couple weeks later, Liz had just finished the first coat of burgundy on one of the second floor's main room walls and was covered in red specks from the roller. She considered a bath, but didn't want to soak in a tub of red water. The shower was in the second floor bathroom, but she hadn't used it yet. In fact, after the name-calling incident, she'd not used the upstairs bathroom at all. But by now enough time had passed, while she recalled the event, the emotional memory had faded quite a bit. In fact, that entire day was such a jumble of hustling and moving and noise and people through the house . . . she had been sleeping before it happened and now two weeks later, couldn't say with all certainty that hadn't been part of it.

She flipped on the light and found it brilliant.

"What the hell wattage is that?" she asked. "Two million?"

Well, it was bright enough; whatever she hadn't liked about this room couldn't possibly be as sinister in this light. She brought her things from downstairs, towel, soap, robe, and closed the door. The bathroom was small and had no windows. It filled with steam quickly.

She lathered up and began to scrub at the paint freckles.

Joey lay sleeping in his bed. He'd finally dozed off with a truck in his hand, sleep claiming him just as the truck topped the crest of Pillow Hill. His leg twitched as he dreamed.

For years, Joey had dreamed about his mother, whom he'd never met. Although his dad never told him, Joey knew his mother had left very soon after he was born. He also knew Liz was just as good as a mother, even if she wasn't the real thing. But he dreamed about his mother a lot. Until recently, anyway.

Lately his naptime dreams had been scattered bits of weird. In the current dream, Joey was playing at the park a few blocks down the street from their house. He was playing hide and seek with some other kids from the park, and Joey was it. He covered his eyes and counted to ten, then yelled, "Ready or not," and twirled to see it was getting dark.

Joey walked around the park, alone and searching for someone, anyone else. For some reason, his parents weren't around, and when he yelled for the other kids to come on out, he couldn't find them. He went behind the bathrooms, but no one was hiding there. He checked in the tunnel on the jungle gym, but no one was hiding there, either. He climbed to the top of the slide, looking out over the entire park. The sky looked pale green, like it was going to storm, and a breeze chilled Joey's legs and arms where his clothes didn't cover.

Then he spotted someone. From the top of the slide, he could see a kid sitting on a bench by the water fountain. Joey slid down, leaped off the edge into the sand, and ran to the bench.

It was a girl. Her head was down and blonde hair hung in her face.

Joey asked, "Where did everyone go?"

She didn't answer, but her feet kicked back and forth, too short to touch the ground.

"I thought we were playing hide and go seek," Joey said. "I guess I'm not very good at it 'cause I can't find anybody." Joey glanced off to the parking lot and realized all the cars were gone. He was really alone at the park with just this little girl, and she wasn't even talking to him.

Joey slid toward the edge of the bench, ready to stand and leave.

"I think I'm gonna look for my dad," he said and leaned forward to hop to the ground.

The girl's head tilted up then and Joey saw her eyes were huge, like hardboiled eggs bulging from her head. Her skin was yellow and cracked and her hair, now that he saw it right, wasn't blonde, it was dirty and closer to brown. A damp leaf clung to it, a small twig sticking out from behind her ear. She opened her mouth and the lips split with long, red cuts.

"Your father's a murderer," she yelled into his face.

Joey flew off the bench and took off across the park, imagining he was wearing his fast shoes. He looked back and saw the girl get up and step up into the water fountain. Joey stopped running and watched, wondering.

Then the girl dissolved into the fountain, her dead, yellow skin dripping off her and slipping down into the waterspout. Joey was alone for real. He looked around, wondering which way was home.

Then his dream changed and Joey was sitting on a picnic blanket and his mother was with him. As always, her dream-face was blurred, but Joey knew who she was.

Liz rinsed away the soap from her arm and saw most of the paint flecks were gone. What few were left she figured would wear off by the end of the day. She wet her hair, lathered and scrubbed it, and turned her back to the showerhead to wash the shampoo from it. A stream of soapy water ran into her eye and she plunged her face into the line of spray to rinse it. All that accomplished was causing it to burn even more. She squinted through the other eye, searching for the cloth to wipe them.

As she pressed the soaking cloth to her face, Liz suddenly felt a series of chills skitter up her spine. The backs of her legs went very cold and she had the feeling someone was watching her.

Had Jack come home early? Was he joining her in the shower for a nooner on his lunch break?

She wiped her face and peered over her shoulder to see a gap in the shower curtain and a small boy, younger than Joey, staring at her. He had glasses and short black hair.

Liz dropped the cloth and stepped back, slipping on the tub floor and tumbling backward. She knocked her head on the edge of the tub and bruised her hip. She must have blacked out for a second because she remembered the sense of waking up when she opened her eyes, then twisted her face out of the line of hot spray.

"Oh, my God," Liz said out loud, shutting off the water and flinging the curtain back. Cold air assaulted her, breaking her skin out in wet goose bumps. She yanked her robe off the doorknob and wrapped it around herself, then stepped out of the bathroom in a haze of steam and confusion.

"What the fuck was that?" She hurried to the middle of the main room and looked back at the open bathroom door, steam still swirling out in white wisps.

The sun shone into the room, casting Liz's shadow large on the floor before her. The smell of paint surrounded her. A valve was released on her skull and it felt as if it would float away.

"Just paint fumes," she said. "That's all."

She gathered her things, turned off the light and closed the door. As she rounded the landing on her way downstairs, she thought, *Forgot to open the windows. Passed out from too many fumes.*

She found Joey still asleep and decided she'd relax for another half-hour or so before waking him. After pulling on a shirt and a pair of shorts, she rolled onto the bed and stared at the ceiling, crossing her ankles and trying to think of parties or shopping, something to get her mind off the look on the boy's face and how real he seemed.

Jack had been two weeks on the job, but it was a job he'd been doing, more or less, for over a year. His last thirteen months in Houston had been spent as acting lead man for the electronics department of a computer manufacturer. The previous supervisor had left suddenly to avoid a nervous breakdown from job-related stress and Jack had been moved in to take over until a permanent replacement could be found. For six months they strung him along, never giving him an official title, but never saying he wasn't in charge. Finally, he decided to find a company that wasn't afraid to commit. Fett Technologies was the company. Their main plant was in Angel Hill, Missouri and, although the money wasn't as good, the cost of living was lower, too, and, after doing some figuring, Jack realized he'd actually be coming out more ahead every month than he had been. So he took it.

Liz offered no resistance. In fact, Jack suspected she might see the move as a chance to solidify the feeling of family and belonging she'd been trying to build since they'd married a year ago. The only person Jack was leaving behind was his brother Allen, and they rarely saw each other except holidays. So to Angel Hill it was.

The folks at Fett Technologies took quickly to Jack, at least it seemed to him. And he liked them. His days were split, spent half in meetings and half trying to track down a late toggle switch or a roll of thirty conductor cable that was supposed to have arrived three weeks ago. What little time he didn't spend sitting or searching, he familiarized himself with as many aspects of the job as he could.

Jack's department consisted of three areas. One built the circuit boards to go inside the control boxes, another made cables to connect the boxes to the utility trucks, and the third put the boxes together, assembling the switches and buttons to the faces, inserting the boards, and connecting the cables. Jack spent the first week helping in the circuit board area, and the second week soldering connectors to lengths of raw cable.

What he liked most about the job were the absolutes. When a part came back for repair, it was only a matter of finding the problem and solving it. In the test phase, if one of the switches didn't light up the correct test button, check it out, fix it, and that was that. The job of building control panels didn't require a great deal of guesswork and that was the solid, logical world Jack had made for himself. He said sometimes, when asked why he went into electronics, that if he'd wanted to deal with unreality, he would have studied the arts instead.

Although he'd been there two weeks, the day Liz thought she saw a little boy in the bathroom was the first day Jack had sat down and talked to Charley Clark. Sure, he'd passed a minute here and there with him, but Jack didn't know a thing about him. He'd never had a conversation with him. When Jack walked into the break room to eat his lunch, Charley was the only one who had opted not to eat out that day. His plate of microwave pot roast sat steaming in front of him.

"Wow," Jack said, "mind if I sit down? It's kind of crowded in here, I don't know if I can fight my way through the mob."

"Go ahead," Charley said. He closed his newspaper and slid it aside. "You haven't decided to get out while you can, I take it?"

"Huh?" Jack asked, setting his coffee and chips on the table. "Oh, you mean the job? No," he replied, tossing a small pizza into the microwave. "This is a great job. I like the company. My last job, they were so screwed up, it's a wonder the company didn't go under."

"Wow," Charley said. "So you just worked for a different division of Fett, right?"

"No," Jack chuckled. "This place is a well-oiled machine compared to that one. At least here, I know what's going on, you know? I know the chain of command and if there's a problem, I'm figuring out who to go to for what. Down there . . ."

"That bad?"

"More so," Jack said. The microwave beeped and he

took his pizza to the table. "No, I like the job. The town's a little different, but I figured it would take a while to get used to a much smaller place."

Charley smirked as he said, "Better watch what you say about Angel Hill. She might come back to bite you in the ass."

Jack looked sideways at him, not sure if Charley was trying to be funny or not. His tone was serious, despite his smile. "What do you mean?"

Charley took a bite of his pot roast. When he swallowed, he said, "There's a bookstore on Dayan Street, Arthur's Used Books. The man sells nothing but old books. Except," Charley said, holding his finger straight to mark his point, "this one book at the counter. *The Outsider's Guide to Angel Hill.* It's a collection of local stories, legends and shit that have sprung up since the town was founded. Some of them are bullshit, but some are right on. Arthur wrote it himself and had it published a few years ago. You won't find a person in town who owns a copy, but somebody's buying it 'cause he sure as shit doesn't keep his business open just selling old books."

"What's that got to do with the town, what did you say, biting me in the ass?"

"Just read it. Halfway through and you'll wonder what the hell's wrong with you to stick around here. Even if you don't believe a word of it, just that any of that crap could be associated with one town--."

Jack had finished his small microwave pizza while Charley was talking and he tossed the cardboard plate into the trash.

"Yeah well," Jack said, "every town's got its stories. I'm sure Angel Hill's are no different."

"Think what you want man, I'm just giving you the warning every new person gets when they move to town."

Jack tossed back the rest of his coffee and rinsed his cup in the sink. He had his chips, unopened, in his hand as he walked out.

"Just get the book, man. 'Arthur's Used Books' on Dayan."

Jack wasn't buying into Charley's bullshit, but what the

man said did get him thinking. If he was going to live here, why not try to learn a little about the place. The main library was on Angel Hill Road, straight across from Holland.

Angel Hill Road was out of Jack's way. Angel Hill sits on the intersection of US169 and the Platte River. The highway and the river, on the map, form an X, splitting the town into four smaller sections. Fett Technologies stood in the lower section, in south Angel Hill. The Kitches lived in north Angel Hill in the top of the X. But the library lay in west Angel Hill and would require backtracking to get home. Jack contemplated the last half of his day whether he wanted to bother today, or wait until the weekend. After all, the drive home was a good thirty minutes with traffic and Fett Tech was on a regular nine-hour workday. If he made the detour today, he'd get home even later, and that meant even less time with his wife and son. And Liz would have been working on the house all day; her mood wouldn't be the best. It would be worse if he got home later.

He'd go this weekend instead.

Jack set his mind for a Saturday trip to the library, then he clocked out and went home.

When he got there, Joey was staring down from a third floor window. Jack glanced up, saw him and waved. Joey turned away and was gone from sight. Jack used the front door this time; he wanted to see the second floor and get a look at what Liz had done today.

He had to give her credit. For someone who hadn't wanted a big job like this house, she was bringing everything together nicely. The fumes hit him and he winced, but he liked the color. As he was admiring the paint job, he heard Joey moving around upstairs. Banging around would have been a better description. He'd never noticed before what a heavy walker his son was.

Downstairs, Liz was on the couch, her feet up and bare. When she saw him, she stretched, popped her back, and smiled.

"I'm glad you're home," she said.

"Oh yeah? How come?"

"Just am. I don't care so much for being by myself here."

He kicked off his shoes and fell onto the couch at her feet. "You got Joey," he said. "He seems to be getting used to everything."

"He doesn't count. I doubt Joey's gonna stop the monsters."

Jack chuckled. "I doubt that if monsters came to take you away, babe, I could do much about it. So I guess it's a good thing that isn't gonna happen."

"Did you see the color upstairs?"

"I did," he said, nodding. "I like it. Hey, this Saturday, I'm gonna go to the library, do you want me to get you something?"

"What?" she asked. "I'm not allowed to go, too?"

"Of course you can go," Jack said. "I figured I could take Joey and give you a day to yourself. You don't even have to do any work on the house if you don't want to?"

Liz smiled with mock glee. "Do you mean it? I get a whole day off and don't have to touch the house?"

"Yeah, yeah," he said, standing. "Hush up. I was trying to be nice."

"Yes," she said. "And it was very nice. And I just might take Saturday and sleep until noon."

A knock came on the back door and Liz said, "There's dinner."

"Pizza?" Jack guessed.

"Yep."

"I'll get Joey," Jack said, walking toward the hall.

"Where are you going?" Liz asked as she got her purse and the checkbook.

"He's upstairs, isn't he?"

Liz laughed out loud, and said, "I don't think so. He's gonna play up there all by himself? Not in this lifetime."

"Yeah he is," Jack replied, nodding. "I saw him in the window when I was coming up the walk. And I heard him knocking around up there when I was looking at the paint. Where'd you think he was?"

"He's outside," Liz said. "I'm the one who let him out. Let me get the food and I'll yell for him."

Sure enough, when Liz returned with the pizza, Joey was in tow.

While Liz got plates and Joey sat swinging his legs at the table, Jack said, "I'll be right back," and he went upstairs.

He made a circuit of the rooms, but all he found was that he was alone. He walked to the window he'd seen Joey in and stared down at the yard. Then he turned back to the room and it was still empty. He made another round, looking in the closets, too, but Joey was still downstairs and when Jack returned, he asked, "Joe, you didn't go upstairs a little bit ago, did you?"

"Huh-uh," Joey said around the food in his mouth. "I don't want to go up there."

"Then we got raccoons or something," Jack told Liz, "'cause I heard something moving around up there."

"What about mice?"

"I haven't found any in the traps yet."

"I thought you said you saw him, too."

"I thought I did, but I guess not. I know I heard something, though. I'll call an exterminator tomorrow. We can't have raccoons and I don't even want to consider that it might be rats."

"Don't say that," Liz cautioned.

"Well, I'm pretty sure the realtor said the house had been empty for six years. I wouldn't be a bit surprised to find out something was living in the ceilings up there."

"Why was it empty so long? A big place like this?"

"I don't know. I didn't think to ask. At the time, I was only interested in finding us a place and this seemed the perfect one."

"Perfect and spooky as hell sometimes," Liz commented.

"What's so spooky about it? I mean, it's big, but so what? I think it's a nice house."

"Me too," Liz said. "I'm not saying it's a dump. I just wouldn't want to spend a night here alone."

The phone rang, then, cutting off Jack's response. They both looked at each other, wondering who could be calling when they still didn't know anyone.

"It's gotta be work," Jack said, then looked at his watch. "It's awful late though. There shouldn't even be anyone there still."

"Maybe it's burned down and they're calling to tell you not to come in tomorrow."

"Right," Jack said, smiling. "Hello?" he said. He was silent a moment, listening, his face growing more twisted with his frown. When Jack pulled the phone away from his ear and turned it off, Liz caught a bit of sound, a loud, distorted screech.

"Who was it?" she asked.

"Just kids," he answered, "playing with the phone."

"What did they say?"

"Just stupid shit. Some moron. Immature crap, that's what it is," he said, turning away from the phone and biting into his pizza. "People have got way too much time on their hands."

Joey took his bath while Liz sat sideways on the toilet reading to him. Jack was in the bedroom with his headphones on, strumming away.

After Joey was dried off and in his underwear, Jack told him it was bedtime. Joey whined, but knew it wouldn't do any good. Bedtime was bedtime was bedtime. Jack tossed him onto the mattress and Joey bounced, laughing. Jack covered him up and asked him, "How much do I love you, Joe?" Joey spread his arms wide and Jack said, "That's right. And who's your hero?"

"You," Joey said.

"And who's my hero?"

"Me," Joey said.

"Good job. Now get some good sleep. And don't let the bedbugs bite."

Jack was almost out of the room when Joey asked, "Aren't you gonna tell me to have sweet dreams?"

"I was getting to it," Jack covered. "Sweet dreams, Joe."

"Sweet dreams."

The door closed and Jack crossed the hall to the bathroom. While he was standing there, he heard a click and a whoosh. He stood still, listening. What the hell was that? Raccoons? No, his mind said. You forgot to lock the front door when you came home.

When he went up the landing, the front door stood wide open, welcoming anything the night might see fit to admit. He closed it, locked it, and went down to his wife.

In the living room, he found her standing, staring at the wall. When he looked, he saw she was looking at a family picture they'd taken just a few weeks after getting married.

"What'cha doing?" he asked.

"Just looking."

"What for?"

"I was wondering if people in town, since we're new, wonder if maybe we kidnapped Joey and are hiding out from his real parents."

"The hair?" he asked, knowing the answer.

"Of course. I mean, really. We just got here, no one knows us, and we're not the most social people ever. You got the dark hair, I got the red. And here we are with this little blonde-haired, blue-eyed kid."

"Who is not the least bit nervous about where he is, because he's with his parents."

"Parent and a half," she corrected.

"Would you stop? He'll do it when he's ready. All right?"

"I know he will," she said, moving away from the picture and leaning back on the couch. "Ignore me. I'm just goofy right now. I think I sniffed too many paint fumes today; I started seeing things in the bathroom."

"Oh, yeah?" he asked, curious. "Like what?"

"Nothing you want to hear about," she said. She rolled her eyes and raised her eyebrows.

"A big sexy guy?"

"Not even close," she said. "Trust me, though, honey, it was nothing I need to see again."

He sat at her feet and rubbed them through her socks. Liz moaned and stretched her back, arms above her head. Then she collapsed in a heap of exhaustion and closed her eyes.

"You ready for bed?" he asked.

"Almost," she said. "I wanna finish this movie first."

"Record it and watch it tomorrow while Joey's taking his nap."

"Hey," she said, "you want this house to look nice, or not? I'll be in in a little bit."

"Well then," he said, leaning up off the couch. Her feet dropped from his lap. "I'll go play some more."

He blew her a kiss and disappeared into the bedroom. The door closed behind him.

He didn't bother plugging in. Instead, he leaned back against the headboard, Lily cradled in his lap, with her neck resting against his bent left knee. Jack's hand went to the fretboard, fingered a G chord, and he strummed. The high E string snapped.

"Shit," he said, looking down at the broken string. He removed his fingers from the fretboard and strummed again. He shook his head; he'd heard right. The other five strings were out of tune. They'd been perfect earlier.

Jack turned the guitar toward him, staring at the snapped string hanging dead from the tailpiece, the other end dangling from the tuning head. A broken string doesn't knock the rest out of tune.

He'd just been in here twenty minutes ago . . . It didn't matter anyway how the others were knocked out, the high E was broken. He reached under the bed and pulled out his case. There was a compartment inside where he kept his extra strings, but when he opened it, they were gone. He knew he had them. He'd just bought them, what, two weeks ago?

He got on the floor and looked under the bed. Not there. He turned on the bedroom light and looked around the room, but didn't find them.

He went into Joey's room.

Joey turned his head, still awake.

"Hi, Dad."

"Joe," Jack asked, "do you know where Dad's guitar strings are? They're in a little square package." He held his fingers up to the show the approximate size of the pack.

Joey answered, "Huh-uh."

"You didn't see anything lying around and picked it up to play with it?"

"No," Joey said, rubbing a tired eye.

Jack scratched his head.

"Hmm. I just bought them and now I can't find them."

"Are they upstairs?" Joey asked.

Jack looked at him for a second and wondered why he would think they'd be upstairs.

"No," he said. "I don't think so. Well, I'll just get some more, and if I find them I'll have them, I guess." He leaned over and hugged Joey, kissed his cheek, and squeezed the boy's face in his hand. His fingers grazed the wrinkled bit of skin above Joey's neck, at the juncture of his neck and jaw, a thin pink birthmark.

Jack had always thought it looked like a scar, but it had been there since Joey was born. He ruffled his son's hair, then went back to his own room. He stood Lily against the stand and went into the living room where Liz had dozed off during the end of her movie.

The phone rang and he snatched it up.

"Hello?"

He held it to his ear a minute, silent, then hung it up again, shaking his head, a disgusted look on his face.

"Same thing as earlier?" Liz asked.

"I thought you were out," he said.

"No, just dozing off a little bit. The phone woke me up. So was it the same?"

He nodded and said, "I can't believe we've been in town three weeks and already we've got to put up with stupid shit."

"Every town's got teenage kids," she said.

"Yeah, I know."

Heading into the bedroom, they heard a soft click and a whoosh. They looked at each other, confused.

"What the hell was that?" Liz asked.

"I don't know. I'll go see."

Liz's mind's eye saw Jack going upstairs only to come down seconds later with a machete buried in his skull and blood running down his face as if it had been poured on. She shoved the bad movie aside and turned on the bedroom light while she waited.

Jack went up the stairs to the landing and stopped, staring, even more confused now.

"Didn't I just lock that," he asked the house. He pushed the door closed and deliberately, consciously, locked it, CLICK. He turned to go back down and a chill skittered through him. He wondered where the draft was coming from and decided he'd have to find it before winter. "But not right now," he said.

At the bottom of the stairs, he stopped to flip on the bathroom light and left the door open a foot; he'd heard Joey, on more than a dozen nights now, coming back from the bathroom in the middle of the night. At least he's getting up to do it, Jack thought.

"No serial killers up there?" Liz asked as he slid into bed next to her.

"Just an absent-minded husband," he answered. "By the way, I'm going by the music store on my way home tomorrow, so I'll be a little bit late."

"What'cha going there for?" She yawned, stretched, and draped a leg over him.

"I broke a string tonight."

"Nice going."

"I know."

They slept.

Liz woke up in the middle of the night and lay staring at the ceiling, waiting for sleep to come again. She checked the clock. 3:25. She listened to Jack's breathing, hoping it would lull her back to sleep. She looked at the clock again. 3:58.

As she waited for sleep, her thoughts went to the telephone and Jack's prank calls. What was it he said they'd done?

Everyone will suffer now.

That's right. And something else, he said, someone else speaking, too.

You can't save yourself.

Who was it calling? No one in town had their number except Jack's work, so obviously it had been a random call. But most pranks started with something like, "Is your refrigerator running?" or "Do you have Prince Albert in a can?"

She hadn't been on the phone, but the voices had been loud enough, she'd caught their tone. They'd been raspy voices, as far as she could tell. Loud and raspy.

Everyone will suffer now. As she lay in the dark, listening to the sounds of the house all around her, wishing she could just go back to sleep and not wake up until the bedroom was flooded with sunlight, she began to hear that raspy-voiced phrase in her head, over and over.

Everyone will suffer now, everyone will suffer now, everyone will suffer now.

When she was in middle school, Liz had been home alone one afternoon when the phone rang. It was her first prank call and all the voice said was, "You're dead."

It had caught her so by surprise, she'd dropped the

phone and hid in her parents' room, ducking between the wall and the bed. That had been the year before they divorced.

Those two words, "You're dead," had terrified her, but even that ominous phrase didn't carry the weight of doom of "Everyone will suffer now." And then even that one wasn't as bad as, "You can't save yourself."

For the first time since moving in, Liz wished their yard weren't so big. It kept the streetlights from shining in. A month ago, she would have killed for a dark room to sleep in. *That was before we moved into the Angel Hill Tomb*, she thought. Now she just wanted something glaring in, something throwing light bars across the wall, something to prove the dark mass in the corner was just dirty laundry.

She rolled over and moved close to Jack. His warmth spread to Liz and after a few minutes, she finally felt herself sinking into sleep. She was about to give in and descend into unconsciousness again, but something nagged at her, keeping her from taking that last step.

"Dammit," she whispered. She wanted to ignore the pressure, and she knew she could do it, if she just pushed it away, she'd go back to sleep. But she knew the sleep would be light and troubled if she didn't get up.

"Crap," she said, rolling out of bed. She tried to keep her steps light as she crept down the hall. She stepped into the bathroom, shut the door, then turned on the light. Hadn't Jack turned that on before bed? Joey must have turned it out after getting up to pee. The pressure wasn't great, but she knew it was enough. Liz sat and the tinkling of the water sounded incredibly loud in the middle of the night. The sound faded and Liz was standing and flushing the crumpled wad of paper. She stood staring into the mirror while the toilet filled up again. When it was quiet, she went to the door.

Liz froze just inside, listening to the footsteps coming down the hall. She'd tried to get up without waking Jack, but now that she had, he had to go, too.

She heard him step across the cold air vent and she opened the door to light the rest of his way. She stepped back to let the light shine into the hall so she could see him. But Jack wasn't there.

The hall was long, dark, and empty.

He's stepped to the side, she thought. He's going to try to scare me.

Liz leapt out, ready to attack. But Jack wasn't there.

She stood unsure in the hall, watching, listening. Jack hadn't been coming down the hall. "But I heard something," she said. Her voice scared her. It wavered and came out unlike her voice. And in the dead of night, the sound was out of place with the rest of the world.

She flipped off the light and walked, a little quicker than she'd come the first time, back to the bedroom. As she reached the door, Liz heard something behind her. She froze, then whirled, hoping to see Joey coming toward her.

The hall was still black, still empty, still menacing. Liz knew there was nothing there, even if she couldn't see. But the footsteps continued, down the hall, away from her, and on up the stairs. She heard them round the landing before she leapt into the bed, buried herself under the covers, and wrapped herself tight around Jack.

He grunted in his sleep, pressed back against her, and was still again.

Liz lay there, praying for sleep or a stroke or anything that would render her unconscious. She knew that, in the light of morning, none of this would seem as terrifying. But for now, while it was still pitch black in the house, a million horrible things seemed all too possible.

She dozed after a while and, as she felt herself slipping, she welcomed it, opened herself to the oblivion, and fell freely into its arms. Until she felt Joey's small hands nudge her shoulder and ask, "Liz?"

She came out of her stupor and rolled back, asking, "Huh, babe?"

Joey wasn't there. But the voice was.

"Can I get in bed with you?" it asked. It wasn't Joey's voice this time, but it was a child's.

The tiredness fell away from her like a limp suit that hangs too loose. She stared into the darkness wide-eyed. Her heart pounded and she wanted to shake Jack, to make him get up and check every floor, every room, and every closet of the house. But she knew Jack well enough.

Get real, she told herself, using Jack's way of thinking.

You were almost asleep. You dreamed it. That's exactly what he'd say, too. She knew it.

But I didn't dream it, she thought. I was almost asleep. But I know what I felt, and I know what I heard.

She lay wide-awake in the dark, clutching her husband. She finally began to feel safe again, and dozed off just as the first morning light crept through the windows.

Chapter Three

In her sleep, tiny hands nudged her again.

Liz jerked awake with a gasp and rolled out of reach. She was wide-awake and staring. Joey beamed into her sleeping face.

"Time to get up," he said.

"I'm up," she murmured into the mattress.

"Time to get up on the floor."

Liz slid her leg out of bed and her bare foot hit the floor. "There." She pushed herself up and stretched. Her back popped. Her other foot hit the floor. Joey bounded off into the living room.

Jack poked his head in. He was buttoning his shirt.

"You gonna get up sometime, lazy bones?"

"Not if I can help it," she said. "Oh, my God I didn't sleep at all last night."

"You didn't? Man, I was out."

She pulled clothes from her dresser and slid past him into the hall, heading for the bathroom.

When she came out again, Jack was in the living room, looking through the phone book.

"Are you going to be here if I can get someone to come and check for squirrels?"

"I should be. Joey can play in the yard if he wants to. Or if they come early enough I can take him to the park later."

Jack found a listing, called, and hung up.

"He said the soonest he could come would be tomorrow."

"That's fine," Liz said. "I'm sure they're not going anywhere."

"Unfortunately."

He kissed Liz and Joey, then left.

Liz sat on the couch. Joey was on the floor, watching cartoons.

I can't sit here all day, she thought. I've got to go up there some time.

It was nearly noon before she did.

Joey ate a sandwich in front of the television. Liz crept up the stairs, watching her feet, wondering where the footfalls she'd heard last night had landed. The landing was bright with sunlight. Dust motes floated by. Liz blew them away. She rounded the landing and looked up to the second floor, expecting . . . she wasn't sure what. Part of her didn't expect to see anything at all. The other half wasn't so confident. She climbed higher and breathed a very small sigh of relief to find the second floor empty.

The morning's chill was gone, replaced by early afternoon warmth and the sunlight shining into the room threw big squares of yellow onto the floor. Crossing through one of them, she was instantly comforted. She stood at one of the side windows and looked down at the empty lot next door. While she stared down, she listened, waiting for footsteps, pounding, a voice.

With her back to the room, Liz knew that any second she'd feel that tiny hand pressed against her again. But in the brilliance of day, she was able to hold off the terror.

The house was silent around her, but she didn't trust that silence.

It's waiting, she thought. Waiting for my guard to be down. Then it'll do something.

As if in answer, something thumped overhead. She looked at the ceiling. Yes, right above her, in one of the bedrooms.

There's no way I'm going up there, she thought.

Then Jack's voice came into her head. It's squirrels.

"That's a big fucking squirrel," she said. When the sound didn't repeat, she relaxed a little and was able to make herself think maybe it really had been a squirrel. Maybe it had gnawed a hole in the ceiling and had fallen out. That might have caused a bigger thump than normal.

Would it, really?

"I don't know," she admitted.

She found herself going to the stairs, but instead of descending, Liz stepped up. Her hand gripped the rail, sliding along as she climbed to the second landing. As she passed under the rail where the third floor looked down onto the stairs, a chill went through her. She looked around and up to the third floor looming over her. The ceiling was high and the room was grey; the middle room had only one window, high over the stairs, on the north side of the house. Very little sunlight ever found this room. She reached the top of the stairs and found the room empty.

No, the sound came from one of the bedrooms, not from out here.

She stood, frozen but trying to work up her courage.

It's just a house, she told herself. All houses make noises. This house is just a little bigger than usual, so the noises here might be bigger.

"That's just stupid," she said.

She moved to take a step and froze again. There was a voice.

"Forgive me," it said. It panted twice, then said it again, "Forgive me." It kept repeating these two words over and over between pants, "Forgive me,"--pant, pant--"Forgive me,"--pant, pant--"Forgive me."

Liz was at the bottom of the steps before she realized she'd even started moving.

She snatched up the phone and dialed 911. The operator took her sweet time answering. When she did, Liz blurted, "I need the police there's someone in my house hurry--"

The operator asked Liz to slow down.

"I said, there's someone in my house. Upstairs. I heard them up there talking, so there might even be two people. My husband's at work and it's just me and my son, so I need them here right now."

"And what's the address, ma'am?"

Liz gave her the address, "On Fourth Street," she added. "Between Roland and Pacific."

"Okay, ma'am, two units are on their way. Do you want to stay on the line until they get there? Or do you have a neighbor whose house you can go to?"

"No," Liz said. "I'll wait for them outside."

The operator said they should be there within minutes, then she let Liz get off the phone.

Liz grabbed Joey and headed out the back door. She took him around the house, down to the sidewalk and led him down to the lot next door. She sat with him on the sidewalk, staring down the street, expecting screaming police cruisers to charge up the street any second, lights flashing, and sirens blaring.

She threw glances back to the house, half-hoping, half-dreading to see someone darting out the front door.

"What are we doing outside?" Joey asked.

"We're just waiting for some people," she answered.

"Is Dad coming home?"

"Not yet. But I wish he was, believe me."

Finally the police arrived and Liz pointed to the house.

"There's two doors," she told them. "The front door should be locked, but I haven't seen anyone come out that way. The back door's unlocked."

The officers split up and one went in through the back while the other waited at the front door. The back door man came up to open the front and both disappeared inside the house.

Liz stood and waited.

"How come the policemen are here?" Joey asked. "Did a criminal get in our house?"

"I don't know," she answered. "But don't worry about it, Joe. Whatever it is, they can handle it. That's what they're for."

"When I grow up," he said, "I'm going to be a super-hero so if any criminals get in you and Dad's house when I'm grown up and live in my own house, you can call me and I'll get them for you. But don't tell Dad 'cause I don't want him to know my secret identity."

Liz didn't know if she should laugh or not. She knew he thought he was serious, but the whole idea was so cute, she couldn't help it.

"That will be our secret," she said.

She kept watching the house, wondering what the hell was taking so long.

It's a big house. There's a lot of ground to cover up there.

After a while, Liz was sure they'd been in there for half an hour already and still they hadn't emerged with a pair of handcuffed trespassers stumbling ahead of them. She looked up at one of the third floor windows and thought she saw movement.

That's where they were, she thought.

Then she heard the voice again, repeating its plea in her head.

Forgive me--(pant, pant)--*forgive me*--(pant, pant)--*forgive me.*

She shivered and looked away.

"So what's your super-hero name going to be?" she asked Joey.

He looked thoughtful for a second, then answered, "Um, I think maybe, um . . . can you guys buy me a motorcycle? I can be Motorcycle Man."

Liz smiled and said, "A motorcycle, huh? We'll see about that one."

"No," Joey decided, "I don't want to be Motorcycle Man. I think I'll be, um . . . I don't know. I'll wait until I get older and then I'll think of a name. But I'll have to start training soon, so I might need one of those, um, big things, you know? That you hang and you punch it?"

"Punching bag?"

"Yeah, that's it, I'll probably need a punching bag so I can train."

"We might be able to do that," she said.

Finally she saw the officers coming down the porch steps. They were alone.

She ran up to meet them.

"Where is he?" she asked, searching behind them, hoping the creep was coming out after them.

"Ma'am," the first cop said, "we searched the entire house and there's no one in there. Now, whoever was in there, if there was anyone, could have gone out the back door while you were waiting out here."

"Yes," the second cop chimed in, "it wouldn't have been anything at all to slip down the back alley and, from up here, you wouldn't have seen a thing."

"The best we can do is advise you to keep your doors locked all the time, the windows, too. Is your husband in the home?"

"You just said there was no one in there," Liz said. She was beginning to think these cops were morons.

"No, I mean, does he live in the home with you and your son?"

"Of course," she replied. Yes, she decided, they were morons.

"Then, Ma'am, you and your husband may want to look into a security system."

"Especially with a house this size," said the other cop.

"And you're positive there's no one in there?" Liz asked. "You went through all three floors and the basement? Both levels?"

The cops glanced at each other, then said, "Yes, Ma'am, we did." She knew they hadn't. She'd bet they'd missed the basement door just like she had the first day.

"Well," she said, "I guess then, I'm . . . sorry . . . for getting you all the way here for nothing."

"That's no problem," said the first cop. "It is a big house. I'm sure you get all kinds of noises you don't recognize. But I doubt there's anything in there that could hurt you."

The cops exchanged another look and Liz wondered what they were thinking.

"It's always better safe than sorry, anyway," the second cop added.

"I guess," she said. "Thanks. And again, I'm sorry I got you here for nothing."

"It's no problem," he repeated, then climbed into his cruiser. The second cop got into his and they both had pulled away by the time Liz and Joey reached the front door.

Liz carried Joey on her back down the stairs, then slid him to the floor. He ran into the living room and collapsed on the floor, his chin in his hands, staring up at the television. It was still on.

"No running in the house," Liz said. "Besides, come on, it's naptime."

"But we just came inside," Joey said.

"I know we did, and look at the clock. What time does it say?"

"But I haven't even had lunch yet."

"Yes, you did," Liz said. "Now come on, it's naptime. Go pee first."

"Are you going to take a nap?"

"I don't know. I just might take one after my bath."

Joey dragged his feet into the bathroom, then across the hall to his bedroom, making whining noises in his throat. He climbed onto his bed and turned toward the wall, still making noises.

"That's enough, Joe," Liz said.

She filled the tub, then sank into warm water, dunking herself under, closing off the world. She came up, breathed, and wiped water from her face. She rested her head against the back of the tub and let the water surround her.

She was trying to relax and not think about the house or the noises or anything else.

But the voice she'd heard upstairs wouldn't leave her head.

(*Forgive me*--pant, pant--*Forgive me*--pant, pant--*Forgive me*)

She'd heard it so clearly, she knew she hadn't imagined it. Had she? Was this the onset of schizophrenia? She couldn't believe that. So who the fuck was in her house? How did they get in? That was something else to consider. They kept the front door locked. She'd been in the living room all day. The living room was next to the kitchen, so she knew no one had come in the back door. How did they get up there?

She remembered Joey's reaction their first day in the house.

"Who lives up there?" he had asked.

No one. But something was very wrong. Liz's mind began to work the equation, adding in the footsteps last night-- they'd walked right past her, she heard them going up the stairs. And that look the cops had exchanged. What was that about?

And there were other things. The phone calls Jack got. And he said he'd heard something thump upstairs.

She lay in the tub, her eyes open, but glazed, as she drifted off into her memory. The room dissolved around her. The yellow walls darkened to stale peach and the ceiling crawled with a billion specks of blurred motion. Liz didn't see any of it.

What she did see was herself on the third floor their first day in the house. Like Jack, Liz had explained the happenings in the house rationally, if not convincingly. Hadn't she heard a scream up there that day? And when she'd fallen asleep while Jack went to the store. Someone had sat on the edge of the bed.

Later, while she was unpacking the bedroom stuff, the front door had opened and closed. Twice.

What else?

The hands that touched her last night, calling her name, asking if they could get into bed with her and Jack. And on the second floor, someone had called her name at least half a dozen times.

All of these things she'd told herself were dreams, because that's what Jack would have done. But she was a horrible liar, especially to herself.

Liz bolted up and climbed out of the tub, wrapping herself in her towel and putting her hand to her face, cradling her chin while she rested the elbow on the other arm. She paced the bathroom, trying to sort out all these memories. How could she not have admitted it before?

Because one of the things she'd fallen in love with Jack for was his mind. He could explain anything and it always made sense, even if the memory of your senses told you otherwise. She loved his rationale and had been trying to emulate that.

But her eyes were open now. The question was how to convince Jack?

He'll rationalize everything you tell him.

She knew that was the truth. Jack's world consisted of facts and right angles and a place for everything.

She stood over the sink, staring into the mirror, trying to figure out what to say to make Jack see what had been happening. Telling him what she'd seen and heard wouldn't do it. But he'd heard things, too. That wouldn't matter, though. Unless it punched him in the balls, Jack wouldn't accept it. And even then he'd give some other explanation for it.

I just pulled a groin muscle, he'd say.

Liz chuckled, knowing that's probably exactly what he'd say.

She suddenly had an idea. Whether it would do the job or not, she wasn't sure. But it would be a first step, and she wouldn't have to tell Jack a thing.

She smiled at her reflection, proud of herself, but the reflection made her wince back, heart thumping, a lump in her throat.

As soon as possible, she told herself. Do it today if you can.

She turned away and stopped, staring into the tub. She hadn't drained the water when she got out. And though it wasn't making a sound, the water inside was . . . moving, as if with the weight of a body. Someone was in the tub, but Liz couldn't see them. She imagined them seeing her and she shivered again. She

52

looked around at the walls and thought, What the hell did we wake up when we came here?

The water stopped moving. She stared at it. A shimmer ran through it, then it stilled again.

Liz stormed out of the bathroom, not bothering to shut off the light, and went into the bedroom. She put on different clothes--the ones she'd been wearing were still in the bathroom, and she wasn't going in after them. It wasn't the water that had made her abandon them. It was that reflection of hers. When she'd smiled at it, she was almost positive it had sneered back. Like it knew something she didn't.

Jack came home a few minutes late that evening, complaining about reed relays and they were supposed to receive eight hundred, but could only find two hundred and that would barely be enough for the day.

Liz had no idea what a reed relay was, nor what it did, but she listened, as she always had when Jack came home. She knew his complaining was a way to get it off his chest. That done, he could come back to reality and live.

"So how was your day?" he asked. "You work on the house?"

"Not much," she said.

"We had policemen here, Dad," Joey chimed in from the floor. Then he made a crashing noise as his Spider-Man action figure pounded Green Goblin in the face.

Jack looked at Liz. "The police were here? What for?"

Liz waved it away. "I was upstairs," she explained, "and I thought I heard talking. I mean, I literally heard the voices, loud and clear. I ran downstairs and called the police."

"And?"

"Well, there was no one here, obviously."

"Then how did you hear voices if no one was in the house?"

"I don't know," she said. "Maybe the television was up louder than I thought and that's what I was hearing."

"Hmm," he said. "Maybe it came up through the vents."

"Could be," she said. "It doesn't really matter. After they came back out and said there was no one in the house, I felt like such a moron."

He chuckled, then said, "You're not a moron."

She kissed him, then went into the kitchen to finish supper.

Jack kissed his son, then disappeared into the bedroom. He was kicking off his shoes and lying down for a few minutes, messing with his guitar. Liz knew his routine as well as he did. She checked the spaghetti. It would be done in a few minutes.

She stirred the pasta and watched the water swirl. She thought of the bathtub and made another mental note to finish calling around tomorrow.

She wanted to get the house blessed and had called a couple churches earlier today, but so far hadn't found anyone who could do it. One church she'd called, the pastor said he'd never even heard of house blessing. She wanted to get it done with no one knowing about it. Jack wouldn't understand her plan and Joey, she knew, would spill it as soon as Jack was in the door.

Liz stirred the sauce, then jumped and flung hot tomato sauce onto the wall. The pressure on her neck had scared her. And the arms around her waist hadn't helped. But Jack was just kissing her.

"Sorry," he said. "I didn't mean to give you a heart attack."

"That's okay. We can just lick the walls for dinner tonight."

"It smells good."

"How come you're not in the bedroom?"

"I broke a string last night, remember? I didn't get off early enough to pick up another."

"I see."

"Don't forget," he said, "the guy's coming tomorrow to check out the third floor. I told him it's probably squirrels, but I wanted him to check for mice, too. Or anything else that might have gotten in."

"I'll be here," she said. "Did you tell him to come to the back door?"

"Uh-huh."

She'd forgotten about that. She'd have to remember to call after the exterminator left. She didn't want to be in the middle of making arrangements and have to stop to explain the noises coming from upstairs. Noises Liz wasn't even a hundred percent sure were from an animal anymore.

Slow down, she thought. You don't know what's causing the noises. It just might be animals.

That's right. The thumping and stomping up there might be squirrels, mice, rats, stray cats, anything. But the voice-- ("Forgive me,"--pant, pant--"Forgive me,"--pant, pant--"Forgive me.")--that had been a voice. It wasn't the television coming through the vent. Someone had been upstairs. Just because the police didn't find anyone--and Liz was sure she could go up there now and not find anyone, but she was also pretty sure once her back was turned, the voice would whisper in her ear--that didn't mean anything.

"Is this done," Jack asked, bringing her out of herself.

"What? Yeah, it's done." She leaned into the living room. "Joey, go pee and come get your plate."

As Jack filled his plate, he talked.

"So we also lost two boxes of hand controllers today. Well, they weren't really lost, they just came in under the wrong number. They were supposed to be thirty-eights, but someone back in receiving must have hit the wrong button or something because they came in as eighty-eights. By the time we'd decided we were going to have to call the company we bought them from, someone noticed a box on the shelf with 'eighty-eight' marked on it and said, 'Hey, we don't even have an eighty-eight.' We popped open the box, and there were the twenty thirty-eights. That saved about five hundred bucks."

Liz hadn't listened to a word of it, but she'd heard him. What she did listen to, was the silence coming from the bathroom.

Going around the doorway and down the hall, the bathroom was located just on the other side of the wall from the kitchen. Whenever the toilet flushed, you could hear it in the other room. Liz noticed Joey'd been in there an awful long time. She banged on the wall and called, "Let's go, Joe. It's time to eat."

Jack was in the refrigerator getting a Coke. Liz made Joey's plate and then her own. He still hadn't come back from the bathroom.

Finally, she set the plates on the table and went down the

55

hall to get him.

She stopped outside the door and knocked. The light under the door went out.

"Come on, it's time to eat. Let's go."

She listened. If he were on the toilet, he'd say so. But she'd seen the light go out, so he wasn't sitting down. If he were doing something he wasn't supposed to, trying to cut his own hair for instance, he'd say nothing and quickly try to cover up whatever he was doing. Liz heard nothing.

She grabbed the handle as quietly as she could. If he heard her, he would have forewarning and be able to hide the evidence. Her head was down, her ears alert. She gripped the handle tighter and began to turn it.

"I'm coming in," she said. "Whatever you're doing better be put up."

"I'm starving," Joey said. Liz jumped and turned to see Joey behind her, a new toy in his hands.

"What are you doing out here?"

"I was getting a different toy to eat with," he said. "I already went to the bathroom but I didn't have to go."

Liz stood silent for a second, wondering where to go from here.

"Why didn't you answer when I called for you?" she asked.

"I was in my closet finding this," he said, holding up an inflatable Spider-Man bath toy.

"It's time to eat. Come on."

They were at the end of the hall when Liz heard something thump in the bathroom. She stopped and looked back, but she and Joey were already turning into the living room, headed for the kitchen, and supper was done, and she didn't want to get into it again. She just wanted to get it taken care of.

Day after tomorrow, she told herself. Get it done as soon as you can.

When everyone went to bed, Joey argued and whined, but in the end, he slept in his own bed. Since a door connected the two bedrooms, Jack told him they'd keep it open for him, but he had to sleep in his own bed. Joey gave in and finally, after too much tossing and turning, he dozed off.

Jack lay back and relaxed, letting the stress of work slough off, into the mattress, and through to the floor where it disappeared. Despite all the problems he faced every day, he had to admit, he enjoyed his job. The chips and relays went in the boards, the boards went into the boxes, the cables were connected, and the finished product was out the door. Jack could rest easy at night, knowing there was order to the world. He fell asleep quickly, his legs wrapped in Liz's.

Liz lay awake long after Jack's breathing had evened out. She stared at the ceiling, wondering what was upstairs. Something was, of that she had no doubt.

The noises, she thought. The voices and footsteps. It figures I had to move all this way to live in a haunted house.

She'd lived a full enough life in Houston. It was only fair that, after moving to Angel Hill and getting away from all that, from her dysfunctional parents, her even more screwed up ex-husband, and the depressing life she'd lived out in the years before meeting Jack, she should have some sanity in her life. Jack built his world on order. Why couldn't she?

But Jack lives here, too.

But he doesn't let himself see anything that's going on here.

And what's going on here?

She rolled onto her side and stared at the wall. She wanted to close her eyes, let herself drift off, but she knew the second she let her guard down, those hands would nudge her again. And what would she do then? Scream? Probably not. But she'd certainly lie awake all night.

She edged backward, pressing her back against Jack. He wrapped an arm around her and she grasped his fingers, holding him close, enjoying his warmth.

Resting against her husband, she tilted her head down and closed her eyes, forcing everything out, welcoming sleep and trying not to listen for bumps or knocks in the walls.

Liz finally slept heavily. She dreamed of her first marriage. Except, in her dream, instead of asking for a divorce, Alex had looked into her face and screamed, "You can't save yourself, you can't save yourself, you can't save yourself--". She moved in her sleep, but didn't wake up that night.

Jack turned over and opened his eyes to darkness.
In the hall, he heard Joey padding back to bed.   Then
Jack   went   back   to   sleep.

Chapter Four

Jack wondered if Liz was having trouble sleeping. She was waking up later than usual. He kissed Joey goodbye, then Liz as she was coming out of the bathroom, heading back to the bedroom to get dressed. "Don't forget about the pest control guy," he said on his way out the back door.

On the way to work, Jack drove past Westgate Music to check their hours. He found them open and decided it would only take a second to get a new string. As he went inside, he passed the white acoustic again and thought once more of buying it.

Not today, he thought. *Of course not today. But soon, I hope.*

He bought his new string, tossed it on the passenger seat, then headed for Fett Technologies.

Turning back onto Tenth Street, Jack found himself behind a school bus going a record twenty miles an hours.

What the hell's a school bus doing out in the middle of June?

He wanted to go around it, but oncoming traffic wouldn't let him. So he trudged along, getting later by the second, and glancing at the new guitar string, thinking, *I should have waited until lunch and come out then.*

The bus turned off on Checker Street and he saw it was a church bus.

Then he put it out of his mind and had forgotten it completely by the time he reached work. He parked, used his ID card to scan the door open, and was there.

He made the rounds of the cells, checking out what everyone was doing. Jack was almost always the last one there. The door was already unlocked in the mornings, and the alarm turned off. One of the night guys in another building usually had to come over and get a part for something he was working on. So everyone on Jack's shift was there early in the morning, not so much out of dedication, as out of trying to get that extra three-fifty a day by showing up fifteen minutes early.

He passed Charley Clark's chair and Charley said, "You oversleep? Stay up too late with the wife?"

"No," Jack chuckled. "I just stopped to get a guitar string on the way. The place closes before we get off at night."

"I didn't know you played the guitar."

"I didn't know you were supposed to know."

"I guess you wouldn't," Charley said, turning back to his work. "But it would be nice to have someone to play with once in a while."

"I didn't know you played," Jack said.

"Didn't know you were supposed to."

"I see."

Jack went back to making his rounds. He checked the list of parts they were short, copied it, and stuffed it into his pocket for his meeting at ten.

He noticed today was country day on the radio. While it wasn't his favorite, he was able to admire the guitar work in a lot of country songs. Fingerpicking was one technique Jack had never been able to grasp.

His ten o'clock part shortage meeting went quickly and before he knew it, it was eleven and lunch would be in thirty minutes. That half-hour passed in what seemed like seconds.

Only half the shop went out for lunch today. Jack took his place across from Charley Clark and said, "So what do you got?"

Charley looked down at his microwave plate and said, "Enchiladas. My wife made them last night. They're hot as hell, though."

"No," Jack said. "I meant your guitar."

"Oh. '57 Gretch Silver Jet."

"Nice. What color?"

"Silver."

"Nice."

Jack bit into his Hot Pocket, then realized he should have blown on it first. Steam escaped and burned the roof of his mouth. He drew back, wincing and trying not to drop the food out of his mouth.

"How 'bout you?" Charley asked before Jack had swallowed.

Finally, he was able to mutter, "White Strat. '87. Lily."

"Good choice," Charley said. "How long have you been playing?"

"Not as long as I've had her. I got her in high school, back when everyone had a guitar in high school. Then she lay in the case for a few years."

Charley knocked back half his Coke.

"What made you take it out again?"

"My wife left," Jack said. He swallowed another bite, wiped his mouth, and said, "My son was only a few months old, and she just left. I was just finishing college and I had a baby and a full time job, and I was not ready to deal with all that by myself."

"I can imagine," Charley said. But Jack wondered if he really could. How could anyone imagine, realistically, what that situation is like without being in it?

"So as I'm starting to go into the requisite depression, trying to work enough to pay the bills and now a babysitter, and trying to spend time with the baby when I am home, I decided I needed something to take my mind off all the bullshit."

"That's right," Charley chimed in. "You'll show her."

"Well, I never got the chance for that. I haven't seen or heard from her since she walked out. Anyway, I decided to take out my guitar and try to learn to actually play the thing instead of just seeing how much noise I could make." Jack took another bite, chewed, swallowed. "Turned out to be great therapy, and I fell in love with it," he finished.

"Cool beans," Charley said. He was nodding, but something in his eyes said he'd moved on to something else. "So d'ya get that book I told you about? Freaky stuff, isn't it?"

"I don't know," Jack admitted. "I haven't got it yet. But I am going to the library this weekend, I might do it then."

"I'm telling you, you got to get that book. You think this place is screwed up, you haven't seen the rest of Angel Hill. That'll set you right on what screwed up is."

"I don't know if I could take more screwed up stuff. It's bad enough this job is the way it is. Plus I got squirrels at home, or something in the third floor making noises." He took his last bite. "But at least that's getting taken care of right now."

"Third floor?" Charley asked. "You got a third floor to your house?"

"Yeah," Jack said. "Why?"

"Well, 'cause there's not many houses in Angel Hill with

three floors. Which one do you live in?"

"It's on Fourth Street. Between Roland and Pacific."

"Man," Charley said, smiling and shaking his head. "You're right, you don't need a book for screwed up stuff. You probably got enough problems living in that house."

"What are you talking about? That's a great house. It needs some work on the top two floors, but it's gonna be really beautiful once my wife and I are done with it."

"Uh-huh," Charley nodded. "Yeah, it needs some work, all right."

Jack watched him, waiting for the punchline. The seconds stretched out, and Charley never delivered. Finally Jack said, "What are you talking about?"

Charley smiled like he knew something.

"I'm talking about four kids dead in an upstairs bedroom and a grown man hanging over the top rail of the banister."

Jack shook his head. "What? No, you got the wrong house."

"Three stories?" Jack asked. "Walkway from the porch to a set of steps leading down to the sidewalk, right? Next to an empty lot?" Jack was nodding. "I got the right house."

"Then tell me what you're talking about."

"You didn't hear the story when you bought the place?"

"No," Jack said, "and I'm beginning to think that with your hedging I'm not going to. If there really is a story."

"There's a story, baby," Charley said. He downed the last of his Coke, crushed the can, and tossed it into the trash can someone had mislabeled "can's only". He belched, loud and from the gut. Then he said, "About, I don't know, nine, ten years ago, this guy and his wife bought the house. They had four kids, three boys and a girl. The guy was a railroad engineer, named Milo Dengler. He was, I guess, never home. You know, out driving the train all the time."

Jack was listening, but kept checking the clock over Charley's shoulder. Lunch was over in eight minutes.

"Well, his wife got cancer and she's dead in two years. This guy, Dengler, he's now trying to work enough to keep the house paid and all that, plus trying to take care of his four kids--I think the oldest was twelve, so he helped out a little, I'm sure-- and trying to deal with his wife being dead, you know?"

Jack said, "I can relate."

"Yours left you with one. Imagine four. Anyway, in the end he goes crazy, gets all stressed out, can't deal with everything like it is. You know, his kids are growing up without him. Shit's falling apart. With four kids and no one to take care of them, he's trying to work enough, but can't do it. So some bills aren't getting paid, stuffs getting turned off, and what have you. I'm sure he got it right back on again. Probably let the phone go. I would have. And the cable. You know, you do without the things you don't need in that kind of situation."

"Really," Jack said. "Shit, cut down on anything that's not a necessity."

"That's what I'm saying. Anyway, I'm sure he was under some huge stress. So, he decides one day he can't deal with stuff the way it is. He snaps, and thinks he'd be better off dead. But then who's gonna take care of his kids? He's got the solution to that."

"No way," Jack said.

"Yep. Took 'em all with him. Cops found them in one of the upstairs bedrooms, all lined up along the wall. He put 'em there, leaning up against it."

"Where was he?"

"Hung himself," Charley said. "Tied a rope to the top of the banister and just let himself drop."

"Christ," Jack said. "How much of that you think is true?"

Charley looked confused.

"All of it, man. That story's been known in Angel Hill practically since it happened. Why do you think no one's been in that house since? Nobody wants to buy that place. If it's any consolation though," Charley offered, "you got one of the most famous houses in town."

"Wow," Jack said, sliding his chair back and standing up, "I'm honored. And how is it you know all this?"

"If you'd buy that damn book I was telling you about, it's all in there. The whole story."

Jack cocked his head. "Are you sure you don't get a commission on this? You seem pretty adamant about me getting this book."

"I'm just trying to give you forewarning about Angel

Hill," Charley said.

"It's just a city, Charley."

"If you say so. But I was born here. I'm telling you, get that book."

It was time to go back to work. Boards needed stuffed and soldered. Cables needed cut. Switches needed to be put into control faces. And all of it needed to be shipped out the door.

Jack went to his office for a while after lunch. He sat at his computer and, to anyone passing by, it looked like he was doing work. The mainframe was up and Jack ran part numbers from his short parts list, checking due dates on delivery. While his fingers did this, his mind was on Charley Clark's *Outsider's Guide to Angel Hill*. If the story he told was really in there, Jack was curious to read it. But if Liz found it and saw someone had killed his family in one of their upstairs bedrooms, there was no way she'd want to stay there. And Liz was into that psychic, paranormal stuff. She'd take one look at the story of the house and instantly swear she'd sensed something wrong with the house the moment she set foot in it.

Too late, Jack thought. We've already got the loan and signed the papers. We don't have much choice.

Liz watched the exterminator go up the stairs to the third floor, thinking *You won't find any squirrels. And anything you do find, I don't think I want to know about it.*

Liz stayed on the second floor. When the exterminator, his shirt read "Carl", came down, she didn't want to have to trudge past the bedroom and wake Joey. She looked at the deep color on the walls and thought she should really get back to work on the house. She hadn't done a thing in two days. If she started slacking off now, the house would never get done and they'd be stuck living in four rooms on the bottom floor.

Who gives a shit, she thought. If all this freaky shit keeps happening, I'd just as soon not be here at all.

She heard him walking around up there. At least, she thought it was Carl. And if it wasn't, did he hear it too? If he heard it, what would he think? What if he did find squirrels?

That doesn't explain the voices, nor the hands on her back the other night in bed, nor a dozen other things. Whether

Carl found squirrels or not, there was something rotten in this house. If the blessing worked, great. If not, she'd been thinking of having investigators come in and look at the place. But so far, she hadn't been able to find anyone who could do the blessing, and that was the first step.

And there would be another step between the blessing and investigators. If the house were blessed, and still nothing changed, if the noises upstairs persisted, if Liz heard footsteps in the hall at night, or felt anything at all brush her skin only to look and find nothing there, she couldn't do anything further until after she'd convinced Jack.

That's the great obstacle, isn't it? she thought. What would it take to make Jack believe there's something in the house?

She didn't know. And, knowing Jack's rationality, she wasn't sure she wanted to find out. Anything bad enough to convince Jack of something out of the realm of normal, definable reality had to be big. Maybe Carl would find large, invisible, talking squirrels and that would explain everything.

In waiting, she began to grow bored. Liz walked into the empty upstairs kitchen and stared out the back window. The back yard was bright and empty. Looking down on it, she could imagine the scent of the grass and water spray from the sprinkler. The sun on her face and arms was nice, thawing the chill of a lonely summer afternoon.

She glanced toward the retirement complex across the alley behind their house, wondering if the naked woman was standing at her window. Before she could remember which window it was, Carl was lumbering down the stairs.

"Mrs. Kitch?" Carl was calling.

"In here," she said.

Carl came into the kitchen and said, "I need to run out for a second and grab the ladder out of my truck."

"I've got one," Liz said, and pointed to the main room where she'd been using theirs to cut in along the ceiling.

"Oh, perfect, thanks," Carl said.

He carried it upstairs and Liz followed. He placed the ladder beneath the crawlspace in the ceiling and climbed up. He lifted the panel out of the way, and got his flashlight from off his belt.

Liz glanced into the empty rooms. They all looked so bare.

Of course they do, she thought. *They're empty.*

But it was more than that. Obviously they were empty, but there's a difference between an empty room and a barren one and these rooms were absolute wastelands. She tried to imagine what they would have looked like furnished by people who'd lived here before.

"Well, the crawlspace up here is too small to get into but from what I can see, there's nothing in the ceiling," Carl said. He stood near the top of the ladder, and his head was up in the ceiling.

"So no squirrels, then?"

"Well, I didn't say that. I just can't see everything up here." He went down a rung and pulled his head from the hole. "And they could get in, really, any number of ways. Through a crack in the dormers, maybe. They could still get into the walls and no holes show up in the crawlspace. It could be mice."

"It could be anything," Liz said.

"It could, yes. I'll also take a look in the basement and around the outside of the house. Where's your basement door?"

"I'll show you."

But before they could move, something knocked above Carl's head. They both looked up.

The crawlspace had two panels. One in the ceiling, and a cap over the top, outside, that had to be lifted and moved aside, which led to the roof. Whatever had made that noise, it was on the roof, not in the ceiling.

"What was that, now?" Carl asked.

"Don't know," Liz said.

It came again, something knocking on the roof.

Carl clicked his flashlight on again and shone it up at the cap.

Another knock and dust fell from the roof, sprinkling his glasses. He climbed higher on the ladder and was reaching up to the cover when a final series of knocks came. All timidity was lost and whatever was out there was *pounding* on the roof, beating at it with everything they had, shaking the top floor of the house and Carl lost his balance, grabbed the top of the ladder for support, but fell anyway, crashing to the floor and kicking the ladder out from under him, across the room.

"Oohhhhh," he said, trying to sit up and rubbing his hip.

"Oh my God, I'm so sorry," Liz said, moving to try to help him up.

"No, that's alright," he said, climbing to his feet. "I'm fine. Just more surprised than anything."

"Really, I'm sorry."

"Don't be. Not your fault. I mean especially in this house, huh?"

"What do you mean?" she asked. "Especially in this house?"

Carl looked like he'd accidentally revealed the secret sauce while sitting in the competition's kitchen.

"Oh, nothing," he said. "Just, you know, big old houses like this, they get reputations. Even when they don't deserve them. You know, people see big houses like this one, they hear a few weird noises, and they think the worst."

"Yeah," Liz said.

"But the truth is, it's just, like you said, squirrels in the walls, stuff like that."

That was no squirrel, Liz thought. Her second thought was *And he's lying.*

"So, let me just put that cover back and we can look in the basement."

They both looked up, staring at the roof cover, waiting for the knock to come again. They watched it for a very long time, but nothing happened.

"That was very strange," Carl said, as if to himself. He stood for another second, looking up, before grabbing the ladder and replacing the crawlspace cover.

Liz led him to the basement, careful on the stairs to be quiet.

"My son's taking his nap," she told him. Carl took the hint and practically tiptoed down the stairs. Liz glanced back at him and Carl was lifting his feet way too high and setting them back down with the utmost caution. Liz thought he must have learned to tiptoe from watching Yosemite Sam or Daffy Duck.

She eased the door open and flipped on the light.

"Now, there are two levels down here," she explained. "You'll go down these few steps here, then turn. You can then either go straight, up a few steps to the laundry room, or turn again and go down to the bottom level, which is where the water heater and the furnace are."

"Gotcha," Carl said. As he stepped down, the phone rang.

"Excuse me," Liz said and tried to get down the hall quickly, but quietly. In the middle of the afternoon, while Joey slept and everything was turned off, the phone rang to shake the walls. She grabbed it before it could ring again. "Hello?"

As soon as the greeting was out, a dread came over her, seeping through the phone lines and penetrating her, making her suddenly wish she'd let it ring.

"You're dead," a hoarse whisper came over the line.

She flashed back to the day in middle school, this same phrase--for all Liz knew, it could be the same voice--scaring her so bad she'd had to hide in her parents' room until someone came home. She stood frozen, listening. It had only said it once, "You're dead," then fell silent and Liz listened to the silence, trying to pick up anything in the background, a voice, a television, traffic, anything that said this was real, that the caller was someone sitting bored at home. But the only noise coming over the line now was nothing. Not even white background noise. The line was just dead. Soon the dial tone started, but Liz hadn't heard a hang up click.

She listened to the tone for a second, then set the phone down She looked around the room, wondering who, what, if anything, was watching her.

She could hear Carl through the vents, moving around in the basement.

She'd go down with him. She wasn't sure what to make of him, but he was company and Liz didn't want to be alone in the big empty house right now.

She got to the hall and turned toward the stairs, then stopped.

Standing on the bottom step was a man. Someone, anyway. The face was blank, blurred out, it looked from Liz's end of the hall. But the figure was facing her. It was still. Liz looked at it, but didn't move. The hall was dim, but light shone in through the front door at the top of the stairs, casting eerie light behind the figure, silhouetting it even more.

She knew there was no one in the house, except Carl, herself, and Joey. She attempted a step toward it. The figure stepped backwards up one step. Liz took another step, echoed again by the figure's backward step. Liz stopped. The blank face nodded once, then the arms raised as if to take its head in its hands. Instead, the entire torso began shaking violently, rapidly. The motion was blurred and Liz thought she heard a droning buzz coming from it. Then the body stopped shaking, suddenly, as if a button had been pushed, or an outlet unplugged.

The body's head turned toward the open basement door where Carl could be heard bumping around in the laundry room. The figure turned and climbed the stairs, vanishing around the landing.

Liz found movement, finally, and ran to the bottom of the stairs. Daylight gave her small courage. She wanted to go up, to see where it had gone, if it was still around, but she heard Joey, faintly, in his bedroom.

She peeked in and listened. He was lying down, curled up, crying.

She went in and asked, "What's wrong, Joe?" He ignored her and kept crying. She moved to the side of his bed and leaned down. "What's the matter? Did you have a bad dream?" He still ignored her and she wasn't sure whether to be annoyed or worried. Was it normal for kids to wake up crying and not know why?

She sat on the edge of the bed and put a hand on his shoulder. "Come on, Joe, tell me what's wrong. You sure were sleeping good. You have a dream about something?"

Joey just whined. He stayed curled up, crying. For all Liz knew, he didn't even know she was there. She pulled him into her arms and rocked him, trying to get him to stop crying and tell her what was wrong, but he wouldn't talk. And of course Carl chose then to come upstairs.

She put Joey down and walked into the hall to meet him.

"No signs down there of anything, either," he said. "Now we can set out a poison for the mice, if there are any--"

"No," Liz said. "I don't like poison. God forbid I come home one day to find dead mice in the middle of the floor. And if they crawl away somewhere, there'd be that dead mouse smell all over and I'd spend a month looking for it."

"Actually," Carl explained, "the poison doesn't work like that. It dehydrates them, so there's no smell when they die. They'll slink off someplace and rot away before you know it."

Liz grimaced. "Great," she said. "Tell you what, I'll talk it over with my husband and he'll give you a call, okay?"

"Sure thing," Carl agreed. "Ask him, also, what he wants me to do for squirrels."

"I thought you didn't find any."

"I didn't. I didn't find any mice either, but that doesn't mean they're not there. It could be they're in the walls themselves. I once had this call, this guy said he had rats in his garage. I went out there, didn't find a thing. No sign, no nothing. So I leave and I get a call again a week or two later. Same guy, he's still got rats in his garage. So I went out again. Still nothing. A few weeks later, I'm driving by on my way someplace, I don't remember where, and I see a big group of guys in this guy's yard, all of them with sledgehammers.

"I stopped to say hi and ask if he'd seen any more rats. Turns out, all those guys are out there, friends of his, to tear down the garage. Well they started bashing away at that thing with the hammer and one of them gets through the wall. Mind you, this is a big cement garage, concrete walls. Well, he busts through and rats just poured out of the wall. There was near three, four hundred of them, living inside the walls. That's why I didn't see any signs. They lived inside the bricks. To this day, I don't have any idea how they got in or out, what they ate, nothing. But I know I saw them fall out of the hole when that guy went through it.

"So just 'cause I don't see them, doesn't mean they're not there."

"I'll be sure and mention that to my husband when he gets home," Liz said. She showed Carl out, then stood at the door a second, staring up, thinking about that roof cover again and wondering just what the hell that was about. Then she went back down to take care of Joey.

Jack wasn't sure what made him turn off Tenth Street onto Dayan and stop at Arthur's Used Books. He'd made up his mind shortly after lunch to leave the book alone, especially after hearing Charley's story. But there he was, pulling the Jeep up to the store and getting out, walking in, closing the door behind him to the tinkle of the bell.

A man he assumed to be Arthur smiled up from his newspaper at the counter and Jack smiled back, offering him a, "Hello."

"Hi there," Arthur replied. "How are you today?"

"Pretty good," Jack said, "pretty good." He wandered to the far end of the store, looking over the shelves, scanning titles and authors.

"Are you looking for something in particular?"

"Not really. Someone at work said you had a good selection here, I thought I'd stop by on the way home. Just taking a look, really."

"Well," Arthur said, turning back to his paper, "you think of something you'd like and you can't find it out here, I got a ton more upstairs and in the back."

"Thanks," Jack said, then turned back to his browsing.

He found a row of childrens' books and went looking through them for something Joey might like. He had no idea what first graders were reading these days. Harry Potter was probably too advanced.

Arthur broke out in a hacking cough, deep, bellowing retches from his chest and Jack turned to make sure he was okay. Arthur hawked something up from his lungs and spat into a paper bag at his side on the floor. Jack turned back to the books.

"You got kids?" Arthur asked.

"Yeah," Jack said. "One. A son."

"There's lots of good kids' book there. Got 'Magic Tree House'. 'Junie B. Jones'. A good stack of them 'Choose Your Own Adventure' books. Remember those?"

Jack did. He'd liked those. Maybe Joey would, too. He meant to ask where they were. Instead, he said, "You know, my wife likes ghost stories. Weird stuff. You got anything like that?"

"Yeah, sure," Arthur said. He came around the corner and headed for Jack.

"She likes the true stories. Small towns, freaky stuff."

Arthur stopped and turned back to his counter.

"Well, sir," he said, "I just happen to have something like that right here."

He picked a book off a stack next to the register and held it out, cover up, so Jack could see Arthur's name in big letters at the bottom.

"*The Outsider's Guide to Angel Hill*," Jack read, "by Arthur Miller." He looked up, confusion on his face. "Arthur Miller, the dance instructor?"

"No," Arthur chuckled. "Arthur Miller the used bookstore owner. But I get that a lot."

"Your book?" Jack said, taking the offered paperback. It was a trade, the size of a hardback, but soft cover. He turned it over, looking at the cover, then scanning the text on the back.

"Proud to say yes," Arthur said, smiling.

"About Angel Hill? Really?"

"Every story in there true to God," Arthur said. He raised his hand in oath.

"Wow," Jack said. "I bet my wife would love it. We just moved here almost a month ago. Is there really weirdo stuff in here? Like secret cults and local witch legends and stuff?"

"If that was the extent of Angel Hill," Arthur said, "I wouldn't have bothered writing that book. I don't think your wife will find exactly what she's expecting in there. But I'm very sure she won't be disappointed, either."

"In that case," Jack put the book on the counter and reached for his wallet, "I'll take it."

Arthur rang him up and told him to have a good day. Jack was at the door when he turned back and asked, "How did you find out about all this stuff? Just talk, urban legends and stuff?"

"No," Arthur said, "everything in there's been well documented. I got a lot from the newspapers, some from old records, a few of them I got from living them myself."

"I see," Jack said. "Thanks again." He turned and left. Arthur waved and went back to his newspaper.

Jack climbed into the Cherokee and started the engine. He slid the book from its paper bag and looked again at the cover. The photo placed between the title at the top and Arthur's name at the bottom was a black and white landscape, some random shot of Angel Hill, he guessed.

"*The Outsider's Guide to Angel Hill*," he read again.

He slid it back into the bag and pulled out, headed home.

By the time he got there, he'd tossed the sack out the window and had the book stuffed into the waistband of his pants. He couldn't say why anymore than he could say why he'd bought it in the first place. He grabbed the string off the seat and went in.

He went in the back, as he usually did, but instead of stopping to kiss Liz or Joey, he passed them in the living room, left them watching television, and took his string into the bedroom. Then he shoved the book under his side of the mattress, far enough back so Liz wouldn't find it when she made the bed. He kicked off his shoes and went back to the living room.

"Everyone have a good day?" he asked.

"It was alright," Liz said. "What's so important in the bedroom?"

"I bought a new string today. I wanted to drop it in there first, get my shoes off."

"Oh. Well, the squirrel guy came. Said as far as he could tell, we don't have squirrels, or mice. But he did say he could set out poison for them anyway."

"Did you tell him that's alright?" Jack picked up Joey and squeezed and kissed him. "You miss me today?" Joey nodded. He put him back down.

"I told him I'd talk it over with you first."

"What do you think?"

"I don't know," Liz said, even though she knew very well where the noises came from. "I mean, if he says we don't have anything, what good is putting the poison out gonna do? But, again, he said just because he didn't see them didn't mean they weren't here. So I don't know."

"Yeah, but it's gotta be coming from somewhere, all those noises up there. I doubt it's termites in the walls making all that racket."

"Probably not," she said. "Your call."

He lay on the couch, stretched his feet over her thighs. "Rub my feet," he said.

She knocked his feet off and said, "Rub them yourself. Why don't you rub my feet? Then you can kiss my butt while you're at it."

"Why do you say things like that when you know well

enough that I will?" He sat up, kissed her, and plopped back down again next to her. "I don't know what to do about it. Maybe we'll have someone else come and check. If they say there's nothing up there, we'll take it that they know what they're talking about. I guess."

Sure, Liz thought. We'll get someone else to go up there, and they'll tell you there's something up there all right. But you're not going to get that from an exterminator. Get a psychic in here. There'll tell you what's up there.

But she didn't say any of that.

She got up a while later to make dinner. Jack went to restring his guitar. Joey played in his bedroom.

Jack got the string changed and tuned up, then played for a few minutes, strumming random chords, shrugging off work's stress and losing sense of the world--the only time he allowed himself to do so.

While his hands and fingers worked the fretboard, Jack's eyes went to the mattress. He watched, as if expecting the book to peek out. When it didn't, he set his guitar aside and pulled it from the bed. He flipped through the pages, wondering what was so special about this book that Charley Clark made a point to tell him about it.

Every town's got its stories, he thought. Why are Angel Hill's any different?

Skimming the first chapter told him why. At least it gave him an idea that Angel Hill's stories might not be like other towns'.

There was a hill on the block surrounded by Rand and Ellison, between F and H Streets. Fett Technologies was on Ellison, crossing with I and J Streets. Jack realized this was the hill he saw every morning turning into work.

The Outsider's Guide to Angel Hill called this hill Splatter Mountain.

The sight commonly known as Splatter Mountain, the book read, *was originally the center of Angel Hill. When the town was founded and the ground broke, Patrick Day drove a shovel into the earth, announcing the official founding of Angel Hill, Missouri. The crowd cheered and drank champagne and no one at first noticed the red stuff coming up from the ground. The one who saw it first was reported to have been Eleanore Gladys, wife of the town's first doctor. Eleanore Gladys screamed, pointed, and fainted dead away. Someone looked to see what she had screamed about and saw, coming up from the ground, a thick red liquid. Someone else screamed, "It's devil's blood!" and the crowd roared with fear and everyone began to go hysterical. There was chaos as everyone scattered to flee the cursed spot.*

Jack flipped forward, passing the detailed account of the town consecration and whatever the people there saw. He found a section break and read.

Soon after the groundbreaking, the details on how long after are vague, but it was within a few weeks, the town hired a geologist from Kansas City to take a sample of the stuff. It had issued from the ground for nearly an hour, running in red streams down the hill, soaking back into the dirt, or drying on the grass. The geologist found plenty of samples to take with him. The crusted powder was scraped from grass and rocks and tested. Results were inconclusive, which is to say no one ever discovered exactly what had spilled from the ground that day when Angel Hill was founded.

Jack closed the book. Odd, he thought. It's bullshit, but it's odd. Unidentifiable red ooze doesn't come from the ground. They probably stabbed a mole or a gopher or something when they broke the ground. And I doubt it bled for an hour. And after a few weeks, the rain would have washed it away. What else you got?

He flipped through the book, stopped in the middle, and read some more.

There was a series of animal mutilations in the late 1800s. During the end, two people were killed, one more presumed dead. A local woman was found dead in her home. The local minister, Pastor Mullins was also found torn to shreds in his living room. His son, Billy Ray, was never found.

Soon after, the town brought in a new minister, Pastor Keeper. Jacob and his family (a wife and four children) were moved in from the small town of Green Lake West across the river in Kansas, about a hundred miles south of Angel Hill.

Jack turned the page, then quickly dropped the book and stood up, grabbing Lily and placing her on her stand. Liz came into the bedroom.

"Supper's ready," she said.

"I was just coming," he said, weaving his pick between the strings just under the nut.

"Come on, Joe," she called into his room. She heard him drop his toy and clomp into the hall.

"Are we having spinach?" he asked.

"No," she said, laughing. "I don't think so, why?"

"Because I like spinach."

"Okay," she said. "I'll remember that next time I go to the store. Tonight we're having tacos. You want hard shells or do you want a burrito?"

"Brito," he said.

"Brito, it is."

"We get any mail today?" Jack asked after dinner.

Everyone was lying in the living room watching television. Joey had a Batman figure on the floor in front of him, ready should he decide to play with it.

"I don't know," Liz said. "I didn't even think to check."

"I'll do it." Jack got up, groaning as he stood. "I'm too young to make old man noises," he said as he strode into the hall. The light was out and he had to see the hall in his head to figure out where he was going. He almost tripped up the first step, but caught himself on the rail.

He unlocked the door, leaned onto the porch, grabbed the mail, and locked the door again. Then he noticed the second floor kitchen light was on. He went up and tossed the mail onto the counter, then shuffled through the envelopes. Here was a bill. Here was an offer for a pre-approved home loan. Here was a letter for this address, but the wrong name. And another envelope for what he figured would be the empty lot next door.

I wonder if there was ever a house there.

He grabbed the two for him, then the other two in the opposite hand. He'd put them back into the mailbox for tomorrow. He turned off the kitchen light and went to the stairs. Then he stopped, watching a bowling ball-sized orb of green light drifting up the wall next to the stairs. It rounded the landing and Jack watched it, trying to see the beam it traveled on, trying to figure out where it was coming from. But it didn't appear to be moving up the wall itself. It looked like it was floating free of the wall, a ball of light hovering in midair, making its way to the third floor.

It vanished over the top banister and Jack stood, listening, wondering.

What the hell was that?

He went to the windows in the main room and looked down. Was someone down there with a flashlight? He cupped his hands against the glass, but couldn't see anyone. And the empty lot was just that; empty. No trees or piles of scrap metal, nothing. No one would be able to hide there. And the lot was empty.

He went back to the stairs, up midway to the third floor landing, then turned and looked up. The light was gone. But his eyes fell on the top banister and Charley Clark's story came to him.

Hung himself. Tied a rope to the top of the banister and just let himself drop.

"There's no way that thing would hold a man," Jack said, staring up at the thick wooden rail. But, standing there in the dark, Jack thought he heard something creak above him. Like taut rope against wood.

"I'll have to make Charley work through first break tomorrow," Jack thought. "That's what he gets for suggestion."

He replaced the mail, took his own mail downstairs, and forgot about the green ball of light.

Liz woke up that night with cool air swirling about her face. She kept her eyes closed and turned over, but the air followed. She knew opening her eyes would prove pointless. She wouldn't see anything, but she'd still feel it.

Forget a second exterminator, she thought. I've got to do something about this now.

I'm getting this house blessed, tomorrow if I can.

She moved next to Jack, pressed her face against his shoulder. The air stopped swirling around her and she eventually went back to sleep.

Chapter Five

As soon as Jack left for work, Liz was on the phone, calling every church she could find. Her search for someone to bless the house revealed something to Liz she'd never have thought about Angel Hill. Listed among the Our Lady of Perpetual Sorrows and First Church of East Angel Hills and a few Angel Hill Assemblies of God were some that made her stomach do a roll. Church of the Hollow Earth? Church of the Priory of Scion? Temple of the Thirteen Holy Attributes?

"Where's a good old St. Patrick's when you need it?" she wondered.

When no one in Angel Hill could help her, she tried the surrounding towns, Gower, St. Joseph, Helena, Easton, Cosby, Cameron. Most of the churches in the smaller towns were Christian. She finally found someone at a Catholic Church in St. Joseph who could do the house blessing. The priest said the soonest he could schedule it would be the following Monday.

"Thank you," Liz said. "I'll be here all day. Is there a certain time I should expect you?"

"Sometime a little after noon," he said.

"That's perfect. My son will be sleeping. I'll assume you need directions."

"Yes, that would probably help."

She told him to take US 169 into town and gave him directions to the house from there.

He said he would see her Monday. Liz thanked him again, then hung up.

Joey asked if he could play outside for a little bit.

"Tell you what," she said. "I'm gonna go up and paint for a while. Why don't you play in your room? Then, as soon as I'm done, we can go down to the park."

"I don't want to go to the park," Joey said. He sounded as if she'd suggested they go play on the highway during rush hour.

"You don't? Okay. Well, then when I get some work done upstairs, we'll both go outside. Maybe we can take your tee to the lot next door and you can hit the ball."

"Yeah, yeah," Joey said. "Let's do that. I wanna hit the

ball."

She left him in his room, then went to the second floor.

Everything was as she'd left it, what was it, two, three days ago?

"My God," she said to the room, "I can't believe I haven't done anything up here in so long." The burgundy paint was long dry. She was pleased with the outcome. Not bad for a first coat. It was darker than she'd thought it would be, but it suited the room. She imagined thick, classy furniture--a couch, a couple chairs--with a bar and maybe they could have the fireplace rebuilt. The mantle was there, but the fireplace itself had been bricked up. With some decent lights and music, this could be the perfect entertaining room. Not that they did a lot of entertaining, but they never had the perfect room before.

"Course, we'll have to make some friends in town first."

She looked down at the wood floor, scuffed and scratched from years of who knew how many different people living here. A big enough rug, she thought, would take care of that, and bring the room together at the same time.

She still had the other three walls to paint and then a second coat. Then again, she thought, looking at the first coat, the one might be enough.

She went to the finished wall and ran her hand over it. Up close, she realized she'd been wrong. Impossible as it seemed, after all those days left alone, the paint still hadn't dried. She pulled her hand back, thinking, *Great, and I just screwed it up. Now I'll have to do the second coat.* She looked at her hand, covered and sticky with red paint. She went toward the bathroom, then swerved away and into the kitchen instead. Since seeing the boy in the shower, Liz hadn't been back. She flipped on the light over the sink and turned on the water. Then she stopped in the middle of putting her hand under the flow.

This wasn't the burgundy she'd used. She stared at it. This was brighter, more vibrant, more red. Her mind played a cliche where the wall had been covered in blood instead of paint and Liz's hand was now covered with it. She thrust her hand under the stream and washed it off. She dried it on her shirt and went back into the main room.

The wall was no longer burgundy and Liz's mind brought the cliche around again. Except this time it wasn't her mind.

She watched as the color on the wall changed, brightened, became red and full and began to drip down the walls as if it had just been applied, and too thick at that. A child laughed behind her and she turned, but she was alone. Liz looked back and watched blood pour off the wall, not just down it, but she could see it seep from the wall like sweat through skin.

She backed up and looked to the side, up the stairs. She didn't know what she expected to see there, but she knew she wasn't alone.

The child laughed again.

Blood ran over the baseboards and began soaking into the wood floor.

The child laughed again. This time the sound came from the stairs.

She looked over to the empty stairs, then back to the wall. The blood was gone.

The wall was burgundy and dry. The baseboards and floor were clean. She went to touch it and found it true. The laugh came again.

She ran to the stairs, then up them two at a time. At the top, she stood brave, waiting for whatever was about to happen. She imagined all sorts of things. Ghosts would rush her and knock her over the rail and she'd break her neck in the fall. Dead arms would reach out from the walls and floor and drag her away. A portal would open in the room and Liz would fall through it into Hell.

The child's laugh echoed up from the landing. She looked back, then quickly turned around to face the third floor again.

"You can't hurt me," she said. "I don't care what you think you can do. But you can't touch my family, or me. This is our house now."

You can't save yourself, the house whispered.

Forgive me--pant pant--*forgive me*--pant pant--*forgive me*, it whispered.

Can I get in bed with you? it whispered.

"You're just memories," Liz said. "You're just energy. You can't hurt me."

Everyone will suffer now, the house whispered.

Liz turned and went down the stairs, slowly, almost

daring the house to do something, but trying to show she wouldn't back down. Still, she left the paint and the walls to themselves that day. On the first floor, she told Joey to get his shoes and they'd go outside for awhile.

Charley asked, "How come with all the witnesses to just about everything you read about, you still can't believe any of it?"

"First," Jack told him, "I haven't even read that book. I've skimmed it here and there, but I haven't sat down and read it cover to cover. I haven't even looked at half the stories in there. As for why I can't believe any of it . . . it's not that I don't believe *any* of that stuff happened, I'm just saying there's an explanation for all of it, if anyone cares enough to really look deep into it. But everyone seems so set on this 'strange things just happen in Angel Hill' line that when someone comes to them with the easy explanation of 'Oh, it's an act of God' or 'It's just one of those unexplained Angel Hill mysteries', that's what people grab hold to and y'all are a stubborn bunch. Really, if you got someone in here from the outside, someone who's not stuck on this Weird Angel Hill kick, someone with an objective mind, I'd bet you'd get actual answers to this stuff in no time."

Charley shook his head and smiled, then turned back to screwing the nuts over the toggle switches on the box faces.

Jack was about to head over to the cable cell when Charley said, "And since you're Mister Objective Opinion, what do you say? Let's start with that house of yours?"

"What about it?" Jack asked. "There's nothing wrong with 'that house' of mine."

"That's not what the people are saying."

"The people? The people don't live in my house. Believe me, the biggest problem in my house is some squirrels in the walls and a front door I can't get to stay closed."

"Nothing else? No voices, no weird lights? Nothing like that?"

Jack stopped for a second and thought about the glowing green ball he'd seen just last night. Was that what Charley meant? But that had been a reflection from outside, a car driving by or something like that.

"No," he said. "There are squirrels and drafts, but that's it. I'm telling you, stuff like what you're talking about just doesn't happen without something--and I mean something real, something you can touch or see--causing it." He picked up a control panel, hooked it up to the tester. "This is reality," he said. "You think the world got to this point, civilization and technology and control panels by some unexplained occurrence? It got here because the world makes sense. One thing leads to another leads to another until you've got . . ." He flipped a toggle switch and a light on the tester glowed red. Jack made a face of mock surprise.

"If you say so, boss," Charley said. He set down the face he'd completed and moved on to the next one. Jack walked away. Under his breath, Charley said, "Wonder if your wife feels the same. Wonder what she's seen."

Jack would be home soon. Liz went upstairs and brought in the mail. As she closed the door, she heard a tap upstairs. She wanted to ignore it and go back down to the living room, but she knew she wasn't going to do that. She climbed the stairs.

In the main room on the second floor, she stopped.

Standing across the room, staring out the window, was a girl. She couldn't have been more than nine or ten. Her back was to Liz. The girl was just standing there. Her hands were raised and her open palms rested on the glass. Her fingers tapped at it making the noise Liz had heard at the front door. She stood and watched the girl, silent, trying not to be afraid. The girl's tapping grew stronger, more insistent, until in seconds she was slapping the window with her palms. Liz wondered if a ghost's hand would be strong enough to break the glass. The girl swung at the glass with such force, Liz thought for sure she *would* shatter it. She grunted with every swing. The pane rattled in its frame, but it didn't break.

Liz lost her concentration and the letters in her hand slipped and fell to the floor. She stooped to pick them up. The noise made the girl stop and turn around. She looked at Liz and Liz looked at her, then the girl looked higher and her eyes grew wide. Liz watched in shock as the little girl's features fell apart. Her pink skin turned grey and cracked. Her hair went limp. Her eyes grew yellow.

Liz gathered her envelopes, stood and turned. Then she

froze at the sight of a man behind her.

"Shit!" she gasped. She backed up and knew the man was going to touch her, but when she looked at him, he wasn't seeing her. His eyes were locked behind Liz, on the girl. His fury shone through in his dead face and he raised an open hand and stepped toward the girl.

Liz closed her eyes, waiting for something, anything, whatever it was she knew it wouldn't be pleasant. But when she opened them again, the room was empty. The mail was still on her floor. It must have fallen again. The girl was gone. So was the man.

She took deep breaths until her heart had slowed enough and her body had stopped shaking.

"I hate this fucking house," she said, going back downstairs, wishing Jack would hurry and get home already.

She woke up that night thirsty. She got a drink from the bathroom, and quickly got back into bed, snuggling up close to Jack. She dozed off and was awakened again a little bit later as Jack climbed on top of her, covering her face and mouth with kisses. His arms pulled her over and he got between her legs. He tasted like onions and he needed a shave, but his body felt good against hers. She wrapped her legs around him and rocked with him, keeping quiet so as not to wake Joey. She let all the past few days fall away as the pressure in her gut built to a climax and for a few minutes, Liz had forgotten all about the voices and the touches and the things she'd seen in the house. It was all lost to Jack's touch and his breath and his body between her legs.

Her breath quickened and she tried to calm it, but the sweat on her body and Jack's thrusting kept her from being any quieter than she was. Jack panted into her ear and she whispered to him, "Come in me."

His fingers dug tighter into her shoulders and he hunched further over her, his pace becoming more measured and frantic. He took a final shot into her, then froze. He twitched inside her and was done.

She came with him, a beautiful release of pressure through her entire body. She strained against him, trying to prolong the agony and the pleasure. Finally, they sank onto the bed. Jack's head resting on her chest. She leaned her head to the side.

Jack lay beside her, eyes wide open, his body frozen.

Liz started. There was Jack beside her. So who was on top of her?

Jack's face said he'd seen the whole thing. But he either couldn't or didn't want to believe it. His expression was a mix of disgust and fury.

Liz looked down to see who was on top of her if not her husband. There was no one.

Liz sat up, waking from her nightmare.

Jack lay sleeping beside her.

She sat breathing quietly for a few minutes, then she got up and went into the bathroom. She locked the door and sat on the side of the tub, crying into her palms.

This was all driving her crazy. She felt herself on the verge of a breakdown. But how could she get help from anyone?

Jack would never believe. Never. She knew it. And what help was Joey going to be? He was only six.

Monday, she reminded herself. I'll get the house blessed Monday. That should help, right? Shouldn't it?

She got another drink, resisted splashing water on her face--she knew it would only wake her up more and she'd never get back to sleep--then crept back down the hall and into bed.

She lay with her back pressed against Jack and when he draped his arm over her, she prayed it was really his.

Joey also lay awake.

He was buried under his thin blanket, in the dark, but the covers would be enough to protect him, he hoped.

He'd hoped Liz would come into his room when she was finished in the bathroom. But she didn't. She'd just turned off the light and went back to her own bed, leaving Joey to whatever was in his room.

He couldn't see it, or them, or whatever, but he could feel them, and he could hear them well enough.

Come and play, they said.

We'll show you the best toys.

Adam, let's go. Up there we can play anything you want.

But Joey wasn't Adam. That was the only thing that offered even a hint of comfort. It made him feel better that, no matter what or who was in his room, at least they hadn't come for him. But in the back of his mind, under more blankets, he thought maybe they really had, no matter what they said.

So he talked to God and asked God to bring his dad or Liz in here so they could drive away the voices that whispered for him to play with them.

He knew what they'd say when they saw the blanket he was buried under, that it was too hot for a blanket and he needed a sheet and he was going to suffocate, but he knew being under here was better than out there. Out there, he might be able to see what was in his room, and he knew he didn't want that.

He heard something from the other bedroom and had a brief hope it was someone getting up to check on him. But no one came and he decided it was just one of them turning in their sleep.

He lay sweating under the blanket until the voices stopped and he finally fell asleep and kicked off the cover.

Chapter Six

The next few days followed much the same pattern as the previous few. Jack went to work, unbelieving. Liz stayed at home, wondering what would appear next, what vision or voice, ready at any moment to take Joey outside to play or for a walk. And Joey was a child, happy to play, uncertain of much else, except that he didn't care for playing alone in the house, and he didn't want to go to the park.

Jack called a second exterminator who came to much the same conclusion as Carl had; no obvious signs of mice or squirrels or anything else, but that didn't mean they weren't there. Jack's conclusion was that, until he saw mouse droppings on the counter, or something skittered past him and disappeared behind a baseboard, he wasn't paying for traps, poisons, or anything else.

When the weekend finally arrived, Jack had forgotten about going to the library. Liz reminded him. His plan of taking Joey so Liz could have the house to herself was thrown out the window; Liz wasn't staying alone in the house. She told Jack she'd like to get a book or two also. maybe something on decoration or remodeling.

Instead, Jack stayed home while Liz took Joey.

She stood on the second floor where the nonfiction was kept. Joey was below her in the childrens' section.

She found a book on kitchen remodeling, tucked it under her arm, and went to one of the two computers located in the middle of the room. She did a subject search for ghosts, and another one for haunted houses. She found two more books to add to the home decoration book.

Joey picked out a Magic Tree House book and sat down at a reading table to flip through the pages while Liz looked for another book about hauntings. When they had everything they wanted, they went to the front desk to get library cards and check out their books. Liz gave the girl behind the counter their information, names, address, social security numbers. When Liz told her the address, though, she could have sworn the girl stopped for a second too long, looking at them. For the space of a blink, Liz thought the girl looked unsure whether to even continue helping them. She looked at Liz, then looked at the pile of books Liz had, and paused. But then the girl shook it off and typed everything into the computer. She handed over the cards and Liz and Joey signed them. The girl scanned the bar codes on the back to activate them.

Driving home, Liz had a second to think about it. The look on that girl's face, she had to have known where Liz and Joey lived. Didn't she? It had been a familiar look, she knew the place. What did she know about it?

"I should have asked her," Liz said under her breath.

"What?" Joey asked.

"Nothing. Talking to myself. Want to get some ice cream before we go home?"

Joey did.

"Alright. Just have to find a Dairy Queen around here someplace." She was looking around as she drove, as if the building would suddenly appear.

"You have to turn around," Joey said. "It's back the other way."

"Oh?" Liz pulled into a driveway and backed out, heading the other way. "How do you know that? Dad took you to get ice cream without bringing me something?"

Joey shook his head no and said, "Just know it's this way."

"Okay, then," Liz said. She found the Dairy Queen a few minutes later, not far from the library, in fact. From the line out front, she could see the library's windows. *That must be where he saw it, then*, she thought.

Jack plugged in, turned up the amp volume, slid into the guitar strap, and played something loud and hard.

It felt good to be able to play without worrying about making too much noise. He let his fingers fly and his mind go, not thinking about anything at all. There were no lost parts, no meetings to hurry to, nothing to ship next day air because God forbid it take that extra day to get there.

With the neck under his palm, his finger running along the strings, he remembered seeing her for the first time. She hung in a music store window. He passed it every day on the way to his afternoon class. She caught his eye one day, then he went to class and forgot about her. A few days later he saw Jimi Hendrix on television, playing a guitar much like the nice white one he'd seen in the window. Jimi went into some hardcore blues song. Jack picked up Jimi's greatest hits collection, *The Ultimate Experience*, later that week and found out the song had been "Red House". When he heard it, he thought, *I've got to know how to do that.*

Six months later, he'd saved up enough for the guitar. Soon after, he met Joey's mother and it was put aside. He didn't pick her up again in earnest until Joey was six months old and his mother was gone. But Jack had decided by then not to learn Jimi's "Red House". He loved playing now and he knew if he learned the song that got him started, he'd never need to play again. So he learned everything he could except that one song. And every time he picked up his guitar, he let the world go and closed himself inside the strings.

It was there, locked away inside the guitar, that Jack let loose his logic and order. For those moments he was playing, fantasy and reality were mixed.

Then his time was cut short and Jack was pulled back to the real world by the ringing phone. He pulled out the amp cord and strode into the living room. He picked up the phone and asked, "Hello?"

"Everyone will suffer now, everyone will suffer now, everyone will suffer now--"

"Who is this?" he asked. He didn't really expect an answer.

"You can't save yourself, you can't save yourself, you can't save yourself--"

He hung up. Before setting the phone back on the base, he thought twice, and took it into the bedroom with him. He tossed it on the bed, replaced the amp cord, and played. He wished he had a bass player backing him up, or a singer, or a drummer, or someone to sit to the side and clap. But he had himself and he enjoyed simply having his fingers on the strings.

The phone rang again and Jack muted the strings and looked down at it. He waited, but it didn't ring again. Then he saw the bed and remembered the book tucked between the mattresses. He looked at the clock. Joey and Liz had only been gone thirty minutes. He still had time.

He set Lily aside, pulled the book out, and leaned against the headboard to look through it.

(from *The Outsider's Guide to Angel Hill*, chapter 8)

The upper right corner of Angel Hill is sometimes known as the garden.

The streets in this corner of town are named Sunflower Boulevard, Rose Drive, and Daisy Avenue after the flowers found growing by the thousands along these stretches of road in 1939.

No one planted them. At least, no one admitted planting them. They just grew. Sunflowers, roses, and daisies. At first, the general consensus was the town had done it in an attempt to beautify Angel Hill, and not much thought was given to the flowers. The next year, they returned and, again, no one gave them much thought. When the flowers returned the third year, it was brought up at a town meeting that gardening on a public lot was illegal, unless approved by the town counsel.

No one planted the flowers, someone mentioned.

Someone must have, the counsel retorted.

A debate arose over who had or hadn't planted flowers in "the garden" and whether the permission to do so had been granted by Angel Hill. After weeks, the counsel realized no one was going to come forward with proof or an admission to planting the flowers. Weary of the whole mess, the town counsel deemed the flowers, "an act of God" and changed the street names to reflect the flowers.

The flowers, however, never returned the fourth year. A new project was then launched to till the ground, hoping to expose remnants of the flowers, but nothing was ever found. No seeds, no dried, discarded petals.

Jack closed the book and tucked it back under the mattress.

Interesting, he thought. I guess. That was over sixty years ago. That's probably the legend surrounding them, and this guy takes it as gospel.

Jack heard Liz open the back door, and he stood up and slid into his guitar. He could see across the hall into the living room. She tossed a stack of books onto the couch and Joey lay out on the floor with one in his hand. He turned on the television and Liz came into the bedroom.

"What'cha doing?"

"Nothing," he said, "just putting her up. You get anything good?"

"We had ice cream," Joey said.

"Shh," Liz said.

Jack gave her a look that asked, "Where's mine?"

"I didn't know what you'd want," she said. "Anyway, I think I got some good books." She led him into the living room and he looked at her selection.

"You get enough haunted house books?" he asked.

"I only got a couple."

"Yeah, but what's the fascination?"

"They just looked interesting," she said.

He tossed them back onto the couch and went into the kitchen to get a Coke.

"I'm gonna make me and Joey something for lunch. You hungry?"

"Didn't you just have ice cream?" he asked.

"That's not lunch, though."

"Yeah, make me something, too, since you didn't bring me anything nice back."

Chapter Seven

It was Sunday and Liz was trying not to be too excited about tomorrow's blessing. She had prayed repeatedly last night and today that it would work.

Joey was asleep. Jack had gone to the music store.

She pulled a bundle of sheets from the dryer, dumping them into her basket. She put the wet clothes from the washer into the dryer, started a new load of wash, then grabbed the basket and headed upstairs.

She untangled the fitted sheet from all the others in the basket, and shook it out in front of her, trying to find the corner with the tag. She got it, and moved to the side of her bed. She raised the sheet over the mattress and let it glide down over the bed.

It fell and draped over the shape of a man. He seemed to be lying curled up on the mattress.

Liz gasped and moved back. She wanted to run, but couldn't. Was it fear or wonder that froze her? She didn't know.

The man's head rose and turned toward her. She saw no features, just the general shape of a body on its side, legs curled up. It leapt from the mattress in a flash, then fled down the hall, taking the sheet with it. Liz moved to the hall to watch. It moved soundlessly. It leapt up the stairs, dropped the sheet on the landing, and vanished.

She stood alone in the hall, praying again, "Please God let it work tomorrow. I can't do this much longer. Please let it work tomorrow."

While Liz prayed, Jack and Charley perused the guitars on the wall at Westgate Music. Charley needed a new amp cord and Jack just wanted to look.

Charley took a Gibson Firebird down off the wall and looked it over.

"What are you doing?" Jack asked. "That's the ugliest guitar in the world."

"Do what? These are classics, man."

"Those are crap. That one there," he pointed to a Flying

V a few spaces down, "that's a classic."

"They're both ugly when you look at 'em."

"Yeah, they are." They moved away toward the basses and Charley looked up at a black Rickenbacker 4001.

"Sweet, isn't it?"

"Since when do you play bass?"

"Not yet, but she's pretty."

"Yeah. Hey, you wanna come over later on and we'll go upstairs and play?"

Charley didn't answer at first, but finally he nodded and said, "Sure, okay."

"Wait," Jack said. "Crap, I forgot, that floor needs re-wired or something. I went up there when we moved in and couldn't get anything to work. Had to settle for the first floor and the headphones."

Charley took the 4001 down and slapped a few notes. He wasn't very good.

"Man, these strings are like playing the streetlight cables outside my house." He looked up at Jack. "You sure it wasn't the ghosts up there keeping it from working?"

"If there were ghosts in my house, sure," Jack said. He grabbed a Fender Precision and plucked a few notes. He was even worse than Charley. "Just old wiring. House hasn't been lived in for how many years?"

"Six," Charley answered immediately. "Since those kids were killed."

"Right. Six years. We'll get that re-done as we work up to it. I just hope it doesn't turn out the entire house needs it. Hey, but you can come over anyway, we can take everything out back. I've got a huge back yard."

"Sweet," Charley said. "I got a couple things to do, but I can come over later."

"Okay. Any time, I'm not doing anything tonight."

Jack stopped and admired his white acoustic while Charley grabbed the amp cord he'd come for.

It was a couple hours later, while Jack sat watching something on the Discovery Channel and Liz sat at the other end of the couch leafing through one of her books, that Joey started screaming from his bedroom.

Liz dropped the book and Jack leapt from his seat. They darted down the hall and burst into Joey's room, but he wasn't there.

What the hell, Liz thought. *Is this what it takes to make Jack believe? Don't make it this.*

"Joe?" Jack asked. "Where are you?"

He wasn't on his bed, or on the floor playing with his super-heroes. Liz looked under the bed, but he wasn't there, either. They stood wondering, and Liz finally heard something. Joey was crying, she could hear it clearly, but he wasn't anywhere. Then she saw his closet door was cracked.

She opened it and found Joey sitting against the wall, crying into his hands, his knees pulled to his chest. He looked up at the light, then at Liz and Jack, and started crying again.

Jack pulled him from the closet and Joey struggled, but Jack got him out. He sat on the edge of Joey's bed, his son cradled in his arms, rocking him, trying to calm him down.

"What's the matter, Joe?" he asked. Joey whined, but wouldn't say anything. They stayed with him to comfort him, and they were patient, until he finally stopped crying and just sat silent on Jack's lap, staring at the wall. "What's wrong, Joe?" Jack asked again.

"You scared me," Joey said.

"I'm sorry," Jack said. "We heard you crying. What were you crying for?"

"Because you scared me, I said."

"No," Jack said. "I mean what were you crying about the first time?" Joey sniffed, then his crying started again, just a few huffs, but Jack knew if he got started, it would go full-blown within seconds. "Calm down, babe. Tell me what happened."

"I was hiding in the closet," Joey said. "I was gonna scare you when you came in here, but you opened the door and scared me first."

"I know that," Jack said. He was beginning to get annoyed. Why couldn't Joey just tell him what had happened? "Okay, why did you scream, then?"

"Because you scared me when you got in the closet."

"No," Jack said. His anger was a knot in his stomach. "Joe, we were watching television. We heard you scream, then we came in here to see what happened. We found you in the closet, then I pulled you out and asked you what happened. So what happened that made you scream in the first place?"

Joey said, "I mean the first time you came in here, you scared me."

"I didn't come in here a first time," Jack said.

"Yeah," Joey said, "when I was hiding and you opened the door and scared me, then closed it again and left."

Jack looked at Liz and Liz hoped her face was showing confusion. She knew what had happened, but she didn't want to go over everything with him right now.

"Joe, I was watching TV," Jack said. "I never came in here. And I certainly wouldn't have scared you then left."

"You must have fallen asleep playing," Liz said. "You fell asleep in your closet, then had a bad dream and it woke you up." She hated saying that. She knew it wasn't the truth and she knew Joey'd never think of her as a mother if he didn't trust her.

"Yeah," Jack said. "That's what happened. Come on, we'll go watch cartoons. That'll make you feel better."

Joey looked at Liz as Jack carried him into the hall. Liz thought his face was pleading, telling her *I didn't dream it. I didn't. Don't make me go with him.* But no matter what Joey thought--and he and she both knew he hadn't dreamed it--she also knew Jack hadn't left the couch.

They went into the living room and Liz hung back. She put her head into the closet and stared at the walls. "Don't ever do that to him again," she whispered. "You can mess with me all you want. I'm not afraid of you, but he is and you'd better keep your fucking hands off him."

She closed the closet door and left the room. Tomorrow afternoon, she told herself for the thousandth time that day. She felt a chill in her spine and knew something moved behind her in the hall.

Suddenly something crashed and Liz jumped, put a hand to her chest, and whirled around. The sound came again. Not a crash, a loud knock on the front door.

Jack came out into the hall and slapped her ass as he passed her.

"Charley's here," he said. "We're gonna go out in back for a little bit."

"If you're gonna be loud, let me know and I'll take Joey shopping."

"His shoes are by the couch," Jack said before taking the stairs two at a time to the first landing.

They played for an hour before either needed a break, both showing off a slew of styles and techniques--Jack watched in silent admiration while Charley fingerpicked with a dexterity Jack knew he'd never achieve--and falling into rhythm with each other like they'd been at it for years.

Jack thought it felt great to have someone beside him, someone to play off of, someone to follow if he wanted to hang back a little, and someone who'd follow him if he had a line he wanted to show off. Watching him, Jack wondered why someone with Charley's talent was working the box cell in a place like Fett Tech.

Same reason you are, was the answer he came up with. *Because this is fun, but it's not my real life.*

Finally Charley lifted his guitar--that big fat Gretch White Falcon--over his head and said, "Okay, I gotta take a piss. Where's your bathroom?"

Charley went inside, rested his guitar against the couch, and proceeded down the hall.

Afterward, he turned off the light, pulled the door closed behind him, and stood quiet in the hall. He heard Jack outside, still playing, but he tried to shut it out and listen to the house.

Stories around Angel Hill were myriad about this house, not just concerning the Denglers, but there were still stories about the first family to live here, the Keepers. The preacher, his wife, and their twins. This place hadn't been good to the families who'd lived here.

Charley wondered briefly how long he'd been gone, then he heard Jack outside again and wondered if he was even missed.

He went upstairs to the second floor.

It was definitely summer in Angel Hill. Even with the open grand room, the air was thick.

"Nothing up here," he said, and turned to go up to the

third floor.

Rounding the stairs on the final landing, he glanced back and thought, *That's where he hung, then.*

At the top of the stairs, he looked around. He took a deep breath, but the air up here was almost too thick to breathe. It hung around him like a plastic bag and his arms were immediately covered in a wet sheet of sweat.

"This is it," he said. He moved through the other rooms, stopping for a second in the corner room to stare at the wall and wonder how horrible it must have been to see those children, dead, lined up along the wall. He shivered despite the stifling heat.

"God, those poor kids," he said. "What the hell made you do something like that, Milo?"

He couldn't answer that. No one in Angel Hill could. Milo'd left no note. And Angel Hill wasn't so small that everyone knew everyone's business. Most of the town had never even heard of Milo Dengler until the day the story hit the news. And the house, it wasn't the only big house in town. But it was definitely the most infamous now.

Charley wandered back to the center room and stood back by the wall.

"How could you?" he asked.

Suddenly a rapid pounding came from above. He looked up and saw he was standing under the crawlspace door. The sound came in a fierce pattern, almost desperate, and it scared him with its intensity.

"Fuck that," he said, and hauled ass back down the stairs and out the back door.

He had to go back inside to grab his guitar, but when he got outside he told Jack, "Hey, I gotta take off. I didn't see it was so late."

"Okay," Jack said. "I'll see you at work."

"Cool." He put his guitar in its case, unplugged his amp and wound the cord, then headed to his car.

Charley drove home as quickly as he could without getting pulled over. He went into the house, put his guitar on the couch and his amp on the floor. Without a word to his wife, he grabbed the phone and dialed.

His sister answered and without a word of greeting, Charley said, "I was in the house."

She didn't have to ask what house, they'd talked about it since Charley told her he worked with the man who bought it.

"And?" she asked.

"And that place is haunted, I don't care what anyone else thinks. I was up on that third floor and I'm telling you I heard some stuff that almost gave me a heart attack."

"Really? Like what?"

Charley told her about sneaking upstairs and about the machine gun pounding on the roof he'd heard.

"On the roof?" she asked. "That's weird."

"Might have been in the crawlspace," he said. "I was right under the door. I don't remember anything about any crawlspace."

"What do you think it was?"

"I don't know. If anything, I hope it was one of those twins and not one of the kids."

"But what if they really did just vanish? Went off somewhere and started over? Couldn't have been too hard back then."

"If that happened, then it was one of the kids, but I can't imagine what it would be doing up in the ceiling."

"I don't know," his sister answered.

"Anyway, I just wanted to tell you I was up there tonight. There's stuff in that house, that's one story you can definitely believe from now on. I'm gonna call Ron and tell him."

"Okay, I'll talk to you later."

Charley hung up and talked to his brother Ron for twenty minutes before finally going back to his wife in the living room.

"What happened?" she asked.

He told her and she shook her head and said the same thing everyone said.

"Those poor kids."

Later, everyone lay in bed.

Jack was dreaming of flowers growing wild when

footsteps next to the bed woke him up. He opened a bleary eye and leaned his head up.

"Joe?" he asked. "What's wrong?"

Before he got an answer, he'd gone back to sleep and the footsteps retreated out of the room.

Liz heard them, too. She wasn't asleep yet and doubted she would be by morning.

The footsteps weren't the first noise that night. Something was going on upstairs. Two floors below, Liz could hear them up there, knocking the walls, thumping the floors. She snuggled closer to Jack, not so much for protection, but for the simple presence of another living person.

Joey dreamed, too. But he didn't dream of flowers. He dreamed of running. He ran because he was being chased.

The dead girl was screaming at him, "Your father's a killer, your father's a killer!" She chased him but when he looked back, she was smiling. Her face didn't show the least sign of meanness. In fact, she looked pretty happy. She laughed as she screamed at him.

He searched the park as he ran, hoping someone else might be here, anyone who could get the dead girl away from him. A grown-up. As soon as the thought formed, he spotted someone. A man stood under a tree at the other end of the park.

I'll never make it, Joey thought. She'll catch me before I get there.

And what would she do, he wondered. He hadn't thought of that. All he knew was that she was chasing him, and when people chased you, you ran. So that's what he did, ran full blast for the man under the tree.

The girl was at Joey's heels, screaming, "Your father's a killer!" But he managed to stay ahead of her. His foot slipped once in wet grass, but he kept his balance and pressed on, pumping his legs and swinging his arms, wishing for faster shoes, and then finally collapsing in front of the tall man under the tree.

"That girl's after me," Joey panted. "She's chasing me and screaming."

He looked up into the adult face and then back at the girl who had stopped just behind him. The faces were the same, dead and green. Puffed, broken skin. Crazy smiles.

"I've been looking for you Adam," the man said.

"I'm Joey," he replied, hoping this correction would save him.

That's when he woke up. His first inclination was to cry, but he decided then that he'd done enough of that and if he ever wanted to get bigger, he'd have to stop crying, because bigger kids didn't cry. Instead, he lay under his thin blanket, his eyes open, his breath even, but his heart fluttering as he listened to the whispers from upstairs, inviting him to play with them.

Chapter Eight

The heat came to Angel Hill that Monday. Liz was beginning to think summers here would be wonderful. Nice weather. Neither too hot nor too humid, breezes every now and then, like an extended, warmer spring. Their house in Texas had had central air, so the Kitches had no fans. Liz would have to buy some when Jack came home from work. She went upstairs once that day, she couldn't remember why, but when she came down again, she thanked God they lived on the first floor. It was darker down there, and cooler. For all its warmth on the bottom floor, the second floor was plain hot. She imagined the third floor was sweltering.

She busied herself the whole morning cleaning, straightening things, and making sure the dirty clothes were actually in the basket, instead of hanging out like limp tongues. Joey spent most of the morning on the floor in front of Cartoon Network. Finally, she was able to give him his lunch and tell him it was naptime.

She'd closed his closet door while she was cleaning. She didn't mention it to him. If he noticed, he might remember whatever had happened yesterday and not want to go to sleep. She had about an hour before the priest should be here, and she wanted Joey plenty gone by then.

She took a chair to the second floor and sat at one of the front windows, going through one of her books while she kept an eye on the front yard, waiting.

He pulled up in a new car, a Cadillac, it looked like. She wondered where priests got such nice cars all the time. She'd never seen one in a Datsun or some ancient piece of crap. It was always nice new cars.

He knocked and she shook her head, loosening all thoughts of cars so they fell out, and she went to answer the door.

He was tall. She had to look up to see his face. His head was rectangular with short-cropped hair. He was thin. She thought he looked like a cardboard cutout in need of a display. He smiled and introduced himself and she showed him downstairs, telling her son was asleep, but they could go into the living room.

They talked for a few minutes, but Liz wished he'd just get on with it. If this didn't work, she'd have to think of something else, and so far none of her books were offering any suggestions. She told him they were new in town, that they were starting over in Angel Hill, and that she wanted to start with having their new home blessed for their family.

"Always a good idea," the priest said.

"Where do we start?" she asked.

"Nothing you need do," he said, "except have pleasant thoughts. I'll start in the kitchen, if you'd like, and just work my way through to the stairs."

"Okay."

He went into the kitchen and set a small case on the counter. Liz hadn't noticed the case at first, then she decided it must have all his stuff. Surely he'd need stuff, wouldn't he? She didn't know. She didn't even know what blessing a house entailed.

She heard him muttering something, but couldn't tell what. She imagined it was a prayer. What else would a priest use to bless a house? He stopped and she thought he was on his way back through. Before he did, she left the room to find something to do. She was curious about the process, but she wasn't sure how he felt about someone watching him work. Instead, she'd go about her business and keep praying it worked.

She went upstairs to check the mail. It hadn't come yet. She stepped out to the end of the porch and looked down the street, searching for the mail truck. It wasn't there. The summer air surrounded her in a cocoon and she wished for Jack to get home so she could buy some fans. Maybe they could get central air by next summer. She turned back to the house and froze, wondering if anyone across the street could see the man standing in the doorway, staring at her. He was grey, vague, but his eyes were all there and they pierced her, full of hate.

"You can't hurt me," she told him.

He sneered and nodded his head once.

What did that mean? Could he? What could he do? No, Liz thought, the blessing has to work.

He went dim and stepped back into the house. Liz heard the priest mounting the steps and the man turned toward the second floor, then vanished. The priest rounded the landing, looked up, smiled at Liz, and went about his prayer, sprinkling holy water onto the stairs. He climbed to the second floor.

Liz went inside and closed the door behind her. The priest blessed the main room. Liz heard a crack behind her. She turned to see the beveled glass in the front door had a lengthwise hairline split down one side. She frowned at it.

The priest blessed the second floor bedroom, the room Jack would use for an office. Liz felt a rumbling in her stomach, a burning that threatened to burst through her skin. She put her hand to it, hoping to calm the pressure. She went downstairs, hoping she didn't puke in the hall.

The priest moved to the second floor bathroom. Liz dashed to the toilet and unloaded a flood of toast and oatmeal.

The priest blessed the second floor kitchen. Liz heaved again, but her stomach was empty and all that came up was a thin trickle of stomach acid. She put her head against the rim and wondered what had made her so sick.

Then she saw the face again, the pissed off man in the doorway. She knew what he meant now. He could do something. He could do this to her. What else could he do?

She heaved again, so violently she ended up coughing out the rest of it, her lungs empty of breath. She wanted to go tell the priest to stop, that he was finished, so this would end, but another part of her said *Let him finish and it will be over for good. No more midnight footsteps, no more thumping, no more dead people in the house.*

She grabbed onto the bowl and heaved once more. She coughed out a wad of blood, then suddenly the pressure in her stomach was gone and she felt fine, if exhausted. A layer of sweat covered her like another skin. She flushed the vomit, then got a drink from sink, swishing it in her mouth and spitting it out. She went into the living room and collapsed on the couch.

She heard the priest going to the third floor. Somehow, down four flights of stairs and a hallway, she heard him muttering his prayers. She sat up with her head in her hands, wondering, for the first time, where they came from, these ghosts. Who were they? Why were they here? She'd never wondered that before. That surprised her. Now she wouldn't know. And she was glad. If it ended everything in the house, she'd give up the chance to know forever. Just end it.

She heard crying. Joey was awake.

What's happened now?

Joey lay curled in his bed, tangled in his sheet and sweating. He wasn't just crying, he was bawling, as if he'd just watched his favorite dog get obliterated by a semi. Liz asked what was wrong, but Joey ignored her and kept crying. She sat on the edge of his bed, rubbing his shoulder, his back, and his head.

"Joe, what's wrong?" she asked. Hadn't they done all this already? "Come on, Joe. Tell me what's the matter."

Then she noticed blood on his pillow. She looked at his face and saw his nose was bleeding. "Shit," she said, and went to the bathroom. She came back with a wad of toilet paper and held it to his nose. But the paper was soon soaked and the blood kept pouring out. She sat him up, still wailing. "Did you hit your nose on something?" He didn't answer, just let go another torrent of howls.

She tilted his head back and held another wad of paper to it, pinching him high on the nose. He squeezed his eyes shut and blood oozed out from between the pressed lids.

"What the hell?" Liz said.

The wad at his nose was full again. She left and came back with the entire roll, holding one wad to his nose while another wiped away the blood that had replaced his tears.

What's he done, she wondered. Was he crying so hard that he burst a vessel? What's going on?

Blood trickled out his ear. Drops of red dotted the sheet. Liz looked at him in horror.

She heard footsteps upstairs and knew this was punishment for bringing the priest.

"Fuck you," she said to the ceiling. "He'll be done soon and when he is you'll be gone. You can mess with us, but you can't really hurt us."

She picked up Joey and carried him outside, through the back door. She took him to the far end of the yard and sat cross-legged in the grass with Joey resting in her lap. He was still crying, still bleeding.

Liz looked back at the house. The man she'd seen on the porch, he was staring down at her from one of the third floor windows. He looked like he was smiling. She stared back at him, her face trying to throw back all the hate she felt, to make him feel it, trying to kill him all over again.

Who was this? Why was he in the house? What the fuck had happened here before they moved in? She decided she had to find out.

She rocked Joey in her lap. His cries were still wild, his nose, eyes, and ears still trickling blood. Then he coughed. She'd known that was coming. He'd cried himself sick. He leaned up and coughed again, a great, hacking cough, reaching down into his core and bringing up a wad of blood that flew from his mouth, hit the grass with a splash. She looked up at the window again and the man was gone. But the house itself stared back at her now and she realized, while the evil may be concentrated on the third floor, it had really penetrated every board and pane of glass, it was in the sheetrock, in the framing, the shingles on the roof.

The house loomed in front of her, daring her to re-enter.

She wondered if the priest had seen anything.

And what was taking so long?

Please hurry, she thought, *I don't know if Joey can keep going. Please finish so it will all go away.*

Joey hacked up another wad of blood, some of it dribbling down his chin. He was in pain, she could tell.

"Christ." She hugged him tighter. What else could she do? Take him to the hospital? For what, upsetting an already angry ghost? How could they treat that? She had to hold out until the priest was done.

And what if it doesn't stop? What then? How do you tell Jack his son bled out while you sat in the back yard and watched it?

"Please finish," she said again.

He stopped crying, leaned up out of her lap, onto his knees, and retched, a violent surge from his gut that brought a wave of vomit and blood all over the grass. It steamed and the smell hit Liz like a fist.

She looked at the house again.

Everything looked different.

It was just a house.

The priest was coming out the back door, smiling. Joey was asleep on the grass, the puddle of vomit inches from his head. She looked at the third floor window, but it was empty.

Was it over? Finally?

She wiped away the blood from Joey's ears and eyes.

The priest came over and said, "Is that your son?"

"Yes."

"Oh, is he okay?"

"He wasn't feeling good. I think the heat was getting to him. Got a nosebleed, then he threw up. I think he's okay now."

"Yeah, the summers in these parts aren't kind."

"I've noticed."

She picked him up. His head rested on her shoulder. The priest noticed the birthmark under his chin.

"That's a nasty scar he's got."

"No," she said. "It's just a birthmark, really."

"Oh? Well, it certainly is a strange one, then."

"Yes," she agreed. Then she noticed the priest trying not to look over Liz's shoulder and when she glanced back she saw the old naked woman duck behind her curtain again.

Liz laughed.

"Well, that's something you don't see every day, isn't it?" he said.

"You do around here," Liz said. "She's always standing there like that. I have no idea why."

They shared a chuckle and Liz carried Joey back to the house. She laid him on the couch, then turned to thank the priest. He said it was his pleasure. They talked another few minutes before he remembered another appointment.

"I hope you and your family have many good years here," he said, walking to the door.

"Me too," Liz said. "And thanks again. I'm sure we'll be very happy here."

"God bless," he said. He walked out.

"Goodbye."

She closed the door and turned around to look at her house. Was it over? Had the blessing worked? She went up to the second floor, stood in the middle of the main room, and waited.

Nothing. She went to the third floor, stood up there a few minutes. She had to make herself stand still. She would probably be nervous coming up here for awhile. But she did it and she heard nothing, felt nothing.

Am I alone? she wondered. She thought she just might be.

"Thank God," she said out loud.

She took another look at the empty third floor, wondering what they'd put up here once the house was done. They really had more room than they needed.

We'll think of something, she thought as she went back down to the first floor.

She got a washcloth from the bathroom and wet it to wipe Joey's face. He was deep in sleep on the couch. Would he even remember any of it when he woke up? She hoped not.

She put the bloody rag in the dirty clothes, then put those in the washer.

She sat on the couch at Joey's feet, leafing through one of her decorating books from the library, at ease for the first time in weeks. Jack would be home in a few hours. She decided to enjoy the peace and solitude for the first real time since they moved in.

Joey slept. Liz relaxed.

Chapter Nine

In the two weeks that followed the blessing, Liz had finished three rooms on the second floor. Two actually, but she was nearly done with the dining room. She worked through the afternoons, setting up three fans on the second floor, while Joey played in the main room or took his nap.

The main room had gone quickly once she'd gone back to work on it. She wondered if Jack had even noticed she'd stopped. But it didn't matter now. The room was done, as was the bathroom, and now she was working on the dining room. Only the kitchen and study up here left to do, then it would be time to decide what to do with the third floor.

Jack had suggested closing off the first floor from the rest of the house, put a wall up down there and add a door to the end of the hall at the side of the house. They could rent it out and the Kitches could live on the top two floors.

"It's not like there's not plenty of room for us up there. There are four bedrooms on the third floor and only three of us. And you and I share a room. What do you say?"

Liz had nodded at his idea, said it was something to think about, but hadn't really considered it.

No matter how long she went without hearing a thump or seeing a blurry figure pass down the hallway, she didn't know if she could bring herself to sleep up there. A hundred psychics could come through, tell her the house was clean, and she wouldn't be able to do it. She knew it like she knew the sun would set at dusk.

But it really was an awful lot of room. More than they needed.

"Forget it, " she said, turning away from her thoughts, and back to the wallpaper.

This would be a beautiful room when it was finished. All they needed now were people to impress with it. All this time in Angel Hill and still they hadn't made any friends. There was the guy at work, Charley, Jack talked to. But as of yet, at work was the only time they talked.

Jack had mentioned going to Charley's house some time to play guitar, but mention it was all he'd done. When the second floor was done, they would have to invite Charley and his family, if he had any, over for dinner.

She looked back through the door connecting the dining room to the main room. Joey was lying on his back, Superman flying above him, crashing down into the floor above Joey's head. Liz lost her concentration and the sheet of wallpaper she held fell back over her. She wrestled with it and climbed up a couple rungs on the ladder to reach the ceiling.

She was papering the last wall when she checked on Joey again and saw he was asleep in the middle of the floor. She'd trained one of the fans on him, but from here she could see he was still sweating.

Liz had taken a break from working and gone downstairs. Joey was asleep and would be, she figured, for a while longer. Joey woke up minutes after Liz was gone.

He climbed off the floor and looked around, wondering where everyone was, including himself. He wasn't used to waking up in the middle of the floor. After a few seconds, he realized where he was. They'd lived in the house over a month, but anything other than the first floor was still alien to him. He moved around the room, looking at Liz's decorations, not forming much of an opinion about them.

It looks a lot different, he thought.

A lot different than what?

He didn't know. He went into what would be the study. It was dark, the shadows keeping it cooler than the main room. This was their bedroom, he thought.

Whose?

The parents, the ones who had the house before us. Their bedroom was in here.

How did he know?

They'd told him, the voices. He hadn't heard them in a while, but they used to tell him things. And this was the parents' bedroom. The kids' rooms were upstairs. Up there was where all the bad stuff happened.

Joey went to the bottom of the stairs and stared up. He listened, but there was nothing. He wondered what had happened up there. And why didn't he hear them anymore? Not that he wanted to, but he had noticed, and was curious.

He took a step up and looked overhead to the high ceiling and then the top rail. Even though he didn't feel he was being watched anymore, he was still scared in the way children are of such places. Looming, dark, empty. He stepped back down and went downstairs, walking into the living room, rubbing his eyes.

"Did you just wake up?" Liz asked.

"Uh-huh," he said, nodding and climbing onto the couch beside her.

"Are you hungry?"

He shook his head and turned to the television. It wasn't cartoons, nor did it look like it was going to be. Liz was watching something Joey had no interest in. A few minutes passed before he got off the couch and went into his room.

"Tell me about the lizards," Jack said.

Charley smiled and nodded. "I remember that one. I was here for it."

"So what happened?"

"Just what the book said. One morning, everyone woke up and found lizards. They were just wandering around, through peoples' yards, under cars. They filled the streets so badly, you couldn't drive anywhere without crushing hundreds of them." He finished his TV dinner lunch, wiped his mouth with a paper towel.

"Where'd they come from?" Jack's lunch was only half-eaten. *The Outsider's Guide to Angel Hill* lay open in front of him. He was going through the chapters, picking them at random, and asking for more details.

"I don't know. We went to sleep one night with no lizards. We woke up the next day with them." Charley had gone over three Angel Hill stories with him and was beginning to regret telling him about the book.

"What kinds were they?"

"All different kinds. They counted about sixty different types, just from the corpses. I don't know the names of any of them, but I remember seeing Angel Hill covered in them. It was pretty freaky."

"I'd imagine so," Jack said. He took a bite and noticed it wasn't as warm as it should be.

"It's getting cold."

"Yeah, it is. But they never figured out where they came from?"

"Nope. But, hell, they only spent about a week on it anyway. After that, they gave up, chalked it up to another Angel Hill Occurrence and forgot about it."

"See," Jack said, trying not to laugh, "this is why you're full of shit. I've been through this book and through it again--I haven't actually read all of it, but I've flipped through it--and I've found, maybe, two or three stories in here that are even remotely plausible. I can't believe thousands of lizards showed up in town one day and no one ever knew why."

"I can't help that. But I remember what I saw. If you're not gonna believe me, why do you keep asking me to tell you about them?"

Jack tossed his lunch, having decided it was too cold to eat and would be less trouble ditching instead of reheating it.

"Because I'm curious. I'll admit that. But I'm curious about details that might not be in the book. You were there for the lizards, you say. What else happened that day, or the day before, that's not in the book? Something else you remember in retrospect that might have possibly explained it."

"Nothing," Charley said. "The book's got all the details. He was very thorough. I can't tell you why, it just was."

"Nothing just is," Jack said. "Everything's got a logic behind it."

"Yeah, you'd think so, wouldn't you?" Charley said. "Forget it. Let's talk about something else. We've still got a few minutes left."

"Like what?"

"How about guitars?"

"That I can do."

They spent the next ten minutes doing just that.

Liz washed shampoo from Joey's hair while the boy squeezed his eyes shut, held his hands tight over them and kept asking, "How many more?" each time she dumped a cup of water over his head.

"Just one more." She wiped his face and told him to look up. She wiped off his neck, clearing shampoo bubbles away from his ragged pink birthmark. She got him out, dried him off, and sent him to bed.

"How about I take the day off working on the house tomorrow and we go have some fun?"

"Are we going to go see Uncle Allen?"

Liz laughed. "No, I don't think we will. He's all the way in Texas."

"So, how far is that?"

"Do you remember when we came to Angel Hill? When we were in the car all that time and driving all day and you ended up falling asleep?"

Joey nodded. "I like driving a lot. We can go see him."

"We might go down for Christmas, how's that? But not tomorrow. I was thinking maybe the park. Or maybe we could take Dad to work and keep the car and just go see what else we've got to do here."

"Yeah," Joey said. "Let's see if they've got horses."

"Horses, eh?" She covered him with a sheet and turned on his fan.

"They used to keep horses in the house a long time ago."

"They kept them in the barn."

"Not this house. They used to keep them inside."

"Okay, Joe," she said, kissing his forehead and turning out his light. "Good night. We'll think of something good to do. Sweet dreams."

She closed the door and went back to the living room, wondering what he meant by saying they kept horses in the house. First, what did it mean and second, where did he hear it? Did he make it up? Of course he did, he's only six.

She woke up later in the dark, nighttime heat just as stifling as afternoon heat. She thought, *We've got to get an air conditioner if nothing else. This is insane, this heat.* Then she heard footsteps in the hall. She froze, listening. *Not again, please*, she thought. *Now what do I do? Dammit!*

Jack came back to bed, climbed in next to her and went back to sleep. Now that she saw it was only Jack, she realized she could hear the toilet running down the hall. She'd heard it flush, had heard the bathroom door open. But with the heat and her exhaustion, she hadn't paid any attention. She let her body relax again and tried to get back to sleep through the sweltering crap of Angel Hill summer. She drifted off finally, thinking, *We've got to get an air conditioner. Jack's just gonna have to do some overtime or something to pay for it. How can he sleep in this?* Then she, too, was gone.

When she woke up next, she was freezing.

The dark told her it was still the middle of the night, the sound of the fan told her it was still summer. She leaned her head up, peering at the foot of the bed. The fan was oscillating, but Liz felt as if ten of them were trained on her. She squeezed in closer to herself, then backed up to steal some of Jack's heat. She yawned and watched her breath vanish over her head. Why was it so cold? Why was it *this* cold? Even with half a dozen fans, it still had to be a good eighty-five degrees outside. She shouldn't be this cold.

A shiver ran through her. She shook it off. Her neck creaked and she stretched. She pulled the sheet tighter over her and tried to bury her head in the pillow.

The temperature suddenly dropped another five degrees and she opened her eyes again. She sat up, looked around. She and Jack were alone, but for some reason, the room seemed somehow too empty. Even with her husband asleep next to her, she felt alone. She shook him, but he was oblivious in sleep.

She got out of bed, walked into the hall. Her skin prickled with chilly goose bumps. Her breath evaporated before her. A cold hand brushed her face and she flinched back, gasping, turning away.

The bathroom door closed. Liz looked into the darkness toward the sound. She moved down the hall to the door. She touched the handle and found it freezing. Something whispered in the dark, incomprehensible words, sounds, noises, she wasn't sure what. All she was sure of was that she hadn't made them.

Whatever had been roaming the house two weeks ago was still here.

Her head told her body to climb back into bed, bury her face against Jack, squeeze her eyes shut until dawn, and spend the night praying. Her body told her mind to go to hell. She was at the foot of the stairs. She climbed to the landing and looked up. The second floor was black. Not even outside light filtered in.

What are you doing? her mind asked. Get downstairs and deal with this in the morning.

"I'm not going to be scared out of my own house," she told no one. *I've waited too long, suffered through too much shit, to get to this point. I've got a good family, a good house, and a good life and I'm not giving it up.* "This is my house now," she said. The house responded with a crack of wood overhead.

Liz was on the stairs to the third floor landing, ignorant to everything around her except the noises and the cold. Up here it was even colder.

Her feet were numb from the stairs and her fingers wouldn't grasp the banister right, they were so stiff from cold. She breathed icicles, exhaled mist.

"You're not scaring me out," she said. "This is my house now."

Another crack of wood from the third floor. She stood on the landing, staring up. She'd braved the dark and the cold past the first two floors, but nothing could make her take that last flight to the top. She just stood in the dark, looking up at it, thinking hatred at it, telling it to go away. Below her, she heard music. A piano played light, cheery notes in the main second floor room. She drew in breath and moved down the stairs.

The notes sounded until Liz reached the main room. When they stopped, the silence was worse than the phantom music. At least with the music playing, she might not hear the whispers. And while she didn't hear them now, she knew they were coming, and when they did, with nothing to drown them out, she'd hear them loud and clear.

She rubbed her hands together, flexed her fingers, and popped the knuckles.

What was coming next? The waiting was just as bad as finding out. The anticipation, the wonder, the uncertainty.

A child giggled overhead, then someone bounded down the steps, rounded the second floor and the footsteps vanished downstairs. The bathroom door opened, then slammed. The study door closed, quietly with a simple click. The door separating the main room from the dining room swung shut.

Liz stood in the middle of the room. The temperature dropped again. She thought she could feel her blood freezing, it was so cold. And she was in her underwear and a T-shirt. That's when she felt the hands on her legs, dozens of them, caressing her skin, running the length of her calf, her thigh, over the knob of her knee. Her hands brushed at them, found nothing, and she stepped away from where she'd been standing. Then the whispers did come.

"You can't save yourself."

"Forgive me--pant, pant--*forgive me."*

"Everyone will suffer now."

Liz turned around, found a light switch behind her, and flipped it. The room was flooded with dull light. The shadows were gone and so, she hoped, were the hands, the voices. It even seemed warmer now. The circulation was restored and her goose bumps were gone. The house was still.

What am I doing up in the middle of the night?

"I don't know," she answered herself. "But I'm going back to bed right now. And nothing can touch us. This is our house now."

She went downstairs, climbed into bed. Her bravado was a front, she knew it. Under the safety of the sheet, she moved against Jack. He shrugged away from her, sticky with heat and sweat. She burrowed into herself, closed her eyes, and tried to keep the house and the things in it from invading her thoughts before she was able to force herself to sleep.

As she finally slipped away, she thought she heard, faintly, from far away, a piano sounding out single hollow notes.

For the third time, Liz woke up.

Did I dream all that? she wondered. She wiped her eyes clean and rolled her feet onto the floor. *Christ, I hope so.*

As soon as she hit the living room, Joey asked if they were going to find horses today, and Liz remembered she said they'd keep the car and do something.

"We'll try, Joe," she said on her way to the kitchen. She got coffee and heard Jack coming out of the bathroom. She headed for the hall and the blessed toilet. When her bladder was quiet and she'd brushed her teeth, she felt much better, but she was still wondering about last night.

I got the house blessed. I haven't heard a noise or seen a shadow for weeks. It's supposed to be over. Please tell me I dreamed it.

But she couldn't be sure.

"Do you mind if we take you to work and keep the car today?" she asked.

"How come?"

"No reason. I just thought Joe and I could get out of the house for a day. See the city for a change."

"Okay."

When they'd dropped him off and Jack had reminded her for the fifth time to pick him up, she glanced back at Joey in the mirror and asked, "So what do you wanna do?"

"Let's find the horses."

"Okay," she said. "I guess we drive around until we find horses."

"I know where they are," he said. "I'll tell you where to go."

Liz smiled and said okay, thinking she was going to spend the day driving in circles. But she didn't have any other plans, so circles were fine with her. At least they weren't in the house. And at the least car had air conditioning.

Jack decided he hated Harris Wilde. Harris was the buyer for the western division of Fett Technologies in Boulder, Colorado. Harris called at least three times a week with a rush order of control boxes and cables he needed sent next day air to the plant in Boulder. And Harris wanted all this made extra, in addition to the regular schedule of work already going to Colorado. But Harris never called in with his "emergency order" until right before lunch, which gave them only three hours to get it filled and shipped in time to make the UPS pick-up.

Jack brought two work orders to the cable cell and gave them to Wanda, the cell leader. He took another three to the box cell.

"These are for next day air to Harris Wilde," he said.

"Cocksucker," Charley said. "Would it be too much to ask that he pull this crap early enough to give us time to actually get it done without rushing?"

119

"And he's surprised when he gets parts that end up not working and have to be sent back," Jack said.

"Hey," Charley said, "you wanna come over some time this weekend and play?"

"I don't know," Jack said. "Saturday?"

"Yeah."

"Okay. I'm sure I can squeeze it into my hectic not-at-work schedule, somewhere between the sitting around and the doing nothing."

"Cool."

"Now I have to call shipping and tell them there's gonna be a last minute next day load."

"Again," Charley said.

"Yep."

Joey directed Liz down Henry Street, right on A Street, up to Parade where she took another right, and down to River Road where he had her pull over. The spot was nice, so she did. They got out and Joey led her down a path leading to the river.

"Here it is," he said.

She looked around, but didn't see any horses. Maybe he was pretending. Was she supposed to go along with him?

"I see," she said, smiling. "And which horse do you want to ride?"

"There aren't any horses here now, silly," he said.

"Of course not. But when they get here . . ."

"I don't know if they're coming."

"Joey, do you even know where we are?"

"Uh-huh." He nodded and looked around again. "This is where the horses are. They used to be."

Liz spotted a wooden sign about fifty feet from where she was and moved toward it until she could read the faded words painted across it.

"Horse Rides. $5.00 Adults. $3.00 Children. No One Under 5. Children 5-12 Must Ride With An Adult."

How the hell did he know this was here?

The sign was old and alone. If there'd been a business here before, it was gone now. She scanned the area, looking for anything at all. There was the river, there was the sign, and there was the impression of an old trail. Weeds grew in patches across it, but the trail was clearly marked. Old trails are hard to erase.

"I'll be damned," she said under her breath.

Joey stood back, watching the river. The sun was bright this early, but the overnight damp hadn't burned off yet. From here the river was black, but the closer she moved, the greener it got until, standing next to the water, it was the color of old toilet water. She couldn't imagine ever swimming in this, let alone eating anything caught in these waters.

"Tell you what," she said. "Let's go to the park instead, huh?"

"I don't want to go to the park."

"Then we'll find something else to do. It's too nice a day to ruin looking at some nasty old river water."

"But the horses used to be here," Joey said.

Liz nodded, wiped her hair back from her forehead and said, "Yeah, it looks like they sure did. I don't know how you knew that, but I'd say there used to be horses here."

"I don't remember," he said. He stared into the water. Liz looked into it too for a second before breaking its spell and taking Joey back to the car.

Jack closed down his computer, clocked out, and waited outside for Liz. From the Fett Technologies front steps, he could see across Ellison Drive to what *The Outsider's Guide to Angel Hill* called Splatter Mountain.

She pulled up in front of him, he climbed in, and they went home.

In the car, Jack mentioned to her going to Charley Clark's this Saturday to play guitar with him for awhile.

At home, Joey went to his room to drag out as many toys as he thought he might need. While he did that, Liz told Jack about the horses and the trail rides that weren't there anymore, but used to be, and had Jack taken him there already, otherwise how did Joey know it was there?

"He's only six," she said. "He shouldn't know anything more about where he lives than what's across the street." She turned on the oven.

"Maybe he saw it on the news," Jack said.

"Doesn't explain how he knew exactly how to get there." She got out a cookie sheet.

"So maybe he's a genius. What are you getting at anyway? So he found a trail ride--that's not even there anymore, so technically he didn't find it--there's lots of old stuff in this house. Maybe he found an old map of things to do around Angel Hill." Jack took a bag of frozen French fries and a bag of frozen chicken nuggets from the freezer.

"You're determined to explain this away, aren't you?" she asked. She took the chicken and fries from him and dumped them onto the cookie sheet.

"That's because there is an explanation. Did you think to ask him?"

"Of course. You know what he said? 'I don't remember.'" She put the food in the oven, then went to the living room, leaving Jack to figure out how Joey found the trail ride, if he was so fucking smart.

Chapter Ten

Days passed--and more importantly, nights passed--without incident. Liz had begun to convince herself she'd dreamed the cold night and the hands on her and the music. On Saturday, Jack took his guitar and his amp and went to Charley's. Liz took another day off working upstairs and cleaned the first floor. She'd given up asking Joey about the trail ride, deciding he either really didn't know, or he just wasn't going to tell her.

She was making their bed, shoving the blanket between the sheets, when her fingers hit Jack's book. She pulled it out, turned it over, wondering what it was, how it got there.

The Outsider's Guide to Angel Hill.

She opened the book and leafed through it, scanning the pictures, the chapters. She stopped on a chapter called, "The Story of Nin Park."

(from *The Outsider's Guide to Angel Hill*, chapter 12):

The story of Nin Park is not one often retold in Angel Hill; everyone knows it and no one wants to repeat it.

Originally, Nigel Naas had purchased the land eventually occupied by Nin Park. He kept his land closely guarded against any intruders and was alleged to have killed and disposed of his share of trespassers.

Then there was the inevitable daring one who "lived to tell" about the other side of Nigel Naas's property line.

It wasn't long before tales of a large glass conservatory with stained glass designs around the top and six-foot weeds, thorn bushes, birds flying around inside with the rotting carcasses of large animals littering the floor. A towering sculpture made entirely from butcher knife blades, some gleaming new, some blood-tinted with rust, stood a short distance from the animals, and further on a fountain sprayed red-dyed water. The statue in the center of the fountain had been a mule-headed monster whose body was that of a lion-man half-breed. The red water shot from the thing's eye sockets onto the carved bodies of three mangled cherubs at its feet.

Not long after the stories began spreading through town,

pressure from those disgusted by the tale had the police knocking on Nigel Naas's door, demanding to be let onto his property, search warrant in hand. A high stone wall surrounded the land and the only way through was Nigel's back door. When Nigel didn't answer after ten minutes of knocking, the door was broken down and a small squad of armed officers stepped into "the worst smelling, the darkest, the dirtiest shithole" they'd seen.

The house was empty. Nigel was gone. Thousands of items were confiscated. Weapons, bloodstained knives, torture devices. While no bodies were ever found on the property, the blood on the knives proved to be human. Police spent a full day searching, documenting, dissecting the house before they found the basement, and Nigel.

The basement had been transformed into a place of hellish worship. The altar, which Nigel constructed in the shape of a huge, erect phallus (the shaft turned out to contain a hollow tube, two inches in diameter, and filled to its five-foot top with drying, yellow semen. Whose was never discovered, but it wasn't Nigel's; scar tissue showed he'd emasculated himself years earlier), had more blades from the butcher knife sculpture sticking out all up its length, some coated with dried blood. Dry pools of candle wax covered the floor, their wicks long spent. Symbols formed a strange pattern of demon worship around the walls. Nigel was found in the middle of the floor, lying on a horizontal wooden cross. Nailed to it, actually, through both hands and feet. How he got there, who did the nailing, and whether he'd died from this or from the shattered spine couldn't be determined with one hundred percent certainty. Nor is it assumed anyone will ever decide to take up the search for the truth.

Nigel Naas was dead and, with no will to be found, soon every sacrilegious thing on his property was destroyed in a mass razing.

The property was turned over to the city of Angel Hill and renamed Nin Park. In an effort to turn the land's reputation around, the park was decorated with statues and fountains again, this time depicting victorious angels wielding swords as if ready to battle the evil, should it ever again appear in Nin Park.

The house was destroyed and a paved entrance was added with a large stone dragon at the front, as if to guard the park, holding a large marble globe in two upturned hands.

(The park planning committee's intention had been to keep anything that may hark back to Nigel Naas out of their blueprints, but hidden clues to Nigel's existence kept finding their way into the park. The name of the park itself is an acronym of Nigel's initials, Nigel Icarus Naas. The dragon symbolized Nigel's soul--he used to say that in a previous life he'd been a dragon. The marble globe was a prison in which, he'd written in a journal, he trapped the souls of trespassers he'd killed. The real globe, if it exists, was never found).

. . . .

Liz closed the book, looked again at the cover.

"Nin Park?" she said. "I don't remember seeing any Nin Park in town."

She flipped the book open again, searching for the pages she'd just read. When she found them, she scanned through the rest of the chapter, looking for something about what happened to Nin Park. She found it toward the end.

Someone had unlocked the Nigel Naas clues--the initials of his name, the dragon, the globe--and it was decided to close the park for good in favor of two new, better, untainted parks. Upper and Lower Hill Parks. Upper Hill Park was a block and a half from the Kitch house.

And that explained why she'd never heard of it.

She looked the book over again, wondering now why Jack had it, why he hadn't shown it to her, and why it was stuffed under his side of the mattress.

She put it back, contemplating whether to ask him when he got home, or to wait and see if he said something about it himself.

Joey's dreams had not only returned, they'd moved from the park to the house.

He was playing on the second floor, pitting his newest Batman figure against an old Power Ranger, when he heard the voice.

He froze, wondering if the little girl had followed him home. But this wasn't her harsh, screaming voice. Someone was whispering. He listened, and realized they weren't talking to him. He got up from the rug, leaving his toys behind, and moved toward the sound. It was upstairs.

He stopped at the foot of the stairs and listened again. Was this anything important enough for him to go up there? Could he leave it alone?

He looked up at the flight looming above him. The stairs, the third floor, the unknown voice in his house.

No, he decided, he would leave this alone and go back to his playing. Maybe his dad would be home soon and they would all go out. That would be nice.

But the further away he moved from the voice upstairs, the louder it got in his head, whispering over and over the phrase Joey didn't understand, but one that worried him anyway.

"*Forgive me*--pant pant--*forgive me. Forgive me*--pant pant--*forgive me.*"

He picked up the Power Ranger and carried it over to the window, staring down to the street, trying to will his father to come home. Then he heard someone coming down the steps, that voice in his head nearly screaming its whispered phrase at him.

"*Forgive me*--pant pant--*forgive me. Forgive me*--pant pant--*forgive me.*"

With his eyes on the street, Joey felt the presence creep toward him, could tell it was reaching out for him, knew its fingers were inches from his skin. He tensed, felt the chill on his shoulder, and leapt in his sleep, on to waking, as Liz shook him awake.

Jack called Liz before he left work and said he and Charley were going out for a bit first.

"Says he wants to show me something," Jack said.

"I'll bet he does," Liz said. "Just remember to use the ones, okay?"

"What?"

"The one-dollar bills," she said. "For the strippers. If you're gonna tip them, use the ones, not the fives and definitely not the tens or twenties."

"Gotcha," he said. "I'll be home soon."

He and Charley clocked out and got into the Kitch Jeep. They pulled out of the Fett Tech parking lot as Charley told Jack where to go, but he wouldn't tell him where they were going to end up.

"Come on, man," Jack said. "What's so important we got to do this now? Where are we going?"

"I just want to show you a couple things," Charley said. "You're so sure everything around here is normal as can be, I want you to see a few things and then you can decide. Turn left up here."

Jack followed his directions and within fifteen minutes he was pulling up outside an apartment building.

"My bother is the manager here," Charley said. "I'm gonna have him show you something."

"I already have a place to live," Jack said.

"Funny. Come on."

Jack followed him inside and to the manager's office where he met Charley's brother, Ron, who was sitting at a desk, rolling a tennis ball back and forth. They traded handshakes and Jack asked, "So what's the big mystery here? The basement infested with giant killer rats or something?"

Charley and Ron exchanged a look, then Ron grabbed a key off his desk and said, "Alright, then. Come on."

They followed him upstairs and he stopped outside a door marked B11. He slid the key into the lock and looked at his brother.

"Ready?"

Charley nodded. "How long?"

"A minute, at the most."

"Okay. Let's go."

"Hold on, hold on," Jack said, hands raised. "A minute for what? What's in here? We're not stepping into a murder scene, are we? 'Cause I'm pretty sure that's illegal."

"No, nothing like that," Ron Clark said. "You'll see. Just be careful, and stay close to the door."

He turned the key, unlocked the door, opened it, and they stepped inside.

Jack wasn't sure what he'd been expecting, but an empty apartment was not it. He looked around, still wondering what was so special about this place. It was small. One, two rooms.

He saw a kitchen off the back of the place, but couldn't tell how big, so it might only qualify as a room and a half. The closed door must be the bathroom.

He took a step into the room and Charley grabbed his arm.

"Stay by the door."

"What for?"

Ron knelt in front of them and put his tennis ball on the floor.

"Here it goes," he said. His fingers came off the ball and it rolled immediately to the center of the room.

Charley and Ron looked at Jack. Jack looked back and shrugged.

"So what? Come on, man, I'm hungry, I gotta get home."

"You say 'So what?'" Charley said. "Didn't you see that?"

"Yeah, he rolled a ball to the center of the room. Wow, you're right, that's pretty amazing, now let's go."

"I didn't roll it," Ron said, getting back to his feet.

"Well, it didn't roll itself."

"Sure it did."

"What?"

He produced another tennis ball. Jack wasn't sure from where.

"You wanna try it?" he asked, offering the ball to Jack.

"What for?" He turned to Charley. "Seriously, come on, this was great, but pointless."

"Here," Ron said, still holding out the ball for Jack.

Jack sighed and took it.

"Fine," he said, "but there's no way it's going to get as close to the middle of the room as yours. I'll overshoot, I can tell you that."

"Just let it go," Charley said.

"Just put it on the floor, and take your fingers off it," Ron said. "Don't push at all. Just let go."

Jack shook his head but went to his knees anyway.

"Anything to get the hell out of here already," he said. He'd only just noticed it, but his head was pounding.

He put the ball on the floor in front of him, looked up at

the ball Ron had rolled and . . . saw it was in the middle of the room, spinning.

Now that's a cool trick, he thought. *What Charley didn't tell me is his brother does stage tricks, too. Apparently.*

Jack aimed the ball, then went a little off center, and pulled his fingers off.

The ball shot off for the center of the room, veering off the crooked course Jack had put it on, and joined the first ball in the middle of the room. The two collided. Then they began to spin around each other.

They rotated like a planet and moon.

"That's a cool one," Jack had to admit. "You got any aspirin or something?" he asked. "My head, man . . ."

"Shit," Ron said. "Too long, come on, we got to get back out."

They all three quickly ducked back into the hallway and Ron had a little trouble pulling the door closed all the way before turning the key in the lock again. When he let go, the door jerked once, rattled in the frame, then stopped. He put the key in his pocket and shook his head, then rubbed his temples.

"That's a harsh one," Charley said, rubbing his head.

"Yeah. And it doesn't get any easier."

"Wonder if it's bad for you. You know? Is it harmful?"

"I wouldn't think so. It's just weird is all."

"So I can go home now?" Jack asked.

They turned to him and Charley said, "That was pretty cool, huh?"

"Yeah, it was alright, but so what? You got a dip in the floor so the balls roll together. Probably got metal inside them and magnets under the floor, that's not a hard one to pull off. Was there a point to this?"

"Couple months ago," Ron said, leading them back to the office, "this guy moves in. He's got all his stuff moved in and he's been here maybe a day, no more than two. Somebody drops by to visit him, but he doesn't answer. Few days later, they come back, and he still isn't home. Now I sat in here for a week and watched people come and go and knock on his door and not once did he answer. I watched the guy move in, so I know he's gotta show up sooner or later. Another week goes by, nothing. Then the exterminator, he's making the rounds, you know, I mean we don't have a problem, but that's because we do this regular to make sure no problems start 'cause once the bugs get in you can't get 'em back out. So anyway, the exterminator knocks on the door and the guy don't answer, so he knocks again, and still the guy don't answer. He's got passkeys, though, the tenants, they know we do this every six weeks and they don't mind as long as we're not going through their stuff, right? So he opens the door, and the place is empty. This guy, he'd paid the full first month, and I watched him carrying boxes into the building and up those stairs, and not once, after that first day, did I see him leave this building, let alone move his stuff back out again. He's just gone. Like that. And all his stuff with him."

Jack shook his head, shrugged his shoulders. "So what?"

"So what," Ron repeated. "So you saw what happened in there, and you felt it to," he pointed to Jack's head. "That's so what. You open this door in twenty minutes, those balls are gonna be gone, that's so what. You spend more than five full minutes in there, you're head starts pounding. Another five minutes, you're throwing up all over yourself. Another five and you're shitting blood for a week. *That's* so what."

Jack looked at Charley.

"Is this guy for real?" he asked.

Charley shrugged and said, "I'm just showing you one of the unexplained mysteries of Angel Hill, one of the things you're so certain can be easily explained. So go ahead and explain it."

"I told you, slanted floor and magnets."

"If it were true, but it's not. And that doesn't explain where the guy went and what happened to his stuff. And how come the physical effects on people when they stay in there too long?"

"The guy bailed with all his stuff, probably decided he couldn't afford the place and moved back in with his parents. The headache, hell, maybe you got something being pumped into the room. You can do that, you know."

"Yeah," Charley said. "I'm that desperate to prove you wrong, I'm gonna go to that trouble. Just realize it, man, there's something in there and we can't explain it."

"Maybe not you," Jack said, "but personally, I'm not worried about it. I told you what I think and that's good enough for me."

"You're impossible."

"Can I go home now?"

"Almost," Charley said. "One more thing."

Jack groaned. He shook Ron's hand and he and Charley went outside.

"You know, we can drive around all night," Jack said. "The only thing it's going to prove is that you'll believe anything."

"Then it's a good thing the next place is within walking distance. Come on," Charley said. "Right over here."

He led Jack over two blocks to an abandoned building. The painted sign across the facade, faded from years of Angel Hill weather, read Four Brothers Paper Mill. The building hadn't been used for paper milling in decades, Jack guessed.

"So what's this?" he asked. "The Haunted Paper Mill of Angel Hill?"

"Cute. But no," Charley said.

"Then what?"

Charley started toward the back of the building.

"Follow me."

Jack did. Charley led him to a loading dock around back.

"You're not gonna mug me back here, are you?" Jack joked.

"Over here," Charley said.

Behind the building a little way was an undeveloped area of woods. Charley was walking into them and waving Jack to follow.

"Naw, I saw this movie," Jack said. "I follow you in there, and you come back out alone. In thirty years, while you're on your deathbed, you finally lead the cops to my body. No thanks."

"Just come on," Charley said. Jack followed him.

They walked about two hundred feet into the woods when they came up on a large concrete slab. *That's a weird place for something like that*, Jack thought. As they approached it, he could see the thing was just what it looked like, a big concrete block. There were no seams, no holes. Just the block.

"What's this, your altar?" Jack asked.

"This is the cover to The Pit."

"Alright, then," Jack said.

"About twenty years ago, some friends and I were playing here in these woods. Like kids do, you know, regular kid games. My friend Doug Parker and I were running through here one day and all of the sudden . . . he was just gone. I mean, I glanced over and there's no Doug. Strange thing was, there was nowhere he could have gone. I figured he'd taken off another direction, and when he didn't jump out at me, well, he must have gone home."

Jack started to take a seat on the slab.

"Don't sit there," Charley warned him. Jack stood up and moved instead to lean against a tree.

"So anyway," Charley continued, "I figured he went home, and the other guys we'd been hanging out with, Steve and Vernon Scotia, they'd left earlier, so I went home, too. Next day, Doug never showed up. Must be busy with his family, right? It happens. So me and the Scotias, we hung out, played in the woods or something that day. When I got home, my dad told me to call Doug's house. Well, it was late, I'll talk to him tomorrow, I figured, right? They called me the next morning asking if I knew where Doug was. They hadn't seen him in two days. Neither had I. I told them we'd been playing in the woods behind the paper mill, and that I thought he'd gone home."

Jack slapped a mosquito on his arm and wiped it away. Charley didn't seem to be bothered by them. In fact, he didn't seem to even notice Jack was there anymore, other than the fact he was talking to him. Or maybe he was talking to himself. Jack thought that's the look on his face, like he's telling himself this story.

"So Doug went missing. And over that summer so did a few other kids. When the police learned the last place they'd been seen was in these woods, right here, in fact, they started searching for stuff. Hair, clothes, blood, anything that might lead them to the kids, or to whoever took them. One day one of the cops came up missing."

Charley took a deep breath, let it out in a long, heavy sigh.

"There were four officers here that day, all working around this area. Two of them right here." He motioned to the slab. "One of them just happened to turn around and see this hole in the ground closing up. His partner was gone. The one that was left about lost his mind, but he was able to tell people what happened. This slab was put here that day."

He stopped and turned around, looked out into the woods, squinted at the sun. He was obviously finished.

"So that's it?" Jack asked.

"That's it," Charley said, shrugging. "You can think that--" he motioned in the direction of the apartment building, "--was set up all you want, but this right here, this is documented fact, and you can look it up. It was in the paper."

"But if just the one guy saw it . . . hell, he could have been the one responsible for the disappearances in the first place and just made up the stupid story about a disappearing hole in the ground. What I really can't believe is that anyone bought it."

"It's Angel Hill, man. We know stuff happens here--."

"Yeah, and that makes it easier to get away with. Someone gives you all a story like this--Oh, I don't know, officer, I turned around and he was gone and this great big hole in the ground is closing around him--you people buy it without question just because you've all allowed this reputation to build over the years. Come on, man, it's just a town. Tell me, after this," he indicated the concrete block, "did anyone search anymore for those kids or that missing cop?"

"No," Charley said, shaking his head. "They didn't."

"There you go, problem solved. He gets away with a few kids and a cop--who was probably just about to dig up something the other guy didn't want found--and gives you a stupid story, everyone believes it, he gets away clean."

"Not exactly. I told you, that guy about lost his mind. He got moved to the Fairfield State Institute not long after that. He was there until they closed it down. Don't know where he is now, but it ain't on the Angel Hill Police force."

"Still," Jack said. "Come on, man. Think about that one for a minute, huh? Whether your story is true or not, or whether my explanation is right or not, you have to admit, mine does make a little more sense than 'a hole opened up in the ground and swallowed them.'"

Charley looked at his watch.

"Come on," he said. "You can go home now, just drop me off to get my car."

Jack followed him out of the woods and drove him back

to Fett Tech.

After an hour, Liz had put the book out of her mind. By the time Jack got home that night, she'd forgotten it completely.

"You wouldn't believe the stuff Charley tried to tell me today," he said, taking off his boots. He told her about the apartment building and the balls, and said, "And now that I think about it, that ball I had did feel kind of heavy. Probably the metal they put in it for the magnets in the floor. Can't believe they tried that on me. And then he shows me this cement block in the woods, saying some hole opened up and swallowed a bunch of people twenty years ago. That guy is desperate to get me to buy all this Haunted Angel Hill stuff."

Liz shrugged, and raised her eyebrows, a *What'reyagonnado?* gesture.

He kissed her on the head, then went into the kitchen to heat up the meatloaf.

Liz remembered the book again as she climbed into bed a couple hours later. By that time, it didn't seem as important as it had. Maybe she'd ask him tomorrow about it. She huddled to him, felt his arm moving down her side, his kisses on her cheek, her jaw, and she knew Joey was asleep, so she wrapped a leg over his and kissed him back.

When Jack had dozed off afterward, Liz felt herself drifting off just as a crash came booming through the ceiling. She leapt up, gasping. She looked at the ceiling, then down at Jack. Why hadn't he heard? Why was he still asleep?

The crash came again. She jumped again.

The piano--(We don't even have a piano, Liz thought)-- sounded its out-of-tune notes.

She pulled on a pair of shorts from the floor, a tank top over her head, and she was in the hall, on the steps, ascending slowly.

Rounding the landing, she saw nothing. On the second floor, the darkness stood fast.

Then someone appeared out of the night, small and dull in the middle of the room. This wasn't the little boy she'd seen in the shower, this person was older, maybe ten.

Liz stood back, uncertain, but not quite afraid.

"You won't scare me away," she said.

The boy stared, but Liz couldn't tell if he was staring at her, or at something past her. Finally his eyes focused on Liz and his lips cracked open in a bad impression of a grin.

"It's not scaring you he wants," he said.

"What does he want?" She didn't have to ask who was "he".

"This place isn't good to families. It tears them up like trash."

"What does he want?" Liz asked again.

"Save yourself from this," the boy said. He took a step back and was swallowed in shadow.

In the main room, the piano sounded discordant notes. While she couldn't place the spot specifically, it was definitely coming from the main room, somewhere by the front windows.

She moved like a dream, drifting from one place to another, now by the stairs, her foot hovering above the bottom one, ready to step up. Her hand clutched the banister and from behind her the piano fell silent, the notes dead on the air. She moved upward as if gliding over the steps without touching them.

She turned her head backward and up to see the body dangling from the rail over her head, its weight dead, the features blurred by rot.

The body jerked, the mouth gaped and screamed, "You can't save yourself," and Liz found herself sitting up in bed, panting, sweating, naked.

She got up, slipped into a pair of shorts and a tank top from the floor, and went upstairs. On the second floor, she turned on the kitchen and bathroom lights then went into the main room. There was no light in here, but the others gave off enough to compensate.

In the middle of the room, she looked at the walls, quiet, listening, waiting. After a minute of nothing, she said, "Come on. Show me something. I thought you were all gone, but I guess I was wrong. I don't know what you want, or how to get rid of you, so why don't you just show me something. Quit fucking around."

The night made its noises, but the house made none. Crickets chirped outside. Traffic down the street on Pacific blew by. But the house was settled out for the night, it seemed. And the ghosts, if they really were still there, had also turned in.

She wanted to go back to bed, to tell herself there was nothing there. But she couldn't do it. Not yet. She knew if she had this chance and passed on it, if she assumed everything was fine, then found out later that it wasn't, she'd regret it. So she waited. She listened. She expected. But still nothing happened. Nothing thumped. Nothing touched her. Nothing spoke to her.

She must have stood there for an hour. By the time she moved, her legs had begun to cramp and her feet were sore from standing. She hadn't spoken again, and neither had the ghosts. Maybe they really were gone. She'd dreamed tonight. She must have dreamed last night, too.

She sighed, relieved, and turned out the lights, then went back to bed. The clothes were drenched in sweat when she stripped them onto the floor. The bedroom was stifling. She draped the sheet over her legs, rolled over, and let herself sink back to oblivion.

Chapter Eleven

Every once in a while, she'd remember the book under Jack's side of the mattress and she'd think again of asking him what it was, why it was hidden. But she only remembered when Jack was gone, and by the time he came home, she'd forgotten it again.

As summer progressed in Angel Hill, the temperature was incredible. No, not the temperature. The humidity. It had been hot and humid if Texas, too, but for some reason this summer was almost too much. She didn't know if it was specific to the region, or if it was a killer summer everywhere.

Jack had called his brother a few days ago and Liz had him ask about the weather. Allen said it was hot, but nothing too bad. Standard Texas summer fare, he said.

They got the air conditioner, finally, and shoved it into the window in the bedroom. Liz said in the middle of the day, she could handle a simple fan in the living room, but that nighttime heat was killing her. They kept the door connecting their bedroom to Joey's open at night, and cooled both rooms.

Then one night in the middle of July, it rained. Blessed, beautiful, cooling rain. It came while everyone slept.

From her dreams, Liz sensed the thunder and lightning, but she was dreaming about swimming. Jack rolled over in his sleep and moved his arm to rest against Liz's back. He pulled the sheet tighter and shivered.

Joey dreamed of a midnight chase through the house, the man dogging his heels while outside everything was black and flashing with thunder cracking in his head.

The rain came in sheets, blown by the wind. Everything was wet. The lightning came every few seconds, accompanied by vicious thunder. Liz moved in her sleep, but didn't wake.

Joey found the first floor and darted down the hall into his parents' bedroom, but they weren't there. He thought he heard them in the living room, but going across the hall would show the man where he was. But he had to find his dad, or Liz. He dreamed he was wearing his fast shoes, and he zoomed across, into the living room. The sound was from the television playing a Scooby-Doo cartoon. The gang was in a haunted house. Velma said "Jinkies", and lightning flashed again. A shadow fell across Joey and he turned around to see the man outside the window, the world glaring behind him. The man raised his arms and screamed rage as his fists crashed into the glass, shattering it and sending shards flying across the room.

Joey screamed himself awake.

In the living room, glass shattered, spraying the floor with shards and rain.

The combination of Joey and the glass woke Jack and Liz.

Liz was up first, yelling, "Something broke." Jack leapt from the bed, not sure what was going on, but he knew Liz had screamed.

He rubbed his eyes and asked, "What?"

"I think a window just broke."

"Where?"

"I don't know, maybe in Joey's room. He's crying."

Jack was in Joey's room but returned just seconds later. "It's not in there. I'll find it, you get Joey."

Liz slid into a pair of shorts and Jack went into the living room.

The window behind the couch was an empty pane and slivers of glass covered the couch and floor. Rain flew into the room. His foot sank into the carpet, cold and wet. He turned on the light and said, "Shit."

Think about it, he told himself. It's a process.

First he had to stop the rain from coming in. Cover the window with something. What? The room behind the bathroom upstairs, there was a roll of plastic up there. And a staple gun in the kitchen drawer. Jack took the stairs two at a time to the top and turned on the third floor bathroom light. Actually, that was the only room on the top floor with a light. He found the plastic leaning against the wall in the storage room and he slung it over his shoulder. He flipped off the light and went back to the stairs.

But he stopped at the top, listening.

Was someone up here?

No. There was no one else in the house, and Liz was downstairs with Joey.

But that sounded like whispering.

He cocked his head toward the darkness and waited.

After a second, he snapped himself out of his daze and said, "No, it's the rain on the roof." And he ran back downstairs thinking, *Which is also getting into the house so I'd better hurry up before anything's ruined.*

He laid out the plastic on the living room floor, then ran to get the staple gun and a pair of scissors from the kitchen. Cutting the plastic was harder than he had expected; it kept sliding over itself and he couldn't get a good enough grip, let alone an even piece. He ended up with a piece that looked as if a blind man with one arm had cut it. But it was big enough to cover the window behind the couch.

Jack hung it, centering it over the open pane, and shot a staple into the center. Then he finished both sides of the top and shot staples down along the sides and bottom. He stood back and looked at the job. Not pretty, but the rain would stay outside.

He brought towels from the bathroom, all the dirty ones he could find, and as few clean as possible, and soaked up the rain from the carpet. Then he brought in the kitchen trashcan and began tossing the bigger glass shards into it. When all he had left were the smaller pieces, he got on his knees and spent over thirty minutes plucking them from the couch and the carpet.

He finally climbed back into bed to find Liz already there.

"What was wrong with Joey?" he asked.

"Bad dream," she mumbled.

Jack was in the bathroom dressing for work the next morning when he heard Liz shout down the hall, "What the hell is this mess?"

He tucked in his shirt, swept his hair to the side with his hand, and came out into the hall.

"That's the glass you heard last night."

"What are you talking about? I didn't hear any glass last night. I heard Joey crying."

"No," Jack said. "You woke me up saying something had broken. You were half-asleep still, so you probably don't remember it, but you did."

"I remember going to Joey's room because he'd had a

bad dream."

"And I came in a bit later because I'd been in here fixing this." He put his keys in his pocket and slid into his shoes. "I'm gonna call someone today to come and fix it right."

"Did you get--?"

"Yes. I got . . . well I got as much as I could. I'm pretty sure I got it all. If there's anything left, it's dust. If you want, I can vacuum it up before I go."

"No," she said. "Never mind. I just didn't sleep that well. I was dreaming something about swimming, but it was so hot last night."

He kissed Joey goodbye. Joey wiped his cheek and went back to his cartoons, slurping cereal from his spoon.

"What are you talking about? It was the coolest night it's been in weeks."

"I don't know. I don't. Forget it. I'm just still tired."

"Well, when he takes a nap, go lay down."

"I'm sure I will."

Jack kissed his wife and went to work. Liz told Joey to watch cartoons while she took a bath, and then they'd find something to do.

For the first time in forever, Joey wanted to go to the park. If Liz had known Joey's dreams, she'd have guessed it was because the terror in them had moved from the park to the house. So for Joey Upper Hill Park was no longer a threat, but his own house was.

Liz watched him from the corner of her eye while focusing most of her attention on a book. After taking the haunted house and remodeling books back to the library, she'd grabbed a few paperbacks and was making her way through them. One sat finished on top of the television, one sat untouched next to it. One rested in her hands, spread open.

Joey yelled at her from the top of the slide and she waved at him before he vanished behind the guard and began the swirl to the bottom.

She turned her eyes back to her book and found her place just as a voice from beside her said, "Cute boy."

Liz looked up and over to see the grinning idiot smiling

at her. She smiled back and said, "Yeah, we're fond of him." She
went back to her book. The grinner persisted.

"Yeah, he's gonna have a hundred girlfriends when he
gets older."

"Yep."

"How old is he?"

"Six."

"Oh, he's big for his age."

"Uh-huh."

Liz chided herself for being rude. *You've been here how
many months already? You don't know anyone here. You have no one to
talk to except your husband and stepson, and this woman--who's perfectly
nice--is trying to say hello, and you're brushing her off.*

*That's because, nice or not, she's a grinning idiot. Do I want her
hanging out with me all the time? No.*

"I kinda figured he was yours," the woman said. Her
grin, so far, had yet to decrease in width. "I wasn't too sure with
his hair, but it's almost darkened to your shade. It'll be there
before too long."

Liz had found her place and reread the same line three
times.

"I'm sorry?" she asked. "What?"

"His hair," the woman pointed to him. "It'll be there
'fore too long."

Liz smiled and nodded, then looked at Joey. And she
saw the woman was right. His hair was darker. It was no longer
the bright blonde it was when they moved here. Now he sported
dirty strawberry-blonde hair. She watched him play for a few
minutes, laughing and running, and wondered when that had
happened. She thought hair was supposed to lighten in the
summertime.

"You live just a few houses down, don't you?"

Liz looked at her for a second, trying to figure out if she
recognized this woman.

"You live in the big house? Next to the empty lot."

"Right," Liz said. "Yeah, we just moved in. You live
across the street?"

"Across the street and up the hill a little way," the
woman said. "I think you'll like it here. This is a good
neighborhood, for the most part."

"Is it? You've been here a while?"

"Of course. I grew up in Angel Hill. Used to live in the West End, but that's no good over there, too many hoodlums. I've been in North End almost twenty years now--ten of it right there in the same house--and you couldn't get me to move back even if it was rent-free."

Liz yelled for Joey and he came over.

"We're gonna go home in a minute, okay? It's about time for lunch."

He protested, whining a little.

"But I'm not ready to go home yet. Can't I have a few more minutes?"

She agreed and they stayed a little longer, then finally gathered their things--Liz's book, her keys, Joey's shoes which he'd taken off soon after they got to the park--and walked the block and a half home.

After lunch, Joey fell asleep quickly, despite his struggles to stay awake. And in his bed, with the air conditioner from his parents' room cooling him, he dreamed.

The same dream; Joey ran through the black house, trying to find something, the best hiding place, or, if he were really lucky, Jack or Liz. He'd covered the bottom floor and found only locked rooms. On the second floor, it was the same. The bathroom was locked; the door between the main room and the dining room was closed and locked as well. Through the beveled glass in the door, he saw people sitting around the dining room table, eating a fancy dinner with candles and bottles of wine, laughing and talking and not realizing he was there. He didn't know these people, had never seen them before, and he found himself stuck between trusting that they were better than the man chasing him, and the fear that they might be the same as him. He watched, but only for a second, trying to decide. Finally he decided that in this place he wouldn't trust anyone, except his dad or Liz.

He turned toward the stairs again and went to the third floor.

Halfway up, he decided this had to be safer; there was light up here. All the rooms downstairs were dark, except for the candles in the dining room.

At the top, he heard voices. And there were footsteps

behind him--the man was coming.

Joey ducked into the closest room, closed the door, and heard voices again. There were children in the next room. He went in and watched them. He'd already forgotten his decision not to trust anyone. He went to one and asked, "Is it safe here?"

The boy looked up from his game of rolling a ball against the wall, then catching it when it bounced back. He smiled at Joey as if he knew him, then said, "Not safe anywhere."

"Then we have to hide," Joey said.

"No we don't," the boy said. He went back to his ball. Joey heard another voice across the room, this time crying.

He went toward it. Then he stopped. The sobs were coming from the dead girl. Except she wasn't dead now. At least, she didn't look dead. But it was definitely the girl who chased him through the park. She looked up from her wet hands and saw him. Joey was glad to see she wasn't rotten and cracked in here. She looked just like any other girl with big wet eyes and a red face.

"Why?" she asked him. "Why did my daddy kill me?"

Just then the door behind them burst open, the man strode into the room, grabbed the girl by the neck and flung her against the wall.

Joey woke up, then covered his head with his sheet, burrowing into himself, and cried.

Liz was in the living room, cleaning. REM's *Murmur* CD played while she worked. She wiped dust from the top of the television, cleaned the screen, put Joey's DVDs back on their shelf. She was bringing in glass cleaner for the windows (minus the broken one) when the phone rang.

She hit mute on the stereo and answered. "Hello?"

"Why did my daddy kill me?" a small, terrified voice asked. Then the line went dead.

Liz hung up, her heart pounding. She picked up the phone again, turned it on. The line wasn't dead; she had a dial tone. She put it back on its base. Then she stood in the middle of the living room, motionless, positive someone was watching her. It was a good fifteen minutes before she could shake it, but she tried to go back to cleaning to get her mind off it. She couldn't deal with all that stuff again, not right now.

Charley Clark asked Jack if he'd finally finished *The Outsider's Guide to Angel Hill.*

"Not yet," Jack answered. "Fact, I haven't looked at it much lately. Just been busy, I guess."

The break room was half full, but there was space enough so everyone was spread out. That was something Jack had noticed. As close as everyone seemed out on the floor, when given the chance, they all claimed their own space.

"Did you ever tell your wife about the house?"

"No," Jack said. "The book's tucked under my side of the mattress and, God willing, she won't find it. We've only been here a couple of months and that's not nearly enough time for her to learn something like that. Especially when she's the one doing all the work upstairs. It'd probably freak her out too much. But I'll tell her eventually."

"And you haven't changed your mind about any of it?"

Jack finished a Coke and set the empty can on the table with a hollow clang.

"What's to change my mind about?"

"About the strange shit that happens here sometimes."

"That," Jack said. As he stood to throw away his trash, he shook his head. "There's an explanation for all of it. I guarantee it. Maybe not always an obvious one like you and your brother and the balls with the magnets--can't believe you thought I'd buy that--but nothing happens without a reason, you can believe that."

"Man, are you this close-minded about everything?"

"I'm not close-minded, " Jack said. "I'm rational. Weird things happen, sure. But nothing unexplainable happens. Everything can be explained, because everything is caused by something."

"Well, we'll see." Charley tossed away his own trash. "Now, I'm gonna take a piss before I go back to work. Are we playing this weekend?"

"Of course," Jack said.

Liz called Jack at work and asked if he could pick up something for supper on the way home. Joey wanted Burger King, but that was in the west section of town and the Grand Prize Diner was on the way home. Jack called in an order before leaving and by the time he got home, he'd eaten half his fries already.

He pulled up in front of the house, got out, locked up, grabbed the food, and saw a light on the third floor go out as he stepped toward the house.

He watched the upper window as he strode toward the door, swallowing another fry and wondering who was upstairs.

Inside, he took the food into the living room and was surprised to find Liz and Joey both there, sitting down, watching television, as if they'd been there for hours.

"Did you call to get the window fixed?" Liz asked.

"Yeah. They said they could come by Friday to look at it."

"Friday?"

"I guess there's a lot of broken windows in Angel Hill right now. Anyway, did you get a lamp for upstairs?" he asked.

"A what?" Liz's attention came slightly away from the television.

"A lamp. I saw you turn it off when I got home."

"What are you talking about?" He was talking about the third floor, she knew it. And now her attention was his. "A light?"

"Yeah," he said. He nodded and looked at her as if they'd been discussing the actuality of two plus two equaling four. "There was a light on up on the third floor when I got home. I got out of the car, grabbed the food, and when I turned around, the light went out."

"No," she said. "I've been down here for a while. Anyway, I'm not even done with the second floor." She got up and pulled wrapped sandwiches and bags of fries from the Grand Prize Diner sack.

"Somebody was up there," he said. "I saw the light go out." Jack grabbed his sandwich and near-empty fry bag.

"Are you sure? There's a streetlight right outside the house. Might have been a reflection from that." Liz put Joey's food on the table and pulled out his chair.

"No," Jack said. "The streetlight's still on. I'd know if it had been a reflection."

Joey lifted himself off his stomach and went to the bathroom.

"Jack, there's no lights up there. None of the rooms above this floor have built-in lights."

"I know that. I asked if you'd put a lamp up there."

"No," she said. "I didn't."

"Well someone did and I don't think Joey's gonna be the one to do it, do you?"

"I'm telling you, I haven't been up there all day. You can ask Joey if you don't believe me."

"I never said I didn't believe you, I'm just--"

"Obviously you don't," she said, "if you're standing here arguing with me over whether I was upstairs when I've just told you how many times I haven't been."

Jack set his food on the table, closed his eyes, and took a breath.

"I'm not saying you're lying," he said. "I'm just saying when I got out of the car, I saw a light on up there and then it went out. That's all."

"Well I don't know where it came from," Liz said, "'cause it wasn't me."

"Fine. Then there's some other explanation for it. We'll figure it out later."

He sat on the couch, unwrapped his sandwich and set it on the armrest. Joey came back from the bathroom, climbed into his chair at the kitchen table and Liz sat across from him. She wanted to tell Jack she could explain it easily. There were ghosts in the house, mainly on the third floor. But she could also easily predict his response. He'd dismiss that quicker than if she'd said a million fireflies had invaded the third floor.

After dinner, Joey took his bath while Liz folded laundry. Jack went upstairs. Liz wanted to tell him not to bother, but she knew he wouldn't listen. Jack unable to explain something was Jack on a mission.

He stopped on the second floor and admired everything Liz had done to it. As far as he could tell, this floor was finished. He knew she had more decorating to do, a number of other little things to get to liven up the space, but overall, he was ready to move their things up here.

Then he went upstairs. He turned on the bathroom light, then propped open the door and headed into the front two rooms where he'd seen the light. The bathroom gave light to one room, but the other was shielded from it in the corner of the house. He walked into the corner room, searching the floor for a flashlight, a desk lamp, a candle, anything. But Liz was right; the room was empty.

Maybe it was *the streetlight,* he thought. *It could have been the streetlight shining on the window and when I moved toward the house, the angle from which I was viewing it changed and I didn't catch the light anymore. I guess that might be it.*

Going back toward the center room, he noticed a large crack running down the door to the corner room. He stopped and inspected it, trying to move it into the light, but the door swung the other way and no matter which way he looked or moved, or how he tried to position the door, he couldn't see as clearly as he wanted. But he could see enough to know the wood was split.

"Man, I don't remember that," he mumbled.

He closed the door and headed back downstairs, still not completely convinced it was the streetlight he'd caught reflecting off the glass.

Chapter Twelve

The next day, Joey's naptime dream found him on the third floor again. And again he was in the corner room with the other children. The house rumbled around him as the man searched its corners and nooks while Joey hid upstairs, knowing he'd be found in seconds, but unable to make himself leave the room. He looked around at the other children and realized he knew them. Not from his old school in Houston, nor from the park, he didn't know how he knew them, but he did. And it wasn't just in the way you know strange people in dreams, he knew he'd seen them before. But where? The girl, he knew where he'd seen her--she was the one from his dreams about the park--but the others. He'd seen them in his dreams before, but he knew them from somewhere else, too.

There were two doors in the corner room and when the man barged through one, kicking it open and splitting it in two pieces, Joey finally found his legs again and darted out the other one. The girl grabbed his shoulder and Joey tried to jerk away from her, but her grip was too strong. He looked back and saw her thrusting something at him.

"Take it, Adam," she said.

He snatched it from her hands and took off, through the center room, and down the stairs. He glanced down and found she'd given him a rag doll.

Then the man's fingers closed around Joey's shirt and he was yanked off his feet. He dropped the doll and looked up to see the man sneering down at him. His eyes were yellow and bulging. Then Joey woke up.

He lay there, trying not to cry from the nightmare, and wondering why he still had to take naps every day.

The first thing Jack did when he came home that night was head upstairs. He came in the front door and walked quietly up. It wasn't that he didn't believe Liz, but he'd spent the day trying to convince himself he'd probably seen the streetlight and he couldn't do it. Because he didn't believe it really was the streetlight, but that didn't give him any other explanations for the light he'd seen. He didn't know what he thought he might find by sneaking upstairs. Liz wouldn't leave anything up there that might prove him right. Still, he had to check one last time.

He hadn't known what to expect, but he sure as hell didn't expect to find the door to the corner room lying broken on the floor. The half that was still attached hung crooked by one hinge. The other half lay on the floor, halfway across the room.

He stood there staring at it, numb from anger.

"Who the fuck did this?" he whispered. He looked around the room. Granted, they didn't use this floor, and they didn't know if they ever would, so a broken door was no big loss, really. But it was the principle. "You just don't go around breaking doors," he said to the house. "What the fuck was she thinking?" Why would she even do something like that? And how? Liz was no wuss, but you don't just break a door in half.

It was cracked last night, he reminded himself. Had Liz done that? Had she been trying to break the door for some reason? No, he couldn't convince himself there was any reason in the world to want that. But there was evidence, lying in the middle of the room.

No, he argued back, that wasn't evidence of any kind of motive, that only showed it had been done. But why? He had no choice but to confront her.

He headed back downstairs, lost his traction when he slipped on something lying on the stairs, and hit his tailbone on the edge of a step.

"Fuck!" he grunted.

He got up, rubbed his tailbone, and looked around to find what he'd slipped on.

It was a doll. He didn't remember Joey having any dolls like this. This was a girl's doll.

He grabbed it and headed downstairs, rubbing his tailbone until he rounded the bottom landing.

Liz was in the kitchen rolling pieces of chicken into croissants. Jack tossed the doll onto the counter.

"You left this upstairs."

Liz glanced at it, then went back to the food. "That's not mine."

"I know that. I assume it's Joey's."

"I don't think so. I've never seen it before."

"Neither have I, but I don't recall having any other kids."

Liz shrugged. Then she asked, "Did you say I left it upstairs?"

Jack took a Coke from the refrigerator. "Uh-huh."

"Where upstairs?"

"Third floor stairs."

Liz put the chicken aside and looked at the doll. She didn't pick it up; she didn't want to touch it. "I've never seen it before."

"Then Joey left it up there."

"Ask him."

Jack got a cookie, bit off half, and said, "I'm going to."

It's not his, Liz thought. *He won't know where it came from any more than I do. I wish I could tell you what's going on, Jack. I'm not entirely sure myself anyway.*

"But the doll's not what's bothering me the most," he said.

Liz went back to her croissants, asking, "What is?"

"The door that's been broken in two up there."

Liz stopped again and looked at him. "What?"

He nodded. "You can act surprised all you want, but unless there was someone here today you didn't tell me about, the only two people here all day were you and Joe, and I know he didn't do that."

Liz was lost now. What the hell was he talking about? Strange dolls? Broken doors?

She folded the last piece of chicken into the last croissant, then turned to her husband and said, as calmly as she could, "Jack I haven't been upstairs all day--." He started to break in, but she held up her hand and he shut his mouth. "I haven't been upstairs all day. If fact I spent most of the day just sitting on the couch. Now, whatever's broken upstairs, or whatever you've found, or whatever whatever, it didn't come from me, and it didn't come from Joey." She could tell he wanted to say something, but she pressed on. "You're gone most of the time and I can tell you, being here, there's a ton of weird shit that goes on here, but until now I haven't bothered even trying to tell you about it because I know how you are. But I'm telling you now, whatever is up there, it isn't from either Joey or me. Hell, maybe the storm broke it. It broke the window, didn't it? Which, by the way, is still a nice sheet of plastic now."

"They'll be here Friday. The storm didn't break the door," Jack said. His voice came out calm, but his tone said, You're a moron. "I was up there last night. The door wasn't broken, but it was cracked. Now it's broken."

Joey came in then and asked, "Are we gonna eat sometime? I'm starving. It feels like I haven't eaten in thirty years."

"It'll be done in a little bit," Liz said. She and Jack exchanged a look they both knew meant, This is over for now, but we'll pick it up here later.

For the second night, they ate mostly in silence, broken by Joey's attempts to get someone talking. After all, he was six and could rarely stand a silent room.

"Dad, we went to the park yesterday and, um, I climbed to the top of the tornado slide and I looked over the top. I'm tall enough now to see over the top. And I saw Liz on the ground and I waved to her, but she didn't see me."

"That must have been when that annoying woman was bugging me," she said.

"What woman?" Jack asked.

Liz had just begun her recount of the smiling woman at the park when the phone rang. Liz cut off her words and Jack leaned back in his chair, tipped the phone from its cradle with his fingertips, caught it, and answered. "Hello?"

Liz could hear the coarse voice coming through, even across the table. Jack squinted against the noise, held the phone away from his head, then hung it up and set it aside on the table.

She almost asked who it was, but Liz remembered the screaming girl in the phone yesterday asking, "Why did my daddy kill me?"

"We've got to get caller ID or something," Jack said. "Then again, I'm sure whoever that is, they're calling anonymous anyway."

Something like that, Liz thought.

Jack went back to eating as if nothing had happened.

You're so damned oblivious, Liz thought. She decided then to tell Jack everything she'd seen and heard in the house. He may not believe her, probably wouldn't, in fact. But she would tell him anyway. And then, with it in mind, at least, maybe he'd start to realize, too, all the spooky shit going on here.

"Maybe we should get our number changed," he was saying, "but we just moved here, it's too soon for juvenile crap like this already. Maybe if we ignore it, it'll all go away."

I doubt this is gonna go away on its own, she thought.

He mumbled something else about stupid kids with too much time on their hands, but Liz was already ignoring him, trying to decide how best to go about telling him about the house.

Joey said he was full, could he have a cookie?

"No," Liz said. "Finish your supper, and, if you eat all of it, you can have ice cream later."

"But I'm full."

"Then you don't need any cookies," Jack said.

Joey slumped into his chair, but reluctantly shoved a piece of chicken into his mouth.

Tonight, Liz decided, she'd tell him tonight after Joey went to bed.

When Liz went to tuck in Joey, Jack went upstairs to get the broken chunk of door. You can't argue with solid proof, and like it or not, Jack had proof someone had broken it. Let's see her say no one was up here now, he thought.

He banged the end on the doorframe as he carried it out of the room and the sudden noise in the stillness made him jump.

A large stained-glass window hung over the landing and from the top of the flight, Jack could see the second floor reflected in it. But for a second, he thought he saw a body. Then he remembered Charley's story about the guy hanging himself. He stopped at the top and looked into the window again, but the image, the hallucination, whatever it had been was gone.

Then he leaned the door against the top rail and went back into the corner room.

He stood in the middle and listened, hearing nothing, but there was something there, just below the surface of what he could pick up. He could almost feel it. He looked around the room, not seeing much in the dark, but the streetlight outside gave enough light to pick out the outline of the walls. He imagined the bodies of the man's four children lined up against the wall like Charley said. For a second, he thought he saw them sitting there, but he blinked and they were gone.

Man, four kids. That must have been a hell of a load to take care of. No wonder the guy snapped.

He shook his head. *What am I thinking? That's no reason to kill them. Guy was a nut.*

"There's nothing here now," he said to himself. He took a last look around, then turned and left. He grabbed the chunk of door and carried to downstairs, thinking, *There's a draft on those stairs. I'll have to get that taken care of, too. This house may turn out to be more trouble than it's worth in the end.*

He dragged the door into the living room where Liz sat with the television gray and silent, and the light shone bright on her.

"Now, you're gonna tell me no one in the world did this, then?"

"Jack, put the door down," she said. "I'll tell you who did it. At least I'll tell you as well as I can."

"That's right," he said. The door-half went on the floor again and Jack sat on the couch across from her.

"It wasn't me. And you're right, Joey didn't do it either. There's someone else in the house. Actually, I think there's a few of them, but there's one in particular I worry about."

Jack held up a hand. "Now you're getting entirely off the subject, because there's no one in this house except the three of us. We've been over this. The door is broken and you did it."

Liz flared at his accusation.

She rolled her eyes, shook her head, and got up. She was halfway to the doorway when Jack said, "Okay, for the sake of argument, let's say you're right. Who do you think did this?" He held out his hand toward the plank against the wall, as if Liz needed help figuring out what he meant.

She stopped and turned around, staring at him, daring him to interrupt her again. He kept his silence, but raised his eyebrows, asking *Well?*

"Hang on," she said, and disappeared into the kitchen.

She came back with a cup of hot tea, blew into it, and took a small sip.

She set the cup on the table next to the chair, but she didn't sit. She glanced at Jack who was still standing in the middle of the room, waiting.

"I don't know who broke the door," she said. "But I know there are other people here. I don't know if something bad happened here or what, but there's at least two up there and I thought they were gone, but they're not.

"You've probably heard them, too, but the way you are, you convince yourself it's something else."

He shrugged.

"Like at night, when you're lying in bed and you wake up and you can hear them upstairs, or sometimes out here in the hall. They seem to like going up and down the stairs, that's for sure."

"And when was the first time you noticed these . . . other people?"

"Don't patronize me. Unlike talking to you, Jack, you can say 'ghosts' and I won't think you're stupid."

"I don't think you're stupid. You know better than that. But there's--"

"There's no such thing, right?"

He didn't reply.

Liz took another sip from her tea. It had cooled a little, but she still had to blow on it first.

"The first time I noticed them, now that I think about it, was our first day here. You'd gone to the store and Joey was asleep in here. I laid down in the bedroom and fell asleep, too. A little bit later, I woke up when I felt someone climb onto the bed with me. I assumed it was you or Joey, so I went back to sleep. But when I woke up, you were just coming home with the groceries, and Joey was still in here."

"And you didn't think that maybe he'd just come back here again after going in there?"

"No, I did think that. That's what I assumed for a long time. But in retrospect, I don't believe for a second now that's what it was. It was someone else."

Jack got a Coke from the kitchen and sat on the arm of the couch, holding the can in his lap. "And that's it?" he asked. "That's your big proof there's . . . ghosts . . . in the house?

Because you felt someone climb onto the bed while you were, as you said, asleep? Yeah, they call those dreams in the real world."

"Fuck off," she shot back. "I've seen them. I've seen the man walk past me. I've seen them in the bathroom, and upstairs in the middle room, two different ones. I've heard their voices. I've felt them. Whether you buy it or not, that's who broke your precious fucking door, and, unfortunately, not believing in them isn't going to be enough to get rid of them."

He stared at her, took a drink, and asked, "So you're the expert. How do you get rid of them?"

"I don't know," she said. "I had the house blessed a couple weeks ago, and I thought they were gone. I didn't hear them or anything for a long time. But the other day, there was a phone call--"

"Oh no, not a phone call. Well that cements it for me. I'm convinced."

"Forget it," she said. Liz went into the kitchen, away from Jack.

He sat for a second, then got up and followed her.

"I'm sorry, okay? I know, I said I wouldn't interrupt. I'm not trying to make light of what you're saying, but you know I can't buy any of this without actual proof."

"I'm not saying you should buy anything. I'm just telling you what I've seen and heard."

"All right. Go on. I'm sorry. Please."

She set her cup on the counter and turned to him, but she kept her eyes down.

"The other day, the phone rang and I answered and it was this little girl's voice. She was yelling something like, 'Why did my daddy kill me?' Now, whether it was for real or just some kids playing around, I don't know, but it freaked me out and it fits, I guess, with the house. I mean if there's ghosts here, that means someone died here, right?"

Jack didn't answer. He was thinking about the story Charley Clark told him about the house. And then he understood.

"I get it," he said, smiling. "You read the book, didn't you?"

"What?"

"Yeah, you read the book and now, because I didn't tell

you about it in the first place, you're coming up with this crap about ghosts. I know, I learned my lesson. I'm sorry. I should have told you in the first place."

"What the hell are you talking about?"

Jack was looking at her, trying to gauge her reaction. Maybe she hadn't found the book.

"*The Outsider's Guide to Angel Hill*," he said. "The chapter in there about the house?"

She shook her head. Then she remembered the book.

"Wait," she said, "I do remember a book. It's under your side of the mattress. What is that? Angel Hill porn, and that's why you hid it?"

"No," he said. "I didn't hide it. I just hadn't gotten around to showing it to you yet."

Liz dumped the rest of her tea into the sink, rinsed it, and set it on top of the dirty pile of dishes.

"And why not?"

"Because of the house," he said. He was beginning to regret mentioning the book. It didn't seem Liz had read that chapter, after all.

"What about the house?" she asked.

He turned back to the living room and leaned back on the couch. Liz followed and stood in front of him, staring at him, almost daring him to answer.

"The house," he said. "The book is all about weird crap that's happened in Angel Hill since the town was founded. There's a chapter in there about our house. Apparently some guy a few years back killed his kids and himself up on the third floor."

Liz's mouth dropped.

"Oh, my God," she said. "You mean you knew about that and we moved here anyway?"

"No," he said, leaning toward her. "I swear, I didn't know a thing about it. I didn't find out until we moved here. Then Charley mentioned this book to me and, honestly, I didn't have any intention of getting it. I don't even know why I did. But I didn't find out about the house until weeks after we'd been living here."

"And you didn't think this information was the least bit important to the person who's stuck here all day by herself?"

"No," he said. "It's not that. But I knew it would freak

you out. I mean, come on, Liz, people die all the time. You think every house that anyone has ever died in is haunted? That'd be almost every house anywhere. There was no point in getting you all freaked out--like you're getting now, I'd like to add--over something that happened years ago."

Liz sat in the chair across from him, listening, but not looking at him.

"You should read about some of the crap that's gone on in this town. It's so crazy, I can't even accept most of it. I keep arguing the logic behind it all with Charley at work, but he insists it's all true. But true or not that someone killed himself in our house, that doesn't make it haunted."

"You're right," she said. "That doesn't make it haunted. But the footsteps, and the voices, and all the other shit I've heard around this place, that does make it haunted."

"Houses make noise," he said.

"Fuck you, all right? I think I know the difference between a house settling and a voice calling my name." She stopped, closed her eyes, and took a breath. After a second, she continued. "You don't have to believe me--I never thought you would anyway. I only told you now because you think I broke your stupid door and I know I didn't. You need an explanation for it, and that's the one I'm giving you because that's the only one I've got."

"Fine," he said, "you didn't break the door. Okay. But it didn't break by itself, and ghosts didn't break it either."

Liz turned on the television and flipped through the channels. Jack watched her for a few seconds before asking, "So what, we're done talking?"

"I guess," she said. "I've given you my side. Believe it or don't, I'm tired of arguing with you."

"Hey, I don't want to argue either. I just want to find out how the door got broken, that's all."

"And I told you." She went through the channels again. She wasn't really looking for anything to watch, but she needed the distraction.

"And that's one possibility. And when we've exhausted all other possibilities, and then come up with a few new ones, we'll maybe go back to that one. But you know I can't take that one out of the blue like that."

She shut off the television, stood up, and tossed the remote on the chair.

"If you paid attention around here once in a while, you'd realize it's not out of the blue."

She left the room and Jack heard the bathroom door close, then water running.

Guess that's it, then.

He grabbed the chunk of broken door and carried it back upstairs. No point leaving it laying around to clutter up downstairs. He'd do something with it this weekend.

Upstairs, he leaned it against the wall, placing it horizontal to keep it from falling. He stood up, stretched his back, and sighed.

"Ghosts, just because some guy kills himself years ago," he mumbled. "Whatever, man."

And before the sound of his voice had faded, he saw a man standing across from him, staring back at him. His arms twitched and his heartbeat jumped once, then he realized it was his reflection in the window across the room.

Thanks a lot, Liz, he thought.

He walked to the window and stared at himself. He was going over in his mind any explanation he could conceive for the broken door. He knew Joey couldn't have done it. And that only left Liz. But she insisted. And he wanted to believe her. But her explanation was crap.

His mind was elsewhere, his eyes were focused on the Jack Kitch staring back at him, but when the shadow passed behind him, he was right back in the third floor room, twirling, looking for whoever was up here with him.

The room appeared empty. And he wanted to think it really was empty.

But empty rooms don't cast shadows by themselves. Certainly not moving shadows. Who was up here?

"Liz?"

No boards creaked, nor windows rattled.

He went to the door leading to the center room, looked out and around, down the stairs. There was no one. The shadow had been in the room, so she couldn't be out here anyway. He turned back in, went into the corner room, then looked into the third room at the side of the house. When he turned back into the corner room, he stopped, staring at the chunk of broken door, still leaning against the wall, but standing vertical.

Jack took a deep breath, listened to the room again, and knew someone was here.

It was Joey. He heard him giggling.

He checked the rooms again, in the closets, then went into the bathroom. He turned on the light, looked behind the tub, and opened the door to the storage room. Cool, stale air wafted out and Jack ducked his head in, looked around, listening, but didn't see Joey.

He could still hear him giggling. He'd heard him giggling the entire time he'd been looking, but he had looked everywhere. If Joey was up here, he'd picked one hell of a good hiding place.

Screw it, he thought. If Joey's up here, he can stay up here. I'm going downstairs. We'll see how funny it is when he's all by himself up here.

He made a show of turning off the bathroom light, clicking it off loudly, and then going down the stairs with heavy feet.

At the second floor, he went down a few steps, quieting his footsteps to make them sound as if he were still going down. Then he backed up onto the second floor and moved away from the stairs, into the shadows, waiting for Joey to cry or come down.

His wait seemed to drag on for a while, but Joey never came down, nor did Jack hear any whining. After a few minutes, Jack edged out toward the steps, head cocked and listening.

He heard a creak on the stairs and when he moved to step back into the shadows, there was another giggle. This one seemed higher, more childlike than Joey, louder, and right behind him.

He turned around, expecting Joey, but was confronted with the empty room, shadows and stillness covering everything.

And now Liz's words came back. *The house is haunted. There are ghosts upstairs.*

No, he thought. That's not the truth.

"Joe? Come on out, it's past bedtime."

He waited again, keeping an eye on the stairs, one on the room in front of him, but nothing moved in either direction. He heard Liz downstairs open the bathroom door, click off the light, and walk down the hall. There's nothing up here, he thought. But another giggle, this time directly in front of him, said otherwise.

The uneasy part of him said there was someone in front of him, a child. But the rational part of him said if there was, he'd see it. And since he didn't see anything, there was nothing there. And since Jack spent most of his time listening to the rational part, he told himself he was right and there was nothing there. He didn't know where that noise that sounded like giggling was coming from, but it was not ghosts.

As he went downstairs, the uneasy part of him said it could feel something breathing down his neck, but the rational side said shut up, I'm going to bed, I'm just really tired, that's all.

Jack slid into bed, turned over, and closed his eyes. A few seconds later, he found himself wishing Liz had come to bed instead of staying up to watch television. At least then he could let himself feel that weight that seemed to rest on the other side of the bed, the weight that he would know was Liz. But since there was no one there, he told himself he didn't feel anything across from him. No, he didn't feel that shift. No, he didn't feel that tug of the sheet. And no, he didn't feel anything pass in front of the fan.

Liz flipped through the channels, knowing nothing was on, but not wanting to go to bed just yet. Wait until Jack falls asleep, then go, but not right now, not while he's still probably awake in there being so smug and superior because he knows everything and if it's not something he can hold in his hands or put in his mouth, then it must not be real. She'd rather spend the next two hours going through every channel conceived than deal with him again right now.

She soon realized she wasn't thinking about Jack, but Alex.

This isn't Alex she told herself. That was totally different. He was an asshole.

Jack's not winning any points right now, either.

Yes, but this is different. Jack's not Alex. This is just an argument. It'll blow over.

What if it doesn't? Here you are how many hundreds of miles from everything you've known and what if it happens again? Can you start over again, and so far from home?

This is home. What happened with Alex isn't going to happen again. I'll see to that, no matter what.

Even if that means telling him you were wrong about the ghosts?

It won't come to that. They're real and if he doesn't want to deal with it, fine. I'll have to handle him *and* the ghosts.

Can you?

I have to.

A few hours, and a couple more cups of tea later, Liz went to bed.

The night hung sticky over them and the air conditioner wasn't doing any good. Through a light sleep, Liz felt the sheet stick to her like another skin and she kept turning, hoping the next position would be the one to take her further under. Hours must have passed by the time she felt a small hand nudge her arm.

"Mama, can I get in bed with you?"

She vaguely registered that Joey had called her Mama for the first time. She wanted to jump and clap and squeal with joy, but she was so tired and hot, she'd do it in the morning, she decided.

"Come on," she mumbled, and scooted closer to Jack to make room.

She felt him climb onto the bed and settle in. She rested her hand on his arm, kissed the back of his head, and sighed, hoping to fall finally into a deeper sleep.

"Mama?" he asked.

Her heart warmed again, but still she was too tired to celebrate.

"Yeah, babe?"

"Why did my daddy kill me?"

Liz's eyes shot open and she sat up, staring down at a dead boy lying next to her.

Liz screamed and brushed her hand through the boy, like knocking a bug off the edge of the counter, but he vanished as Liz's hand passed through him.

Jack sat up, clicked on the lamp next to the bed and

asked, "What? What's wrong?"

Liz looked at the bare spot on the mattress, then looked at Jack, and knew he wouldn't believe her.

"What is it?"

"Nothing," she said. "I was just having a dream. I think I almost fell off the edge of the bed."

"Be careful," he said. "Why don't you move over here?"

"I will," she said, "in a minute." She went to the bathroom and the door clicked behind her. Jack shut off the lamp and went back to sleep.

She sat sideways on the toilet with the lid closed, her face in her hands, trying to keep from crying.

There's nothing to cry about, she told herself. It's nothing that can hurt you. The most it can do is make noises and move stuff. But it can't hurt you. This is your house now.

Is it? She wondered.

She rubbed her eyes, then went to the sink to splash cold water on her face. She avoided the mirror by keeping her face down. She remembered the demon-Liz that had sneered back at her a few weeks ago. She didn't want to go through that again, not right now.

I just want some sleep, and when I get up in the morning, then I'll figure something else out. I have to; I can't keep doing this night after night. Not on my own.

Maybe if Jack had some kind of proof, he'd wake up and see things as they are, too. Then you'd have someone on your side.

That's not going to happen. I can't control how and when things happen. And unless the girl or the man swung him around by the nuts, I don't see him believing.

You're probably right, she thought.

Of course. His rational mind was one of the things you liked about him in the beginning.

I know. God, I can't believe that thing touched me. Worse, I kissed it. Christ, if this whole thing weren't bad enough, I'm going to have nightmares about it for a month now.

Shit, she thought. She just remembered the doll Jack had brought downstairs. What did he do with it? Was it still sitting on the kitchen counter?

She dried her face and turned away from the mirror

without looking into it, then left the bathroom. She found the doll where Jack left it, staring up with its painted face. She grabbed it, keeping her mind on what to have for dinner tomorrow night, or who was supposed to be on Oprah tomorrow afternoon, anything that wasn't this doll.

She carried it to the second floor and wouldn't let herself go any further. Liz flung the doll up the stairs to let the house have it back and if she came up to check tomorrow and it was gone, well, she'd deal with that nervous breakdown when it came.

Back in bed, Jack was already fast asleep. Liz slid in next to him, keeping a little closer to him. She tried to find a middle ground where, on the one hand, she wouldn't be close enough to the edge of the bed that the boy could touch her again, and on the other hand, there wouldn't be enough room for it to lay next to her again.

Joey felt his way along the staircase in the dark.

He'd run up here to get away from the man, again. He'd expected to find the children up here, but this time the third floor was empty. And even though all the lights in the house on the first two floors were burning and glaring, the third floor was black.

He heard something creeping on the stairs above him. He moved down a step. Then he heard something coming up toward him from below. He froze, his six-year-old heart ready to burst, and a short, quiet whimper escaped him.

Suddenly the man roared above him, "Come here, boy!" At the same time, the little dead girl appeared glowing from the darkness below him. She held her hand out to him, clutching a doll. "Take it Adam," she said. "It will protect you."

Joey moved to avoid touching either of them, stumbled on the stairs, and fell.

He woke up crying on the floor in his room.

Liz came in to see what was wrong.

Chapter Thirteen

Liz looked at the shirt Joey wore and when it didn't come down as far as it should, she thought, I guess it's time for some new clothes.

She tied his shoes, despite his protest that, "I know how to tie them. Cross over, pull through."

"I know you do," she said. "But I like doing things for you." He winced at the tightness of the shoes and she asked, "Are your feet getting too big for them?"

"I don't know."

She kissed his head and reminded him not to leave the backyard, and not to look at the old woman across the alley. He said okay and ran out the back door. Before the clang of the closing screen door faded, Liz heard the knocking on the front door and thought, We've got to either get a doorbell or a sign that says to come to the back. But her frustration faded when she saw the two Angel Glass-uniformed men standing outside.

"Is this the Kitch residence?" asked the first.

She told him it was and invited them in, telling them how happy she was to see them.

"I can imagine," said the other one.

She led them downstairs, telling them where the broken window was. They followed, making small talk about the heat and "nice house", but she could tell by their voices that they weren't thrilled with being here.

"So, how long have you lived here?" asked the first man.

"Only a couple of months," Liz answered. "We moved up from Houston."

"'We'?"

The second man went to the plastic-covered pane and measured it.

"Yeah," Liz said. "Me, my husband, and our son Joe."

"Only three of you?"

"Lots of space here for only three people," the second man commented.

"That it is," Liz agreed.

While Liz entertained the glass repairmen, Jack stood against the wall of the break room during the monthly Fett Technologies communications meeting.

"As you've all noticed, no doubt," Bill Sten said, "things have slowed down a bit here . . ."

Like hell, Jack thought. Maybe they've slowed down in the other departments, but we've got plenty of work to go around if you want to send some people our way.

" . . . And that is mostly due to one of our biggest customers having gone bankrupt. In all, Fett Tech is out just under a million dollars with the loss of this one customer."

The talk around the plant lately had been about a cut in hours, which was supposed to last at least six months. The upside was that the hour cut was instead of a layoff. For that Jack was glad. He may have a fairly important position, but he was still the new guy.

"On the bright side," Bill Sten continued, "we had a tour come through here just a few days ago. A customer we've been dealing with for a good three or four years brought in a busload of people to show them where he gets his product. One of the gentlemen on this tour commented to me about how impressed he was with what he saw."

Just get to the point, Jack wanted to say.

"He was impressed, not only with the way things are run here, but he said it was mostly with the people we've got working here at Fett Technologies. He was impressed with their level of motivation and with the general attitude throughout the plant."

Blah, blah, blah, Jack thought. I've got a load of start/stop modules that need to be on the way to Aurora in two hours, so let's get to the damned point.

It was all Jack could do to keep from sighing out loud. Finally, Bill Sten made his point.

"What this means for all of us is that, within the next month to two months, Fett Tech should be able to regain some of that loss. However, until that time, the only way we can be able to keep our level of quality is by keeping the staff we've got. And the only way to do that is we're going to have to cut back our work week from forty to thirty-six hours."

The groan of four lost hours of pay flowed through the whole crowd.

"That means, instead of four nines and a four, we'll be working just the four nines for the next several weeks."

There goes that acoustic I've been wanting, Jack thought. At least for a while. I wonder if that's going to affect the people on salary. I do still have a house payment, after all.

As the meeting broke up and everyone ambled back to his or her areas, Jack caught up to Charley and asked, "We playing this weekend?"

"I don't know now," Charley said. "Looks like I might be out looking for a part-time job. I don't make the big bucks like you."

"Please, you've been here a lot longer than I have. I'm sure if you break it down hourly, you make a lot more than I do."

"Well, nevertheless, I'm not going get all the bills covered on thirty-six hours."

"And we're not going to get all the work-orders covered that way, either," Jack said. "I'm going to have to talk with him to see about that. 'Cause we get enough crap from Aurora on forty hours. I don't need more pissing and moaning from them because Fett Tech in general lost a customer; that's not my fault."

"Well, you see what you can do. I'm gonna get those start/stops finished up."

"You got an hour and a half."

As they packed up their tools and the first repairman, whose name was Art, wrote out the bill, Liz noticed the second man, whose name was Richard, seemed suddenly anxious. He shoved the last of his tools into his toolbox and had his keys out and ready before standing up.

"You ready?" he asked Art.

"Yeah, in a minute." Art didn't seem the least ill at ease.

Richard shivered and brushed at the back of his neck. Liz watched and felt sorry for him. She knew what was touching him, but how did you talk about something like that, and with people you didn't know, in your own house?

"With tax, that comes to--"

"I'm gonna wait outside," Richard said. He headed for the hallway and Art said, "Yeah, I'll be there in a second."

He handed Liz the bill. She got her purse from the hall

table and dug out the checkbook. She heard Richard close the front door.

"He doesn't seem too eager to leave, does he?" She filled out the check.

"He's okay," Art said. "I guess it's really my fault. On the way over here, I was telling him stuff."

"About my house?" Liz asked.

"Oh, man, I'm sorry," Art said, realizing what he'd said. "No, it's just that, I mean, well, you know, you're new in town and, I really didn't mean anything, I was--."

"That's okay," Liz said. "I heard. Well, I heard something anyway."

Art appeared relaxed, but she could tell he was going to watch everything else he said the rest of the time he was there.

"So, you know what happened here?" she asked. "I mean, the whole story?"

"Uh, not really. Just what was in the papers, but that was a long time ago. And I'm sure the papers didn't know the whole story anyway. I mean, something like that doesn't just happen without a whole bunch of stuff leading up to it, you know?"

She signed the check, tore it out, and handed it over.

Art took it and filled out the receipt.

"So what did the papers say?" she asked.

"Just, you know, guy and his kids. Look, I'm sorry for bringing it up. I shouldn't even be thinking about it, and certainly not talking about it with the person who has to live here. Not that there's anything at all wrong with living here."

"Oh, there is," Liz said. "Believe me, there's nothing you could say about what's happened here that would make me feel any worse about being here."

He handed her the receipt which she stuffed into the checkbook, then the checkbook into her purse.

"Well," he said, "okay. I just read that, um, the guy who used to live here and his kids, four or five of them, I'm not sure, were found dead one day upstairs."

Liz glanced toward the back door, making sure Joey wasn't around to hear.

"And he killed them?"

"I don't know. That's what they said, but I wasn't here and like I said, there's probably a lot of stuff that led up to it, so, you know, who kno--."

The phone cut him off. Liz wanted to finish the conversation, but the ring bore into her, and she finally grabbed the phone to shut it up.

"Hello?" She didn't expect a response, just another ghost call, but Jack said, "What'cha doing?"

Art took his cue, mouthed, "I'm gotta get going," and backed out. She hadn't wanted him to go yet, but Jack's tone said he had something to talk about.

"Nothing," she answered. "Just paying the window guy. It's fixed."

"Good," he said. "It's a good thing they got to it when they did."

"How come?"

He told her about the hour cut and that he didn't know if that was going to affect his paycheck or not. Joey came in and got a glass of water.

"I hope not," Liz said. "Just realized today Joey's about to grow out of his clothes. He's gonna need a whole new wardrobe for school, unless you want him to be the kid showing off his socks 'cause his pants are too short."

Joey put the glass back and went outside again.

Since when can he reach the faucet by himself without leaning over the sink to do it? Liz wondered.

"I'm going to talk to Bill Sten later, I hope, and find out. Hell, if it's a small pay cut versus a lay-off, I'll take the pay cut for a bit. A smaller paycheck's better than no paycheck."

"We could always go back to Houston."

"No, thanks," he said. "We've already got too much time and money in that house to leave now."

Too bad, Liz thought.

"Well, tell me what you find out when you get home."

"I will."

They hung up and Liz stood back to look at the new window. Then she looked around for Art. She'd seen him leave, but she wasn't finished talking to him.

"Damn," she said. But at least she had some outside confirmation. Someone had killed himself, and his children. Art said he didn't want to say it was a murder/suicide, but Art didn't have to; the girl had told her enough.

(Why did my daddy kill me?)

She stood for a minute, dazed and lost in these thoughts, then she suddenly snapped out of it, shook it all away, and went outside to find Joey.

She'd expected to find him running and jumping, kicking his ball around the yard, or just being Joey. Instead, she saw him sitting toward the back of the yard, by the alley, with his back against the wall that separated their yard from the parking lot of a condemned church on the next block. He was looking up at the house.

"What'cha doing, Joe?"

"Nothing." He brushed away a fly that landed on his cheek, and went back to doing nothing.

"We got a new window," she said. "No more plastic-rattle while you're watching cartoons."

"I know."

She sat next to him.

"You about ready for lunch?"

This was where he usually asked, "Will it be naptime after I eat?" Instead, he kept staring at the house and said, "I'm not hungry."

She looked at him, then at the house, trying to figure out what he was looking at. She expected to see the man looking out from the third floor window, or maybe the little girl. But she was pleased to find only dark glass staring back.

Then she saw it.

It wasn't anything staring at them from the windows, but the house itself. The sky overhead was bright with summer sun and everything around them shone with it, but the house was dark, as if the sun were afraid to illuminate it.

It wasn't as if she saw a face in the house, nothing so cliche. It was just a house, but looking at it, Liz could see it challenging them.

She looked around the yard, thinking, *We own this. This is ours. We can do with it as we please.* She looked back at the house, and thought, *And that includes the house. It belongs to us, not the other way around.*

"What's the matter, Joe? You looking at something?"

"Huh-uh."

She sat next to him and put her arm around him.

170

"You know," she said, "if there's something wrong, you can talk to your dad or me about it. We're always here to listen to you."

"I know."

"And if something's scaring you, we'll listen to that, too."

He seemed to wake up a bit from his daze. He looked at her, then back at the house.

"But what if talking about it doesn't help?" he asked.

"Then the best thing to do after that," Liz said, "if talking doesn't help, is to face it. The best way to get over something that's scaring you is just to face it. Most of the time, you realize that whatever it is is really nothing that can hurt you."

"How?"

"Well, for example, when I was a little girl, I was afraid of heights. So one day I climbed the highest tree I could find, all the way up close to the top. And I stood up there and looked all over the place as far as I could see, and then I just climbed back down."

He leaned his head toward her, resting against her chest.

"So you're not afraid of heights anymore?"

"Oh, no," she said, "I still am. But at least now I know that, as long as I keep hold and stay calm, I'll be fine. Anyway, it's not the heights that scare me so much as the falling."

Joey chuckled and Liz hugged him.

"So, you about ready for lunch?"

"Is it gonna be naptime after?"

"Probably."

"Can I have chips and cookies with my lunch?"

"You can have one. Which would you like?"

"Chips."

"Okay. Come on."

He seemed fine now as they walked back to the house, but then Liz had the feeling the house was watching her and she wished she could sit at the back of yard, outside, away from the house. Instead, she went inside with Joey, like being swallowed up.

Chapter Fourteen

Bill Sten told Jack the hour cut wouldn't affect his own paycheck, but it probably wouldn't have much affect on his hours either. There was still paperwork to be done, shop orders to be entered, orders to be placed. So Jack would be spending his Fridays at work, like usual, but he'd be doing it alone most likely. And no, Bill told him, the problems with Aurora would have to be worked out and their orders filled within those thirty-six hours.

Charley Clark spent the weekend looking for a part-time job, something that wouldn't take up too much time and that he could slip out of quietly when Fett Tech went back to a regular schedule.

Instead of going to Charley's, Jack spent the weekend on the second floor, helping Liz finish. After what seemed like a marathon session of painting, hanging, and moving, they stood back on Sunday evening and looked at their finished second floor.

All they needed was to move the furniture up here.

Liz, however, wasn't sure she was ready for that.

Twice during the weekend something brushed the back of her neck while she was painting. The first time she'd almost dropped the roller. The second time, she was sure it was Jack; he'd been behind her the second before. But when she turned around, she saw Jack was gone and she felt very alone in the house.

More times than she could count, she caught shadows out of the corner of her eye.

They're just curious, she told herself. Like animals that want to see what you're doing.

Except these animals could scare the shit out of her in the middle of the night by putting their dead hands on her skin while she was sleeping.

"Do you want to start bringing stuff up when I get off tomorrow?" Jack asked.

"I don't know," she said. "I think it can wait. At least for the week. I'm so exhausted from yesterday and today that I don't even want to see this floor again for a while."

Or pretty much ever, she thought.

"I know how you feel. Hell, you've done more work up here than I have. I'm surprised you even had the steam to finish it up."

She raised her eyebrows, shrugged.

"You want me to go get something to eat?" Jack asked.

"Like what?"

"What do you want?"

"A bath and a bed and fifteen hours of sleep."

"You can have those after we eat."

Jack ordered a pizza, then went to pick it up instead of waiting the forty-five minutes to an hour for delivery. While he was gone, Liz ran the bath water.

Joey asked, "Am I taking a bath, now?"

"Not this time," Liz said. "You can watch anything you want, because I'm taking a bath until your dad gets home with supper."

"Can I watch *Naruto*?"

"If it's on, but I don't think it is. *Avatar* is, I think. You can watch that."

Joey turned to run into the living room, but Liz called out, "Wait! Joey, come here for a second."

He came into the bathroom and Liz leaned over to look at him.

"What?" he asked.

She stared at him for a second, then said, "Never mind. Go watch cartoons."

He left, and she closed the door, then undressed and sank herself into the water, exhaling and moaning.

Avatar wasn't on, but a *Justice League* rerun was. Joey watched until the first commercial, then he heard something upstairs.

He listened, hoping it was his dad with supper because he was hungry and he didn't want that noise to be something else in the house.

While a toy commercial played on the television, Joey moved toward the door, listening into the hall, hoping to hear his dad coming down the stairs.

But dad comes in the back door.

And the noise came again, right above him.

Liz was taking a bath, dad was gone. Joey was right here. The man was upstairs. Or the girl. Or one of the other kids.

And whomever it was up there, they'd find him, because they'd been looking for him since they moved here and they'd find him sooner or later.

Justice League came back on. Down the hall, Liz splashed water.

Joey stepped into the hall. Another noise came right above him again. He moved toward the stairs, and the noise followed.

The best way to get over something that's scaring you is just to face it.

Was Liz right? He had the feeling she'd seen things, too. And she didn't act afraid. Had something happened to her here and she faced it and now she was fine?

Joey went to the stairs and listened.

He didn't hear anything this time, so he stepped up, quietly so Liz wouldn't hear. She'd wonder what he was doing and he didn't want to tell her. If he was wrong and she hadn't seen anything in the house, he didn't want to tell her what was up there because ghosts were scary and he didn't want her to be scared like he was.

He could hear her humming a song in the bathroom as he crept up. He got to the front door landing and turned to look up. The noise had been right above him, so if there were anything up here, it would be on this floor. But he couldn't make himself keep going.

He was trying to be brave and face it like Liz said, but his legs wouldn't go any further.

He looked up the stairs. The lights were on. He stood on his tiptoes, but couldn't see very far past the top of the stairs. He listened again, but still didn't hear anything.

He turned to go back downstairs, and then he heard it.

Something creaked above him. Not on the second floor, higher. Joey moved on the landing so he could see between the railings, up to the third floor.

He dreaded what might be staring back at him, but Liz

said "Most of the time, you realize that whatever it is, it's really nothing that can hurt you."

I hope not, Joey thought.

He looked up, focused on the dark, heard the creak again, and saw the boots moving back and forth in a tiny circle.

Something whispered "Adam," into his ear, and Joey screamed and bolted down the stairs, tripped in his rush, and fell face-first to the floor, tumbling over and over until he came to hit the back of his head on the hardwood hallway floor.

Liz heard the thumping, and plunged her head under the water to keep the ghosts out. If she couldn't hear them, their noise wouldn't bother her and if the noise didn't bother her, she might pass five seconds without thinking about them. She was already paranoid enough half the time just undressing, knowing someone or something could be watching and she wouldn't know for sure.

She'd heard the television in the front room and wondered if Joey'd heard the thumping on the stairs. She was pretty sure he knew what was in the house, too, but she also thought he was trying to keep the reality of it out of the front of his mind. He was like Jack sometimes in that, if he didn't think about it, it wasn't there. Except Joey wasn't the straight-arrow thinker Jack was. Not yet. He still had his perfect childish logic where anything he thought could be real.

Liz decided those few seconds under water were enough--God forbid she open her eyes and find something dead grinning down at her--and she sat up, swept water and hair away from her face, and rubbed her eyes with the rag.

She'd better get dressed before Jack got home so she could grab the food and eat as soon as he walked in the door.

She unplugged the tub, dried herself, and dressed in a pair of sweat shorts and a T-shirt. She ran the brush through her hair and cleaned the water from her ears. She opened the door to head toward the living room, and froze in horror when she saw Joey lying unconscious on the floor.

"Oh, Jesus Christ!" she yelled. She leaned to wake him up, then remembered something about not moving someone who's unconscious in case they've broken something.

She ran to the phone instead to call 911. What would she tell them? That she wasn't watching her six-year-old son? That in her negligence he'd fallen down the stairs? Was that even what had happened? Yes, she told herself.

Shit, she thought. And I heard it happen, too.

But you thought it was ghosts, she heard Jack saying. *How stupid are you?*

I'm sorry, I just heard noises, I hear them all the time, I didn't realize it was Joey.

Then maybe you're not stupid. Maybe you're crazy. Maybe that's the problem.

No, she protested. Joey's seen things, too. Ask him.

I would, but he's unconscious at the bottom of the stairs.

Fuck, get an ambulance. She remembered, but before she could dial, Jack walked in the back door with the pizza.

"Jack," she said.

He didn't notice the look on her face and he said, "Are you starving?"

"Joey."

"Huh? I'll get him. You get the plates."

"No, Jack," she said. "Joey. He's in the hall. He fell or something, I don't know, I was taking a bath and I heard something in the hall and by the time I got out, Joey was--"

"What happened to him?" he asked, dropping the pizza on the table and rushing toward the hall. He found him at the foot of the stairs as Liz had left him and was immediately on his knees, trying to shake him awake.

"What the hell happened to him?" he yelled over his shoulder. "What happened to him?" a third time.

"I don't know," she said. "I told you, I was in the tub. I heard the television, I thought he was in the living room. I don't know what he was doing upstairs."

"Did you call an ambulance?"

"No," Liz said. He looked back at her. "I was about to when you walked in the door."

They both waited for the other one, but neither moved nor spoke.

"Well do it, then!" he shouted.

Liz jumped and ran for the phone.

While she dialed, Jack shook Joey's shoulder as if waking

him up from a nap.

"Joe," he said. "You okay, babe? You alright? Did you hurt yourself? What happened, huh? You gonna get up?"

Joey's eyes fluttered and Jack wondered if he was having a seizure, but then he opened them and tried to sit up.

Jack put his hand on Joey's shoulder and kept him down. "Don't get up, Joe. Just a second."

Joey went back down and began crying. Jack ran his hand over his son's head, through his hair, murmuring, "You're alright, Joe. I'm here. You're okay."

Liz came back and said the ambulance was on its way. Then she saw Joey was awake and asked if he was okay.

"I don't know," Jack said. "I'm hoping he's just scared. He's not bleeding anywhere I can see, at least."

Liz sighed and put her face in her hands. Jack exhaled and rubbed Joey's head.

By the time the ambulance got there, Joey's crying had calmed to a scared whimper.

They put the neck brace on him and loaded him into the ambulance. The trip to the emergency room was, for Jack and Liz, a week long. But when they got there, Joey was fine. The ER doctor, his nametag read "Owen Cambridge", told them nothing was broken, nothing was bleeding, neither in- nor externally. Joey had a knot on his head and his body was sore. There was a bruise on his shoulder. They'd taken X-rays, but everything else was fine.

When we get home, Liz thought, he can have all the chips and cookies he wants.

When we get home, Jack thought, he can have all the Batman toys he wants.

Joey just wanted something to eat and to go to sleep.

They were going to let him stay the night. After all, he had passed out and you can never be too careful with kids. By the time he was admitted and in his own room, it was almost midnight.

Jack was going to stay, but Liz told him she would.

"It's already late, and you've got to work tomorrow. He's fine, so you can go home and get some sleep. If they let him go tomorrow before you go to lunch, I'll call you and let you know."

"Then I'll come and take you home then," he said.

Jack kissed his wife and son and went home. Liz asked the nurse if it was okay if Joey had a shower.

"He's been outside playing most of the day," she said.

"Of course," the nurse said, "as long as you help him."

"I will."

She led Liz and Joey to the shower, showed her the towels and the soap and left.

The shower was a stall. She stood outside while Joey washed his hair, then his body, and shut off the water. She wrapped a towel around him and drew him out.

He stood with his arms up to his chest, trying to draw himself close and keep warm, while Liz dried his hair, then moved to his face and neck, and down to his body. She knelt in front of him and dried his back and his legs. She happened to glance over and caught sight of something that made her drop the towel and back away.

Joey frowned, looking up at her, wondering what was wrong.

"Am I all done?" he asked.

She couldn't say anything, but she stared at him, into his eyes.

Joey asked, "What?"

She still didn't answer, but she managed to move a little closer.

"I'm cold. Am I done?"

"I think so," Liz said. She tossed him the towel and he wrapped it around himself. He pulled on his clothes and rubbed his eyes. Liz put the towel into a basket sitting outside the room and led Joey back to his bed.

He climbed up, got under the blanket, turned over, and was asleep within minutes.

Liz sat in the chair next to his bed, facing the window, not wanting to look at him, but still able to see his reflection in case he got up in the middle of the night and tried to touch her.

Jack turned over in bed. The sheet was drawn around him with the air conditioner on low. Still he was freezing.

He wondered, in a half-asleep way, if they had any blankets anywhere. But if they did, he was too tired to get them. He was practically asleep anyway. He'd doze off completely soon enough.

When he did, he dreamed it was a different night and Liz and Joey were home. Joey was playing in his room. Jack heard him walking around, moving toys and creaking the bed with his weight. Liz lay next to him, rubbing her hand up and down his arm.

He moved his feet to her side of the bed, rubbed his toes over her legs. She was cold, though, and he pulled them back.

"Christ, you're cold," he said.

She leaned into him and whispered in his ear, "Everyone will suffer now. You can't save yourself."

Jack jerked out of sleep and sat up, looking around, wondering what had just been touching his arm.

The room was dark, but he could see it was empty. He was just dreaming. Liz was still at the hospital with Joey. Lay back and go to sleep. Have to go to work in the morning.

He took one last glance around the room, then turned over to go back to sleep. Before he could begin to slip away, he was shivering so badly he had to get up and turn the air conditioner off altogether.

It's like winter in here, he thought.

He slid under the sheet again and pulled it close around him, burrowing into the bed, trying to force himself to sleep.

After ten minutes, he knew it was hopeless. He sat up again and scanned the room, trying to figure out where Liz had put the thin blanket they'd had on the bed when they moved here. There was no closet in their room, and Joey's closet was stuffed with toys.

He got up and looked under the bed, but the only thing under there was his guitar case. He checked the towel closet in the bathroom, but it wasn't there either. And he wasn't going to call Liz at the hospital to find out where it was. He'd just have to look for it because there was no way he was going to get to sleep if he couldn't stop shivering.

He stood in the middle of the hall, trying to decide where to look next. The sound of something pounding upstairs made up his mind for him.

"Something fell," he told the house. He himself was a little unconvinced. A fall is a single sound. This had been over and over. Four, he thought.

He topped the flight to the second floor and the world seemed as if it had slowed down. Jack stepped off the last stair and moved toward the main room. The night hung thick about him, heavy with darkness and heat.

And I was just thinking of sleeping in my clothes to keep warm, he thought.

He checked the main room, but everything looked in place. He turned, still moving slowly, toward the kitchen. Nothing touched in there, either. The bathroom, the dining room, the study. Everything where they'd left it.

Echoes of his dream came again and he heard that voice in his ear, *"Everyone will suffer now. You can't save yourself."*

A shiver went up his back. He recalled Liz's talk of something in the house with them. Had she said it was strongest on the third floor? No, that wasn't Liz. It was another voice, an inner voice in his own mind. But he ignored it because there was nothing upstairs and if he started convincing himself otherwise, he'd be just as blind as Liz. The only things upstairs were the empty rooms, the broken door, and all the junk in the room behind the bathroom.

And there was his answer. Something up there had fallen. Something big, obviously, if he'd heard it downstairs. But there was so much crap up there, it wouldn't surprise him to hear it in the basement if it all fell. And Liz said the exterminator had said there were no animals in the house. Jack would bet Charley Clark's thirty-six hour paycheck the exterminator didn't check in there. He probably thought it was a closet and didn't bother.

Slack-ass, Jack thought.

He climbed the stairs again, still seeing the world crawl around him. But if everything was in slow motion now, when he reached the third floor, they were simply frozen. Everything was still. Even his breath, when he exhaled, hung suspended in the air around his head. A bead of sweat stuck to his temple, refusing to roll any further. He moved toward the bathroom, trudging across the floor as if through thick mud. He flipped on the light and everything jumped a second ahead. His breath caught and the sweat bead was gone. He looked around, fighting with himself over whether there was anyone behind him or not. His mind said No, his creeping flesh said Most definitely!

What am I doing up here? he wondered.

Trying to figure out what fell and if anything's broken, he answered. Then you're going back to bed and getting some sleep before it's too late.

He crossed the bathroom, freezing and moving back a step when the reflection that passed in front of the mirror wasn't his. He looked again, closer, blinked his eyes, and there was Jack Kitch looking back.

I'm tired, he thought.

He opened the door to the storage room and was wafted with cool air. His skin grew gooseflesh and his nose wrinkled with the smell coming from the dark.

He pressed the door back against the wall to let in more light, then peaked in. He scanned the room, the shelves, the stuff leaning against the walls. Nothing seemed out of place, but there was so much crap in here, it would be hard to tell. He searched, hoping, looking, willing something to be broken, something heavy that could have fallen from a shelf and made enough noise to be heard on the first floor. But, dammit, no matter how badly Jack wanted it, nothing in here had made that noise.

He pulled back, closed the door, and sat on the edge of the tub to think. He'd heard the noise. No, he'd heard *a* noise. Who was to say it came from upstairs? Who was to say it came from inside the house? No one. He'd assumed it had because of his dream, because of Liz, because of everything else in his life right then adding to his stress and wearing him down.

He went out into the middle room and everything was moving normally now. The room was hot, but the heat wasn't pressing in on him, the air didn't try to strangle him with its stillness. He stood center-room and thought, *There's nothing up here but me. Liz is out of her mind and I need to stop letting her influence me because I'm alone up here, the rest of the house is empty. It's just me.*

That decided in his mind, he went to turn off the bathroom light. He caught another glimpse of himself in the bathroom mirror, just a half-second flash, but it was a trick of the light and motion because Jack wasn't really beaten and bloody as the reflection suggested.

He flipped off the light, went to the stairs, and suddenly

everything was again frozen. He looked behind him again, and he was still alone. But there was something touching his back. He could almost feel the individual fingers pressing and flexing on his skin.

A muscle spasm, he told himself.

The hand moved up to cup his shoulder muscle. It squeezed.

Jack was still frozen at the top of the stairs. The world had stopped around him, everything except his heartbeat which came double-time and pounding. More sweat formed on his brow, his back, under his arms, but none of it moved. The air around him stank like rot and hung thick in front of his face.

The hand on his shoulder squeezed tighter and he felt a rush of hot air against his ear. A voice was saying, "*Forgive me--* (pant, pant)--*forgive me.*"

Suddenly the noise came again, that pounding, heavy, almost desperate, but not up here. Outside. Something on the roof, it sounded like.

Jack shook off the paralysis and darted down the stairs, rounding the landing and feeling the banister loosen in his grip as he used it to haul himself around the corner, then down to the first floor. He walked into the bedroom with heavy feet, slammed the door behind him, and slid into the bed. He pulled the sheet around his chin, buried his face in the pillow, squeezed his eyes shut, and stayed that way until he fell asleep. The last thing he heard was crickets outside, and nothing else that night banged upstairs, and Jack thanked God for it as he waited for sleep.

C. DENNIS MOORE

Chapter Fifteen

When Jack hadn't heard from Liz by eleven, he decided to go to the hospital at lunch anyway. It was halfway between Fett Tech and home, he could be there and back in half an hour. And if they weren't ready to send Joey home, at least Jack could find out how he was feeling.

He found Joey alone in his room and figured Liz had gone to get him a snack or a drink.

"Are you feeling okay?" he asked. Joey nodded, but kept his eyes on the television. Jack glanced up and saw Bugs Bunny. He looked back and asked, "How's your head?"

"Better," Joey said.

"Good. Has Liz said when you get to go home?"

"I don't know," Joey said. His eyes stayed on the television, but his head turned slightly toward Jack, as if he would look at him if his eyes hadn't been drawn inexorably to the screen. "I haven't seen her since last night."

"What?" Jack said. "Where's she been?"

"I dunno," Joey said, shrugging his shoulders. "She gave me a shower and then I came to bed. She was gone when I woke up."

"You don't know where she is?"

Joey shook his head. Jack kissed his forehead and said, "I'll be back. If a nurse or someone comes in, ask them when you can go home. I'm going to see if I can find your stepmother."

Joey didn't respond and Jack closed the door behind him.

What in the hell did she think she was doing leaving him alone like that? And where the fuck did she go?

For the first time in their marriage, a voice of doubt spoke up.

She's alone all day, it said. *Who's to say what she does at home? Maybe she's seeing someone else. Maybe that's where she is.*

Shut up, Jack told the voice. That's ridiculous. She's not seeing someone else.

How do you know?

Because I do.

That sounds logical.

Shut up.

He stopped at the nurses' station and asked, "Has anyone seen my wife? We brought my son in? Joseph Kitch? I had to go to work and my wife, Liz, was supposed to be staying with him. But I can't find her."

The nurses hadn't seen her.

Angel County Hospital had a huge glass birdcage set off from one of the waiting rooms. Jack looked there, but didn't find Liz. He found a pay phone and called the house in case she'd, for whatever reason, called a cab and gone home some time after he left this morning. No one answered. He looked in the gift shop. He checked the chapel. He checked the cafeteria. There was Liz sitting alone in a booth along the wall, sipping coffee and smoking a cigarette. Jack slid into the seat across from her.

"When did you start smoking?"

"When I was fourteen," Liz said.

"Hmm. I seem to have missed that the past couple years."

"I quit a week or so after Alex left."

"A test of willpower?"

"Something like that."

"Where've you been?"

"Pretty much right here," she said.

"Pretty much?"

She puffed, inhaled, and sighed smoke out the side of her mouth. She rubbed a red eye and said, "Well, you know, I wandered around the hospital for a while. After a while I think I started scaring the nurses--they were looking at me pretty weird-- so I came down here. Been here since late last night."

Jack sat silent for a minute, biting the inside of his lip.

"Want to tell me why?"

Liz had apparently been slipping into a daze; when Jack spoke, she had to focus on him and ask, "Huh?"

"Want to tell me why you left Joey by himself in the middle of the hospital and went off to roam the halls?"

"I don't know," she said.

"What do you mean you don't know?"

"I mean, I don't know if I want to tell you. You aren't gonna believe me, so why waste the time?"

Jack looked at his watch.

"Time is one thing I don't have a lot of, Liz. I'm supposed to be back at work in about five minutes, so spill it. What's wrong with you?"

Liz tried a laugh and looked down at the table.

"There's nothing wrong with me," she said. "You want to find out what's wrong, go to the house and try the third floor. Whole bunch of stuff wrong up there."

Jack got a hot flash as last night came back to him. He'd spent the day trying to shove it away and convince himself he'd dreamed it, a nightmare brought on by stress from Joey's fall and Liz's insane insistence of ghosts. He'd almost convinced himself, except for the small nag at the back of his skull.

"There's nothing wrong with the house," he said. His voice cracked on "house". He cleared his throat and hoped Liz didn't call him on it. One look at her told him she was only half-listening anyway. "And I'm sure nothing from the house had anything to do with you walking the halls here."

"No, why would it?" Liz said.

Jack looked at his watch again. He was late. Leaving now wouldn't matter, he wasn't going to make it back on time. I'm on salary anyway, he thought. If the engineers can take an hour lunch at least twice a week, I can once in a month.

He rubbed his eyes and said, "Just tell me why the hell you left Joey alone all night when all you had to do was sit with him. You could have slept, you could have stayed up watching television, you could have got a book from the gift shop, I don't care what you did as long as you did it with Joey there. So why did you leave him all night?"

Liz crushed out her cigarette and took two more sips from her coffee before she set the cup aside and asked, "What color are Joey's eyes?"

"I take it that has something to do with this?"

"What color are they?"

Jack thought for a second before saying, "Brown."

"Not anymore."

He raised his eyebrows, squinted his eyes, a *Huh?* gesture. "And now they're . . . ?"

"They're green. Well, pretty much. There's still some brown in them, but they're almost all green now. I noticed it last night, but it was after working all day upstairs and I wasn't sure if

187

I was just tired and confused or if his eyes had really changed color."

"His mother had green eyes. They've probably been a mix forever. Lots of peoples' eyes are a mix of colors."

Liz sighed.

"I knew you were going to have some kind of explanation. I told you it was a waste of time."

"I just want to know what this has to do with why you were so irresponsible?" Jack said. "If I'd known you were going to go off and leave him alone, I'd have stayed and watched him myself. You know, just because he's not your son doesn't mean--"

Liz cut him off with, "Don't you ever say anything like that again. Who's the one who stays home with him every single day? Who's the one who feeds him, bathes him, talks to him? It sure as hell isn't you. I'm more parent to that boy than you've been since we moved here."

"Sorry for being the one to have a job," he said. "But that house isn't going to pay for itself."

"Fuck that house," she replied. "That house can burn down for all I care. What I'm trying to tell you through your stupid fucking logic-haze is that Joey's brown eyes are now green. His blonde hair is now red--in case you hadn't noticed--and last night after his shower, while I was drying him off, I saw the boy--your *six*-year-old son--has pubic hair. Not a lot, but a dozen is more than any six-year-old should have."

Jack had turned away from her, trying not to hear because none of it made any logical sense and as soon as she shut up, he'd be able to think and figure out what she was talking about and at least two good ways to explain it.

"Now, I may not be the electronics genius you are," she said, "but I know enough to see things that are going on right in front of me and not dismiss it because I can't explain it. I'm telling you what's going on and I'm telling you that fucking house has something to do with it. I want you to tell me everything you know about what went on up there."

Jack shrugged. "I don't know anything," he said. "A guy killed his kids, then himself. That's it."

"When?"

"I don't know," he said. "Few years ago, maybe. Five,

six, I don't know. I wasn't here, I was in Houston, remember?"

"There's got to be more there," Liz said. She pulled a half-empty cigarette pack from the seat beside her, shook one out, stuck it in her mouth and lit it with a match from the book tucked into the pack. She puffed, blew smoke. Sighed. Watched an old woman in blue scrubs buy a carton of milk and a salad.

Jack put his hand on her wrist and she snapped back to look at him.

"I want you to tell me what the hell's wrong with you," he said.

She looked at him and he could see she wanted to say something, but she decided she didn't have the words she needed and she looked down at the table instead.

"I don't know," she finally whispered. "I don't even know. Everything's so fucking crazy. I got stuff at the house, voices and shadows and people killing their children upstairs. Then Joey's different and you're you and that ain't helping a bit and--"

"Thanks," Jack said.

"I'm sorry. You know me, Jack. You know I'm not crazy--"

"I never said you were."

"No, but you look at me like I am. When I tell you what I've seen and heard in that house, you look at me like I just said the invasion forces had landed from space. I'm not talking about anything that hasn't been documented a thousand times over already, but you just won't listen and you don't see any of it. I don't know, maybe because they know you don't believe in it and that when I say there's ghosts you'll think I'm insane."

Jack leaned over the table and kissed her forehead.

"I don't think you're insane," he said. "I think we just need to get Joey and you and me home and we'll figure something out from there, okay?"

She kept her eyes on the table. She stubbed out the half-smoked cigarette and let herself be pulled up as Jack led her back to Joey's room.

She stayed in the room with him while Jack went to see about getting him signed out. She kept her back to the wall by the door and didn't look at Joey. He lay in the bed watching television, neither speaking nor looking her way.

The ten minutes Jack was gone seemed like an hour and Liz stood there, dreading a word from Joey because she was suddenly sure the voice that came out wouldn't be his and that would be one more thing in the long list that Jack would choose not to see. She wished sometimes she could just punch Jack in the face, just once, just hard enough to open his eyes to the possibility that not everything in the world fell into his stupid, narrow-minded classifications.

Jack came back. "They said they could let him go just as soon as the doctor releases him."

"How long?"

"They're trying to get hold of him now." Jack used the phone to call work. He told Bill Sten where he was and that he'd be back just as soon as he could.

The doctor came in ninety minutes later to look Joey up and down, then said he was good to go and once the paperwork was done, Joey was wheeled to the front door where Jack had the car waiting.

The ride home was quiet and once they reached the house neither Liz nor Joey was eager to get inside. Liz kept her eyes on the third floor windows as she shuffled to the door. Joey kept his eyes down. No one spoke.

Soon after, Jack went back to work. He said he might be a little late in case anything had come up with Aurora while he was gone. He kissed his wife and son, and went out the back door. As soon as the door clicked shut, Liz heard the bathroom door close down the hall.

She suppressed a shudder and sighed.

Joey sat on the couch watching cartoons. Liz knelt next to him and said, "Joey, I want you to tell me if you know what's going on."

Joey stayed focused, but his mouth opened as if he were going to talk.

"I'm sorry I left you alone last night," she said.

"That's okay," Joey said. She wanted to hug him when she recognized the voice as the Joey she'd known the past two years. "You were just scared."

"Yeah," she said. "I guess I was. I'm sorry. Do you know what's happening?"

He shook his head, but didn't say anything. Then he

looked at her and asked, "Do you?"

"No," she said. "I don't."

"Something bad?"

"I don't know."

"Bad stuff happens here a lot," he said.

"Does it?"

"Uh-huh. People get hurt here. Are we going to get hurt?"

"No," she said, even though the best she could come to certainty was a strong hope that everything might be okay.

She left Joey where he was and crossed to the bedroom, keeping the corner of her eye on the hall, hoping to God nothing was coming down the stairs toward her. In the bedroom, she thrust her hand under Jack's side of the mattress, searching, finding the book she knew was there, and pulling it out.

Jack knew something, she knew he did, but he wouldn't tell her. That's okay, she thought he might have gotten it from this book, and if he did, she'd find out what he knew.

She thumbed through it, glancing at the chapter headings, then flipped to the front for a look at the table of contents.

There were three chapters on ghosts, and two were haunted house stories.

Liz turned the book over for another look at the cover, then looked at the back, checking to see if there was any word about how true the stories in here were. The front cover had a banner pasted across the bottom: "TRUE STORIES OF ANGEL HILL ODDITIES". She flipped back to the contents and picked one of the haunted house stories.

She turned to the chapter then scanned down the page. This wasn't her house. This house was in west Angel Hill and was supposedly built on the site of a Civil War battle. Not what she was looking for.

She turned to the other haunted house chapter and read.

It told pretty much the same story Charley Clark had given Jack. Milo Dengler's wife dead from cancer. Four kids. Dengler signs off from work one day and a few days later the police show up. The book didn't say how the police came to be at the Dengler door, but it did tell what they found. Milo Dengler hanging from the rail at the top of the third floor and his three sons and a daughter dead in the corner bedroom.

Liz shuddered, closed the book with her finger between the pages, then turned around, sure there was someone behind her.

Joey was still in the living room. From the bed, she could see *Naruto* on television.

She turned back to the book, flipping through the pages again, hoping for pictures or names or anything else. She didn't know much more now than she did before. Except that she'd been right when she first wondered if someone had died up there. She would never have guessed it would be so bad, though.

To kill, not only yourself, but also your four kids. She couldn't imagine there was any reasoning behind that good enough to make it even the germ of an idea in anyone's head. But she wasn't him, she told herself, and she didn't know anything more about him than what this book said. For all she knew, the book itself was so much conjecture. Who knew how much truth there was in its pages? But there was a nudge at the back of her skull that said it was true. No matter the motive behind it, this was what had happened.

The book offered nothing more than the story and she closed it, then slid it back under Jack's side of the mattress.

In the hall, she peeked in on Joey who was still sitting quietly, watching cartoons. At the stairs, she saw the bathroom door standing open now and wondered when that had happened. She knew she heard it close when Jack left. As she stood staring at it, the light clicked on, shocking her into action and she quickly went up the first flight of stairs.

At the door, she looked out, saw the mail hadn't come yet--but who was this? Someone was coming up the front walk. Liz stared at her for a second before she recognized her. The woman from the park, the one who lived up the street. What was her name? Liz didn't think she'd ever asked for it.

The woman came up the porch, but before she could knock, Liz opened the door. The woman was startled for a second, but then she saw Liz and smiled.

"Hi," she said. "I'm sorry to barge in, but I saw the ambulance last night and just wanted to make sure everything was alright down here. Do you need anything?"

Liz wondered how much of this was genuine concern

and how much was nosy neighbor.

"No," she said. "Everything's fine down here. We just had an accident with my son, but he's okay."

"Oh, I see. Well, you want to be careful with kids in a big house like this," she said. "There's got to be lots of opportunities for them to hurt themselves."

"Yeah, well . . . " Liz said, then trailed off. She stood for a second, wondering how to proceed, then a thought occurred and she said, "Hey, can I ask you something?"

"Oh, sure," the woman said.

"You've lived here, you said, what, ten years? Did you know the people who lived here before? The Denglers?"

"Oh," the woman said. "What a sad story that was, huh? It makes you wonder why they let people like that be parents."

Liz didn't know about all that. From the way the book told the story, it was just one bad thing after another, but up until that point it seemed the Denglers had been a pretty solid family.

"Yeah," Liz said. "I heard about what happened, but I was just wondering if you might know anything about them before all that? I'm curious to know what kind of people they were?"

"They were fine people," the woman said, "until that happened."

"Well, was there--I'm sorry, we're out here on the porch in the heat. Please, come inside."

"Thank you."

Liz led her up to the second floor and gave her a seat.

"You know," she said, "I don't think I ever got your name in the park that day."

"I'm Judy," the woman said, and held out her hand.

"Liz," she said, and offered her own hand.

"Yes, they were good people," Judy started. "At least, I always thought so. I was only beginning to know them when she got sick, but I very much enjoyed their company when I came down here. I didn't know the husband too well, but his wife, and the children, wonderful people. It was a shame and a waste, to lose someone like that."

"Cancer, wasn't it?" Liz asked.

"Yeah. Took her way too fast."

"Tell me about the children."

"You want to talk about a tragedy," Judy said. "What he did to those children, that's a crime against the world. They were the brightest, warmest children you've ever met. The oldest, Adam, he was always the man of the house, what with their father out on the trains all the time. I used to come visit after she got sick, to check in on her, you know, and Adam was always taking care of the younger ones. Getting their lunch, making sure they had clean clothes, all that. He was so grown up for such a young boy."

"And how old was he?" Liz asked.

"I don't know exactly," Judy said. "Young, just getting into his teen years, I think."

Liz was thinking that she hadn't seen this one. She'd seen the man, and two of the children, but none that old. The ones she'd seen had been children.

"And then Sarah," Judy said. "She doted on her big brother. She was pretty young, maybe ten. She used to practice her piano and if I walked my dog past the house at the right time, I could hear her from the sidewalk. Let me see . . . Jason was the eight-year-old, and then Kyle was five, I believe. I mean, they were a terrific family, they had everything in the world going for them. But that cancer, you know, it just swoops in and takes all that away."

"Yeah," Liz said. She wasn't listening anymore, she was thinking about the children. This woman was taking away their anonymity; they were no longer nameless shapes that touched her in the night. She pictured Joey, perfect and sleeping downstairs, and then she imagined having that four times over and what kind of hole does your life have to sink into before you do something so horrible?

She glanced over and Judy's lips were moving, so Liz tuned in.

"--this color, too. It all looks so different, but I really like it. Are you going to open up the house and finish all three floors?"

"I don't really know yet," Liz said. "We've been living on the bottom floor and that works out just fine so far. There's really no reason to move anything up here, other than we've got the space and we might as well utilize it. But, to be honest, we don't *need* this much room. I love the house, but sometimes I wish we'd bought a smaller place."

"Yes," Judy said, nodding. "And knowing what happened here can't make it any easier."

"No," Liz confessed. "It doesn't."

Judy looked at her watch.

"Oh, I should be going, I'm going to be late. I just wanted to say hello, and to make sure everything was okay. You know, you see an ambulance down the street where something so awful happened once before . . ."

"Oh, God no," Liz said. "That's too horrible to even think about."

She walked Judy back to the door and said goodbye, stood there watching as the woman went down the steps to the sidewalk, then turned up the street heading back to her own house.

She locked the front door, then turned and went up to the second floor.

She looked around at all the work she'd done up here, and for what? How could she move up here? And if Jack ever got it into his head that they should use the third floor, what then? She couldn't do it.

She climbed the stairs again, toward the third floor, and her mind asked, *What are you doing?*

I have to see, she thought. I have to see where it happened.

Why?

I don't know. But I know I have to.

Well, leave me out of it.

Come on. Let's go see.

She rounded the landing and stopped, frozen again.

At the top of the stairs, sitting with her chin in her hands, looking solemnly down at Liz, was the little girl. Sarah? Her hair hung dead and dirty around her shoulders. Her dress was faded and grungy. Her eyes hollow, sunken.

Liz stared back, waiting, wondering what was going to happen.

And for the first time in months, Liz wasn't afraid. She saw the girl now as she was, a victim, not some menacing figure sent to torment her out of the house. She suddenly found herself feeling sympathy for this girl.

Then Sarah's lips parted, mouthing the silent question: *why?*

Liz felt the lump rise into her throat and she wanted to give a reason, but she didn't know. She would have done anything then to make the girl feel better, but she found herself empty of solutions.

"I don't know," she said back.

The girl stood up and Liz didn't know whether she should stand her ground or run.

The girl took a step back, away from Liz. Liz took a step up, too. The girl moved back another step, and before Liz could follow, Milo Dengler was hanging dead and green beside her, dangling from the top rail and staring at her, his face full of anger. Liz caught him from the corner of her eye and as she turned to look, Dengler lunged toward her, arms out and his mouth open in a roar.

Liz backed away, then leapt to the landing and turned, suddenly aware she couldn't get downstairs without passing him, without going under him. What if he dropped from the rail and landed on top of her?

He's a ghost, her mind said.

That doesn't make it any less terrifying.

He can only scare you, he can't hurt you.

I hear a heart attack hurts plenty.

Dengler hung limp above her now, his arms at his sides and his head lolling forward on a broken neck. But his eyes were open and rolled up to stare at her.

She looked up and saw the girl had vanished from the landing. She was alone with the killer and any empathy she'd felt for the girl was replaced by bald fear. And Joey was alone downstairs. Were the others down there with him? Was the man just a distraction to keep her from Joey while the children did something to him?

No, she tried to convince herself. The sorrow in the girl's face had been real. Whatever all this was about, it wasn't something they'd done, but something that was done to them, something they were led into. At least, she hoped.

She watched him, waiting, wondering. The body turned sideways in a breeze Liz didn't feel, but a chill still ran up her back and gooseflesh rose on her arms.

The dead eyes still stared at her, but he hadn't moved again since she'd reached the landing. She took a cautious step down, ready to leap back again if he even twitched. Another step down and Dengler was still. But the eyes followed her. She imagined she could see the evil grin beginning to spread across his cracked lips, but another look proved her wrong; his face remained the same solemn, dead look.

She'd gone down five steps now and Dengler's body hung a foot from her face, her head even with his chest. Liz wished he'd vanish into whatever other place he'd come from, but it didn't look like he was going to, and she couldn't stay here all day, trapped on the stairs by a ghost. She swung her feet over the rail and used the overhang on the stairs to climb down, inching past him. She slid her hand down the rail and her feet off the edge of the step, down to the next one. Her eyes stayed on his body, watching for any sign of movement.

She kept trying to tell herself *He's just a ghost, he's just a ghost, he's not really there, it's just an image, not real.* But a smell came from him that contradicted that. And a heat washed over Liz's face when she passed him. The body swung sideways again and she glanced up quickly. His face was only two feet above Liz's, and his eyes were still locked on her. She stared into them and this time she didn't imagine it; the lips really did part and he showed a row of ugly teeth sneering at her.

She gasped and her foot slipped off the stair. Her knee banged the banister and her arm flung out to catch something and keep her from falling and breaking her back.

Maybe that's what he wants, she thought, to kill us all so there's more of them.

But why, she wondered. *What would be the point in that?*

Maybe there isn't a point. Who knows? Who cares?

Right. Get out of here. That's all.

Her arm found the banister for the flight of the stairs leading to the bottom landing, right behind her, and she hauled herself backward over it, flinging her feet over and backing up toward the wall, then she looked up and saw Dengler was still hanging there.

His head was cocked sideways, his face dead, his eyes staring at her, and his arms were outstretched, the fingers flexing, reaching, grabbing for her. She heard the knuckles pop when he curled the fingers. She leaped down the stairs to the landing, then took the last flight down to the first floor three at a time, trying not to trip over her feet and land on her head.

Is that what happened to Joey? He'd come up here that night and he'd seen something? What? Dengler? The little girl? Something worse?

What could be worse?

Nothing she could think of.

She stopped in the hall midway to the living room and put her back against the wall, her face in her hands, and she cried, as silently as she could. When she realized the torrent was too much for her, she went into the bathroom--the light was off now, and Liz had to turn it on--and closed door. She sat on the edge of the tub, bawling into her hands and wishing all of it would go away. She thought she'd be able to handle it, that she was strong enough to deal with a ghost or two, but the scope of it turned out to be bigger than she'd thought.

This wasn't the ghost of some unfortunate person who'd died in the house, it was a man who killed his four children and then himself, and anyone who could do that wasn't someone Liz wanted to have to deal with.

She knew there were things she would have to do now, things she was hoping to avoid. If Jack didn't want to believe it all, that had been fine, but now it was getting to the point if she didn't convince someone else she was going to have a nervous breakdown.

Blessing the house hadn't worked. So what would? She'd have to find out. How? The library's resources had been limited and she'd come away with nothing.

Okay, maybe Jack would have something--he was good at thinking his way through things--once she convinced him. So that was the first thing.

What would make Jack believe the ghosts were more than just house-settling creaks or the wind or prank phone calls?

He'd have to see it.

From the living room, the sound of the ringing phone came dull through the walls and Liz got up, wiped her eyes, and went to answer it.

"Jack's probably at work, isn't he?" Allen asked.

Liz smiled. Finally, something familiar. She was

homesick for Houston, and their old neighbors, and their old non-haunted house.

"Yep," she answered. "He said he might be a little late tonight, too. Do you want me to have him call you when he gets here?"

"That's alright," Allen said. "I didn't really want anything. I just had some free time and thought I'd see how Missouri's going for you. How's Joey?"

Liz almost said *I'm not sure; he's not Joey anymore*, but she caught the words in her mouth and changed them to, "He's fine. Do you want to talk to him?"

"Sure, for a second."

She handed the phone to Joey, then sat back in the chair, listening to Joey's one-sided conversation, asking if Allen was going to come up or if Joey could come down there. She smiled and breathed easy for a while, happy for the distraction.

The second Judy was in the door, she went to the phone. The front door stood open and she came back to shut it as she dialed, but the phone was her first priority. She had to call her brothers. Charley was first.

"It's me," she said. "I just came from the house."

"The house? How'd you manage that?"

"I saw the ambulance there last night--did you know the boy went to the hospital?"

"Yeah," Charley said. "I work with his dad, remember?"

"Right. Anyway, I met her at the park a few days back, talked to her a little bit. Told her today I wanted to make sure everything was okay, play the concerned neighbor type. She brought me inside and we went upstairs--"

"Did you hear it?" Charley asked. "That pounding in the ceiling?"

"No," Judy said. She went into the kitchen and poured some tea, then dropped a handful of ice cubes into it. "We were only on the second floor. She's really done a nice job on it."

"Yeah it looks great. No pounding, then? Did you see any of them? You know sometimes they're seen standing at the windows, especially Sarah."

"No," Judy told him. "That was the only problem, I

didn't see or hear anything. And she didn't talk about it. She did ask me about them, though."

"What did you tell her?"

Judy pulled the phone away from her face for a second and took three long gulps of the tea. Then she filled in her brother on the conversation, at the end of which he said, "I wonder what she's seen. If she's asking about them, do you think that means she's seen the kids? He never talks about them, but I get the feeling he wouldn't believe it if he did. But I don't know her. What's she like?"

"She seems nice enough, I guess. I wasn't sure that first day in the park, but today she seemed a lot friendlier. But all she wanted to talk about was the house and the kids, so maybe she was just curious."

"But you didn't see anything?"

"Not a shadow." She sat on her couch and leaned back. She sighed. "You think that maybe it is all just talk?"

Charley was silent a second, thinking. Finally he said, "No, what I heard up there wasn't just talk. There was something up there. I know it."

"You could be wrong. Raccoons?"

"Could be," he admitted. "But what I heard didn't sound like any animal. I swear it sounded like something knocking on the ceiling, trying to get in."

"But if they're there, then they're already in. Aren't they? What do you think it could have been?"

"I don't know," he said. "I don't know anything about any of it, except that I'm ninety-nine percent sure they're still there."

"I wish we could help them."

"I know. You gonna call Ron and tell him? He'll want to know, too."

"Yeah," Judy said. "I called you first, but I'm calling him next."

"You know, I took Jack to see Ron a few days ago."

"What for?"

"I wanted him to see that apartment. That guy is a rock. He came out of there thinking we'd played some trick on him."

"I hate that apartment," Judy said. She shivered.

"Yeah."

Judy got up and went to her front window. She looked down the street at the Kitch house, formerly the Dengler house, formerly the Keeper house. "But if those kids are still in there and that house is holding them, I hate it even more."

"You and me both," Charley said. "You call Ron.

Jack had a crisis and didn't even realize it. Aurora had called while he was gone and asked for twenty intercoms to be sent next day air. B.B. Whitaker had answered the call. He'd only been moved to Jack's department a few days earlier and hadn't had to deal with Aurora yet. He didn't know not to promise them something without discussing it with the cell in charge of that part first. Better yet, B.B. shouldn't have been promising them anything at all; that wasn't his job.

Granted, Jack had been nowhere around--still at the hospital at the time, or driving Liz and Joey home--but B.B. was new and should have passed the phone to anyone else who'd dealt with Aurora before.

And just two minutes ago, Jack found out their UPS pick-up for next day air items had been moved back an hour. That gave them forty-five minutes to finish the intercoms and get them boxed and moved to the shipping area.

And all Jack could think of was the house.

He'd dreamed those things last night, that's what it had been. He knew it because, in his dream, the house had been cold, but that house hadn't been cold in weeks. He'd only dreamed he couldn't sleep. And that was an odd thing to dream, but given the things he dreamed he'd seen upstairs, it was nothing.

And that was why he was so tired today, because his sleep had been so troubled with nightmares, not because he'd been up all night trying to sleep. It had to be why because the alternative was to listen to Liz's claims and say the house was haunted, which it wasn't, because ghosts weren't real.

What about all the times you've gotten up in the morning and found the bathroom light on?

That doesn't mean anything. Joey could have went to the bathroom in the night and left the light on. His room is right across the hall from it.

And the sounds in the walls?

201

Squirrels. Mice.

The exterminator said there was nothing.

The exterminator's a moron.

The light you saw go out on the third floor that night?

That was a streetlight reflection. We've been over that one already.

While the cut-off for the UPS load got closer--Jack normally would have been on the floor helping get the intercoms done in the time crunch--he sat at his desk playing "What about" with himself, trying to convince himself the house might be haunted, then coming back with an explanation as to why that didn't mean the house might be haunted.

When he got home that night, Liz told him to come upstairs with her.

"I want to show you something."

He followed her, wiping sweat from his forehead. The heat the higher in the house you went was almost unbearable at times. If they ever moved anything to the top, they'd need an air conditioner up there for sure, maybe two.

On the stairs from the second floor to the landing, Liz skittered up them far ahead of Jack, once glancing over her shoulder as if she expected someone above her. Jack glanced up, too, when he passed under the rail, thinking, *That's the spot. If the story was right, that's where he hung himself.*

At the top, Jack asked, "What is it?" He looked around, expecting to see something different, any noticeable change, but everything looked exactly as it did the night before. When he'd been up here alone, in the dark, when something touched him.

He repressed a shiver and told himself again that he'd dreamed it. Of course he dreamed it because this house wasn't haunted. Ghosts weren't real.

"This," Liz said, and he turned toward her, then squinted and backed away from the flash of light shot into his face. The Polaroid clicked, hummed as the picture slid from it.

"What are you doing?" he asked. He hadn't even noticed it in her hand before now.

"Just taking some pictures," she said.

"What for?"

She shrugged in answer and aimed the camera at him again. He blocked the sight with his open palm. "You're gonna blind me."

"You'll be fine," she said, and raised the camera. He moved his hand and turned away. Liz shot another picture, then set the prints on the top step while she shot a few more.

"You a photographer now?"

She shook her head, but took another picture, set it aside, and aimed the camera at him again.

"What are you doing?" he asked again. His voice had raised. He hadn't meant it to happen, but he was tired, he was hot, and he was stressed.

"I'm just taking a few pictures," she said. "Relax. I want to see something."

"You can't take them without me? I'd like to go sit down."

"No, I can't. I want you to be here when I take them."

"Whatever," he muttered and wandered into the bathroom.

Liz took another picture of the stairs while Jack pissed. He flushed and came back out to another flash of the camera. His vision danced with colored lights. The heat pressed in on him. The air clung to the insides of his lungs, heavy and thick.

While Liz amused herself, Jack looked around, wondering what they would ever use this floor for, wondering why his wife was crazy, wondering why it was so fucking hot up here.

Finally, he threw a hand up and said, "All right, you can stay up here all night, but I'm sweating to death." He went down the first step.

"Wait," Liz said. "One more."

She aimed the camera next to Jack, toward the banister, and clicked off a final picture. She scooped up the others, glanced at them and saw they were almost finished developing, then followed Jack downstairs.

In the kitchen, Liz peeked out the back door and saw Joey wandering around toward the back of the yard. She set the camera on the counter and fanned out the pictures. Jack was in the living room, taking off his shoes and lying down on the couch.

The last picture was coming into final focus and she looked at each one in turn, moving her head out of the way of the light. There was Jack, looking surprised and annoyed, and the backdrop of the third floor's main room behind him. Her eyes roamed the surface, hoping for that outline, that spectral light, that bit of proof Jack would need in order to believe. But in this light, all she saw was Jack.

She collected the prints and took them to the bathroom. She closed the door and fished around in the towel closet until she found an old make-up mirror, the kind with the small light bulbs at each corner. She plugged it in, set it on the closed toilet lid and sat down on the floor in front of it. She put the stack of pictures in front of the mirror and tilted it forward so those small light bulbs shone directly into the pictures.

Here was the first one, catching Jack by surprise. The lights showed nothing else. She moved on to the next one.

In the second picture, the last one taken, Jack on the stairs, Liz aiming at the banister, she saw a faint streak of light over Jack's shoulder, but whether that was movement on her part, or the dead man Dengler, should couldn't say. And if she didn't know, it would never convince Jack.

In the third picture, she struck what she thought was solid gold proof.

Jack's back turned to the camera and his face reflected in the bathroom mirror. There, hovering right above Jack, Liz saw two tiny white points of light, like eyes. And in the mirror, more detail. Along with the eyes, she thought she saw the outline of a head.

She swiveled the light bulbs closer, leaned her head in, and strained to see into the picture, trying to make sense of the light before jumping to conclusions. She had to be sure before she took it to Jack. If he found any weak spot in her proof, he'd seize on it.

She set this picture aside to come back to, and moved on to the rest of the stack. But that one shot was the only one that revealed anything other than Jack. She set the rest on the floor and put that other one back on the toilet lid.

Then she pulled two more shots from the back pocket of

her shorts. She'd taken these before Jack got home.

She looked down at the translucent image on Milo Dengler's dead body hanging from a phantom rope over the top rail. He looked just like he had earlier when he'd trapped her on the stairs, except this time he wasn't staring at her.

The second picture she'd taken outside. It showed Joey in the foreground with the house behind him. She'd taken this picture soon after they moved in. It was only today, though, that she'd taken another look at it--at first, just trying to find the changes in him, thinking that might be proof enough for Jack-- and saw one of the children watching them from one of the third floor windows.

That was when the solution came to her. She had rummaged through the bedroom until she found the camera again, and was hopeful to see she still had almost the entire film cartridge left.

She ran upstairs, stood on the top landing, aimed at the railing Dengler had hung from, then snapped the photo. Then she hurried down, not wanting to stick around in case he decided to show up again. And standing in the kitchen, watching the grey film darken, then see shapes forming and color and light crystallize, she saw him, Milo Dengler, dead and transparent.

"There it is, Jack," she'd said out loud. "You can't deny this one."

And then she realized Jack could deny anything he didn't see for himself.

She set the camera aside and would take more when he got home, when he was there to see her snap them, to see them shoot from the bottom of the camera, to see them develop, and then he couldn't deny it anymore.

But they'd all come to nothing, except the vague implication of eyes above Jack's head. And looking at it again, now, Liz thought, I don't know. It's all just faint enough, he might be able to not see it.

"Shit."

She looked again at the picture of the figure in the window, then looked at Joey just below, standing mid-yard between Liz and the house. He stood with his head titled back, one arm raised high with the fingers spread wide. His mouth was pulled back in a wide smile. Spring was only then beginning to wind down and the constant apprehension of when the next shadow would pass the corner of her eye or the next dead voice come down the hall were still weeks away.

She wished she could go back to that time, just after moving in, when everything was still good and the future was still hopeful. Now what did she have to look forward to? Wondering if she was going to be able to sleep through the night, or if something was going to shock her awake with its frigid touch?

Fuck that, she thought, I'd just go back to a month before we came here. Tell Jack to find some place else. Christ, I should have made him bring us up to look at it before we just moved right in.

But that wouldn't have helped, and she knew it. At the time, she just wanted someplace that was home again, someplace where she wasn't worrying every time she came home that the house would be empty, that Jack and Joey would be gone. Even now she found herself with that nibble of worry at the back of her mind, and she always had to stomp it and tell herself again that Alex was years ago and she was better off.

And now she had her family. And Jack wasn't going anywhere. And whether Joey called her Liz or mom didn't matter because she loved him like he was her own and she was pretty sure he felt the same way.

She looked up, wiped her eyes, and realized she hadn't even been aware of crying.

She blew her nose and gathered up the worthless pictures, stuck the other three back into her pocket, and put away the make-up mirror.

Jack was in the bedroom, lying down with his guitar draped over his stomach and his fingers strumming near-silent chords. She heard him and turned into the living room before he could stop her. She went outside and sat in a lawn chair against the house.

Joey was kicking a ball against a tree by the alley, then trying to catch it when it ricocheted.

Liz pulled the picture of Joey from her pocket and held it up. He was taller, and his hair was darker now. She tried to think back, but couldn't remember getting his hair cut since they moved to Angel Hill, but it looked, if anything, a little shorter than it did in the picture. Comparing the picture-Joey to the one in front of her now, she thought if not for the wrinkled pad of pink flesh at the top of his neck, she might not recognize him at first.

So just take Joey and go back to Houston.

And go to jail for kidnapping. Even if I took him to Allen's, he's not my son. I can't take him, and I won't go without him.

Then you'd better find some proof.

No shit.

She looked at the other two pictures, Dengler hanging from the rail, and the lights above Jack's head. Would he believe they were eyes? Would he see the outline of the head in the mirror, or would it be something else for him? Glare from the flash? Sunlight from outside bouncing off the mirror?

While Joey chased the ball across the yard, she went over the possibilities if she showed Jack the two she took earlier.

Best case scenario, he saw the pictures and it would all click in his mind. He'd see them for what they were and they'd all get the hell out of here.

Worst case, he'd think she was trying to pull something on him and get pissed. And right now wasn't the best time for them to go without talking to each other. She could tell he was still bothered by this afternoon at the hospital, even if he wasn't coming out and saying anything about it.

In the middle there were other possibilities. He could see the pictures and it would click for him and they'd try to figure out a way to deal with it. Not great, but better than nothing. Or he could see the pictures and at the very least notice the change in Joey. That might be enough to make him realize something was going on, even if he wouldn't accept what it was.

Joey's laughter broke her concentration. She looked up and saw him standing at the back of the yard, pointing and laughing. She followed his finger. He was pointing at the window across the alley. Was the naked woman standing there again?

Jeez, she thought, get a nightgown, or something.

"Joey," she called, "don't point. And don't laugh."

She glanced over and saw the old woman's eyes peeking out from behind the curtain.

"Liz?"

She jumped a little, then looked over her shoulder. Jack was at the screen door.

"Yeah?" She tucked the pictures under her thigh.

"Come here for a second?"

She got up, shoving the pictures into the back pocket of her shorts. "Stay in the yard, Joey," she called before going inside.

Inside, she waited for Jack to speak, wondering what he was going to say. A tingle at the back of her skull said, *He's going to leave you. Just like Alex. You can't hold anything together, can you?*

Shut up, she answered. He's not Alex.

And Alex wasn't your parents. Remember telling yourself that when you first got married? You spent the first month wondering when he was going to leave you, just like your father left your mother. And then he finally did, didn't he? Your father, then Alex, and now Jack. And not only Jack, but he'll take Joey, too, and that'll be four men you've lost.

SHUT UP! she yelled inside her head. He's not going to leave me.

We'll see.

"I want to talk to you about this afternoon," he said.

She came back from herself and looked at him, certain he was going to say she was a horrible step-mother, and if she couldn't be a step-mother, there was no way she could be a mother.

"Okay," she said. Her heart pounded and her stomach fell three feet inside her. "What about it?"

"I want to know, right now, and with no bullshit, why you left Joey alone all night."

What was she supposed to say? She'd already told him why. Did he want her to lie? She couldn't, because that wouldn't solve anything. She'd have to tell him again and hope it got through.

"I left him alone because I was afraid."

"Of what?" he asked. His voice had a tone to it, an unasked question: Don't you know there's nothing to be afraid of? It's obvious. How stupid can you be?

"I'm not sure," she said, careful not to jump into anything she'd regret later. "He was taking a shower and then I was drying him off and I looked at him and he was totally different. I mean, it wasn't just the hair color or his eyes, but it was like I wasn't even looking at the same kid anymore, like he'd been replaced by a very bad duplicate."

"Aside from being ridiculous, that makes you leave him alone all night in a strange place?"

"I told you," she said, "I was scared. It freaked me out. I mean it wasn't just that, it was a lot of stuff, that was just one."

"So what else was it?" He turned to look out the back door and watch Joey. Liz heard Joey's high squealing laughter and wondered what he was doing now.

"It was just stuff, I told you." You're losing him, she thought. If you don't give him specifics, he's going to blow it off again. Tell him, dammit. "It was . . . I don't know. The house, and the heat, and I haven't slept for shit lately and--." Then she had an idea. Let him find out on his own.

"Let me show you this picture," she said. She pulled one from her back pocket, hoping it was the right one. She handed it to him, a silent prayer on her breath, and he looked down.

"Picture of Joey, so what."

She breathed easier at having grabbed the right picture.

"Well," she said, "just look at him. I found this yesterday," she lied. "I took it about a week or two after we moved in. Look at him, then look outside and tell me you don't see a huge difference. I don't know what to do, I don't know if there's something wrong with him or if maybe I'm the one going crazy, or what."

She stopped, urging him with her mind to look further into the picture, to see the girl in the window, to ask what it was so she could act surprised herself.

"You're not going crazy," he said. This time his tone was more *Don't be a silly goose*. She was glad. "He's just getting older. Kids go through growth spurts, you know?"

He stared at the picture and Liz looked outside. Joey stood at the back of the yard still, but now he was looking at the house, toward the top windows. Liz wondered what he was seeing and whether she should go to him, take Jack outside, leave it and keep hoping Jack saw the picture, or what.

He was taking his sweet time seeing her and Liz had to fight the urge to point it out to him. He had to see it himself, otherwise he'd rationalize it away.

She looked over again and saw Joey was walking around

now, kicking his ball in front of him, then following it at a slow pace. Whatever he'd seen in the window was gone, but he was bothered by it. Would he come inside? Would he say something to them about it? No. She knew he was seeing things, too, but he hadn't said a word about it yet. And he wouldn't, she figured.

Why not?

Hard telling.

What's happening to him?

Don't know.

Look at the fucking picture, Jack. What doesn't belong there? In the corner. In the upstairs window, you dumb bastard!

"Speaking of pictures," he said, "you wanna tell me what was so important upstairs I had to go up there as soon as I was in the door? Because, really, I didn't see much point. If you wanted pictures, you could have done that without me."

She was blank now, because she hadn't thought to come up with an excuse for her behavior on the off chance nothing came of the pictures. She'd been so sure something would appear.

"I just," she stammered, "I didn't want to go up there myself."

Change the subject, she told herself. If you start blathering idiotic crap, you're better off not talking at all.

"Let me guess," he said, "because of the ghosts?"

She shrugged, glanced out the door, then turned around to the refrigerator.

"We're having pork chops for supper. What else do you want with them?"

"What I want is for you to quit playing stupid and tell me what's wrong with you? You don't leave a six-year-old boy alone in the hospital all night because you think he looks a little different. I'm not going to drop this until you tell me. This isn't some kid off the street, Liz, he's--"

"Your son?" she finished for him. "And let me guess, he's not mine, right? Is that where you were going?"

He stopped, looked down, but tried to shake his head no.

"Let me tell you something, I may not have given birth to that boy but I would die before I let something happen to him. I'm here with him every day and I see things changing, because I don't have my head up the Fett Tech ass or out playing with myself at someone else's house every weekend. So don't you dare give me that He's my son crap."

"I wasn't," Jack said. "I just meant--"

"What else do you want with your pork chops? I have to get it started."

He looked at her and her face was disgust.

You stupid asshole, she was thinking. I tried to come to you with this and you had to be a prick, didn't you?

"I don't care," he said. "Whatever we've got."

"Fine, I'll make mashed potatoes."

She turned around and started supper.

Jack recognized his cue and left.

I can't believe that came to nothing, she thought. I was so sure this would be it. And he'd see the girl in the window and ask me what it was and then he'd see it all and we could do something about it together. Christ! She got the pork chops from the fridge and tossed them on the counter. She kicked the refrigerator door closed. She banged a skillet. So sure.

Jack went into the bedroom, tossed the picture on the bed, and lay down next to it. He turned toward the wall, away from the door, and stared at Lily on her stand. She never yelled at him, nor misunderstood. She never jumped to conclusions. And she didn't insist the house be haunted.

He wasn't trying to draw lines between parent and step. He was just going to say Joey was his son--okay their son, was she happy now?--and she should have known better, should have more responsible, than to just up and leave him alone because she was freaked out over something so stupid as Joey looks a little different than he did when they moved here.

It's called growing. Everyone's doing it.

He reached out a hand and gave the strings a light strum.

And what the hell was that crack about playing with himself all weekend?

How about if he took Lily and swung her into the side of Liz's smart-ass mouth? No, he told himself. She's getting me pissed off over nothing. She was just aggravated when she said that. There's something going on alright, Liz. It's not ghosts, but there is definitely something. You're acting too strange.

He grabbed the picture of Joey again and stared at it, comparing this two-dimensional boy to the son he had in his mind, the one he saw every day.

Yes, there was a difference. Joey was smaller in the picture, but he was how many months older now?

There was nothing wrong with Joey. And Jack knew there certainly wasn't anything wrong with himself. That only left Liz and he didn't have to think hard to make a list of her strange behavior lately.

He heard her in the kitchen banging things around as she made supper.

Then again, another part of him pointed out, you have to admit, you don't really see him that much. Not as much as Liz does.

All the more reason I'd notice changes in him, he reasoned. Because if the change is gradual, she won't see it if she's here all the time. But I would. It's like seeing a person gain or lose weight. If you're around them all the time, you don't notice the change until afterward when you're looking at the before picture.

He looked at the picture again, scanning the whole thing this time, looking at Joey, at the house, at the girl in the third floor window--

He blinked, furrowed his brow, and looked again.

Yes, there she was, faint and half-obscured by sun glare.

But I'll be damned if it doesn't look like there's someone standing in the window.

Is that what touched me last night?

Shut up. Nothing touched you. You dreamed that.

Right. I forgot.

He looked at the picture again and she was gone, if she'd ever been there. Yes, there was still something in the window, but now that he really studied it, it could be anything from reflected light to distortions in the glass or smudges on the camera lens when Liz snapped the photo, all of them made to look like a girl in the window by suggestions from Liz and Jack's subconscious working together.

Then he wondered if Liz had seen the image. Maybe unconsciously she had and that had been the seed of her ghost theory. That made sense, didn't it? And ever since, every noise or shadow suddenly becomes a ghost.

Yes, that was it. His wife wasn't crazy, just impressionable.

Everyone will suffer now.

You can't save yourself.

The words went through him via his spine, expelling themselves through the goose bumps on his arms.

That had been his dream. And he'd heard it before, from the prank calls they'd gotten.

But that's all it was. Everything was fine. The world was normal. He'd figured it all out.

While his mind worked to convince him of this, Jack turned over and stared at Lily.

Liz had lost count of the dinners they'd eaten in silence.

While her frustration had begun to fade, she didn't know about Jack and if she tried to talk to him and he came back with a sarcastic or spiteful response, she knew she'd be right back to pissed, too.

So she kept quiet, ate her pork chops, shoveled mashed potatoes into her mouth, and tried like crazy to think of something to say that would have nothing to do with ghosts.

Joey had eaten half of his mashed potatoes, a few kernels of corn, but hadn't touched the pork chop.

Jack and Liz noticed it simultaneously, and they both said, "Joey, eat your supper."

Joey laughed at the stereo quality, but still only brushed at the food with his fork. Jack and Liz chuckled, glanced at each other, then stopped and looked down at their plates.

Joey said, "I'm full."

"You're not full," Jack said. "Eat."

Joey poked his fork at a piece of corn, but couldn't pierce it.

"Scoop it up," Liz said, demonstrating with her own fork.

"I like doing it this way," Joey said, then continued to try to spear the kernels that eluded him.

The silence dragged on another few minutes before Liz said, "So did anyone say anything about you being gone so long today?"

"Who's to say anything?" Jack asked.

Liz shrugged. She cut off another bite of pork chop.

"No," Jack said. "The load wasn't leaving today, so everything went okay."

"No calls from Aurora?"

"Oh no, they called. They always call. God forbid a day goes by that they don't call half a dozen times with three dozen things they need next day."

"I can't believe no one says anything to them about that." She chewed her pork chop. Joey slid some of his corn toward the potatoes, trying to hide them. "Eat your corn," she said.

"Why would they?" Jack said. "They pay for the shipping and every part they get from us they have to buy, also. Each plant is individual and anything that goes from one place to another better come with a bill and a receipt."

"Is that normal?"

"I don't know, really. It makes sense, I guess."

"I kind of figured company property meant company property no matter where it was."

"Maybe," Jack said, shrugging. "I don't know."

After Jack and Liz finished their food and Joey had convinced them he was done, too, Liz sent Joey in to take a bath.

After she put the dishes in the sink and threw away what little was left, she headed for the bathroom.

Jack was in the bedroom, leaning against the headboard with Lily resting against his knee. When he saw her pass by, he leaned toward the hall.

"I'm sure he's capable of washing his own hair."

"I'm sure he is," Liz said. "He's also capable of drowning if he slips and falls."

Jack went back to Lily, knowing he wasn't going to convince her of Joey's independence on this issue.

Liz closed the door and sat sideways on the toilet lid. Joey filled a plastic cup with bath water, then dumped it out, watching the silvery-clear stream fall.

Liz's breath caught and her vision blurred, then cleared and she wiped sweat off her forehead. The few stray strands of hair she'd found on Joey last night were thicker now, and there were more of them. She tried not to stare, and tried not to let it affect her like it had last night.

She'd had the day to think it over and she knew now that Joey was involved, too. She could handle this now.

She dumped water over his head, washed his hair, and rinsed it. He asked if she was going to wash him off, but Liz said, "No, I think you're old enough now to do that yourself."

He said okay and rubbed soap over his stomach from side to side like children do.

Liz stood in front of the sink, staring into the mirror, silently praying to be able to get through this without her reflection doing anything Liz herself wasn't doing, too.

She looked down into the sink and asked, "Joey? The day we went to find the horse rides . . . how did you know where they were?"

"Adam knows."

Her heart jumped a few beats and her stomach felt as if someone had shoved a large rock into the middle of it.

She took a deep breath, looked up into the mirror and asked, "Is Adam someone in the house?"

Joey was silent a second, then she heard the water pouring from the cup again. She glanced over her shoulder. Joey looked up. "Uh-huh."

Finally, she asked, "And when does Adam talk to you?"

"I don't know. Sometimes."

"What kind of stuff does he say to you?"

"I don't know. Stuff. He tells me about the people who used to live here."

"The Denglers?" Liz asked.

Joey nodded. "Uh-huh. But not just them. There was a preacher who lived here, too."

"And does he visit you, too?"

"No. But Adam tells me about him."

Liz felt her chin beginning to tremble and she ground her teeth together to stop it. She wiped her forehead again and sat back on the toilet seat.

"Like what?"

"They built the house for him."

"Who did?"

"The town," Joey said. He scrubbed at his face with a wet rag, then wiped his hand across his eyes. "Angel Hill. The preacher lived some place else, but Angel Hill wanted him to

215

come here so they built the house for him as an insensitive."

"An incentive?"

"Uh-huh."

Liz heard something in the hall and she stood and moved toward the door. The noise faded and she heard Jack in the bedroom, strumming his guitar. Whatever had passed outside was gone.

"And what else does Adam tell you?"

"The preacher had some kids and he made them leave."

"What for?"

"Cause they were doing bad things to each other."

Liz frowned. She guessed at what he was talking about, but the whole matter was too disturbing for her to be discussing with her six-year-old stepson.

"They were twins," Joey continued. "A girl and a boy and they slept upstairs all the way and he came up one night and caught them and they had to leave and he didn't see them anymore."

"Does Adam ever tell you things about us?"

She took another deep breath, half-dreading the answer, half-hopeful it would be a no.

"Yes."

Her stomach sank another three feet inside her.

"What does he say?"

"He told me you're going to have a baby."

At this, any thought of further revelations from Adam were out of the question.

It was true; Liz had missed her period. But she hadn't told Jack, she hadn't even said it out loud to herself. And she couldn't be more than a few weeks along, nowhere near showing.

How did he know?

He just told you. From Adam.

"Joey, who's Adam?"

"He's one of the boys who used to live upstairs before his dad killed him. He hit him in the head with a big board. But that didn't kill him, so when Adam came back, his dad swung it at him again and a nail cut his throat and he died."

She could feel the onset of hyperventilation. She hadn't expected this level of knowledge from him. She knew he'd seen things and heard things, but she hadn't known he was talking to them. She stifled the urge to lose it, got control of herself.

"And have you ever seen Adam?"

"Uh-huh."

She got a towel out of the cabinet, set it on the toilet seat.

"He's older. He's got short dark hair, and he's taller."

"Do you know how old?"

"He said he was--" he stopped and looked up--thinking? Or talking to Adam?--and said, "twelve."

She handed him the towel and he took it and stood up. She unplugged the drain. Joey made a clumsy attempt to dry his head and Liz had to take the towel from him to do it. When he was standing on the rug, dried and slipping into clean underwear, Liz forced herself to ask, "Do you know what's going on up there, Joe?"

"Uh-huh."

She waited, but he didn't continue. She had to ask, "What? What are they doing up there?"

"They just want to get out."

"Who?"

"All of them."

"The children? Adam?"

"Not Adam. Adam's down here now."

"Where?"

He didn't say anything, but he stared at her and his eyes weren't his and the face, mostly Joey's, showed signs of someone else in the slopes and tones and the way he held it. She looked at the birthmark under his chin, the ragged run of pink flesh that everyone mistook for a scar. (*The nail cut his throat and he died.*)

Then she hugged him and felt herself beginning to cry for the six-year-old boy she'd fallen in love with and who was now only partly here anymore.

Chapter Sixteen

Jack spent that week conducting tours through the department. With Fett Tech in desperate need of customers, they'd invited busloads of people to take a look at their plant in the hopes of winning them over. Jack cringed every time a new group walked through the doors, knowing every second he spent with these people--showing them where the wave solder was, explaining to them that the dope room was for doping compound that went into the junction boxes and some of the cables to make them waterproof--would be time spent letting everything else fall to the side.

How many calls from Aurora was he missing? Not that he didn't enjoy the break from them, but he knew that just because they couldn't get hold of him wouldn't negate their need for box loads of parts sent next day air.

And what about all their other customers? Were their parts supposed to be put on hold, too, just to explain how an intercom is rewired to a bunch of people who probably aren't even that interested? Of course not. And with the hours cut to thirty-six, that didn't leave them a hell of a lot of time to do any catching up.

But God forbid any of that matter. Got to get the potential customers through here before dealing with the ones we've already got, right? He couldn't believe he'd ever been impressed with the way things ran here. Those few months ago seemed like years, already.

Someone asked why it was called a "Y" cable.

Jack pointed out the configuration of the assembly, how three separate cables ran from a center box in the form of a "Y", and he wanted to wrap the thing around the moron's neck until he stopped being so stupid.

Liz spent the week going through *The Outsider's Guide to Angel Hill*, wondering at all the weird crap that had gone on here. She wondered how much of it was authentic and how much hearsay.

On Thursday, she called Arthur Miller personally--the

bookstore name and phone number was printed on the back cover--and asked him about her house.

"You live in that house?" was his initial response.

"Yes," Liz said. "We moved here a couple months ago. My husband bought your book and it's very interesting--." He chuckled and thanked her. "--but what I'm wondering is, has anything other than the Dengler thing happened here? Do you know anything about anyone who lived here before or since?"

"Well, the second part's easy," he said. "No one's lived there since Milo Dengler. Just about everyone in town knows the house and knows what happened there. Your case, someone from out of town, is about the only way they were going to unload that place."

I'm not surprised, she thought.

"And what about before? Do you know anything about the first people to live here?"

"Yes," he said. "Some. I know the first occupant was a preacher named Keeper. He and his wife and their children--he had twins, boy and a girl--lived there. Why a preacher with only two kids needs that a big a house, I don't know, but I do know that when the kids was in their teens, Keeper found 'em upstairs together."

Yes, Joey had already told her that.

"Story goes he kicked 'em right out and never saw them again. Now, the story also says the kids were sharing a bedroom upstairs, one more thing I don't get, but that's the story. I mean, even a preacher has to know better than to put two repressed teenagers together."

"But they were brother and sister. Worse, twins," Liz said.

"I'm not saying it was normal, that's just the story. I'm only saying, there are a lot of rooms in that house. Surely those kids could have had separate rooms."

Liz moved away from the phone for a second and listened. Joey was in his room.

"But the preacher kept that extra room for guests, as I hear it."

"There's lots of rooms here," Liz said.

"There's more now," Arthur Miller said. "At first, the bottom floor was a stable. The Keepers only lived on the top two floors. I believe there's a room on the second floor he used as a study. And the bedrooms were upstairs. Well he came up for bed one night, heard 'em in there, and when he looked in to tell them to go to sleep, he found 'em doing stuff no parent ever wants to see their kids doing."

"What happened?" Liz asked.

"He kicked 'em out. Told 'em the devil had no place in his house and he gathered up their clothes, tossed 'em out the window, and that was that. They were gone."

"What happened to them?"

"I don't know," Arthur Miller said. "So far, no one's got a story for that. And since it was almost a hundred years ago, I doubt anyone will."

"And what about after the Keepers? Anything happen with the people who lived here after that?"

"Nothing I've heard of. The Keepers lived there another twenty or so years before the preacher died. I think his wife sold the house and moved away. I don't know, maybe she died, too. It was years before the Denglers moved in, surely someone else lived there in that time, but if they did, nothing happened to call attention. The Denglers were there for a while before . . . it happened."

Liz got off the phone with Arthur Miller with only minimal new knowledge. She wasn't even sure what she was looking for in the first place.

All work on the house had ceased, but she still went upstairs once in a while. She'd sit on the top landing, staring at the spot Milo Dengler had hung from, and daring him to reappear. Her courage came from looking at Joey, wondering where he was going and what would happen when he was gone. She'd watched the air in front of her, expecting to see him form from nothing, but he never appeared.

The girl moved through the room a time or two. And when Liz went downstairs, the noises on the third floor started again. During the night, the thumps and giggles coming down the stairs were almost every few minutes. How Jack could sleep through it, she didn't know.

She'd watch Jack sometimes when he came home from work, wondering if he was going to see the changes in Joey yet, wondering what he would say if he did.

He'll see sooner or later, she thought. *He has to. Eventually it's not going to be something he can deny or rationalize away.*

But will it be too late by then?

I don't know.

But he hadn't noticed yet.

How could he not? Was he blind, or stupid?

After the night in the bathroom, she never questioned Joey again about what was happening. She saw herself as knowing too much already. She could barely sleep and her appetite was gone. She told herself she had to deal with this and get on with her life because if she really was pregnant, she had more than just herself to think about.

But I have to think about Joey, too.

And you're not going to do him any good if you ruin yourself.

She'd try to take naps in the afternoons, but she could rarely sleep. She'd try to force food down her throat, but after a few bites, she felt she would puke if she swallowed any more.

During the long hot afternoons while Jack was at work, she'd start to feel helpless, knowing something was happening but neither knowing what it was, nor what she would be able to do if it happened right now. Despite the many rooms and three separate floors, the walls of the house began to close in. She'd go outside, but even then the feeling of something inside the house watching her remained. And if not that, the Angel Hill summer sun beating down would drive her back inside.

She wanted to blame most of her discomfort to the house and everything in it, but that nagging in the back of her head finally became too loud and she decided she couldn't avoid thinking about it any longer. Adam had told Joey something that Liz hadn't even admitted to herself yet. So finally she'd gone to the store alone, and when she came home, already stuffed into her back pocket with her shirt draped over it had been a pregnancy test. After seeing the results, she put the test back into the box, but the box in the bathroom trash can and changed the bag right then. It wasn't full, but she just wasn't ready to tell Jack yet that they were going to have a baby. There was something about it, something about Adam knowing before she knew that made her uncomfortable.

But even after seeing the results, knowing it was true, she knew she could only attribute some of her problems to the baby.

There was still the matter of the house and that feeling that something big was coming.

The entire week following her conversation with Joey in the bathroom became one long series of hours stretching into forever with no purpose and no end.

Once, she wished for whatever it was to just hurry up so she could eventually move on from it and lead a normal life again. And then she looked at Joey, so different now, and prayed for it to hold off a while longer.

Finally the weekend came and Liz breathed a small sigh of relief. Whatever was coming, hadn't yet.

On Saturday she woke up and that expectant feeling in the bottom of her stomach had lifted. Maybe whatever it was had decided it wasn't time yet. Jack said he was going to Charley's for an hour or two and when he got back they'd go to a movie maybe and then to eat.

Liz lay on the couch, exhausted from a night of waking up at every sound, wondering when the lot of them would thump down the stairs, toward the bedroom, coming for Liz, or for Joey. She had lit a cigarette, then remembered she couldn't smoke anymore. She wanted to lean up and stub it out in the ashtray, but she was so tired.

While she floated away, she kept an ear out for Joey in his room.

Since they'd moved in, Liz knew he'd grown at least three inches, and added at least twenty pounds. It was all she could do to keep him in clothes that fit. His face had thinned. His voice was deeper--not puberty-deeper, but not the high tones of a child anymore, either.

The birthmark under his chin was also a deeper red. This scared her the most.

Once during the week, she wanted to hit Jack in the head with anything hard to knock realization into him. How could he not see the change? He had to see it. Maybe he just wasn't letting himself see it consciously. Because then he'd have to admit something was happening and that would disrupt his perfect ordered world.

Still, he had to see it. He had to. He had to see that his six-year-old son looked more like a twelve-year-old boy he'd never met. There were still traces of Joe Kitch, but they were buried beneath the mask of Adam.

And if not for Liz having spent ninety-five percent of last night wide awake and listening, she'd take him outside right now, away from this house for five minutes. Maybe she would have driven Jack to Charley's and then taken Joey shopping or something. She would have done anything else besides lie on the couch and let the nothing of the house put her to sleep.

She would. If she weren't so damned exhausted.

But the rhythmic rush of the air conditioner in the bedroom across the hall, and the sunlight falling through the window to warm her shoulders, lulled her into the dark.

Jack pulled Lily from her case, wiped off her body, and sat across from Charley on a small stool in the Clark garage. He slung the strap over his shoulder and went down the strings, checking to see they were in tune.

Charley had tuned his before Jack arrived. While he waited for Jack, he asked, "So your wife still pissed?"

"I don't know," Jack said. "I don't think she's so much pissed now as she's just annoyed. It's not like a temper anymore-- she's just on edge, I guess."

"About what?"

"I don't know," Jack lied. He knew exactly what was bothering Liz. She hadn't mentioned ghosts since Monday, but he knew it was on her mind. It was in the way she jumped sometimes when the air conditioner kicked on, or when the phone rang with one of its stupid prank calls. Jack made another mental note to himself to call the phone company and get the number changed just as soon as work quieted a bit and he could think. No, Liz hadn't said anything, but he knew she was thinking about it.

Was she at home now mad at him for going off to "play with himself"? She hadn't seemed mad when he left, but over two years with Liz told him she didn't have to act mad to be fuming. She knew how to hide it, and then when she let it go, watch out.

But she really did seem fine. And anyway, he was only going to be here an hour, maybe a little more. And they were going to spend the entire evening out together.

"So what's it gonna be today?" Charley asked.

"I'm thinking some--" and he played a Texas blues lick, something he'd heard on a Stevie Ray Vaughan record once, or at least an imitation of it.

Joey'd heard them talking to him all day. He could hear their voices floating down from the third floor and vibrating into his brain. He sat on the floor in his room with an army man forgotten in his hand, staring at the wall, into it, and on past, seeing only shadow. When his legs began to move and his body to stand, his brain was still focused on that dark. When his hands reached into the toy box in his closet and dug down, searching, and finally pulling free the rag doll, the plastic softball, the toy truck they'd left him, his brain saw only dark. When his feet moved him toward the door, into the hall, and up the first step, his mind was dark.

Adam looked down at the toys in his hands, clutched them tight in his fingers, and climbed.

Liz had dreams of Houston. She was coming home from work and when she walked in the door, she knew something was wrong. It was nothing apparent at first, because Alex hadn't taken much, just his clothes, a dozen or so CDs, and whatever knickknacks and whatnots he'd brought to the marriage. She sat on the couch, put her feet up, and sighed. She didn't notice the sheet of yellow paper taped to the television screen for a good ten minutes. But when she did notice it, she knew exactly what it was and she knew exactly what that feeling was, she knew what was wrong.

Her actions were in slow motion. She crossed the room with syrup-soaked feet, reached for the note with a reluctant arm, and pulled it from the screen with fragile fingers. Her chest expanded and sank in exaggerated motions as she read.

Wake up, Liz, because Joey's gone now and Adam is going upstairs and you have to wake up. Dengler is up there waiting for him. You have to WAKE UP!

She frowned. That's not what the note said. It had said he didn't see the marriage going anywhere, that he wasn't happy and he didn't think it fair to her to stick around just for her sake because he'd resent her sooner or later and he still cared about her enough not to put her through that.

She looked at it again. Her fingers shook because she remembered what it had said and she remembered how she'd reacted to it.

Liz! Wake up! The birthmark is bleeding and Jack won't make it in time. Wake up!

No, this was all wrong. She remembered it. And this wasn't how it happened. What was wrong? Why couldn't she see it? There was something. What? She looked at it again.

Joey is gone. Adam is here. Joey is gone. Adam is here.

Why was that familiar? Adam? Joey? She couldn't remember and it kept changing and she'd just come home to find her husband gone. But this wasn't how it happened. She looked around and noticed, now that she looked, what was missing from the apartment. Alex was gone. Joey was gone. Adam was here?

Joey!

She remembered and she looked at the note again. This time it had stayed the same.

Joey is gone. Adam is here. Joey is gone. Adam is here.

Christ! What did it mean Joey was gone? And Adam is here? Where's here? What did it mean? Where was Jack? She didn't even know Jack yet. Alex had just moved out and she wouldn't meet Jack for another few years.

She dropped the note. It floated to the floor and vanished before it hit. She went for the door to find Joey, but the door was gone and she ran from one wall to the next searching for the way out. Then she heard a piano. Someone was playing in another room. She went into the bedroom--the only other room aside from the kitchen which opened from the living room, and the bathroom which was way too small for a piano--and

226

found the little girl. Sarah. Her back was to Liz and she sat facing an upright piano, her fingers doing scales back and forth.

Liz stared at her for a second, wondering what this person was doing in her apartment when she should be in Angel Hill, haunting the third floor. And that thought brought something to mind, some piece of what was wrong, but it was just out of her reach and she couldn't fully grasp it.

She moved toward the girl and a final chord was struck. The tone hung in the air, vibrating in Liz's head, then faded.

"Why are you here?" Liz asked. Sarah sat up straighter at the sound of Liz's voice. Then she turned, rotating sideways toward Liz. The face was dead, but not rotted. The hair was lifeless, the skin pale. The eyes were glazed over. The girl opened her mouth.

"WAKE UP!!!" she screamed.

Adam topped the second floor and moved into the main room. His sister sat at the piano, ethereal, vague. Since their mother's death, the Denglers had done without a number of things, and while she hadn't taken a lesson in months, their father insisted she practice, knowing their mother would never want her to quit something she showed so much promise at. So she practiced. On the bench next to her sat her doll.

A shadow that resembled his youngest brother rolled a truck over the hills and bumps on the couch.

The middle brother had sat at the window for hours, rolling his plastic ball back and forth across the sill while he waited for their father.

Adam turned away from this scene, knowing it wasn't real, that the things he saw before him were just recordings the house had made, images, not even as substantial as the ghosts that roamed the house. These were just memories.

He passed the kitchen and saw himself making lunch for the others, just as he'd done that day. More memories, more images projected by the house. But not real.

He started up the stairs again and the front door banged open. The glass shattered and fell in a shower of sparkles. Stomping footsteps came toward him, up the stairs, and his father's image flickered in and out, hung over, haggard, and murderous.

The ghost-image Adam came from the kitchen to intercept, knowing how bad their father could be when he'd been drinking.

Adam stood on the stairs and watched the scene play out with transparent people.

"I've got their lunch done," the Adam-image said. "You can go lie down if you want. I'll take care of them."

His father grunted something and disappeared into his bedroom. In the past few months, he'd been trying to get the bottom floor turned into a separate apartment and renting it out for some extra money. The kids' rooms were on the third floor and Milo's was in the room off the second floor's main room, which they'd made the living room. They'd all been living only on the top two floors for a while and he'd learned to keep down the noise when their father was in bed.

The door closed, the children ate their lunch, and Adam sent them outside to play in the back yard. He stayed in to straighten up while their father slept. While he gathered a few toys scattered next to the couch, he heard something in his father's room. Creeping closer, careful to be silent, he listened closer. It sounded like crying. This was nothing new. Since their mother died, his father cried almost regularly. Whether in mourning or from stress, Adam didn't know. Since his father had started coming home drunk, Adam had learned to stay clear of his path and try to keep things at home in order.

While the Joey-Adam stood watching, the ghost-image Adam passed by on the stairs, went into the room that used to be his, and the door closed.

He waited. His heart beat hard in Joey's chest. Within seconds, his father's door opened and he watched a shadow that resembled his father float up the stairs. In its hand was a thick wooden board.

The day all this had happened for real, Adam wondered for a second where the board had come from, just before it slammed into his skull. Now that he saw his father brought it out from his room, he wondered again, *Where did it come from? Had he been planning this?*

The rest he didn't need to see; he knew it. His father came into Adam's room, caught him off guard, and swung. The board knocked him out, bringing a swell of black across his vision and a thump against the floor.

His father came out then, wiped his brow, and panted, "Everyone will suffer now."

Jack played a rhythm pattern against Charley's blues lead, letting himself sink into the sound and motion of playing. He didn't pay much attention to his fingers or the changes; he'd let himself go and his hands went where they should automatically.

While Charley went off on another run, in the back of Jack's mind, a thought was forming.

It grew form and substance and soon moved further up.

Charley turned toward Jack and did a fret-long slide to the top of the neck, slid his fingers into the rhythm Jack had established, and Jack took over the lead.

The divorce, raising Joey, supporting the both of them and still finding someone to take care of his son while he worked--through all of it, this had been Jack's release. At first, it had been hard to deal with and he saw himself having either an anxiety attack or a heart attack by the time he was thirty. But once he picked up Lily and began learning to play her in earnest, every night after Joey went to bed, this was his tranquilizer, this was his joint, his cold beer, his cigarette, his cookie, his orgasm, everything one might ever need in order to relax, Jack had found in this chunk of wood with the metal wires.

His first inspiration had been, of course, Hendrix. But after a while, Jack realized no one was ever going to emulate Hendrix. You could learn to play a Hendrix song, but that's all it would ever be, you playing a Hendrix song. So he went down a few steps, learning the original blues styles, then moving up again to the Texas Blues, Stevie Ray Vaughan in particular. SRV had been a huge Hendrix fan and his style was similar while not being as wild.

He bought as many SRV records as he could find and then got whatever videotaped concerts he saw. He bought the Stevie Ray Tribute video and watching that had led him to a number of other guitarists he would study. Within a year, he'd drowned himself in so much blues, he could play it without thinking. He let it come up from within, down in his gut, flowing out through his fingers.

It was something he didn't have to think about, just something that was, something that existed as its own thing with no other logic or thought. His fingers flew and his mind was free and his gut churned with deep things that came out and filled Charley Clark's garage with sound and feeling.

And that thought in the middle of Jack's mind came further toward the front while he played and fell away from the real world, a thought that said not everything had to have a logic behind it, because some things--like this--could just be because they were and that was all.

A part of him fought this notion, but another part felt the music rising up and felt the strings bend and slide under his fingers and this part knew that that might be right.

For one fraction of a second, he let himself listen to that thought and he found it spoke with Liz's voice.

"You want to find out what's wrong, go to the house and try the third floor. Whole bunch of stuff wrong up there."

And once that much was in, it was easier for other bits to sneak in.

"What I'm trying to tell you through your stupid fucking logic-haze is that Joey's brown eyes are now green."

And that was true, wasn't it? But how could that be possible?

The same way it's possible you didn't have a nervous breakdown after Joey's mother left. Feel those strings under your fingers, feel the neck against your palm, and the weight on your shoulder from the strap. Feel the sound coming from the amp, feel the way your spine tingles when you get the slide just right and it makes that sound that makes you feel like your slipping backwards out of the world. Some things just are because they are, without reason or thought. Sometimes there is a pattern, but it doesn't always fit the world you know. Like a chord pattern. Any combination of chords will fit together, but only certain progressions will make a person smile. So why can't Joey's eyes be green?

Because that means there really is something wrong.

That's right. So do something about it. Quit playing with yourself and do something about it!

His fingers broke off mid-note and the pick hit the concrete floor.

"Shit," he said.

Charley stopped strumming.

"What's the matter? That was gold, man."

Jack slid out of Lily's strap, set her aside on her stand, and switched off his amp. He dug his keys from his pocket.

"I'm sorry," he said. "I forgot I've got to get home for a little bit. I'll get Lily later, I've got to hurry. So, uh, keep playing. With any luck, I'm a moron and I'll be back."

With that, he was out the door. Charley stood dumbstruck, holding his guitar with his fingers positioned to strum again. Instead, he ended up standing there for at least two full minutes wondering *What the hell?*

Liz sat up with a gasp, wide awake and panting.

Where was Joey? She ran into his room, found it empty, then ran down the hall again, through the living room, into the kitchen, out the back door, hoping--praying--he'd gone outside to play.

He was nowhere. At the back of the yard, Liz called for him.

Across the alley, the old naked woman peeked out from behind her shielding curtain.

Liz looked up at the house, dread at seeing Joey, or worse--the little girl--staring down flooded through her. The windows were empty. But the house was different. She could see that. The white exterior had darkened to a dull yellow. The windows stared back, the back door hung open, inviting her, daring her.

A shadow passed over the house--the entire house, like a huge invisible cloud--and she took off at a full on run for the door.

"You can't save yourself," Milo Dengler whispered as he shambled down the stairs. "Everyone will suffer now. You can't save yourself."

The ghost-image walked through Adam on the stairs. Adam's skin broke out in gooseflesh. He wiped sweat from his eye and rubbed at a spot on his neck. When he pulled his hand away, he saw blood.

The ghost-Dengler disappeared before reaching the second floor. Adam went to the top and into the bathroom, stared into the mirror, saw the pink, wrinkled flesh on Joey's neck was an open wound and running with red in a sluggish flow.

From downstairs he heard Milo Dengler calling the others in from outside through the kitchen window. *Stay outside*, he thought. *Stay outside and be safe. Run.* He tried to push his thoughts outward toward his sister, *Take the others and run!*, then he remembered this was all past. Nothing he saw was real, just memories the house dredged up.

The ghost-Dengler came back up the stairs, followed by the three other children, wondering what their father wanted with them upstairs. Did he have presents for them?

No, Adam wanted to tell them.

He stood by helpless, bleeding, while the scene played out again before him. The wood, his father's desperate blows, the blood, the screams of terror from his brothers and sister, the hitching sobs from his father when it was done.

From the corner of his eye, he caught motion, and he looked and saw himself stumbling from the room, dazed, dizzy, shaking his head, wondering what was going on.

His father hears movement, he looks up from his wet hands, and he acts before he can think. The board swings around, cracks Adam in the jaw. He flies to the side, hits the wall, then looks over and sees his brothers and sister lying dead. He screams, then lunges forward. His father swings the board again, Adam tries to duck out of the way, the board misses, but a nail poking from the end catches the flesh below his chin, at the spot where his jaw meets his neck, and tears him open. Adam goes down, gurgling and sputtering blood. He dies within a minute.

And that's all Adam saw the first time.

The next few minutes are new to him.

Milo Dengler brings clothes from the childrens' rooms, dresses them, and takes them into the corner bedroom, Adam's room. He lines them up against the wall, sitting with their backs pressed against the wallpaper.

He kneels before them and whispers, "Forgive me," over and over, panting between words.

"*Forgive me*--(pant, pant)--*forgive me*--(pant, pant)--*forgive*

232

me."

While he pleads, his hands work a rope into a noose. When he's finished, he secures the noose to the top rail, slips it over his neck, climbs over, lowers himself so his face is even with the banister, then he drops. The fall isn't far enough to snap his neck, but the rope tightens around his throat and Adam can tell he wants to struggle, but as tears fall down his red, puffed face, he keeps his fingers clenched, one hand holding the other so he can't fight.

When the ghost-image dies, Adam stares at it, wondering.

It's still there. It hasn't vanished. In fact, it seems to have gained solidity.

Then the eyes snap open and move sideways to Adam. The mouth opens in a grin Adam can't discern between malicious and gleeful.

"Let us go," Adam says. The words barely make a sound in the silence.

The ghost stops grinning and mouths the word, "*No*."

Jack tried to use his mind to make the stop light turn green, but the damned thing seemed stuck on red as car after car after car passed him. He turned his attention toward the opposite green light, trying to will it yellow, but nothing happened. He closed his eyes, banged his forehead on the steering wheel, and yelled, "Let's go!"

When he looked up, he faced a green light.

He took off, squealing the tires, and leaving the driver behind him wondering what was with the crazy guy in front of him.

He'd made the drive from Charley's to his house over a dozen times, but couldn't remember it ever having taken so cocksucking long. It wasn't even that far. Hell, nothing in Angel Hill was far; the town wasn't that big.

Ahead he saw Roland Street and he knew he was close.

A truck pulled out in front of him and Jack slammed on the brakes. He skidded to a stop less than a foot from the truck. The driver flipped him off, yelled something, and then pulled away.

Jack's heart thudded. He looked over his shoulder and saw the stop sign he'd almost ran.

I have to pay attention, he told himself. *If not for myself, then for Joey and Liz. Get home, but do it in one piece.*

Adam moved away from the staring ghost that hung in front of him. He climbed to the third floor, then set the toys on the top step. The doll, the truck, the plastic ball. Then he stood back, turned toward his father again and asked once more, "Let us go."

His father didn't answer and Adam took that as a no.

He sighed. He looked at the toys and saw what looked like steam rising from them. Milo Dengler saw it wafting up and his face twisted, questioning.

He seemed to get an idea what might be happening and he opened his mouth. His voice came out dead and cracked, like an old record that's been played too many times. When he moved, his old skin broke like distressed paper.

"You belong here."

"No," Adam said. "You decided that. Why?"

While Adam talked, the steam from the toys rose, took shape, gained substance. His brothers and his sister stood at the top of the stairs, looking over the rail at their father.

Milo looked at his son, then over his shoulder and he saw the others.

He looked back at Adam, then he vanished.

Jack was out of the car almost before the engine stopped running. He leapt up the steps from the sidewalk, and was at the porch in almost four strides. He bounded up to the door and tried to go through, but it was locked. He fumbled with the keys, knowing which was the right one, but somehow unable to find the bastard. Finally another key fell to the side and revealed the front door key. He jammed it home, turned, and pushed. The door banged open, and then Jack noticed the broken glass. He could have stepped through at any time. He wondered for a second why the glass was broken, and if it was all connected to the third floor and whatever was happening up there.

He had to find Joey.

He flew down the stairs, ducked into Joey's room. It was empty. The house had an almost unreal quality, something he couldn't place, something foggy and dreamlike. There was a ringing, high-pitched whine in the air.

"Joe?" he called.

In the bathroom. Nothing. In their bedroom. Nothing. "Joe?"

Under the bed? No. He turned, saw smoke, ran for the living room.

Liz beat at flames that sprang from the floor and couch, coughing smoke and fighting the sting in her eyes.

Not a dream quality, Jack thought. Not foggy unreality, but totally real danger.

"What the hell is happening?" he yelled.

"I was asleep," she said over the smoke detector. "I had a cigarette. I guess it fell and caught the carpet."

You stupid bitch! Jack wanted to yell, but he had more important things to worry about right now.

"Where's Joey?"

Liz stopped batting at the flames and looked up at him. Her face was dumb and numb. "I don't know," she said. "I couldn't find him either. I went outside to look for him, but he's not out there. I came back in to look upstairs, but I saw the fire."

Jack turned back and ran for the stairs. Liz dropped the cushion she'd been using to beat at the flames, and took off after him.

Adam stood in the third floor's main room, a circle of ghosts accompanying, his brothers and sister, surrounding their father who'd reappeared semi-solid from the wall, stumbling and dead.

They caught him between them. He stood in the middle, looking from one to the next, first furious, but slowly calming, and finally looking at them pleadingly.

"Let us go," Adam said. Joey's shirt was soaked and stained, deep red. Blood flowed in a regular stream from his neck, but he seemed neither bothered nor weakened.

His father looked over. "No," he said. "You all belong

with your father. We didn't let anything split us up when she died; we won't let anything split us up now."

"Let us go," Adam repeated.

Then his father's calm face went back to angry and he sneered, "You can't save yourself."

"Let us go," Adam said for the last time.

"Everyone will suffer now!" Milo Dengler roared as he lunged for Adam.

His hands found the bleeding throat and inertia carried them both into the wall. Adam banged his head and reeled from the shock. He noticed a high ringing sound, wondered what it was, then his attention was brought back to the stinking, rotted, green thing in front of him.

It smiled, showing dead, grey teeth. Its eyes were mad yellow orbs. The breath it blew into Adam's face when it spoke made his stomach churn, like breathing old diapers and rotten fruit.

"Please," Adam said.

"No," Dengler yelled, then yanked Adam's arm, swinging him around and tossing him across the room. He flew through his sister, hit the opposite wall, and stumbled around.

He realized suddenly that he didn't know how to end this. There'd been no plan, just a wish. Since the death, they'd been trapped here, invisible in the house, but present, roaming, floating, haunting. Their father had been stronger and his hold unbreakable. But Adam was physical now and that surely had to count against the wraith.

He looked around and saw, for just a flash, his brothers and sister dead again as they'd been that day, bloody on the floor, and when he blinked it changed and their spirits stood again in the center of the room, their eyes big and begging, looking at their father.

"You can't go," he said. Adam saw his anger had once again washed away. The look he showed now was one Adam had seen countless times in his original twelve years, a father's love. "I didn't mean to hurt any of you," Dengler said. "I was trying to spare you."

"Then let us go," the girl said.

"I can't."

"Why?"

"I can't be alone. And if you go, I can't follow."

Adam took a step forward, calmly. There came a pounding from the roof--Liz and Jack would have recognized it, as would the exterminator Carl and Charley Clark--heavy, frantic, and Dengler glanced up for a second. Adam used that glance and lunged at the man, pinning his arms back and doing what he could to hold him in place.

He looked over his shoulder at the other three and said, "Hurry."

Jack and Liz bounded up the stairs, yelling for "Joey!"

On the second floor, they searched the rooms, hoping to find him, hoping he wasn't upstairs. The rooms were empty. They ran up the last flight and found Joey--no, this wasn't Joey.

Jack stared, wondering what had happened in the forty-five minutes he'd been gone. His son was gone. No, he could see bits of Joey in there, but it looked as if someone had done a bad job erasing Joey and then drawing this new person on top of him.

His chest thumped, his stomach sank. His throat had acquired a curious new lump.

How did this happen? How did I not see it?

He looked at Liz who was watching, in shock.

Joey stood hunched and pressing something into the wall. They had to stare at it for a second before they realized it was a man, struggling against the boy, but having a hard time of it.

"Oh," Liz said and Jack followed her eyes.

They saw three others, two boys and a girl--Liz recognized them--climbing the walls like spiders with their hands and feet. They stopped every few steps and looked back at Joey and the old man. Joey's face was strained. He was getting weak, they could see it in him.

The children scurried up the walls and crawled along the ceiling.

Where are they going? Liz wondered.

She saw where they were headed and heard the pounding coming from the roof again. She thought, "So simple. All they have to do is get out."

They were headed for the trapdoor, which led, not only to the crawlspace, but up to the roof as well.

"What's happening?" Jack asked.

Liz said, "They want out."

Jack's head pounded and he had to stop and think--he was forgetting. What was it? Then the drilling, shrieking sound woke him up and he remembered.

"Liz, the fire."

"Shit!" she yelled, and took off down the stairs. She got to the top of the last flight before seeing how far it had spread in such a short time. They'd only been upstairs just over a minute--maybe--and already it had grown down the hall. Flames licked upward, threatening to catch Liz if she came down any further.

The phone was down there; there was no way to call for the fire department. The most she could hope for was to get Joey out of here and hope one of the neighbors called. If not, they could call as soon as they were out.

She ran back up and told Jack, "We've got to get him and get out."

"What?"

"The fire," she said. "It's covered the first floor and it's coming up the stairs. We have to get Joey and get out before it blocks the door."

"How?"

"I don't know."

Jack looked at his son, struggling to hold the big man in place.

"Joe, we have to get out of here," he called.

Joey either hadn't heard him--which Jack didn't think likely, he was ten feet away--or he wasn't listening. Jack didn't know exactly what was happening, but whatever it was didn't lessen the urgency to beat the fire to the front door. Once that was blocked, so was their only exit.

The man shoved Joey off him, into the rail where he almost went over the side. Jack lunged to catch him, but Joey got his balance and held himself up.

Before anyone could stop him, the man ran to the wall below the crawlspace and snatched the children from it, tossing them to the floor again. One dodged him, but couldn't lift the trapdoor out of the way.

Something crashed downstairs and Liz took off to see what it was. Jack hesitated a moment, not wanting to leave Joey, then followed anyway. He had to know what was happening down there, how much time they had, whether anything was blocking the door besides the fire.

They got halfway down the flight leading to the front door when they saw how far the fire had reached. On the bottom landing, looking through the flames, Jack could see patches of unscorched wall, but the flames were closing in on those, too.

"How?" he asked. "How does a fire spread this quickly?"

"Maybe the house is doing it," Liz said. "Maybe whatever's going on up there with Joey is screwing with things in the house and it's trying to get rid of it all."

"Houses don't have wills," Jack said. "It's just a house. Despite anything inside it, it's just a house."

The flames took over the first flight of stairs. They retreated up the second flight to the second floor, then saw the fire was moving to the ceiling. In the case of the stairs, it was burning the underside of the flight leading to the third floor landing.

"Shit," Liz said.

"Go call the fire department," Jack said.

"On what?"

"Across the street. Hurry! Go!"

He gave her a shove toward the stairs and she finally got moving, dashing down the flight, close to the wall, away from the fire. At the door, Jack saw her stop, wondering how the glass got broken, then he yelled down, "Just go!" and she went, out the door and out of sight.

Jack leapt up the third flight. Halfway, the entire thing collapsed under him. He fell onto the bottom flight, knocked his head against the charred wood, and was out.

The heat awakened him and he couldn't have been out for more than a few seconds. But that was enough time to be pinned under more falling burning wood. He pulled himself up and hauled his weight to the landing. He glanced out the door and saw Liz across the street, banging on a door.

She fell asleep, he thought. *She was smoking and she fell asleep.*

239

All this from a cigarette?

The frame above him cracked and creaked. He had a split-decision to make. Out the door or risk going up again. The decision was made before it had fully formed. Joey was upstairs.

Jack got to his feet and hopped to the second floor. He must have knocked his knee in the fall, too. Standing on it hurt and it wouldn't bend very well. How swollen would he be all over by the time he and Joey got out of here?

A run of four or five stairs were missing from the third flight, leaving a hole Jack didn't think he could bridge with his sore leg, never mind the flames dancing up through it.

But he'd have to try.

Looking up, he heard a voice cry, "Don't leave me alone!"

What was going on up there?

The front door was nearly blocked now, but he would have to chance it anyway.

The smoke in the house was horrible now, stinging his eyes, filling his lungs. It made forms in the room, swirling ethereal shapes. One looked like people, a boy and a girl, arm in arm. Parts of the smoke evaporated and the boy and girl changed to look like skeletal, rotten figures, still arm in arm.

What in the hell had happened in this house?

There you go again, he told himself. *Wasting time trying to figuring it all out. Just don't fucking worry about it and get your son!*

That's what he had to do.

He moved back a little, flexed his leg. The pain in his knee shot up his back, but he flexed it a few more times anyway, trying to work it out. He took the best, widest stride toward the stairs he could, up the few that remained, and leapt, reaching with his arms straight, his hands open, his fingers searching for purchase, through the flames.

His hands closed, one on a step, the other on the rail. His chest rested on a step. He wrenched himself up, straining from the struggle, sweating from the fire, fighting against the burning in his chest.

He got himself up enough to lessen the pain and finally wriggled himself to his feet. On the landing, the wood cracked. He rushed a prayer through his head, *Please, God, keep the house together long enough*, and went up the last flight, limping.

The third floor was shrouded in smoke.

"Joey," Jack called. He waded through the fog, heat rising behind him, sweat pouring down his face and blurring his vision, watching for Joey or one of the others he'd seen up here, careful not to bump them.

You can't bump a ghost, he thought. Still, he kept his eyes out, just in case, for all the good they did in this mess.

The landing crackled again, then collapsed behind him. He turned, saw, then turned back and called again, "Joe! Come on. We've got to get out of here."

"Help me," Adam called.

Jack found him through the smoke, standing below the trapdoor.

"Where is he?" Jack asked.

"They're holding him while I get this open. But I can't reach it."

"Here," Jack said and lifted Joey onto his shoulders. This new version of his son was much heavier, but taller too and with Jack's help he was able to slid the trapdoor aside and lift himself high enough into the crawlspace to lift the roof hatch cover out of the way, too. The pounding from the roof stopped and when the cover was clear Jack looked up and saw someone staring back at him.

"Wha--?" he asked.

A woman. Her face beamed with something that looked like relief and then she thrust her arms into the hole in the ceiling, fingers reaching.

The children saw this and immediately leapt off their father and climbed the walls again. Their mother grasped their hands and hauled them all up through the hole and out of the house.

The man, Dengler, clutched Jack by the arm, spun him around.

"You won't take them from me," he said. Foul smoke blew into Jack's face. He winced.

"I just want to get my son. We'll leave. Just give me my son."

"These are my children."

Jack pulled out of the dead man's grip, turned, and dove into the smoke in search of his son again.

"Come on, Joe!" he called.

There were screams behind him, whether from pain or fear, he didn't know, but the sound they made sent shivers up his back. His hands stuck out in front of him, the fingers flexing, searching. The smoke had gotten worse and he could see almost nothing at all.

"Joe!"

"Go, Jack!" someone said. It sounded like Joey, but it was deeper, older. "You can't help him now. I'm sorry."

"What?" he yelled through the smoke.

"I really am."

Rough hands shoved him out of the way and the dead man held his hands up to the hole in the ceiling, reaching for the children as they rose out of sight.

"Don't leave me alone!" he screamed up at them.

The children looked down, their faces peaceful, brilliant.

"Don't leave me alone!" the dead man yelled again. He roared and thrashed his fists about, knocking them into the walls, nearly shaking the house in his rage.

Jack looked back at the stairs. The fire had claimed the second floor and the stairs were blocked. He was trapped.

He went to his knees and crawled across the floor, his hands out in front, still searching.

The house crackled and popped around him. The smoke in his lungs threatened to choke him, but he couldn't give up until he found Joey.

Then his fingers hit something warm and fleshy.

He grasped it and pulled it to him. Joey's skin was red, but the red came off on his hands and he saw it was blood.

"Jesus Christ," he said. "Joe." He shook him, tried to sit him up, opened his eyes and checked his pupils. He found the wound under Joey's chin, the birthmark of pink skin, now turned into an open wound. Joey's shirt was soaked in blood. He saw beneath the red how pale Joey's skin really was.

The dead man roared again, knocked Jack aside, stumbled across the room, vanished into the wall, and the smoke closed in around him. Jack heard a thunderous crack, felt the floor shift beneath him. He reached for Joey, then lost everything to blackness and gravity as the floor collapsed under him.

Chapter Seventeen

When Jack found out that the Fett Tech layoff included everyone hired in the past six months, he wasn't disappointed.

He could always find good work, and the further from Angel Hill, the better.

They'd live off the insurance from the house for a while, though. At least until the cast came off his leg. The fire inspector, who'd lived in Angel Hill all his life and remembered the day the Dengler children were found dead up in that third floor bedroom, ruled the fire was caused by old wiring. The house was about a hundred years old, after all. Neither Jack nor Liz mentioned the cigarette.

The insurance check came while Jack was in the hospital. Liz had handled everything. Charley Clark and his wife let her stay with them while Jack was laid up, but she spent most of her time at the hospital anyway.

One day Liz was sitting in the Clark living room, going through the phone book, when her eyes fell on a picture hanging across the room. She got up and crossed the room, staring, trying to figure out what it was about the picture that drew her eye. There were four people, two men and two women. One of the men was Charley, about ten years younger, but definitely Charley Clark. And then it hit her. One of the women in the picture was Judy. Her neighbor from up the street, the one who said she'd known the Denglers. As Liz stood staring at it, Charley's wife, Susan, came into the room and Liz asked, "Who are these people with Charley?"

"Those are his brother and sisters," she said.

"I think I've met this one," Liz said, pointing to Judy.

"Yeah, Judy. She just lives up the street from your old house, didn't you know that?"

"Nope. I've met her once or twice, but I didn't realize she was Charley's sister. Hmm. And the other two?"

"Boy, Charley just doesn't tell people anything, does he? That's his brother Ron and their other sister, Rachel. She lived in your house, I can't believe he never told your husband about her."

"She lived in my house?"

"Well . . . yeah. Her husband was Milo. She died, though. Cancer. It was really rough on Charley and the others, but when Milo did that . . ." she stopped. She shook her head. "I'm sorry, I just can't believe Charley never said anything about it to you guys."

"Well, we knew about what happened there," Liz said. "Obviously. But we didn't know you guys were related."

There was a moment where neither knew what to say next, broken with the ringing of the phone. It was Jack, asking if Liz could bring Lily with her when she came out.

"No, I'm not bringing your guitar. They're not gonna let you play that thing in the hospital."

"I'm bored," he said.

"I'll bring you a book, you goon. Read something for a change."

He told her which book to bring.

When she got there, she handed him the book and Jack opened it and started leafing through it.

"I told Charley once that someone rational enough to seek the honest answers could explain everything in here," Jack said.

"Still think that?"

"I don't know what I think anymore." He set *The Outsider's Guide to Angel Hill* on the tray beside his bed. His original copy had burned with everything else in the house, so Liz had had to stop and pick up another copy. "But I'm very happy to still be an outsider, and very eager to get out as soon as possible and never come back."

They talked about where to go. Houston was brought up, but it was decided to set their sights on someplace new. Maybe use the insurance check to build a new house somewhere. A small house. One story.

When Liz told Jack the house would have to have an extra bedroom, then she rubbed her stomach and smiled, Jack's grin wrapped almost around to the back of his head.

Then Jack asked, "Hear that, Joe? You're gonna have a baby brother or sister."

When the third floor collapsed, it crashed into the

second floor not far below. Jack's head thudded against the floor and his vision went blurry for a second. He leaned forward and found Joey's leg, then wrapped his fingers around it and tugged. He pulled his son to him, hauled him into his arms, and forced himself to his feet.

What remained of the ceiling above him rolled with fire, threatening to fall on top of him at any second. He buried Joey's face against his chest and went to the front window, staring down and trying to decide whether he thought they could make the jump. If he laid himself out flat and took the impact on his back, Joey's fall would be muffled. Jack, however, may break his back. Okay then, that would be plan B.

Limping into the kitchen and dining room proved just as useless; the first floor living room was under the second floor dining room, and that's where the fire started. The closest he could come to the dining room was looking at it through the doorway.

The front door?

The stairs were ablaze and bright with orange and yellow and red, dim in places with thick black smoke.

If he was quick enough, he might make it.

The fire wrapped them like a blanket. Jack slipped out of the world and let memory take him down, telling him where was the last step, where was the door, without Jack having to see for himself, since the smoke was too thick and the fire too blazing to let him see anything. He hugged Joey closer to him and moved down the stairs, through the heat and smoke, going in a blur, not thinking, just moving, just getting down and out and into cooler air and clearer vision. The fire snapped and reached for him, trying to draw him back in. Then he heard broken glass crunch underfoot, felt his shoulder bump the open front door, stumbled to the side, out the door, leaping past the stairs down the porch, and finally tumbling over himself into the yard, still clutching Joey to him.

He crawled out into the yard with his knees and one arm, the other wrapped around his son. At the edge of the yard, he collapsed, then rolled over and let himself pass out. Before he did, he looked up at the inferno raging before him, fire spilling from the windows and roof, and thought, *That's really beautiful.*

The fire department came, as did paramedics.

Jack was unconscious, so they asked Liz what had happened to Joey; he was covered in blood. She said she didn't know. They found no wounds. They asked about the scar under his chin. She began crying and said it was just a birthmark.

It had only been a week, but Liz could see the changes in Joey. Whatever had happened to him, whether he'd become Adam, whether he'd always been Adam somehow (Joey was six, Adam died six years ago, after all), or whatever, she thought it was reversing itself. Quicker than it had come upon him, things were different. He was shorter, for one, and in those seven days, his hair was blonde again.

Jack and Liz hadn't been alone since it happened--what would they do with Joey? And anyway, neither of them wanted him out of their sight--so they hadn't had the chance to talk about any of it. The thought on both their minds was *What does Joey remember?*

He'd been unconscious for almost two days.

At first the paramedics thought he was dead, then they got a pulse and slight breath sounds. Smoke inhalation had gotten to him, and there was all that blood they couldn't account for, but he would be fine. Even the fact he didn't wake up for two days didn't alarm them too much. Whatever'd happened had left him drained and his body would take time to recharge.

If asked, he'd say the only thing he remembered was waking up and not being able to see. Everything was blurry and mixed. There was something above him, some vague, faceless form. He would have thought (but not said) it looked just like his mother did in his dreams and he'd felt happy. Then the blurriness faded, replaced by form and detail, and Liz stood above him, and he'd felt even happier then.

On the day Jack left the hospital, Joey was a smiling six-year-old. Maybe not fully back to his old self yet, but he would be.

Liz decided she wouldn't tell Jack that the children who'd been murdered in their house were the niece and nephews of his friend Charley. If Charley thought it was important that Jack know, he could tell him himself.

Liz, Jack, and Joey had other things to concern themselves with now, new lives to start, not just the one inside her, but for all of them.

The house had been destroyed. The stone walls stood empty and charred, but everything inside was ash. Liz drove by on the way to get Jack from the hospital. Joey was asleep in the back seat. She stopped the Jeep and stared at the ruins, then smiled. The whole event had been a hell of a thing, but they'd all come through it. It was like she'd thought all those weeks ago. No matter what happened, they could only scare them, they'd never be able to really hurt them. And, bruises aside, that was the truth.

She wondered if the children had got what they were after. What had happened to Milo Dengler? What would happen with the land? They certainly weren't keeping it. If, sometime, a new house were built here, would thumping sounds in the hall awaken the occupants?

"I think it's all done," Joey croaked from the back seat.

Liz put her foot on the gas and the car lurched up the hill, away from the house.

"What's that, Joe?"

"I said I think it's all done. They got out. He just didn't want to be lonely there by himself. But they got out."

She nodded and smiled into the mirror at him. "I see," she said. *Change the subject,* she thought. *Don't talk about it right now, not yet, not this soon. Don't ask him anything. Let him be a six-year-old again for a while. Maybe later, some other time.*

"What color would you like your bedroom to be in our new house when we build it?" she asked. "You can pick any color you want."

He was quiet a second and she wondered what he was doing. She glanced back, saw he was watching the ceiling with roving eyes and a grin on his face, and she knew he was thinking it over.

"How about," he said, "um, how about . . . waffles."

Liz smiled. "Waffles?"

"I like waffles," he explained.

"Waffles it is," she said.

The empty lot faded behind them.

247

Good riddance to it, she thought. This place was never home, no matter what she'd felt or thought. She rubbed her stomach. Next time. That'll be home. And for the first time, she felt secure in that.

She turned the corner, glanced into the rearview, and took her last look at the ruins.

Thanks for reading THE THIRD FLOOR. I hope you enjoyed it. For more on Angel Hill and the house on 4th street, please enjoy this free bonus story, "In the Presence of Loneliness":

IN THE PRESENCE
OF LONELINESS

"Are you into weird situations at all?"

Now there was a question. It was certainly the last thing he'd expected to be asked when he called looking for an apartment to rent, but over the past month his desperation level had risen to unknown heights and his reply was immediate and without hesitation.

"Man, I'm into whatever situation gets me out of my parents' basement. I'm 35, single, and I can't be 'that guy', you know?"

"Well, I do have a house that I need to get someone into," the landlord said over the phone. His voice wavered briefly and Tom couldn't tell if it was bad reception or hesitation. "It's near downtown--"

"Perfect," Tom blurted.

"Well, it's, like I said it's a weird situation. My wife and I manage some properties for a company in California who are expanding out here and they need someone to occupy this house while it's being renovated."

Again, he didn't care about the specifics, as long as, at the end of the day, he was out of his parents' basement for good. Then a thought occurred to him.

"Would I have to help with any of the renovations? I'm not great with stuff like that."

"No," the landlord said. "That's all taken care of, we've got a contractor working there with a couple other guys and they're doing all the work. All you'd have to do is live there. Rent free. Pay for your food and cable, if you want it, and stuff like that. The owners just don't want the place to stand empty while the work is going on and all that equipment is there. I mean, you'd obviously have to keep the place clean, take out the trash and stuff."

"That sounds perfect. Can I take a look at it?"

"Sure, any time you're available."

"Is now too soon?" He didn't want to sound pushy, but his excitement was getting the better of him. If asked, he'd have said it had been the words "rent free."

"Sure," the landlord said. He gave Tom the address on Fourth Street and said he could be there in ten minutes. Tom hung up, pocketed his phone and left his parents' through the garage.

His "situation" had been far from ideal the past month. The split had been sudden and he'd had time enough to grab the essentials. His clothes, tooth brush, computer and a handful of CDs went with him and that was basically all he'd been living with the past four weeks. He still didn't fully understand the break-up but when he looked back he saw how distant Julie had been and, when he thought about it, he knew the signs had been there. But none of that helped him to understand why. Most likely he never would. All he could do, he felt, was try to get on with things the best he could, tackling the issues of the present.

His room in the basement was cozy, furnished with a couch--on which he slept--and a TV, plus a bathroom over to the side where the washer and dryer were situated. A door to the garage provided private access coming in or going out. But there was that damn door at the top of the stairs.

Tom told himself he liked his privacy and when he came downstairs he shut the door behind him. But when his mother came down to get laundry or otherwise check up on him, God forbid she make sure the door click behind her on the way up. So Tom was left in the basement watching television or reading with a half-opened door, which was placed midway between his parents' dining room table and their television, either listening to his aunts cackling around the table as they played cards or the crime shows his father always watched with the volume blaring because the old man was nearly deaf.

This is what he told himself, but it wasn't the whole truth. The truth was, all that noise and laughter upstairs just made him miss Julie and the times they had together. He missed having someone to watch television or even just share a meal with. He could go upstairs, sure, but it wasn't the same and, he felt, would probably just make him feel even lonelier. There would be people and company, sure, but it wasn't home.

So he decided to get his own place and get back to living.

And once he saw the place, Tom's first thought was, "Oh hell yeah."

The house was three stories if it was an inch. The top two floors were still under construction and a sheet of plastic hung in front of the stairs leading to the second floor. The front door entered onto a landing with stairs to the left going either up or down. The bottom floor, where Tom would be staying, opened onto a long hall running the width of the house, with two rooms on either side, two bedrooms at the front of the house and a living room and kitchen at the back. The bathroom was to the right of the stairs.

The place still held onto a faintly smoky smell, but the landlord assured him it would be gone when everything was done.

Tom loved the house immediately and the landlord gave him an application to establish character and employment and they parted ways. A few days later, Tom was moving in.

To make the house feel like home he borrowed the couch from his parents that he'd been sleeping on plus a chair and a television, then bought dishes and groceries and a small table which would double as a desk when he was on the computer. His parents had an old box spring, which he bought a mattress for and Tom suddenly had a real bed again

He liked the house the first couple of days. He liked the feeling of coming home to a place that was his. He liked the quiet. On the third night, however, the quiet closed in around him like a cocoon and he had to escape and go for a drive. That too proved to be too solitary as he found himself driving past restaurants where he and Julie had eaten or stores where they'd shopped, and while those places were full of people in the midst of living, none of them were Tom. The emptiness had followed him. So he went home and went to bed, hurrying the process of morning and work, which always kept him busy and too preoccupied to think about how much he hated his new life.

That was the night he thought he heard mice, scratching behind the walls, scurrying through the plaster and lathe, trying to get out.

It didn't take much to convince him to get out of bed

and go buy poison right away. Thirty minutes later, the green blocks were in place and Tom was back in bed.

The next day the workers returned to the house and his loneliness was gone.

He met the lead man, Henry, and they shook hands and Tom asked if there was anything he could do and Henry said, "Just don't touch anything and let us know if the dust gets to be too much."

"I will," Tom said. He met the two other workers, shook eagerly, glad to have more than his own presence in the house for a change, but Rodney and Taylor--those were the names of the workers--didn't seem interested in letting Tom into their club, so he went back down to his part of the house and tried to decide what to cook for dinner. A frozen pizza would do, but he had a better idea and he went upstairs and asked, "Anyone up for pizza? My treat."

At "My treat," Rodney and Taylor both said, "Hell yeah," but Henry shook his head and said, "No, we can't do that. Thanks, though."

"You can, really," Tom said. "I'm ordering one anyway, and it's just me; I'm not going to eat the whole thing tonight.."

"We'll help," Rodney said from behind a drywall lift.

"Alright," Henry agreed. "Fine. If you say so. Thanks. Now you two get that ceiling up, no one eats anything until it's all up."

Tom nodded and returned to the first floor, smiling inside, and for the first time in a long while, feeling like he was part of the world again.

The workers left that night with full bellies, leaving Tom and an empty pizza box behind. Tom took a bath, then spent an hour watching television with the volume too loud as he tried to fill the house with voices and laughter. Then at one point he heard Henry walking around upstairs. He wondered at first what the man could be doing up there, then decided he'd probably forgotten something and had come back for it. Tom went up to say hi and help him look if Henry wanted him to.

He pushed through the plastic and went upstairs, but the grand room at the top of the stairs was empty. Tom looked in what would be the dining room, asking "You forget something?" But the dining room was empty, too. So were the kitchen, the bathroom and the study.

He heard something out in the hall and thought it was the plastic being rustled, so he went out to look and found the front door standing open. The storm door was shut, and Tom cupped his hands around his eyes and pressed his face to the glass, but didn't see Henry or either of the other two outside.

"That was quick," he said. "Guess he found it." He closed and locked the door and went back downstairs, deciding he might as well go to bed.

Tom didn't do well living alone. He had never done it before, had always had roommates or lived with a girlfriend, and so didn't have years worth of tricks to pass the time and stave off the solitude that seemed to plague his every lonely moment in this house, binding him like a straitjacket.

On the days the workers didn't show, he started movies he never finished or went for drives to nowhere or, more often than not, just went to bed sometimes two hours earlier than normal.

He came to hate being alone in the house. So when the noises began, he told himself it was his own wishful thinking, his own loneliness, creating companions where none existed.

First were the footsteps. Someone walked back and forth over his head, up and down the second-to-third floor stairs. But in his heart, Tom knew it was just random sounds houses make at night that his mind was distorting into something else because he wished so much he had someone to talk to.

The night after the footsteps, after the workers left for the evening (two hours of which time Tom had spent upstairs just observing and soaking in the companionship), he heard drunken weeping, which he told himself was a bum crying over a wasted life in the empty lot next door to the house. In this part of town, he assured himself, the homeless were many, and that lot belonged to no one as far as he knew, so it was entirely possible.

The third night he stayed up as late as his eyes could stand, watching television with the light on, sitcom after sitcom, each set decorated with vibrant colors, each character dressed in perfectly "regular" clothes, each line delivered with stark precision. It was like attending a party where everyone was happy and every corner lighted and no one ever heard anything that wasn't there, and they never left him alone or told him they just didn't want to be with him anymore.

He woke late in the night, disoriented and frightened to find himself in this strange place. When he finally realized where he was he turned off the television and crossed the hall to go to bed. But halfway there, he stopped in the dark hall and listened. He'd heard footsteps out here just now. He knew he heard it. He leaned in and turned the living room light back on, but the hall was empty.

Tom stood there in the semi dark, waiting, wondering. He was alone. But he felt eyes on him just the same. Someone was here, staring directly at him, and whoever it was, they were just as desperate as he was. He felt this in his veins.

Then he said, "No. Not real," and he went into the bedroom and shut the door, leaving the living room light on all night so a slim bar of white seeped in under the door.

Before he was finally able to find sleep again, he thought he heard one or two steps ascending the staircase.

He soon came to realize that, despite his protests of the night in the hallway, the noises were very real. They never became obnoxious or overwhelming, but they were there, and when he was woken in the middle of the night by the front door opening and closing again, he lay in the dark, terrified he would then hear those footsteps coming down to the first floor, praying they would go upstairs.

On that particular night, they went nowhere, and that image of something just standing there on the landing, all night, that was even worse.

On that night, he broke down and called Julie.

He'd been wanting to for a while, but had been putting it off. Now he felt justified; she was responsible for his situation, after all.

She answered on the second ring, her voice still heavy with sleep.

"It's me," he said, then realized "it's me" might not carry the same weight if she was seeing someone else, and he didn't know if she was. Then again, maybe someone else was there with her. He regretted calling.

"Tom? What are you doing up?"

"I don't know," he lied. "I just woke up and felt like I needed to talk to you."

"Is anything wrong?"

He was still in bed and he pulled the cover up to his shoulder and wrapped it around him, settled his head into the pillow and held the phone to his opposite ear.

On the landing and throughout the house all was quiet.

"I guess that depends on how you look at it, huh?"

"God, Tom, I'm not waking up at whatever time it is so you can tell me what a bitch I was."

"That's not why I called," he said. "Nothing's wrong. I just wanted to talk."

Julie was silent, waiting for him.

Now that he had her here, what next? He wasn't going to tell her about the noises, he just needed some human contact and hers was the number he dialed.

After ten seconds, Julie said, "Look, if you're not going to talk, I'm going back to sleep. Sounds like you need to do the same."

"Do you miss me?" he asked. Again, regret settled in immediately.

"Don't do this. Just go back to sleep, okay? We'll talk eventually."

"Yeah," he said, already knowing her answer to his question. "Sure. Good night--." He had to stop himself before calling her babe.

Julie hung up and Tom lay there in bed looking at the display on his phone. Those few seconds with Julie had lifted his burden somewhat, but it had also only made him want more. He scrolled through the contacts in his phone, but didn't find one person he felt comfortable calling at this time of night just to talk, and that realization hit home like a sledgehammer. Even his parents were out; a call at this time of night just because he was lonely and he'd never hear an end to her insistence he should come back and stay with them.

"Jesus," he told the house. "All these numbers and not one friend."

He'd never felt so . . . singular in all his life. Nor so alone.

There was crying again, but this time it came from upstairs and there was no convincing himself it was from anywhere else.

Tom couldn't stay in the house and continue to live with its noises without knowing what they were. So after nearly a week of wondering who was walking around upstairs after the workmen left, he asked them. The main room on the second floor was finished and they'd moved into the kitchen. It was small and cramped and Tom didn't spend a lot of time in there with them. He was supposed to occupy the house, not pester the crew working to restore it. So he didn't stay upstairs too long, just invited them to help him with some Chinese food. He knew how long they worked before taking their breaks, so he knew when to bring it up. When everyone dug in, he asked his question.

"So did the previous owners die in the fire here when the place went up?"

"No," Henry said around a mouthful of noodles. "They all made it out and moved away, I think."

"Guy I know, Charley, worked with the guy who lived here," Rodney said. "They were from Texas before they came here. He thinks they moved back there."

"Well that's good," Tom said.

"No, what you're hearing isn't the previous owners, it's probably the one before them. This place was empty for a long time before they came here and torched it. Whatever you're hearing moving around, it's not them."

This stopped Tom and he paused for a second before asking, "Whatever I'm hearing?"

"It's no secret," Henry said. "But we don't pay any attention to it. Whatever it is, it's long dead. Can't hurt you if you just ignore it."

"You knew about it?" Tom asked.

"Of course, who in Angel Hill doesn't?"

"Me!" Tom said louder than he'd intended.

Henry shrugged and ate some more noodles.

"And the landlord knows?"

Rodney and Taylor were both nodding.

"And he didn't say anything?"

Rodney and Taylor both shrugged.

"What about full disclosure?"

"You're not buying the place," Henry said. "You're living here free, he doesn't have to tell you anything."

Tom was stunned, both by the revelation and Henry's attitude. Yes, Tom was here rent free, but Henry's words and tone stung a little, as if relegating Tom to the role of hired help, only his compensation wasn't in wages, but in room and board. Which, when he thought about it, was actually the case. But still.

"Well, it's a little hard to ignore when it's right over my head all night," Tom said. "He should have said something before I moved in."

He went back downstairs soon after, his mood ruined.

The men left a couple of hours later and Tom dreaded hearing that front door close, because he knew the footsteps would start soon after.

As he tried to find something to watch on television, debating whether to put in a movie or go out for a while, Henry's words kept repeating in his head. Just ignore it. How was he supposed to do that?

No, he thought, I can't ignore it. But I can confront it.

Given the things he'd had to confront in his own life lately, Tom thought facing what may or may not be a ghost should be child's play. He waited a few more minutes, staring blankly at the TV screen while he worked up his courage. Finally he stood up from the couch and, before he could give himself a moment more to think about it, he set himself in motion.

He went upstairs and stood in the middle of the grand room, which was above his bedroom. He wondered if anything would happen with him here, the whole watched pot syndrome. He listened and waited, expecting any second to hear footsteps clumping past him.

Instead, he heard them overhead, on the third floor.

He looked up and quickly took off up the stairs, hoping-- no, not hoping, that was too enthusiastic a word; trying was more like it--trying to get up there before what- or whoever it was could disappear. The footsteps met him at the top of the stairs and when Tom got there he stopped, unable to take that last step onto the floor. He just stared at the darkness, his heart beating like a rabbit's and his stomach expecting to drop when some ferocious and decayed visage rushed him from the darkness.

But nothing came out of the darkness. Tom just stood there, knowing that whatever was walking up here had stopped at the top of the stairs and in whatever dimension it existed it was probably staring him down right now.

A chill crept up his back. He swallowed and felt a dry click in his throat. His eyes scanned the dark, but there was nothing to see up here.

Finally he took in a breath and asked in a voice dry and brittle, a question that took all of his strength and one, if he was being honest, he didn't want answered.

"What do you want?"

From out of nowhere, from the air in front of him, came the reply.

Tom's heart sank and everything he'd been through since moving in came at him in a rush of emotion and he went to his knees with his face in his hands and cried. When he was done, he went back downstairs, but only for a minute. Then he came back up.

The crew didn't work on the house for a few days. Henry had traveled out of town for his daughter's wedding, and when he got back he took another day off before returning to work. When he and his crew showed up, the house was hot. Summer had come to Angel Hill and a stink hung in the air. Their voices broke up the stillness in the house as they opened the door and all filed in together.

Rodney complained, "I can't wait to get this place done and be out of here."

"I hear that," Taylor said.

"That's up to you two," Henry said. "Up to how much time you waste. Get to work and leave that guy alone. I want to be on that third floor by next week."

They shoved the plastic aside, then everyone froze as the

sight hanging from the third floor banister registered in their minds. He'd tied an extension cord to the banister, the other end around his neck, and lowered himself over the side. On the stairs below him Henry found Tom's note.

"There was a sense of loneliness during my entire stay in this house. At first I thought it was my own, brought on by a recent break-up after two years together. I'd never lived alone before and in this big house, once the guys left at night, the solitude always came crashing in. So I thought it was just me.

"But when I came upstairs and felt that presence before me and asked what did it want . . . its answer was one I immediately recognized as I'd felt that very same thing almost every night I spent in this house.

"'Company,' it said. That's all it wanted. It didn't want to be alone in this house anymore. In that moment, I felt the pain it felt and I understood how deeply it hurt. Every night I spent in this house, that's all I wanted, too. Just some company. Another presence to fill some of that empty space, another voice to break up the silence, another mind to interact with.

"I cried when it spoke that word, but they weren't tears of pain or loneliness. It was joy at having found someone who would be able to make it go away. That's not asking too much, is it?"

Henry put the note back where he found it and said, "Naw, that's not too much. I'm sorry for not noticing." He lowered his head and gave Tom a moment of silence before taking out his phone and calling 911. While he reported the death, he felt the presence around him. He always felt it. But like he'd told Tom, you had to learn to ignore it. This time it was stronger, though, and he knew it was because the presence wasn't alone anymore. And then he had a feeling burn through him, as if it hadn't been a presence at all--not like he'd thought. He felt the house open up, then close in around him again and suddenly feel very small despite its three floors. And then it was big once more, only not just big, cavernous, full of stark, empty rooms with walls that echoed and corners that swallowed light and even with Rodney and Taylor just a few feet away, Henry felt totally alone in the house. He felt it like a solid object, as if the loneliness were touching him, weighing on him. But it had what it wanted and maybe, for a while, that would be enough. Maybe now it wouldn't be so restless. Maybe now the crying would stop.

AFTERWORD

The novel you've just read, THE THIRD FLOOR, is very loosely based on a true story. While the main events of the story didn't happen, many of the smaller occurrences did.

The novel is set in a house I lived in during my last year of high school with my mother and her then-husband and later, when they closed off the first floor from the rest of the house, where my wife and I lived for a few years with our then-three-year-old son.

That house was very haunted and very few people who entered it left doubting. For the entire time I lived there, the front door opened and closed so many times I lost count. Several nights while we lived on the first floor, I woke up to the sound of my son walking across the floor in our bedroom only to get up and find him still sound asleep in his bed. And these weren't the half asleep imaginings of a dreaming mind, I always sat up and listened carefully to make sure I *hadn't* been dreaming and almost every time, unable to see anything in the dark, I still heard him, usually across the room on the opposite end, near the bookcases.

The incident in Joey's closet really happened to my son. He was in his room playing, the closet door open, and he was in there trying to find a toy when he came into the living room upset, nearly in tears, asking why I'd come in and scared him. I hadn't left the living room.

The incident with Joey in the bathroom at dinnertime is also based on a real event.

While the story of the Denglers and what happened to them is fictional, the house and the atmosphere surrounding it are real. Hopefully I was able to put my experiences there to good use in this novel, and if THE THIRD FLOOR creeped you out even half as much as living there did me, then I've done my job.

Up next is the prologue to a novella, "The Man in the Window." I include this excerpt here because this was the very first Angel Hill story.

Following the "Man in the Window" excerpt is another excerpt, this time the first chapter of my first published novel, *Revelations*, which was published in 2012 by Necro Publications.

My last excerpt is the first chapter of a novel by my friend David Bain, *Death Sight*, the first novel in his Will Castleton series. Will is a "slightly psychic" investigator and ex-US Marshal whom Dave and I have discussed possibly having visit Angel Hill some time in the future. If that adventure ever becomes a reality, I figured now would be just as good a time as any to give readers of my book a chance to meet him.

THE MAN IN THE WINDOW

Prologue

Caleb had lost count of the days he'd lain here. It was long enough for the cockroaches to infect his bedsores. He watched them lay eggs and he was helpless to stop them. He couldn't move. He lay there with tears in his eyes. The sun shone outside and through the window across the room it looked like a beautiful day, but he was denied the enjoyment, trapped here in his own body.

His nurse would be in a few hours later to feed him, but he thought "nurse" was a bit of a stretch. A nurse would have kept the bugs out of him.

He felt no pain, and he supposed for that he should be grateful; whatever was wrong with him, it didn't hurt. But sometimes seeing a thing is bad enough without feeling it.

Having no family, Caleb figured he should count his blessings he had that woman to feed him, because stuck up here in this bed twenty-four hours a day, as inept as he thought she was at her duties, he was always glad for the company.

And then a thought occurred to him: count his blessings? What blessings? Was it a blessing to be a prisoner of himself and not even know why it was happening? Was it a blessing that the only person he ever saw shoveled cold soup into his mouth twice a day, but couldn't be bothered to bathe him or to make sure his muscles weren't completely atrophied? Where was the blessing in this life?

Whatever was happening to him, it was no blessing. Whatever was happening to him, God certainly had nothing to do with it. God the creator, God the loving father to all. As far as he could see, the "generous God" myth was one of the biggest hoaxes ever pulled on humanity.

I would gladly turn my back on all He has created for just one more day of mobility.

As that thought formed, then dissolved in Caleb's head, he noticed a man in his room. This man was perched atop the bedpost like a gargoyle, smiling down at him.

"Would you, now?" he said to Caleb. "Because I think

we can work something out, you and I."

Who are you? Caleb thought. Paralyzed within himself, thinking it was all he could do.

The man made a brief motion with his eyes, looking up. Caleb's eyes followed and saw horns sprouting from the man's forehead. "Now do you know who I am?" the man whispered. "I can get you out of this bed. I can make it so you walk again, so you can clean yourself and feed yourself again. No more cold soup, no more soiled sheets." He leaned in closer, his feet still clinging to the bedpost but the man was so impossibly close to Caleb's ear now, Caleb wondered how he didn't topple forward and fall to the floor. "There's a world out there, and you're missing it. I can change that. Just say the word and it's done."

Caleb lay mute and terrified.

"Sorry," the man said. "I guess you can't. I tell you what, if I make it so you can talk right now, I'll trust you to fulfill the rest of the bargain afterward. If it's a deal, blink once."

If this man can make it so I talk again, Caleb thought, *I'll give him whatever he wants. Even if I don't walk or move again. If I can talk, that would be enough.*

He blinked.

The man's eyes lit up and he leapt from the bedpost to stand beside Caleb. He touched Caleb's throat and heat invaded the invalid's body where the man's hand rested. He took his hand away and asked, "Do you accept? Speak."

Caleb croaked the word and his mouth was still numb, but he could tell it was moving, his tongue thick and heavy between his teeth. "Yes," he said.

"Yes," the man repeated. "Perfect." He laid his hands on Caleb's face this time, his thumbs resting over Caleb's eyes, and that heat swept through him again, this time through his entire body. He felt it in his chest and his stomach, he felt it in his legs.

"Sleep," the man told him. "In the morning, you'll get up, dress yourself, and go downstairs." Before Caleb had time to think of anything else, he passed out.

Night fell and the nurse came, but Caleb was sleeping so she let him rest and would check on him again later. Before she could do so, she fell asleep on the couch.

Meanwhile, Caleb was upstairs having the most horrible

nightmares. He wouldn't remember the details, but there was darkness and heat and cockroaches. Good God the bugs he dreamed. Millions of them, more even. Every cockroach to ever populate the Earth must have been in his dream.

And then before he knew it, the sun was shining again and outside his window he heard a bird chirping. Caleb opened his eyes, rubbed them, and lifted his head off the pillow to look about the room.

He suddenly realized what he was doing and he shot up in bed. He looked at his hands and watched the fingers flex and relax. He swiveled his head about. He pulled the cover off and stared at his legs.

The bugs were gone, the bedsores were healed. But, even if his body were fixed, wouldn't the sores still be there? He wondered for a moment if the dream he'd just woken from had been the sickness and maybe all that time he'd spent trapped up in this room had been the real nightmare, from which he'd now woken only to find it all a figment of his imagination? Could it be?

He climbed out of bed and pulled fresh pants and a shirt from his dresser. He stood before the mirror and watched his body at work. Dressed and ready for the day, he took the glasses off the nightstand--it seemed like he hadn't worn them in months--and headed downstairs. Excited, Caleb did a foolish thing and leapt down the first two stairs. He overstepped and his foot came down on the edge of the plank, slipped, and Caleb went tumbling head over heels to the floor. He smacked his head on the stairs as he went down, then once more on the hardwood floor. His vision went blurry, then black, and his head rang with bells and his skull felt as if it were vibrating. A vision appeared on the ceiling above him, a thousand scurrying cockroaches swarmed from cracks that opened up and they all sat there, upside down on the ceiling, watching him.

"Bugs," he said before losing consciousness.

REVELATIONS

Chapter 1: In the Year of the Scavenger

Ashley and her family had left early in the morning along US 54 out of Kingsdown, and had just cleared the infected zone after Waterloo. They wanted to put as much distance between the zone and themselves as possible by tonight. It was late afternoon and the sky was red with grey and black clouds. The air was close and thick with mid-summer, and the caravan's engines were the only noise for miles.

A lot of the families were on the move, they knew, but so far they'd seen no one else. As conditions grew worse, as the infected zone expanded, the people fled. They drove busses, RVs, eighteen wheelers hauling trailers loaded with possessions and people., whatever it took to keep going.

Ashley and her family traveled in smaller groups: two trucks and three cars. The trucks had campers over the beds. Shoved into the back of Millie's F-100 was everything they owned. In the back of the Viewliner, sitting quietly and seeing nothing, were four seemingly comatose old men.

Ashley squinted against the glare of the sun that glowed white against the red sky, and pressed on. Phillip sat beside her stroking his sandy beard, almost tugging on it. Neither spoke. What was there to say, comment on the weather? Remark on how black the landscape was, stretching out on either side of them? Or maybe talk about how they hoped they came to a town before nightfall because the barren, blackened fields surrounding them were too creepy?

Ashley rubbed her eyes, flipped the visor down to shield them, and pressed the gas pedal further, the speedometer needle sweeping past eighty.

The cars and trucks sped up with her.

They passed a sign announcing Garden Plain before Phillip broke the silence.

"Getting hungry?" he asked.

Ashley leaned her head to the side, glanced up at the sky to judge the time, and said, "Yeah, I could use something. I can't believe we're still in the middle of nowhere."

Phillip grabbed the CB mic and told everyone the plan.

Ashley pulled over and killed the engine and Phillip was out before she could even get her seatbelt off. As soon as his door slammed shut, he screamed.

She thought maybe he'd slammed his finger in the door or stepped on something, but when she glanced over, Phillip was gone. In his place was a bird. She could see it easily from inside the car, as they were over half the size of any man--four feet at least. Its thick wings folded back and fluttering, she knew the thing was perched on Phillip's stomach as its foot-long black beak tore into his throat.

Phillip gurgled. The bird craned its golden-feathered head back, dropping a chunk of bloody red meat into its gullet, then went back for more.

Ashley didn't hesitate. The Challenger sped away, spraying road gravel and almost fishtailing as the tires gained purchase. The caravan behind her was doing the same, all of them watching the birds flock toward them. A few birds had landed. Elle and Steven had fallen, but this wasn't the time to mourn or try to help. There was nothing they could do, and they knew it.

The caravan was a mess of metallic beasts rumbling down the highway, but by the time Ashley had reached fifty on the speedometer, the single-file line was back in order.

A few miles down the road, the CB crackled and a voice asked, "Where are we going?" Her name was Sara. She was a dainty twenty-one, blonde with green eyes and she'd been with the family since she was fifteen.

Ashley grabbed the mic and answered, "I don't know!"

"We have to get shelter," Sara said.

No shit! Ashley thought.

Another voice came on, Derek's. He was driving the Charger with Sara in it. "We're just driving until we find something?"

"Have you got a better idea?" Ashley yelled.

Neither Sara nor Derek had an answer.

The birds swooped to attack the rooftops, but never gained the foothold they wanted, and when the drivers hit the gas or the brake or swerved to the other lane, the birds fell tumbling to the highway, flipping end over end until they came upright and took to the air again, screeching their dissatisfaction.

One tried to come straight for Ashley, but she hit the headlights and honked the horn, disorienting the bird, which missed the car. A second later the first truck clipped its feet and it went face down into the camper, then slid off and just missed being flattened by the second truck.

"Sack of shit!" Ashley yelled back before it vanished from the rearview.

She almost reached for the Colt, but instead, she focused on driving and kept her eyes open for a place in which to take refuge until the Scavengers went away again.

She looked at the empty space next to her and thought *It's too bad about Phillip.* She enjoyed his company. He was a few years older, but had always seen Ashley as an equal. She thought maybe that was because of how he felt about her, which, she thought, was how she'd begun to feel about him, too. It would have been nice, she mused, to marry and have the strength of two leading the family instead of Ashley alone. It had been almost three years since her father died and she still made decisions with a secret feeling of trepidation. Her father never felt that, she told herself. Her father was the greatest man to ever live. If he'd lived *before*, she thought, he surely would have been taken.

She passed a sign announcing Goddard but saw from the highway that it was no good, all fields and rundown houses. She shook her head. Wichita was next. She gazed around, hoping something would be out there, a large brick hospital, a grocery store, a school building, anything. But she sped almost another ten miles down US 54 before seeing anything other than black fields and killer birds.

What she saw in the distance, through the dust and the glare of the red sky, was more than Ashley would ever have hoped for. She grabbed the mic again and said, "Everyone see that building?"

She came to the access road and turned off 54.

The place loomed in the distance, but the more she sped ahead, the closer and more defined it got, and the clearer she saw it, the more her heart sank because she suddenly knew they'd never get inside. And if by some stupid lucky chance they did, there would be a family already in there--but surely there's room for two--or the place wouldn't be secure at all. Gaping holes in the walls, or broken windows that wouldn't keep the Scavengers out.

She tried not to let these thoughts kill her hopes before they reached the place.

One of the birds dive-bombed her hood, got its beak caught in the metal, then flopped down onto the windshield, shattering the glass. The windshield held, but it was covered in a spider web of cracks.

She yanked the wheel to the side, the car fishtailed, and the bird fell over. The tip of its beak snapped off where it was lodged in the hood, and the bird slid off the car. She didn't turn to see it get up again, but she knew it would.

Ashley saw the front door of the huge building. There was an attached carport with stone pillars holding up the concrete roof. Ashley steered for it. A bird was on the ground in front of her car, but she didn't swerve. She slammed into it instead and the monster flew back, tumbled somersaults in the dirt, then landed upright, spread its huge wings, and took off.

Ashley was close enough now to read the faded and peeling letters on the door: WELCOME TO THE TRUST.

A bird swooped down and rammed the shattered glass. It fell inward, knocked Ashley sideways, and the car swerved, slammed into a pillar, and she was thrown into the steering wheel.

The caravan pulled in around her in seconds and Sara's window went down. "Climb over!" she yelled.

Ashley looked up from the steering wheel, a dark bruise already starting to swell over her brow. She tried to focus, but through the birds' shrieking and the cars honking and the voice yelling for her to "Come on!", all she could do was notice the swirl of colors and shapes blurring in her eyes.

She had clear passage from her exposed hood to Derek and Sara's Charger. If she were quick enough, she'd be in before the birds could flock to her.

She got her feet on the front seat and prepared to slide across the hood which would bring her directly to the other car. Then she stopped. A bird stood on the ground ten feet from the car.

She couldn't stay put, not with the windshield gone. But the bird was right there. The gun might hold it off long enough for her to switch cars.

"Pull back," she yelled. Sara turned and relayed it to Derek who pulled alongside Ashley's window. Ashley grabbed her Colt.

She brought it up and trained it on the bird's face. It peered into hers with its golden eyes, those pinprick black pupils issuing their challenge.

She put one hand on the open window, lifted herself, and kept the gun steady in a nervous hand. Her eyes never left the bird's. Her eased into the open space between the cars. The bird cocked its own head. Its tail feathers twitched. The roof of the car obscured her view for a second and she glanced into the air. Dozens of the fuckers were up there, circling the place like they were only waiting for the inevitable.

Then the bird was back in her line of sight. It didn't seem too worried about the gun. It twitched its tail one last time, then it leapt into the air, flapping its ugly wings and screeching.

Ashley unloaded five bullets into its chest, sliding her body into the other car, ducking inside and still shooting.

The bird flinched with every impact, but it never stopped screeching and it never stopped coming. Ashley rolled up the window just before it slammed its beak into the glass, its tongue stretched and shaking with the ferocity of its screech.

"Go," she yelled at Derek, who slammed on the gas and peeled away.

"How do we get in?" Sara asked.

"I don't know," Ashley said.

They drove around the building, the caravan following and honking their horns. The birds flew around, dive-bombing the cars and waiting for someone to expose the thinnest scrap of flesh to their hungry mouths.

Of the Scavengers, the birds were the lightweights. They were big enough to swallow a newborn whole, but flashing lights and noise confused them.

They circled the complex three times. The building was much bigger than Ashley had first thought. She'd figured two families could rest here easily, but now that she saw the entire thing, this place could comfortably house three or four families.

"Hang on," Derek said, turning around to the back of the building. Ashley looked out the window beside her and saw birds soaring overhead. None were attacking, but that didn't mean they weren't keeping an eye on the small bags of meat below. "Maybe if we can get one of the trucks backed up close enough," Derek said, pointing to a black metal grate, "we can get someone back there who's quick enough with a screwdriver to get that cover off and we can slip inside that way."

"That's a ventilation duct," Ashley said, "and if the system is working and the fans are turning, that could be dangerous. You wanna take that risk?"

Derek didn't answer.

"I'd take it," Sara said after a minute.

They looked at her.

"I would," she went on. "It's not any worse than being out here going round in circles, is it?"

"No," Ashley said. "We already lost Phillip today."

"We lost Phillip because they caught us off guard. Otherwise we wouldn't have been out in the open like that. This is my choice. No one to blame except me if it's the wrong one."

"We'll be out of gas sooner or later anyway," Derek said, and Ashley flashed him a look that said Stay out of it.

"See?" Sara asked. "We'll have to stop eventually, and when we do, it'll just be the glass between us and them and we've already seen how effective that is."

"I'm pulling up next to it," Derek said.

Ashley stared at Sara and Sara stared back, but neither said anything and neither wanted to back down from their position. Finally Ashley spoke.

"I'll do it."

Derek rounded the corner again and slowed near the vent cover, then backed in against the building. Ashley took the CB and said, "Millie, back in here beside us, up against that vent cover. You see it?"

"I see it," Millie came back. Millie pulled the F-100 as close to the Charger as she could, close enough the side-view mirror tapped the chrome against Ashley's door.

"Come on," Sara said. "Let me go. It'll be no big deal, I can get through it."

"It'll be a big deal to me," Ashley said. "You're not going. Derek, I expect you to keep her in this car. If I can get in through there, I'll come back and give everyone the all clear and you all beat ass into the truck and out the back into the building.

But not until I say. Got it?"

Derek nodded. Sara ignored Ashley, but when Ashley repeated, "Got it?" she nodded, then looked at the floor.

"That space is two feet square at most," Derek said. "What about all our stuff?"

"We'll worry about ourselves first," she said. "From there we'll find a door we can unlock from the inside. We'll come back for the vehicles and our stuff then."

Ashley turned toward the window, but stopped straight ahead, staring out the front windshield. Derek noticed her freeze and looked. Sara noticed both of them frozen and looked. She screamed, then clamped a hand over her mouth. A bird perched on the hood of the car, its beak inches from the glass, it's eyes glowing. Even with the windows rolled up, they could still smell it, like fifty years of rot and blood and Hell on earth, because that's exactly what it was.

"Get it off there," Ashley said.

"How?" Derek asked.

"I don't care," Ashley said, "just get it off."

Neither saw it at first, but when the bird moved its head in their direction, they understood why Ashley was so upset. Snagged on a ragged edge of its beak was a scrap of cloth, the color of the shirt Phillip had been wearing.

"Rotten piece of shit," Ashley seethed at it through the glass.

The bird shrieked back and tapped the glass with its beak.

Then they were all blinded and deafened and the bird flapped and shrieked at the air, taking off again. Tuck's car was grill to grill with theirs, flashing the brights and laying on the horn. Tuck gave her a thumbs up from the driver's seat. Ashley tried to spread an appreciative smile across her face, but seeing that piece of Phillip's shirt in the bird's beak made it feel forced.

She looked back at Sara and Derek and saw they knew what to do. Sara would stay put; Derek would make sure of it.

The windows went down simultaneously, Millie shoved herself across to the other side of the cab, and Ashley slithered through and over in a flash. The windows were up again before the birds could dive down to them.

Ashley vanished through the small window into the back

of the truck. It was only a matter of waiting now.

The back of the truck contained all their belongings. Food in white plastic coolers, clothes folded into suitcases and paper sacks lined against the back of the truck's cab, and a pile of blankets and sleeping bags. Tucked under this pile was a toolbox. Ashley pulled it out, opened it, grabbed a screwdriver.

She flipped up the camper shell's window and went to work on the screws--had the first two off--when she heard the clatter of talons overhead. She looked up and saw they were wrapped around the rim of the window. The bird lowered its head, twisted it to face her, and glared at her.

Her first instinct was to drive the screwdriver into one of those eyes, but before she could move, it lunged for her and she fell back, her arms covering her face.

Millie yelled, "Shit!" and started the engine, then pulled away from the building.

The bird snapped. Ashley ducked sideways, then lashed out and grabbed it's neck. The flesh was like cold, dimpled, raw meat. And when it shrieked, it felt to Ashley like a thousand crawling beetles moving in her palm.

"What are you doing?" she yelled to Millie.

The bird pulled back, opened its beak, and dove forward again.

"Shove it out the back window," Millie said. "Then we'll back over the fucker."

The bird dug its talons into Ashley's stomach, sinking them into the tender flesh.

Blood seeped through her shirt and Ashley screamed. It brought up a foot, scratched at her face, opening a cut on her cheek.

She shoved and it toppled backward, its talons ripping free of her. She scrambled to her knees, one hand out for balance, the other still closed tight around the bird's neck.

She maneuvered it closer to the open back window. It tore free of her grasp, jerked backward, squawked, snapped at her face. She threw herself backward, fell again, hit her head against the tool box, and kicked wildly until she connected with something. She landed a solid blow to the head, then another in its leg. A final kick to the body and the thing went out the window, squawking and flapping its wings.

"Now!" Ashley yelled over her shoulder.

The truck's inertia shifted, then a huge THUMP bounced them as they rolled over the bird. The truck came back down hard and Ashley hit her head on the toolbox again.

"Shit!" she yelled, rubbing the newest bruise.

Millie put the truck in drive and ran over the bird again. Another THUMP and crash as everything inside shifted. Ashley sat up and looked out the back window. The bird stumbled to its feet. She lifted her shirt and put a hand to her stomach, wiping away blood. Looking at it, the bird hadn't dug in as far as she'd thought. It still hurt like hell, but she'd be fine.

For now she had to concentrate on getting inside the building.

"Now, let's get back to that shaft and get inside."

"Got it," Millie said, and swerved the truck in a wide circle to get back to the side of the complex.

Ashley slipped again. She didn't hit her head, but she did get a particular view through the side window.

She saw a second floor window that she thought may save them a lot quicker than a shaft that may or may not lead to safety. The glass was gone, and normally that would have signaled to them to move on, that this place was no good. But this window was barred. Spaced wide enough so they could slip through, but close enough to keep the birds out.

"Millie," she said, "Look over there."

She pointed and Millie had to crane her head to the side and slow the truck down to see it. "Uh-huh," Millie said.

"We can fit through there, can't we?"

"Speak for yourself," Millie said. She patted her stomach which, although not fat, was sagging with age.

"Just pull over there," Ashley said. "We'll get you through. The only thing I'm worried about is getting The Dead up there."

The truck stopped alongside the building. Millie spoke into the CB, "Over here, everyone," and the other vehicles headed for them.

Ashley climbed back into the cab. "We're going to try for that window up there," she said into the mic. "Luther, you grab your shotgun and cover us while we're outside."

She grabbed her own gun off the front seat and climbed

out, then unhooked the extension ladder from the side of the camper shell.

A bird shrieked behind her and she whirled, firing.

It broke off its attack and fled back into the air.

She leaned the ladder against the building, then looked over her shoulder at Luther. He was watching her every move and his shotgun's barrel poked out through his driver's window. He nodded to her and she slid the gun into her waistband, then extended the ladder up to the window.

"Millie," she called. "Grab one of the coolers and get up this ladder."

She could imagine Millie grumbling about fitting through, but the engine cut off anyway, and the door opened. Millie hauled one of the food coolers out through the tailgate and started up.

Ashley stood below her, keeping her eyes on the birds. She drew the gun and covered Millie while Luther covered her, and for the first time she honestly felt they might get inside with the family intact. Except for Phillip, that was. And Elle and Steven. She made a promise to herself then that when the Year was up this time, she'd go back to that stretch of highway and put up markers for them.

Just then she came from her thoughts with a scream. Not hers. She focused and had one second to see Millie falling. Blood on Millie's head, a bird swerving away, and Millie was suddenly on the ground, one leg tangled in the ladder rungs, and the bone below her knee was now twisted in a direction it was never meant for.

Millie was still screaming. The cooler lay open a few feet from her, its contents spilled for whichever bird was quick enough.

Ashley yelled, "Shit!" and without thinking she slid the gun into her waistband again and went to Millie. "Are you okay?" she asked. One look at that leg and anyone would have known Millie wasn't okay. And if that didn't do it, her screams surely would.

How did she miss it? She was staring right at Millie, she had the gun raised and ready to shoot any bird that came near her. Why didn't she see it?

Because she'd been thinking about Phillip instead of

concentrating on her task. And now Millie had a broken leg for it and if someone didn't get that food, the family would suffer for that, too.

Stupid, she thought.

"Tuck," she yelled over her shoulder. "Gather this food and help me get Millie up the ladder. Luther, keep lookout."

The door opened and Tuck was there in seconds, scooping the food back into the cooler. He carried it to the truck, then helped with Millie. Ashley held Millie's feet, while Tuck had her from behind, his arms under hers, wrapped around her chest. He took a backward step up the ladder.

With each jostle and bump, Millie groaned again.

"I'm sorry, Millie," Ashley said. "I don't know what happened."

Millie didn't say anything other than, "Ugh!" when Tuck backed up another rung.

Ashley had her gun in her waistband again, and Millie's leg draped carefully over her shoulder, easing herself up the ladder with Millie and Tuck. The top was only a few more rungs away, but the closer they got, the clearer Ashley saw another problem. From the ground, the bars looked spaced far enough apart for a tight fit through, but nearing the top of the ladder, they looked closer than that. So close together, in fact, that Ashley was mentally going through their stock of supplies, hoping to come up with a hacksaw or a torch, something to get rid of one of those bars. They'd still be able to slip through, but the birds were way too big.

And once the others came? Ashley wondered. The bugs wouldn't come that way. The bats may be able to squeeze through, but they were still six months away and by then they could replace the bar. And the dogs weren't a consideration at all, not that far off the ground. So, she figured, getting through was the problem and, for now, the only problem.

Tuck had gone as far as he could. His arms drooped with Millie's weight and Millie just lay there, trying to hold back the pain. Ashley craned her head to the side, looking at the bars.

"You think there's any way to fit through there?" she asked Tuck.

He looked over his shoulder, then back down to Ashley. "Probably," he said. "Don't know about pulling her in with me," he added.

A shot sounded and they both looked down, Ashley nearly slipping on her rung and pulling them all down with her. Luther was leaning out his window, gun pointed off in the distance.

"Fucker was trying to creep in," he called, keeping his eyes on the bird.

Then came another shriek and Millie was suddenly torn from their arms.

Ashley and Tuck stared dumbfounded as the bird opened its talons and let Millie drop to the ground. It wasn't a long fall, and normally she would have been fine, but with her leg already broken, she landed with a new scream. And they'd never even seen this one coming, both looking at Luther.

Ashley pulled her gun, fired. Luther redirected his aim as well. Tuck had left his gun in the car.

The bird retreated as soon as the shots came, but by then it had already torn out Millie's right eye, bit off her nose, and one of its talons had sliced open her throat.

Ashley emptied her gun in the bird's direction, her eyes red and watering, her mouth set in a grimace, and her mind repeating over and over, "Failure, failure, failure."

Millie wasn't dead when the bird flew off, but there was nothing any of them could do for her now.

Ashley listened to Millie's gurgles and death chokes and did the only thing for her she could; she shot her in the head. Then she finished climbing the ladder and tried pressing her body through the bars.

Tuck was too thick, but Ashley was young and fit. She grabbed the bars in both hands, lifted a boot, and slipped through with a little effort.

Then she was inside the building and all she wanted to do was sit on the floor and cry. Why couldn't she cover her eyes and shut out the world and the hell and the birds and the family, and just cry herself to sleep right here?

Because there were still ten others out there who needed her.

She knew that's what the next year would come down to. No matter how many times she wanted to give up and let the Scavengers take her, she couldn't. Her grandfather had formed this family, her father had held it together through two Years of the Scavengers, and Ashley could do no less. So if not for herself, then for the ten people still alive outside, she had to straighten up.

She told Tuck to send Sara up. She at least would be able to fit through the bars, and with both of them inside, Luther and Derek could keep watch and Tuck could bring the dead up the ladder one at a time. Ashley and Sara could help them through.

"Tell her to see if we have a hacksaw in the truck," she called down. "Have her bring it up if we do."

Sara came up five minutes later.

Ashley went to work with the saw, and wondered what kind of place this was. From outside, Ashley could see the walls were close, the floor bare. There was a door with a small window. Sara tried to see as much outside the room as possible without having to open the door.

Ashley's breathing came in harsh pants and the squeak of the blade through the metal was piercing, but in another minute she yelled, "Got it," just before the blade broke through the other side.

She pulled the severed bar from the window, and looked down.

"Bring them up," she called.

This time Luther and Derek stood to either side of the ladder, guns ready, eyes skyward, while Tuck helped the Dead up the ladder and into the building, one at a time.

The twins, Matt and Mary, followed, then Tuck and Luther who went up together, hauling one of the food coolers. The box was too big to fit through the bars, so Ashley took out anything that wouldn't go bad, and the cooler was put back into the truck which was then closed and locked until they could come back for it. Luther and Tuck went up and in, and then Derek pulled the ladder up and in after him.

As soon as everyone was in and safe, they all collapsed on the floor. After allowing for ten minutes' rest, Ashley cleared her throat, and said, "Alright, let's see what we've got here. We need to get the cars and trucks inside and seal off any exits."

They explored as they went, opening doors and going down hallways to see where they went. From what they'd seen so far of the building, they couldn't tell if they were in a school, a hospital, a prison, or an office building, because they found rooms along the way that would have been at home in any of those places. Here's a classroom across the hall from an exam room. On the bottom floor, a corner of the building housed five padded cells. If necessary, they could erect a barricade in front of the doors just using the empty desks they found.

"Welcome to The Trust," Ashley said.

"What?" Sara asked.

"Welcome to The Trust," she repeated. "That's what the sign said when we pulled up. Welcome to The Trust."

"What's The Trust?"

"No idea."

"This place is huge."

"Which should work to our advantage, I hope," Ashley said. She opened a door. Another office. "Doesn't this place have a kitchen? Some place to store the food?"

"A place this size, you'd think so."

"Yeah, you'd think."

She had sent Tuck and Derek to find a way to get the cars inside, while Luther took the twins to find a safe place for the Dead. Meanwhile Ashley and Sara explored.

The electricity was still on, and there wasn't as much dust as either had expected.

"It's almost like the place has been waiting," Sara said.

"That doesn't fill me with hope."

"Why not?"

"What if we're not what it's been waiting for. If there's someone else due here?"

It made sense. Power to all the abandoned buildings had been cut off decades ago, and the last place Ashley had been in like this had had a carpet of dust.

"Here," Sara said, bringing Ashley out of her own head. "Cafeteria."

"Sure?"

They went in and Ashley was greeted by a room longer than it was wide, and lined in five rows across from one end of the room to the other with long tables and light blue plastic chairs.

"Great," Ashley said, heading for the back of the room.

"If the power's on in the rest of the building, there might be a refrigerator where we can put the food."

They found it and went to find the others and bring the food down.

The plan was to meet back where they'd split, on the second floor. When Tuck and Derek returned, they'd bring the tools to close this door off and make sure no one else entered the building, at least through there. But by the time Ashley and Sara found the way back--opening the door to make sure it was the correct room and Ashley saw one of the birds clinging to the bars, its head in the room, squawking and shrieking, but not able to force its body through--Tuck and Derek still hadn't returned.

They leaned against the wall, waiting, listening to the birds on the other side of the door trying to claw their way into the room. One squawked so loud, Sara jumped. Ashley, however, seemed too zoned out to notice. She had her elbows on her knees and her face in her hands. Her eyes were closed and she was thinking about Phillip and Millie.

Tuck and Derek returned and they went to work covering the door. They took the top off one of the desks lying around the place and nailed it directly to the doorframe.

"You got the cars inside?" she asked, sliding up the wall to her feet.

"Yeah, pretty much," Derek said. Tuck handed him a nail and Derek drove it through the desktop.

"Pretty much?" Ashley asked.

"The Viewliner," Tuck said. "There were a few birds in it, so we left it out there."

"We should be able to get it later, maybe tomorrow," Derek said.

Ashley nodded.

She let them work while she wandered to the other end of the hall.

She still wasn't sure what this place was, but she'd make finding out a priority. Get everyone settled and then explore and find out where they were. Who knew what they might find lying around here, but if it was something that might help them-- canned goods or extra clothes, maybe--it would be nice to find out.

She opened a door, looked in. She'd never heard of it

before, The Trust.

"All done," Tuck called down to her.

Ashley closed the door and joined them again at the other end of the hall.

"Now we wait for Luther and the twins and they'll take us back to where they took the Dead. We'll set ourselves up somewhere near them and . . . " she trailed off.

"Then we'll start the wait," Sara said.

"Get comfortable, folks, and take it all in 'cause this is home for the next year."

"If we last that long," Derek said. "We don't have enough food for a year."

"If it comes down to it," Ashley said, "we'll last as long as we can then send someone out to loot a store."

"Send someone where?" Tuck asked. "There wasn't anything for miles."

"In case you hadn't noticed, I'm not having the best time of it right now, so please, if you have a better idea, give it to me."

Tuck shook his head, kept his mouth shut.

"Then like I said," she went on, "we go as long as we can. If we don't find anything here--."

"There is a cafeteria," Sara blurted.

"Right," Ashley said. "There's a cafeteria downstairs, so I see no reason to believe we won't find something here. But if we don't, we send someone out. I'll go if I have to."

Tuck nodded. Derek looked like he was going to say something, but before he could, Luther and the twins, Matt and Mary, returned.

The group was led downstairs and Luther showed them where the Dead were staying. Then he led them down another hall, around a corner, and into another room. This one looked like a gymnasium.

"Big enough?" Luther asked.

"This is fine," Ashley said.

The doors were propped open, and Tuck and Derek took them to the vehicles. A little over an hour later, the family's belongings were stashed in the gym and they all stood back and looked at home.

DEATH SIGHT:
A WILL CASTLETON NOVEL

David Bain

PART ONE:
DROWNING

1

The dead stared at him with dark, empty, accusing sockets that formerly held their eyes.

Will's feet were rooted in a nightlit desert. A full moon. A dry, coppery odor to the air. Cacti. Rocks. Low dunes rising out of the ankle-deep water.

For the desert was also the sea.

Will and the dead stood in the ankle-deep waters of the desert, staring at each other.

One of him.

Hundreds of them.

Everyone who would now die because he was still alive.

Everyone already dead who would come into his life.

All the ghosts he would ever create, ever encounter.

He could not make out the faces of most of the throng of shadowy figures.

Those in front he recognized, however.

They were the faces of an entire SWAT team, cops from several branches of law enforcement, still in their tattered uniforms.

Horribly disfigured, all of them.

Only half their flesh still on their raw faces.

Limbs missing.

Their eyes infinite wells of unfathomable dark.

He knew the corpse, the spirit that stood at the forefront. Cummings. A decent, if overbearing cop in life.

Will could see Marshal Cummings' tongue through the hole in his flesh, through the gap in his teeth, his jaw.

Will could see the tongue move like a thick worm as Cummings said, "Look down, Castleton."

The water wasn't water.

It was blood.

"The tide will rise," Cummings said. "You'll drown in an ocean of blood before you're through."

Then Will would realize he was already covered in the stuff.

***

The vision would wash over him, even when he was wide awake.

Will would come out of it screaming.

Thus, the powers that be sent him to see Smith.

***

"The blood and the darkness," Will said. "The death. The outright *evil.*"

"Not what you signed up for," Smith said.

"I mean, to put bad guys away, yes. To do some good in the world, yes. But a U.S. Marshal's supposed to protect federal witnesses, oversee major meth lab busts, that sort of thing. *My* life since the accident, though…"

"Not what you signed up for," Smith repeated. He clicked his ballpoint pen, working his thumb, making a sound like a castanet. Maybe it was good this shrink had a nervous habit. Will had thought the whole thing about psychiatrists scribbling in a notebook while you talked was a myth, but not with this guy.

"We can't always predict the directions our lives will take."

Will straightened in his chair, frowned at the man. "Are you being funny?"

Smith laughed. Guy with silver, slick-backed hair, suspenders, red tie, blue button-down shirt, his sport coat slung casually over his high-backed leather chair. A guy whose clothes were probably worth more than what Will paid for his new apartment here in the city per month: laughing at him. Will in biker boots - he'd rode his Harley here - jeans, Hold Steady concert t-shirt, black leather jacket which he'd refused to take off so he could leave faster.

"Sorry. Poor word choice." Smith clicked his pen again, reclined slightly in his chair. Smith sat behind his big faux-mahogany desk. Will hunkered in a seat to the side. Open space, between them. There was indeed a couch, but Smith hadn't suggested he use it.

Smith looked at Will as if he expected Will to speak.

Will chose not to.

Mist had collected on the window which took up the entire eastern wall of the room. Lake Michigan loomed beyond, cold and gray and choppy. Wind buffeted the building.

Something hissed like a cat and Will flinched involuntarily - an unseen timed aerosol canister had sprayed an artificial pine scent into the room from high atop Smith's numerous heavily-laden shelves of psychology texts.

"Listen, Mr. Castleton. *Will.* Do you think you can trust me?"

"Tell you the truth, I'm afraid I'm going to end up in some scholarly journal as Patient X. Or, worse yet, in a tell-all book. I have trust issues when it comes to telling the skeletons in my closet. With good reason, but I think it's one of those things I'm supposed to 'reveal to you, like it's a deep, dark secret."

"I'm my own boss. I don't need to publish. All the confidentiality laws apply to what you want to do here. And I can't write for shit. My girlfriend - wife now - wrote all my papers in college."

"You must be a great psychiatrist then. How'd you pass your exams?"

"I might be exaggerating a little. But I won't write about you."

"You could get a ghost writer. That would be particularly ironic in my case."

"So you're ready to talk about that aspect of your life? The alleged ghosts and such? I understand about the extreme nature of the cases you've been involved with. Your accident in Florida, the dead girl in Michigan, what you witnessed in Arizona. These things couldn't have been easy. But the claims of supernatural involvement..."

"They're *not* 'claims.'"

"Sorry. Bad word choice again. Let me put it this way.... These waking nightmares you've had - "

"Visions. *Before* the fact."

"The ones in Michigan..."

"Okay, those were after the fact. Obviously."

"I think it's important we talk about these visions."

"Look, I get it. You're saying I've experienced terrible things and I'm having waking nightmares about them. You're going to try to convince me my claims they were visions are some sort of mental compensation on my part, my way of dealing with latent guilt or something."

"Why would anyone feel guilt when they've helped solve crimes? When they've put bad men in jail for what they've done?"

"I don't feel *guilt*. That's just it. What I feel is *spooked*. What I feel is … manipulated by some higher force. Like my life's not my own. And whatever this thing is, it keeps wanting to draw me back in. To draw me back *under*. I feel like I'm *drowning* again. But this time I'm drowning in blood, not saltwater."

"Interesting. Why don't you start by telling me about the accident."

Will opened his mouth. Closed it.

"Okay, they're just claims. I didn't really have visions. I just got lucky in the hospital in Florida. I just did some spectacular detective work in Michigan. I was just in the wrong place at the wrong time in Arizona. Can I get a pass now? Can you tell my bosses I said what they wanted to hear? Can I go back to work now?"

Click, click, click went the pen.

"I think it's important we talk about these events in your life."

"Is there an echo in this room? But okay, let's talk. You've got to make your money some way."

"Your accident. There was a death involved."

The guy wasn't going to be rattled.

Will sighed. He clasped his hands in his lap, stared down at them.

"A death. Yeah."

He looked up and met Smith's eyes - which he hadn't really done up until this point. They were a washed-out blue. Surprisingly mild. Interested. Non-judgmental. And there was, perhaps, a depth Will hadn't expected to see there.

"Okay, if we're going to play this game," Will said, "let's play it full on. I'll tell you this much - if I feel guilt for any of this bullshit my so-called superiors are making me come here and talk about, it's for what happened on that god-damned boat…"

C. DENNIS MOORE

C. Dennis Moore is the author of over 60 published short stories and novellas in the speculative fiction genre. Most recent appearances were in the Vile Things anthology, Fiction365.com, Dark Highlands 2, What Fears Become, Dead Bait 3 and Dark Highways. His novel, *Revelations*, is available in hardcover, trade paperback or ebook formats from Necro Publications.

Also by C. Dennis Moore

Free Downloadable ebooks:
Welcome to the Trust

Short Story Collections:
Terrible Thrills
Icons to Ashes
Dancing On a Razorblade
With Just a Hint of Mayhem: The C. Dennis Moore Short Fiction Omnibus, Vol. 1

Mini Collections:
Five Fates
Five Fantasies

Novellas:
The Man in the Window (an Angel Hill story)
Camdigan
Safe at Home
Epoch Winter

Novels:
Revelations

Nonfiction:
The C. Dennis Moore Horror Movie Guide, Vol. 1

Printed in Great Britain
by Amazon.co.uk, Ltd.,
Marston Gate.